Ride the Laughing Wind

Books by Blaine M. Yorgason
and/or Brenton G. Yorgason

Ride the Laughing Wind
The Miracle
Chester, I Love You
Double Exposure
Seeker of the Gentle Heart
The Krystal Promise
A Town Called Charity, and Other Stories About Decisions
The Bishop's Horse Race
The Courage Covenant (Massacre at Salt Creek)
Windwalker (movie version)
The Windwalker
Others
Charlie's Monument
From First Date to Chosen Mate
Tall Timber (private printing)
From Two to One*
From This Day Forth*
Creating a Celestial Marriage*
Marriage and Family Stewardships*

*Coauthored with Wesley R. Burr and Terry R. Baker

Tapes

Charlie's Monument
The Bishop's Horse Race
The Miracle (dramatized)
Caring and Sharing (Blaine Yorgason speaks)
Things Most Plain and Precious (Brenton Yorgason speaks)

Ride the Laughing Wind

Blaine M. Yorgason

Brenton G. Yorgason

Salt Lake City, Utah

Library of Congress Catalog Card Number: 84-70642
ISBN 0-88494-530-8

First Printing, 1984

Lithographed in the United States of America
PUBLISHERS PRESS
Salt Lake City, Utah

For Michael Terry Hurst and Francine Shumway Sumner
who have the laughter of the wind in their souls

Contents

Acknowledgments

Grateful appreciation is expressed to Devar and Madge Shumway and their sons Dan and Casey, and to Jim and Jeanne Redd, who opened their hearts and their homes and showed us the way.

Authors' Note

Ride the Laughing Wind began in a farmer's field in San Juan County, Utah, in September, 1983, where we had the privilege of assisting in the discovery of the bodies of two Anasazi people, a man and a woman. The sight of them, and the few remnants of their belongings that their families considered important enough to bury with them, gave us many thoughts, and these thoughts ultimately jelled into the basic story.

Still, these were the "Old Ones," gone more than seven hundred years. Who, without literal inspiration, could really know the ways of their thinking? While we indeed sought inspiration, and felt we received some choice insights, we also turned to written sources so that we might better comprehend their culture, their mores, and their environment. These sources not only provided data but oftentimes generated new ideas that added to the story and carried it along. There were also a few passages here and there that were so poetical and so lovely in form, so lyrically beautiful, that we felt impelled to use them as they appeared in print, merely adapting words and format to our story and style.

To the authors and publishers of all the works listed below—which is by no means a comprehensive bibliography of available sources but only a list of the sources *we* used—we give heartfelt thanks.

Sources Consulted

Baars, Donald, *Red Rock Country,* New York, Doubleday Publishing Company, 1972.

Bahti, Tom, *Southwestern Indian Tribes,* Las Vegas, K.C. Publications, 1980.

Barnes, F.A., *Canyon Country Geology for the Layman and Rockhound,* Salt Lake City, Wasatch Publishers, 1978.

Barnes, F.A. *Canyon Country Prehistoric Rock Art,* Salt Lake City, Wasatch Publishers, 1982.

Barnes, F.A., and Pendleton, Michaelene, *Canyon Country Prehistoric Indians,* Salt Lake City, Wasatch Publishers, 1979.

Broder, Patricia Janis, *Hopi Painting, The World of the Hopis,* New York, E.P. Dutton, 1978.

Brooks, Juanita, ed., "Diary of Thales Hastings Haskell," *Utah Historical Quarterly,* vol. 12, 1944.

Collier, Michael, *An Introduction to Grand Canyon Geology,* Grand Canyon Natural History Association, 1980.

Day, A. Grove, *The Sky Clears,* Lincoln, University of Nebraska Press, 1951.

Dutton, Bertha P., *Indians of the American Southwest,* Englewood Cliffs, N.J., Prentice-Hall, Inc., 1975.

Evers, Larry, ed., *The South Corner of Time,* Tucson, University of Arizona Press, 1980.

Hamblin, Jacob, "Journal 4," Salt Lake City, Historical Department, The Church of Jesus Christ of Latter-day Saints, 1863.

Hibben, Frank C., *The Lost Americans,* New York, Thomas Y. Crowell Co., 1968.

Highwater, Jamake, *Ritual of the Wind,* New York, The Viking Press, 1977.

Hobson, Geary, *The Remembered Earth,* Albuquerque, University of New Mexico Press, 1980.

James, Harry C., *Pages from Hopi History,* Tucson, University of Arizona Press, 1974.

Kilpatrick, Jack Frederick, and Kilpatrick, Anna Gritts, *Walk in Your Soul,* Dallas, Southern Methodist University Press, 1965.

Little, James S., *Jacob Hamblin,* Salt Lake City, Juvenile Instructor's Office, 1881.

Mails, Thomas E., *The Pueblo Children of the Earth Mother,* 2 vols., New York, Doubleday and Company, Inc., 1983.

Mays, Buddy, *Ancient Cities of the Southwest,* San Francisco, Chronicle Books, 1982.

Neruda, Pablo, *The Heights of Macchu Picchu,* New York, Farrar, Straus and Giroux, 1966.

Nequatewa, Edmund, *Truth of a Hopi,* Flagstaff, Museum of Northern Arizona, 1967.

Parsons, Elsie C., *Pueblo Indian Religion,* 2 vols., Chicago, University of Chicago Press, 1939.

Pike, Donald G., and Muench, David, *Anasazi, Ancient People of the Rock,* New York, Crown Publishers, 1974.

Rahm, David A., *Reading the Rocks: A Guide to the Geologic Secrets of the Canyons, Mesas, and Buttes of the American Southwest,* San Francisco, Sierra Club, 1974.

Rosen, Kenneth, ed., *The Man to Send Rain Clouds,* New York, The Viking Press, 1974.

Schaefer, Jack, *The Canyon,* Albuquerque, University of New Mexico Press, 1980.

Stokes, William Lee, *Scenes of the Plateau Lands and How They Came to Be,* Salt Lake City, Publishers Press, 1973.

Talayesva, Don, *Sun Chief: The Autobiography of a Hopi Indian,* by L.W. Simmons, New Haven, Yale University Press, 1942.

Tedlock, Dennis, trans., *Finding the Center,* Lincoln and London, University of Nebraska Press, 1972.

Tedlock, Dennis, and Tedlock, Barbara, eds., *Teachings from the American Earth,* New York, Liveright, 1975.

Thompson, Laura, *Culture in Crisis: A Study of the Hopi Indians,* New York, Harper, 1950.

Thompson, Laura, and Joseph, Alice, *The Hopi Way*, Chicago, University of Chicago Press, 1950.

Waters, Frank, *Pumpkin Seed Point*, Athens, Ohio, Swallow Press, 1969.

Waters, Frank, and Fredericks, Oswald White Bear, *Book of the Hopi*, New York, Ballantine Books, 1963.

Watson, Don, *Indians of the Mesa Verde*, Colorado, Mesa Verde Museum Association, 1961.

Wormington, H.M., *Prehistoric Indians of the Southwest*, Denver, Colorado Museum of Natural History, Popular Series, no. 7, 1947.

Yava, Albert, *Big Falling Snow*, Albuquerque, University of New Mexico Press, 1978.

Zepeda, Ofelia, ed., *When It Rains*, Tucson, University of Arizona Press, 1982.

Prologue

If you can find a very old map of North America, do so. It might help. If you can't, then be content with a new one, but keep in mind the old names, the old places, for they carry with them the spirit of the past, and that will also help.

Start on your map at the *p'aso* (where the land meets the sea) at the extreme southwest corner of the United States. Moving rapidly, trace inland along the old wagon road from La Punta that almost marks the magical line between California and Mexico. Skirt the top of the Sierra de Juarez as you move east, pass New River Station and Cooks and Seven Wells, and halt just shy of Yuma. Now just as quickly move north, letting yourself follow the drunklike wanderings of the Rio Colorado, the mighty River of Red. Go past Olive City, Bradshaw's Ferry, and La Paz, all long gone now, to Threnberg (now Ehrenberg), Aubrey, and Fort Mohave, then through the incredible land below Black Mountain past Camp Eldorado to Callville, where Lake Mead now stands.

Now you are there, at the beginning of the plateau country of the American Southwest. This Colorado plateau lies like a lazy pyramid across huge portions of Colorado, New Mexico, Arizona, and Utah, and its apex points south and west. It is a vast tableland of buttes, mesas, hills, and mountains—of gullies, washes, arroyos, and canyons. Especially, however, it is a land of canyons, perhaps the most elegant canyons in the world—Labyrinth and Stillwater, Westwater, Cataract, and Glen. Their walls of Navajo and Cedar Mesa sandstone rise and fall like the tentative chords of an orchestra rehearsing for a concert. And as the rivers lead one toward the apex of the pyramid, this canyon music swells to almost unbelievable heights.

The plateau's names are a cornucopia of the languages of those who have lived there: Coconino, Kaibito, and Defiance plateaus, Black Mesa and Mesa Verde, the Sierra Abajo and Navajo Mountain, Oraibi and Polacca washes, and so on.

The plateau is 130,000 square miles of sedimentary stone that has been lifted, largely uniformly except for places like the Waterpocket Fold, to a mile or more above sea level. It is a land of little moisture, and with the exception of the large rivers, the places where water collects are almost surely the result of altitude.

Moisture-bearing clouds from the southwest, borne on winds from the Sea of Cortez, collide with updrafts from the high mountains and mesas. Lifted heavenward they precipitate, and the water forms seasonal streams that eat their way down across the rock, or else it filters through the porous sandstone to collect in low areas and become tiny seeps and springs.

This pattern has determined in large measure what sorts of vegetation can be found on the plateau, and where. Low down, where water is generally more scarce, sagebrush, mahogany, cactus, and juniper abound. Higher, above six thousand feet, where there is more moisture, pinyon, oak, serviceberry, snowberry, strawberry, raspberry, squawbush, and pine prevail. And yet every so often one will find a particular spot, unusually favored with water or shelter, where the pattern will be broken and a small concentration of high-altitude flora such as Douglas fir, willow, and quaking aspen will flourish at lower-than-usual altitudes. That is the plateau country.

Turn east once more and follow the tortuous curves of the great river through Big (now Grand) Canyon, to its confluence with the

Flax or Colorado Chiquito (Little Colorado) River. Push northward again, through the canyon we call Marble, past the modern Glen Canyon Dam and onto Lake Powell. Drift still eastward past Navajo Mountain and Rainbow Bridge Canyon, thence up the Rio San Juan, noting as you pass the huge Chinle shale formations exposed there. Cut through the Monument Uplift that made Monument Valley out of de Chelly sandstone, and then past the strange sand-rock formation called Mexican Hat, a lovely example of nature's balancing ability. Move easterly still, through the massive slickrock sandstone monocline of Comb Ridge and on past Old Bluff, and pause only when you reach the diminutive Recapture Creek.

Catch your breath for a moment, and as you do, look around. Feel the distance. Touch the earth and sense the life, and death, that is held there. Gaze in awe or perhaps even fear at the broken and rolling desert that rises suddenly, both near and far off, into abrupt sandstone mesas and buttes, jaggedly carved by wind and rain and the deep-cutting rivers. The size of those mesas and buttes is awesome, their ruggedness breathtaking, their colors infinite. They, of course, are the rock.

As you stand there, listen carefully to the wind, or, on a rare day, the silence. But most especially, listen to the wind. Listen as it drifts across the mesas, sighs through the juniper and pinyon, whispers through the occasional patches of long grass, moans as it passes above the old canyons and the ancient hollows in the rock. Do you hear the laughing? Is there perchance a soft chuckling of good-natured humor that you detect? If so, rejoice, for you are in tune with the powers of the earth, and the joyful Kachina people, the ancient ancestor spirits, have you in mind. Pay close attention, for often they ride the breezes, laughing, giving good counsel and advice. These are the laughing wind.

Move north again, going more slowly now, up Recapture Creek. Take a drink from the spring beneath McCracken Point, and then take another. It is good water, and cold. Now look upward at the rimrock and consider that the ruins of ancient man abound here. Pictographs and petroglyphs are painted on or etched into the desert varnish of the massive sandstone ledges. And the ruins of those peoples' stone dwellings crouch low on the mesa tops or nestle in caves beneath the sheer rimrock. Watch carefully or you will miss these things, for they are rendered in earth-toned hues of soft reds, ambers, rich browns, and bleached tans that are the natural condition of this land of wind and sun. They have weathered well, these old creations, and have retreated only into a more harmonious union with the face of the land from which they sprang. They, like it, speak of permanence, of eternity.

So continue north. Leave behind you Recapture Pocket and Chimney Rock Draw, drift beneath Cowboy Pasture and Big Bench, pass Horse Canyon, go slowly through Fiddler's Green and remember that good people have long inhabited that place, pass Ute and Road Canyons, skirt Shumway Point, move beneath White Mesa and beyond the sight of Posey's sad and lonely little war. Continue past Ute and Murphy Points, Brown Canyon and Lem's Draw, and at Bullpup Canyon, turn right.

All these are names that now grace our maps. They were not names then, nor were there even maps upon which to write them. Far to the east of where we are, across a continent and then an ocean, it is the Christian year 1278, and the Hapsburg family has gained sovereignty over Austria, beginning a dynasty that will continue until 1918.

In England, Roger Bacon, 64, is still suffering imprisonment for heresy, and will do so for fourteen more years. Additionally, the British government has cracked down on coin-clippers. The punishments are unequal, however, for while 278 Jews are hanged for the offense, convicted Christians are let off with a fine and a warning.

In the East, paper money is first put into use, and Marco Polo serves the Kublai Khan. In Italy six more years will pass before ravioli is created, and in that same sixth year in Hamelin of Europe a story will be circulated about a piper who leads children away because the townspeople have refused to pay him for piping their rats into the river Weser.

On the seas there are only a few who dare sail beyond sight of land, and a full century will pass before the great European voyages of discovery will begin. It will be more than two centuries before a man called Christopher Columbus will sail westward to search for the Indies.

And throughout the civilized world, the cause of pride has reason to rejoice, for at last the glass mirror has been invented. This is the time.

Here and there upon the plateaus we have described live small clans of "The Peaceful Ones," nearing the end of their third migration and, as a civilization, just passing their first millennium. These are the builders of the stone cities and cliff houses. Each year the leaders grow stronger and so the people more weak, planting their corn, beans, and squash, plucking their turkeys, fashioning their wonderful pottery and baskets, moving and remodeling their homes, becoming constantly more rigid in their traditions, giving up as they do so a few more of their freedoms, and thus losing a little of the vitality that has made them such a wonderful people. They don't know it, of course, but they are about to vanish, about to become *The Old Ones Who Have Gone.* Centuries from now, the Navajo will call them *Anasazi,* The Ancient Ones, or Ancient Enemy. The Americans, for want of a better name, will call them Cliff Dwellers. These are the People.

Moving northeasterly up Bullpup Canyon, look carefully for the right rock formation, the ancient marking upon the stone, the correct grouping of trees. If you can find these, and if you can turn to your right again at the precise spot in the dry bed of the wash, you might be fortunate enough to spot a hint of a trail leading upward.

Hesitate now, and consider carefully. Do you truly wish to take it? Are you prepared to change? For, as surely as you climb that trail, you will become a different person. No one who has climbed it all the way has not. It is indeed something to think long thoughts over.

But meanwhile, the wind is drifting through the rabbit brush and snakeweed, midges swarm around your face, a dust devil dances up the wash ahead of you, and you feel a longing, an urging.

Nature, softened through eons of nearly endless time, deals easily with its structures, using for the most part curves and circles and gentle contours to amiably weld creation together. Man, on the other hand, who is very new at the business, seems bent on building with square corners and sharp angles, fighting the elements as he forces and crushes them together. Knowing that, it is usually a simple matter to spot even the most hidden of his handiworks.

And so it was for Arah "E" Shumway on that bright October afternoon in 1910. It was the too-square shadow in the red and white rock high above him that caught his attention.

Arah Shumway was the son and grandson of Mormon frontiersmen Peter and Charles Shumway, both of whom had spent their lives, under the direction of their prophet-leaders Brigham Young, John Taylor, and Wilford Woodruff, helping to carve out settlements in the vast wildernesses of Utah, Arizona, and New Mexico. But now the days of establishing communities were past, and it was the time for sinking roots. With that in mind, Peter only months before had moved again, planting his almost-grown family for the last time on some acreage he called Fiddler's Green, located a few miles south and east of the small community of Grayson (Blanding), Utah.

Now, with winter coming on, nineteen-year-old Arah, home from more than two years of living with the Navajo, was after the last of his father's cattle. Once they were gathered he would begin his long-neglected schooling. He might also look around for a wife, but he wasn't certain how to go about that, as he felt he knew so little about women. Of course he watched his mother, Mary, carefully. He loved her singing, and it gave him a reason to seek out her presence and so learn of her ways. Arah also watched his father, and though he loved him equally, he wondered at his silences, at the distance the man seemed to have placed between himself and his wife and children.

Arah worried about that, for now that he was home again, it appeared more obvious than ever. Of course his father was gone a lot, and that could not be helped. A man had to earn a living, and the Church also required a great deal of time. In fact, it was about the same in almost every home he knew. But why was it that a man could not be a part of his home when he was there? Why was it that so many of the men he knew seemed to grow as silent as the wilderness in which they lived? Did it have to be that way? If so, he was not at all certain that he would ever wish to marry. Somehow it seemed to him that if a man and a woman loved each other enough to marry, then the closeness they felt ought to carry over and to grow even greater through the years, rather than diminish.

Drawing rein, Arah Shumway backed his horse gently until the juniper trees were out of line, and carefully he looked again.

Square. A tiny, too-square hole in the rock near the top of the draw to his right. *Anasazi.* It had to be.

For long moments he sat his horse and studied the bluffs above him, searching for something else, some other sign of ancient habitation. But there was nothing that he could see, nothing at all. Perhaps the only thing up there was a granary, a storage bin. If so, it wouldn't be worth the climb to find out. But within young Arah Shumway was a feeling, a sense of something undefined that drew him upward.

The horse stamped its hoof impatiently, eager to be moving; Arah glanced down, and that was when he saw the petroglyph etched onto the darkened sandstone. It was a swastika-like sign that he saw, and below it were a frog, a snake, and a strange humpbacked flute player. And beyond the rock upon which those were etched, drifting upward, almost invisible if he had not known what he was looking at, was the ghost of a tiny trail.

Dismounting, Arah tied his horse to a juniper and set out, climbing easily but carefully. He wondered that the Old Ones would build there, with only seasonal water for miles, but he did not question. How could he, when he knew so little of their ways?

The trail wound and twisted up the steep slope above the bank of the wash, and he paused for breath, looking upward. Now he could see nothing but sky, that and a turkey buzzard circling overhead. Arah watched it, breathed deeply of the pure air, caught a momentary draft of something that smelled like cool, wet earth, wondered at that, and continued, picking out the way of the old trail as he climbed. And suddenly he was over a sheer lip of sandstone and there it was, spread tightly but beautifully before him.

For a time he stared at the tiny hanging valley, breathing deeply of the lush atmosphere of the place, listening to the insects, feeling the silence, wondering that such a place could be. In the valley's warm, moist air flourished cottonwood, spruce, willows, and aspen, grass thigh-deep grew in profusion, game trails seemed everywhere, the quiet gurgle of water laughed playfully from nearby, and there was a gentle singing in the air, a singing of peacefulness and serenity. Arah heard, and his heart almost ached with the beauty of it. That was the place.

Quietly Arah Shumway moved forward through the grass beneath the trees, wishing not to destroy the spirit of the place. He paused at the clear spring that flowed into a deep rock tank, knelt and took a long drink, wondered again, this time at the cold sweetness of the water, and looked up at the cliff that towered above him.

Notches. They were there, as he had somehow known they would be, carved centuries before by the hand of someone who had used this water but who had chosen to live above, where it was more difficult.

Carefully he reached up, placed his hand in a notch that was higher than the lowest one, and pulled himself upward. Toeholds up to the first notch were tiny, but he found them, and slowly he worked his way up the bulging face of the sandstone, from notch to notch, wondering as he climbed that another had made the same exertion, both upward and downward, many times, carrying water and other burdens.

Perspiration soon streaked his face and ran in tiny rivulets down his body, but still he climbed, determined. And then Arah Shumway was there, on a narrow ledge tucked back beneath the rimrock, gazing at a small home constructed long ago by the *Anasazi,* the Old Ones whom many of the Navajo had chosen to call Enemy.

The structure, of layered stone fitted carefully without mortar, was not large. Two rooms for living, low ceilinged, deep only as the cleft in the stone. Two other rooms lay beyond them, and then there were two others, much smaller and farther along the ledge, that had been for storage. And before them all, in the earth below the ledge and into the living rock itself, was the nearly filled-in hole of a small pit, a kiva.

He hesitated, almost feeling that he was intruding. But then quietly he stooped and entered the first room. For a moment he saw nothing, but as his eyes adjusted to the gloom he saw pottery, several pieces of it. Some of the pots were broken, but most were not, and remained as they had been placed so many years before. On a fitted stone shelf were three seed bowls, a mug and dipper, and some dishes. From a protruding rock hung a large water *olla*, its webbing of grass and yucca fibers and human hair still miraculously holding it.

Gently Arah touched each of the items, noting their neatness, sensing that their placing had been the work of a woman who had been much as his own mother, a woman seeking to make a stone cabin into a home. For the home in Fiddler's Green was indeed his mother's. It bore her look; it carried the signature of her life. It was, now that he thought of it, almost as if his father lived outside of the home, and thus of the family, and so was not a part of those things at all. And that, Arah suddenly knew, was not what he wanted when he married.

In the next room was more pottery, but Arah did not look at that, at least not carefully. He looked instead at the two people, for they were still there, staring empty-eyed at him from their partially mummified remains. On their feet were yucca sandals; draped over the disintegrating bones of their bodies were small robes woven of yucca, rabbit fur, and feathers, and beside them were many woven and hide robes and more empty dishes. A digging stick fashioned from wood and the horn of a bighorn sheep lay on the earth, a few projectile points were strewn about, and a stone axe, carefully hafted, leaned precariously from another shelf.

These were all haphazardly scattered, and Arah sensed without even thinking that the man had last been here, had left *his* signature upon this home, for in this room things were placed as a man might place them.

Arah had seen more spectacular ruins, many of them, but the occupants of this one somehow made it seem special. They were a man and a woman. Both here in this harsh land, both living together, closely, both lying together in death, both, apparently, loving equally.

In respect Arah removed his hat, gazed for long moments at the two, and wondered. He wondered at their beginnings, he considered their endings, and he found himself longing, as he stood there, to one day clasp hands with those two, thank them, question them, and seek to increase the understanding that seemed suddenly to exist between their hearts and his own. For, strangely, such an understanding was forming, and in his mind he was seeing these two, together, coming across the rock of the mesa.

Of course no one who yet lives knows exactly the ending, for that is not given to mortals to know. But perhaps for these, Arah's mind was whispering to him, the beginning of their closeness might have been in a manner such as the following.

Book One

ONE

The Dark Wind

1

The scream, long and anguished and filled with the sound of disbelief, stretched upward into the night sky, drawing out, piercing, and ending abruptly in the soft sighing of death. There was the whispering sound of racing feet, another choking sigh, and another death—then another, and another, and yet another.

The cold rays of the moon streaked down out of the star-filled sky and bounced off the rolling white rock of the mesa, lighting everything as though it were hazy daylight. The land stretched almost level, softly undulating and speckled with the black of juniper and pinyon, rolling on until it reached the rim of the nearby canyon. There it dropped suddenly away into the fathomless depths of darkness; there the world seemed to end.

The silver light from the moon also illuminated the mud and stone walls of the small village, and it showed clearly the faces of the People of Peace as they stumbled forth from their dwellings to confront the unknown horror that awaited them. Their expressions ranged from surprise to fear, but even in the moment of death the woman who watched from hiding could see no anger.

Only horror, that and confusion, filled their faces as they faced the dark wind of death.

Suddenly an old man stumbled from the entrance to a second-level dwelling directly below, an old woman followed, and the woman who hid caught her breath. It was she! It was the ancient grandmother who had the third eye, who had seen this time of dying and of great dryness, and so much more.

Together the two old ones, helping each other as well as they could, scrambled and slid down to the mesa top. Then they started running. Suddenly the old man fell, and the woman, sensing this, turned back, and her very being showed her great compassion.

2

The one who watched had been born, her mind suddenly remembered, in the windbreaker moon of April, to a mother who was of the Blue Flute Clan, and to a father who had come from another village and who was a kind man of many thoughts.

For nineteen days she had been kept by her mother from the light of day, for that was the custom of the People. On the twentieth day, when it was still full dark upon the mesa, she had been taken to face the birthing of the sun and to receive a name.

All of the people were there, and upon them all, as light began to grow a little in the east, had come a great hush, a great stillness. The Creator, Tiaowa, was doing something wondrous in the sky, something truly fearful. He was painting it a strange color of green, and as the people saw it, they feared. Even Taláwsohu, *the Star of the Eastern Day Breaking, was this strange green, and the infant girl's mother and father looked at one another in great fear.*

And in that moment the ancient grandmother, by far the oldest of the People in the village, had stepped forward. She, too, like the infant's father, was not originally of the village, and had been born to another clan altogether. Long before, she had wandered amongst them, all alone, an old woman even then, had been chosen as a wife, and so she had been invited to remain with them. The people liked her, liked the quiet dignity of her ways, and thus she had stayed. Now she was very old, older than anyone could imagine. Yet within her was much wisdom and many memories, and so she was well respected.

There was another thing as well, and because of it the ancient woman was also feared. Within her was the hidden eye, the third eye, the eye for seeing, and through it she could see far ahead, yes, and far backward as well.

"O People," she called out, her voice a high and quivering thing, "hear this voice I send out, this voice of truth and of fear. Yonder is a great greenness, and truly it is a sign from Tiaowa, who is the Giver-of-all-life.

"As you know, the land of the People grows dry with drought, and life is becoming hard for us. Yet truly is this deserved, for we have departed the old ways given us by Bahana, the lost white brother. We have lost the pure way of peace; we have thrown away the good character which should live always within our hearts.

"Within the thoughts of the People lives instead much selfishness, yes, and much in the way of grasping for power over others. With the passing of the seasons this great evil grows greater. Men live in fear of the grasping ways of other men, women are considered less than nothing, and these ways are not good. They are the ways of the Pawaca, the two-heart. Thus is the great Tiaowa displeased, and thus has he taken away the greenness from our land.

"But now is the sign given, the sign that the Great One would give us greenness once again. Do you hear my voice, O People? Do you hear my voice of power? Cast aside the ways of evil, and the greenness will return to our mesas. Hold this evil close to your breasts, O People, and you will be driven and smitten as dry leaves before the winter wind.

"The sign has been given, and even now, as you can see, the green in the sky is fading. But the child remains, and she will be, to us, as the reminder of the sign. Her name will be Taláwsohu, the Star of the Eastern Day Breaking, but you will call her Tala. And as the star now shines green with promise, so too will the green of that promise live within this infant.

"Thus I have spoken, and thus will it be."

A great silence lived upon the mesa. The people stood still and watched the strange green fade into the red and gold of the breaking of day, and in each mind lingered the words of the ancient grandmother. Some believed and feared, but others grew silently angry.

The old woman's words were strange always, and usually powerful. But this, this was more than even she had the power to declare. Who was she to know the thoughts of the great Tiaowa? Who was she to see such a thing? And more, who was she to declare that the infant girl was to be as a sign as well? How could a tiny girl carry the greenness of that strange morning sky?

Suddenly, from the mother of the infant there came a small cry, a cry of surprise and fear. Her husband followed her eyes, saw, and his own eyes opened very wide. A few others moved forward, and in the first light of the sun they also saw, and drew back quickly, fearing.

More crowded forward, looked, there were both cries of fear and great silences, and soon all the People of the village knew of the power of the ancient grandmother.

The infant's eyes were open, she was gazing quietly upon them all, and she was doing so from eyes that were strangely blue-green, the same green as had been within the eastern sky of the dawning.

3

The old woman tugged at the arm of the fallen man who had taken her as the wife of his old age, helping him to rise. He struggled, did so, and she reached up and touched him softly on the face. There was a look that passed between them, a tender look, and then the old woman turned to flee. The man behind her started as well, took no more than two steps, and then in the cold moonlight the young woman who watched saw the arrow slam brutally into his back. He grunted and fell forward, and the ancient grandmother, now desperate, turned back once more.

The young woman gripped the pile of stones surrounding her and dropped her face. What was happening below was exactly as the old woman had told her it would be as they had sat together upon the mountain when it was yet the season of cold. But still, it was too horrible, too far beyond belief.

Another scream drifted across the mesa, another dying, there was an evil laughter in the night, the woman lifted her eyes in spite of herself, and thus she saw.

The old man raised his hand, feebly, telling the old woman to go on, and with a look of agony on her face, the ancient grandmother hesitated. She truly understood the danger, but because she was who she was, she thought more of the man who lay dying than she thought of herself.

4

"This is a thing such as I have never heard," declared the mongwi, *the chief of the village. "Never has a young woman seen in vision the man she is to be united with."*

"Never has a woman seen a vision!" another declared. "That is for the mongwi, *and perhaps occasionally for the other men as well. But it is never a woman's task or right!"*

"But what of the ancient grandmother?" one of the young men who was a neophyte asked, forgetting for the moment his lowly place.

"Silence!" ordered the mongwi. *"You are to listen, all of you neophytes. The elders will do the speaking* and *the questioning."*

There was a long moment of stillness, and then the mongwi *spoke again. "Still," he said, "that old woman truly has the third eye. And the young one here has a great understanding of many things."*

"It is an evil thing!" charged a clan chief who sat near him. "It is evil for the old one; it is evil for this young one as well."

"Perhaps," the mongwi *conceded. "But this woman is the carrier of the sign. How . . . ?"*

"She has become a two-heart," another growled. "It is evident, and if she is not cast out, she will bring destruction upon us all!"

"How so, my brother?"

"She is only a woman," the man stated. "It is well known that she carries the strange sign, but I do not think it is a true sign. It was declared by a woman, it is carried by another woman. My brothers, women have no such powers. For us to give ear to them will bring the wrath of the great Tiaowa upon us all."

There was a long silence, and Tala stood before the council as was proper, with her eyes downcast, her body still. Yet within, her heart beat wildly with fear. Was she indeed a two-heart? Was it indeed an evil thing to see such a wondrous vision or dream as she had seen?

"It is truly a strange vision," the mongwi *stated thoughtfully. "It is well known that a woman has no say in the selection of her mate."*

"That is correct," another of the elders quickly agreed. "A woman's function is to bear children so that the clan may go on. Such is the way it has always been."

"Brother," another declared, "I do not know that this is so. The ancient grandmother has said that in the very old days—"

"Fool!" a young man who sat on the council snapped. "Would you believe in the crazy ideas of an old woman?"

The other stared hard at him, and at last dropped his eyes. He dared not go against the young one who was called Saviki, for it was well known that all who did so suffered much bad fortune.

"O mongwi,*" Tala said fearfully, "I . . . I would speak."*

There was intense silence, and at last the mongwi *responded. "You may do so," he declared with resignation.*

"O men, I would speak of the strange feeling I had when I saw the m . . . man in my vision, the unknown man who is to come. I . . . I would . . ."

"Ha! Brothers," the young Saviki shouted, his voice triumphant. "This is truly evil, and she is indeed a two-heart! I will not listen as a woman, especially one so young, makes Móńglavaiti, *Priest Talk, by speaking of things to come."*

"Saviki is right," the clan chief agreed. "Why, this woman has never given a birthing, has never been a vessel for creating life. How could such a one as she ever have a vision?"

The mongwi *stared at the earth, his mind whirling. He agreed with these men, but truly he feared the power of the ancient grandmother. With her third eye she could see much; he had watched her, and much that she had seen had come to pass. The great dryness on the land was such a thing.*

He feared this one with the green eyes almost as much. She understood things that others did not, she knew the ways of the People as they had been anciently, she had been taught a great deal by the old woman, and now she had seen a vision.

Still, the voice she had sent out concerning her vision could not be true. It must not, for it went contrary to the ways of the People. Of course, if the ancient grandmother was right, then in the very old days things may have been different. But even so, these were not the old days.

"My brothers," he said finally, "I would have a solution. In one sun we will return to this kiva, and a decision will be made. I have spoken."

The others nodded, and in silence the woman Tala was escorted from the kiva and to the dwelling of her grieving parents. She worried, but the ancient grandmother, her great teacher, had told her many times that all would be well in her life.

"My brothers," the mongwi *said as the council sat within the kiva, "I would hear your voices."*

The silence was profound, and Tala stared at the earth, her heart within her throat. A log popped on the small fire, a man shifted position, and at last the clan leader spoke.

"Hear my voice. The woman is a two-heart."

"Hear my voice in the same manner," another declared.

"My voice goes instead for her," a third man stated quietly.

There was suddenly a great commotion as all spoke at once to argue for and against this man who had voiced for the woman. The mongwi *was powerless to bring about order. But suddenly, over the noise, a powerful voice rang out clearly.*

"My brothers, hear my words!"

Silence came quickly, and the man Saviki, his spear of power laid at his side, spoke quietly.

"Brothers, there is a way to test this . . . this woman."

"Speak, Saviki," the mongwi *declared, relieved that the chaos had ended. "We would hear of this way."*

Saviki smiled at the young woman Tala, and she shuddered with sudden fear. His thoughts were in his eyes, and never, among all the men of the People, had she seen such thoughts.

"It is true that she is a two-heart," Saviki declared. "It is also true that if she continues in the manner of her evil, she will bring a great curse upon all of the People of Peace. Therefore, give her a husband. Choose a strong man for her this day, and let her produce life from him. If she accepts this, and is humble before him, then we will know.

"No," Tala whispered as her eyes came up. "No! Such is not to be, for in my—"

"Silence!" the mongwi *ordered, his voice filled with great authority. "Women do not speak within the kiva unless invited. Nor have you been invited, woman."*

"O mongwi*," Tala began, "I—"*

"I demand your silence!" the man thundered.

Tala dropped her eyes in obedience, and the mongwi *turned to the man Saviki. "Is it within your mind to suggest such a husband for this woman?" he asked.*

Saviki's eyes dropped in an expression of humility. "O mongwi*, hear my words. It is within my mind that this woman is truly a two-heart, and very dangerous to the existence of our People. For that reason, I could not recommend her to any man. Yet I have sent out the suggestion, and so fearfully I accept responsibility for it. If the* mongwi *so desires, I will take this woman personally . . ."*

Tala stared at the floor, her mind reeling. Such a union was unthinkable. She could not let it come to pass. Why, it was the very thing her dream, her vision, had shown her. Somewhere along the hidden pathway of her future there was a man, a fine, clean man who would come to her with understanding and with love. She had seen him clearly in her dream of the night, or at least she had seen all clearly but his face, which seemed to be shadowed. Still, she had felt his love, and she had returned it with honor. That man of her vision would be her husband, and there could be no other! Certainly it could never be this man called Saviki, whose eyes burned with such lust.

The mongwi *looked at Saviki with pride and gratitude. Truly, he thought, the man was wise and had great courage. He himself would certainly not care to take this woman as a wife, not even though she was as beautiful as the star she was called after.*

"O Saviki," he declared, and his gratitude was high in his throat, "I have heard your words, and it will be as you say. Take this woman, and make her to be with child. Then will we truly know concerning her heart."

Again Saviki dropped his eyes. But there was also a smile that he was hiding, a knowing smile. "Come," he ordered brusquely as he grabbed the woman Tala's arm. "We will go at once to begin the ceremony."

With great fear Tala struggled free. "No!" she cried, "it is not to be in this manner!"

For an instant Saviki stared, and then with power and viciousness he struck her face and once again took hard hold of her arm. "It is my order," he declared through clenched teeth, "that you come. . . ."

Desperately Tala broke free once more and fell to the earth, stunned that a man of the People would behave in such a bad-faced manner. Saviki stepped forward to subdue her, and Tala, desperate, grabbed the first thing that came to her hand, the man Saviki's power spear. Without thought she lunged forward with it, aiming directly at Saviki.

There was an instant's silence that seemed to her to last forever, a great scream, and to Tala's horror she saw the chipped blade of the spear buried high in the inner thigh of the man Saviki's leg.

Blood gushed forth. Saviki angrily pulled the spear from the great wound, turned toward the woman with hatred clear and bright within his eyes, and in that instant the mongwi *held up his hand.*

"It is as you said, O Saviki," he declared solemnly. "This one is

truly a two-heart. From this day forth, I declare her Outcast. She is mokee, *as one dead. Thus it will be, for I have spoken."*

"No!" Saviki cried, for he too understood the sentence. "I will still have her! I will— "

"My brother," the mongwi *declared, "it is the law. You are truly brave to desire what you do, but now it cannot be. The woman is Outcast, and none of us may see her or speak to her or touch her again, in any manner whatsoever. Should that happen, it is said that all of us will be destroyed."*

"You will be destroyed anyway," the high, thin voice of the ancient grandmother suddenly and bravely declared from above the opening to the kiva. "O People, destruction is coming among you. . . ."

5

The old man struggled in the moonlight, arched his body out away from the rock, fell back, and at last was still. The old woman who was the ancient grandmother slowly rose, and sobbing quietly she spun about. Grabbing at the branches of a juniper she plunged into the shadow of the tree and vanished. For several seconds she scrambled in darkness, and then the woman who watched saw her come out once more into the moonlight, reeling toward the darkened rim of the canyon.

The running would not do her any good, the woman thought as she held tightly to the pile of stone and gazed down upon the terrible violence that was taking place below. It had been her prophecy, and now it was coming to pass. But she would never make it to the edge, never.

More screams sounded in the night, more people died, but the hidden one had eyes only for the old woman who fled erratically across the mesa, her and the dark forms of the two men who followed.

6

In the mind of the young woman who watched, the memory of the night in the kiva still lived. She could remember the eyes of the men as they turned toward the voice of the ancient grandmother, but nothing could be seen in the opening but the ladder and the dark. Still, from outside, she remembered, the old voice had droned on.

"The sign was given, and you declare the sign corrupt. I look down upon you! The voice of interpretation was clear, and you declare the voice powerless. I look down upon you with contempt! The sign is carried daily within the woman's eyes, and you declare her a two-heart and make her Outcast. I look down upon you with pity! Hear, O men. Soon your bones will lie scattered upon this mesa, picked clean by the wings of the air, for you have allowed evil to come among you."

"S . . . Silence!" the mongwi *finally ordered, his voice filled with anger and frustration. "Be still, old woman, or* your *bones will be scattered upon this mesa immediately!"*

"I will still my voice, O mongwi,*" the thin old voice called from the darkness. "But with the third eye I see this, and you will hear and remember. These old bones of mine will never lie upon this mesa, nor will the bones of the green-eyed woman. Thus it is, for I have spoken."*

Silence came then, heavy and strained. The mongwi's *face worked with anger, but he feared, he truly did. The old one should be sent off to die as Outcast, just as the young one was being sent, but he did not dare. She had too much power.*

"O mongwi,*" the one called Saviki said, "I am saddened by the evil in the words of these women. Such a thing as the old one declared can never be, for we are the People of Peace."*

"Your words are true," the mongwi *declared.*

"They are," agreed the clan chief.

"I state further," Saviki went on, "that should destruction ever come upon this people, it will be because of the evil in the two hearts of this green-eyed witch. Now I too have spoken."

"It is so," agreed the clan chief.

"It is so," agreed as well the mongwi. *"Now, woman of the green eyes who is dead, I do not see you, for you are Outcast. If you can hear these words, I order you to depart! Never again will you hear the voices of our People, nor will you ever speak to them again. Thus it is, for I have spoken."*

Tala, stunned by the horror of the thing, staggered forth from the kiva, not seeing the burning lust that raged in the eyes of Saviki, not seeing the tears in the eyes of one or two of the men who were there, not seeing her parents as they turned away, not seeing the ancient woman who slowly followed after her, not seeing anything at all.

She was Outcast!

7

The old woman had reached the last lift of the mesa before it dropped away into the darkness of the canyon, and the woman who was hidden above watched in fascination as the drama below her unfolded.

Suddenly the old woman hurtled forward and slammed face down to the rock, and the woman knew she had been hit by at least one arrow. In the moonlight she watched as the ancient grandmother struggled forward, her legs and arms working furiously, digging into the sand and the dirt, clawing for survival. Yet there was no grass there, no trees beneath which to hide. She was in the open, and the two who followed slowed and then walked easily toward her struggling form.

The hidden woman waited, suspending emotion, erasing pain, a human sponge accepting impressions without comment or mental indentation. She knew that the destruction was because of her own great evil, yet she could not accept that, could not think of it—not if she was going to survive. And truly she had been told to live by the one she watched, the ancient grandmother.

8

"My daughter, I would join you."

Tala stared up, surprised. She was far out on the mesa, Outcast and starving, living in a small cave, and she had seen no one since she had been driven from the village. But now the ancient grandmother was there, where no living person should be.

Suddenly Tala gasped. What if the old woman was not living? What if she too were mokee, *dead, and had come to torment her?*

"Your heart is filled with fear," the old woman observed as she groaned and sank to the earth. "Let it be filled instead with peace. I am no spirit, nor will you be if you can find within yourself the power to live."

"But . . . but I am Outcast!"

"So you are," the old one croaked as she pulled forth from her robe a little food. "But then, my daughter, who among the women of the People is not? Yes, and who among the men who dare to defend the old ways is not Outcast as well? No one! All are Outcast from the truly two-hearted ways of those others."

"But . . . but you are not allowed to speak with me. No one is so allowed."

"Who tells me that I am not so allowed?" the old woman asked. "Are these your words? Is this your desire?"

Quickly Tala signaled no. "I long to hear your voice," she said, her voice a whisper, "but I fear for you. What if . . ."

The ancient grandmother smiled and held up her hand in the silence sign of the men. "My daughter," she declared, "in all the world there are only the two of us. Now eat, and then we will speak of much that is important."

Tala stared for a moment, hesitantly took up the food, tasted it, and then ate ravenously. The old woman watched her in silence, and the trace of a smile was again upon her withered old face. At last the Outcast Tala was finished, and only then did the ancient grandmother speak again.

"My daughter of the blue-green eyes, hear now my voice. There is great danger in this place, for I have seen it. Come, and we will make a walking away together."

Tala stared, quickly stirred out her small fire, and within moments she was following the old woman south across the mesa. Despite her great age the old one moved well and easily, and as the hours fell away Tala grew more and more surprised. Truly this was no ordinary woman.

With nightfall they had come to the white sandstone cliffs at the bottom of the mountain foothills. At the base of these were shallow overhangs with sandy floors. They slept wrapped in the sand, and during the night Tala awoke to the call of a young owl. The sky was bright with stars and a half-moon, it was very cold, and so she shivered and buried herself more deeply in the cliff sand, and soon she slept once more.

In the morning they gathered tumbleweed sprouts that were succulent and tender. As they climbed the cliffs there were wild grapevines, and under the fallen leaves around the roots, the old woman uncovered dried grapes shrunken to become sweet raisins. By noon they had reached the first of the mountain streams. There they washed and drank water and rested.

The old woman frowned and pointed at Tala's leather footwear. "Take them off," she said. "Leave them here, for where we go there is no need for such things."

Tala wonderingly pulled off the leather leg and foot wrappings and put them under a lichen-covered boulder. Then she relaxed, feeling the coolness of air on her bare feet. She watched the old woman, who now was dozing, and for the first time she saw a weariness in her face, a weariness she had never seen before.

"She is preparing me," she said softly to herself. "She knows she is going to die, and then there will be no one at all who will speak with me. Oh, how will I ever live if she is gone?"

Then, ashamed of her own great selfishness, Tala closed her mouth and dropped her eyes.

It was early spring, but the sun was warm and, at least where they were, there was no snow. Slowly the two climbed, and the young woman marveled at the things of the mountain. There was snow on the shady side of the trees, there were green shoots growing already where the sunlight reached, and she could hear melting snow—icy water trickling down into little streams and the little streams flowing rapidly into the big stream. Here, truly, there was much water. Why, she wondered, did it not get down onto the mesa where there was such need?

The sun was warm on her body, touching her, but her breath still made steam in the cold mountain air, and her feet were growing numb. "Do not your feet feel the cold?" Tala finally asked.

The old woman looked at her for a long time, and at last she signaled no. "Look at these feet," she said. "Do you see age there?"

Tala signed no.

"That is true," the old one said. "My feet are beautiful. No one has feet like these. Especially you people who wear foot coverings all the time."

The ancient one walked on, then continued. "You have seen babies, have you not?" she asked.

Tala signaled yes, her mind already filled with a great wondering. What had babies to do with her feet?

"Then, my daughter, you have noticed the mothers and grandmothers of babies as well, always worrying about keeping the feet of the babies warm. But the babies do not care. They play easily in the snow, without foot coverings, and they are not cold."

The old woman hiked along, obviously excited about her thoughts, and then she stopped at the stream. "But the People being what they are," she concluded, "it is not long before the children are taught to be cold, and then they cry because they are."

The old woman took up a crooked stick and dug around the stream. "Here," she said, handing Tala a fat, round root, "eat this."

Tala squatted at the edge of the rushing, swirling water, full of mountain dirt, churning and rolling, rich and brown and muddy with ice pieces flashing in the sun. She held the root motionless under the water. The coldness felt pure and clear as the ice that clung to the rocks in midstream, and she thought of the old woman's words.

She pulled out her hand, felt its stiffness, the old woman laughed and started up the hill, and Tala followed, still chewing the milky fibers of the root.

At the top of the hill was a grove of aspen. The air was colder, and the snow was more deep.

"Those feet," Tala said wonderingly, "now they will surely freeze."

The snow was up to their ankles; it was very cold, Tala's own feet throbbed, and she was truly concerned. The old woman sat on a fallen aspen, held her hands out to the sun as if it were a great fire, and with her eyes closed she smiled and relaxed.

"Do a wolf's feet freeze?" she suddenly asked.

Tala stared, and then signaled no.

"Well, then," the old woman said.

"But . . . but my mother, you are not a wolf."

The ancient grandmother's eyes opened wide and she looked hard at the young woman. Then, lifting her head and closing her eyes once more, she gave a long, wailing wolf cry with her head raised toward the sky.

Everything was white—the sky, the bare aspens, the snow, all were white. The cry echoed off the rocky mountain slopes around them, and in the distance Tala thought she heard an answering wolf call.

"You see, my daughter," the old woman said as she smiled widely, "I am a wolf because I choose to be a wolf. I am always what I choose to be. Now tell me, what have your feet declared concerning the ways of our People?"

Tala stared at the snow-covered ground and felt the great cold that was burning her feet with pain. "Perhaps some of the ways of the People are not . . . not good," she answered slowly.

"Is there anything else? Something that your feet declare concerning you?"

"I am what I am," Tala whispered, "because I have been told that I am so, and have come to believe it."

"Is there power within your heart," the old woman then asked, "to understand your own words?"

"My mother," Tala answered honestly, "this I do not know."

"Say then what it is that you feel."

Tala looked down again, and tears were within her eyes. "My mother," she whispered, "I feel only confusion, for I am truly Out-

cast. Yet still you speak with me, and I with you. I long to be as you say, but I am already this other thing, and . . ."

Tala could not continue, for her grief and shame were within her throat, and her voice was gone. For a long moment the old woman sat with eyes closed, considering. A robber jay flew into the trees above them, waited, saw no food, and departed, going from tree to tree. Finally the ancient grandmother spoke.

"Truly you are the one that has been sent," she declared softly, "for the eyes of the blue-green sea are within you. Yet even for you it will be a hard thing. Do you know that when the heat of summer comes to the mesa, I am to die?"

Tala dropped her face.

"Do not sorrow," the old woman said softly. "I have waited long for this, and am more than ready. However, I fear for you, and hesitate to leave you alone." Suddenly the old woman grew silent, and in her eyes was a strange light. "But . . . but then," she whispered, and her whispering was filled with reverence, "perhaps you will not be alone at all."

The old one stared outward off the mountain and over the mesa, her eyes unseeing, and her thoughts went back and back and back. She saw the land, and it had not changed much at all. It had been dry before, and it had also been very green. Yet still the land of rock was the same. She saw too the People who had lived upon the land, and truly, over the seasons they had changed a great deal—at least, almost all had changed.

"My daughter, long ago there were three who had great power, who did much good among the People."

"Three?" Tala questioned. "I do not understand."

"They are wanderers; three who were anciently called prophets or seers because they could see so much. Perhaps they will come, though so far as I know, they have not been seen in more seasons than a person can count. Still, if the need is great . . ."

"But . . . who were they? And why—"

With a wave of her hand the old woman suddenly ended the discussion. "It is probably nothing," she declared. "I should not have mentioned such a thing at all." Then, abruptly, she changed the subject. "Do you know the Kachina people?"

Wonderingly Tala signed yes. "I have heard stories of them," she answered, "and I have seen the masks. . . ."

"Those are not the Kachina people, my daughter. Those are representations only. The true Kachina people live on this mountain, in a place much higher than this. They also live on other mountains and in the underworld, and come out often through their sipapus, *their holes of emergence. They fly on the winds in all seasons, they are great jokesters and love to laugh, and if you will listen and believe and be true to the old ways, they will be your friends and will tell you many things. If, however, you are a two-heart, then you have great reason to fear them.*

"Perhaps they will help you when I am gone. Perhaps they will even dispel your confusion and tell you the way of becoming who you truly are.

9

In the cold light from the moon-woman the young one watched from the boulders as the two men stood over the ancient grandmother. One prodded her with his bow, she twisted away, and their laughter carried easily to the distant pile of rocks. The men turned partially from the old one, and in that instant the woman somehow lunged to her feet and spun toward the darkened rim that yawned just ahead. But the men were waiting, and with a wild laughter they turned and each loosed an arrow.

The old woman's body arched up and forward onto the rock, her close-cropped white hair bobbing as she fell. Still she twisted, squirming forward, somehow on her knees now, her hands reaching out toward the dark edge. Another arrow slammed into her back, pushing her down, and then her hand found the sharp drop of the rimrock.

Grimly she pulled, and as the young woman stared with stilled breath, the old one hitched herself forward, hung for an instant on that awful edge, smiled as the two men scrambled to grab her—and then without a sound the old woman who had been as her grandmother plunged over the edge and into the darkness below.

Truly, the one who watched thought as her mind whirled in dizzy circles and prepared to leave her weak and sickened body, the ancient grandmother's bones would never lie scattered upon the mesa.

TWO

The Betrayer

10

High on the watchtower a man observed the violence below, and within him was a churning and pounding that seemed to be tearing him apart. The great height of the tower made him dizzy and weak, for he feared heights more than he feared anything else in his life. But that was not the trouble now. It was much more than that.

As the old woman with the third eye dropped over the ledge, he fell back, his eyes closed, beads of perspiration streaking down his face. That was it, then. She had done it. She had fulfilled her final prophecy, and though he would have liked to stop it, such a thing no longer mattered. The ancient crone was dead, as were all the others. They were *all* gone. Every one of his people was dead, including those who were his parents, and he with his great cunning had brought it about.

His eyes felt tight within their sockets, his head pounded, his mouth was dry like the desert sand, and for a moment he wondered. Had he done the wise thing? Would not the great Tiaowa, the great Giver-of-all-life, strike him down for the terrible killing he had brought to pass?

He and the dead ones below were the People of Peace, they always had been, and now he, one of them, had brought the Outsiders among them, spreading death and horror everywhere.

Suddenly the man grinned into the darkness. Now it was he who was being foolish, not those weak ones who had died below. What he had done had been a necessary thing, necessary for his own plans to succeed. He had learned the truth; he had gained an understanding of the pathway to power over others. And this, this was the first great step! There had to be an example, a clear-cut example of his power, or there would be no fear, no restless looking about within the darkness for the sudden appearance of the ones his people called the Angry Ones.

About him blew the winds of night, and within his mind was suddenly a great laughter concerning the beliefs of these People among whom he had been reared. They believed that on those winds rode the Kachina people, ancient, long-dead spirits who helped or did not help, according to foolish notions of right and wrong. They believed as well that the great Tiaowa watched over them and blessed them for their good countenances. That was another foolishness. There was no great Tiaowa, no great Creator to strike him, none at all. They believed also in the goodness taught by the myth called Bahana. That was the greatest foolishness of all. The young man knew that such things were not so, and thus he laughed.

A man was only as strong as his own arm, as powerful as his own mind. Yet with those, and knowing the truth concerning the foolish beliefs of the People, a man could become very powerful indeed. It was only a matter of deciding what one wanted, and then planning very carefully.

Besides, the people of his village had never given him the respect he deserved, and so they should be dead. Additionally, there had to be an example, a total annihilation.

Suddenly the man's eyes opened wide. They had not been annihilated, at least not totally. There was one who yet lived! The green-eyed one who was Outcast—she must be found! She must be found and brought to him.

11

So in the darkness of the night a young man sits in silence on the watchtower from which he has betrayed his People. He is known as Saviki in this village, but he is known in other places by other names as well. He is a finely formed young man, of great strength both in mind and body. Yet within his eyes burns a deep fire, and it is not a fire of goodness.

He closes these eyes now, and before him he sees, as he has seen constantly since the council in the kiva, the comely form of the green-eyed woman. He sees the clearness of her skin, he sees the way her body moves when she walks, he feels in his mind the softness of her being as if his hands were already upon her, and within his mind grows a great lusting. He will have her, of that he is certain, for he has found the way to obtain *all* the desires of his heart. The green-eyed woman is such a desire.

12

"It is good," he signaled as the ones who were called the Angry Ones clustered about him in the pale light of dawn. Here and there in the village and out on the mesa lay the gory forms of the ones he had called his People, his friends, his family. Now they were no more, he mused, and it was his own doing.

Angry at this slight indication of his own weakness, the young man pulled his eyes away from the dead and his mind away from the butchery. This was not the time for such foolishness; this was not the time to be womanish.

"As you say," signaled the leader of the bloody men who stood before him. "We have done as you requested. Now to the bins that bulge with food. Our people are very hungry."

The young man held up his hand. "I will take you to the bins," he signaled, "and truly you will not be disappointed. Moreover, they are but the first of many, and in the seasons to come, you and your people will be very well fed. All you must do is hearken to my words, as you have done this day.

"However, I can not yet show you the stores of food, for you have not as yet completed your task."

The leader's eyes flashed with anger. "What?" he demanded through his signals. "Other than yourself, there is not another of this feeble, womanish people who still draws breath. That was the demand of your voice, and that has been accomplished!"

The young man signed with his hands his placating agreement. "As I said," he signaled, "you have done well, but there is one who yet lives, a young woman of comely form, enticing ways, and strange green eyes. Find her and bring her to me, and you will have not only the food, but your way with this beautiful young woman as well."

In the pale light he saw the men look quickly at each other, sensed their eagerness, and again the young man smiled. Truly did he have the power over men that would take him far.

"Come," he said easily. "I will show you the area where this woman was last seen. As surely as my name is Saviki, I swear that this green-eyed one will be destroyed!"

THREE

Waítioma—The Running Away

13

The slick-rock mesa was white-hot with early summer. Heat waves danced before the young woman's eyes, distorting the junipers, pinyon, and greasewood. Far off a dust devil burrowed angrily at the dry earth, seeking its lost *sipapu,* its hole of emergence.

Fearfully she stared after it, wondering if it was, as some of the People claimed, a sign. She knew that the twisting winds came only with heat and dryness, and that troubled her. But worse, those whirling, spinning creatures seemed as lost souls, like herself, and that troubled her even more.

The woman stopped to rest her aching arms, legs, and bleeding feet, thinking suddenly not so much of herself as of the same sufferings felt by the little ones who followed. Without a sound the three children sank to the stone and were still, and the woman, tears of pity and pride falling freely, hitched the baby higher on her hip and looked away.

Through red-rimmed eyes she glanced toward the brassy sky. No cloud people. No sign of rain. But the *wisoko,* the buzzards, were there, circling as they had done all day, and she was even more afraid.

In four suns she had seen no sign of the Angry Ones. Yet still she pushed the children on, fleeing as rapidly as the small ones could move, sending out prayer-thoughts constantly that they might keep ahead of the evil ones who sought her.

For the first time in her life she feared, she truly feared. Even the thought of what she had seen brought a horror before her eyes that blinded her and seemed determined to force her to the rock with agony. Nor could she blank the memory of it from her mind. It was there, through light and darkness it remained, and often she wanted to scream out, to cry to Tiaowa that the sight of it be taken from her. But such did not happen—even after her pleas it did not happen.

Shuddering, the woman, who was fourteen summers, still unmarried, and now alone with these suffering children, forced from her mind the thoughts of the killings, the lost twisting wind, and the fat-eating bird of the afterlife. She must go on! For their sakes, and perhaps even for her own, she must!

Around her the great tableland of the plateau shouldered against the blazing sky, lofty pinnacles loomed higher still, and over all that red and broken land the sun lay hot and dry, dead heat gathering quietly and lying in wait in the sullen canyons below.

Tala could not recall ever having felt such heat so early in the season, and as she wiped the perspiration from her face she wondered at it. The time of dryness was indeed bad, and on the mesas there was no water at all.

Far and away beyond the broken land, both to the south and to the west, great peaks reached at the clouds, purple with distance, cool, remote, and lost. In those mountains would be water, and there would also be the green of new growing grass. Thus she remembered.

But within her now was a great fear of the mountains, for upon the high-up peaks that loomed in the distance lived the Kachina people, usually friendly spirits who were also mischievous jokesters and even avenging demons, especially toward two-hearts.

Nor did they live only upon the mountains. She knew that, and worried about it as well, for the wind was blowing, drifting across the mesa and twisting at the junipers and the pinyons. Kachina people rode those winds, and if a person's countenance was bad, if a person was a two-heart like herself, an evil one, their wrath might be fearsome.

14

The sun beat down with intensity upon the mesa, the winds of heat kicked up dust and threw it at the little group, and one of the children coughed, and then coughed again. Tala, her mind coming back into her body, looked at the young ones, saw again their great suffering, and quickly she turned away.

She could not bear to see such suffering! It was not right. *O Tiaowa!* she cried in her mind as she sent her prayer-thoughts upward toward the sun. *Where is the water the exhausted children need? Would you not show me? Could you not lead us to it? Surely you, the powerful God of this the fourth world and of all the other worlds as well, giver of life and death to all creatures, father of Bahana, can do that.*

But it was a time of dryness, and so what could she expect of him? The Kachina cloud people had stayed in their kivas and the rains of spring had not come. No, nor had the ceremonies of the people helped. There had been no water, nor was it likely that she would find any, especially here upon the rock of the mesa.

She thought then of dying, and wondered if it was time. But no, that would make no sense. If it had been the time for dying, either for her or for the children who still sat glass-eyed in the shade of a juniper, then all of them would have been with the others of the Blue Flute and Bow clans, and so would have been destroyed by the Angry Ones.

But they hadn't been. None of them. Instead the four little ones had been sleeping elsewhere in a near but well-concealed place, and she had been Outcast, hiding and watching as the old one had directed.

But water! Where in this land of red and white stone and shimmering heat would—no, *could* she find the fluid of life?

"Come," she signaled at last to the children. "It is the time once more for going."

"But my mother," the next-to-youngest whimpered, his eyes brimming with tears. "I thirst, and my feet are very sore. See? They are bleeding and full of thorns. Are there truly no more sandals?"

Tala signaled no, but felt deeply moved by the boy's formalized acceptance of her as his mother. He had been digging in the bit of earth beneath the juniper as they rested, scraping holes, and Tala smiled. It had not been for nothing that the boy's parents had called him *Honani,* the Badger.

"No, Badger," she answered gently as she put her hand on his head. "I have no sandals. Nor do I have water. But you and each of us must keep our *kópavi,* our door in the crown of our heads, open. Only in that way can the great Tiaowa lead us to water."

In a manner that showed her good countenance the woman then lifted the young boy to his feet. Reaching out she took the hand of the silent girl, *Kuwányauma*—which interpreted meant Butterfly Showing Beautiful Wings, or more aptly Butterfly—who was next oldest and almost nine summers. Gently she helped the girl to stand. She then lifted the baby, called Magpie because of his almost constant chatter, and placed him on her hip. Magpie had been whimpering, but now, secure in the arms of the woman, he plopped his thumb into his mouth and was contentedly still.

For a brief instant Tala hesitated, but then she also offered her hand to the eldest of the children, a boy of nearly twelve who was called *Kelnyam,* which interpreted meant the Hawk. But ignoring the hand that the woman held out to him, the boy pushed himself painfully to his feet.

"Woman," he said, using the term as though he were speaking to a creature of no consequence, "I am nearly a man, and am well able to care for myself."

Instantly Tala dropped her eyes after the manner of a woman in the presence of a man. "I meant no offense," she said humbly.

Hawk looked up at her, victory in his eyes because she had submitted so easily. "Perhaps you did, and perhaps not. But woman, do not forget your place. You are only a woman, and Outcast as well. I brought you along only to serve the needs of the little ones. As a man of the People I have no need of such aid. Furthermore, as a man of the People I have final say in all things. Do you understand?"

Tala slowly raised her face until she was looking directly into the boy's eyes, a thing no woman ever did. Yet the ancient grandmother had taught her that it was a good thing, and was very disconcerting to the man so gazed upon. She assumed it would work upon a boy as well, and quickly she learned that it did.

"I hear your voice," she replied carefully, "but I question the words."

Hawk, shaken, stared back into the strange greenness of the eyes, stammered, and grew still as the woman continued.

"O Hawk," Tala declared, pleased that her gaze had had such an effect upon him, "you are a fine boy, strong and full of much courage. But still, you are only a boy. You have not lived enough seasons to accomplish all the things a boy must accomplish in order to be a man. Nor have you learned enough. Yet you will, and in time you will be a fine and a strong man indeed."

She paused so that her words would sink into his thinking, and when she was certain they had and that he was not going to show a bad countenance toward her, Tala continued.

"Yet, my son, in this one thing you are right. I am a woman without a man, and so in many ways I *am* weak. Truly will I need the help of one such as yourself if we are to take these little ones to safety."

Hawk glared at her, his eyes wavered, and at last he looked away. Those eyes of hers, so strangely blue-green, were disconcerting. They made one think of things other than the thoughts he wished to consider.

"And the decisions?" he asked, suddenly recalling. "Who will make them?"

"It is within my heart to say that the decisions will take care of themselves," Tala answered. "Now, is your countenance open so that you may freely offer help, O Hawk?"

The boy glanced back up, saw the strange greenness that looked levelly upon him, and again he turned away. But within him was little in the way of anger. He was only confused, for she was not as other women in the village. He had never truly spoken with her, but now he sensed a power he did not understand, and it gave him worry. Women should not have such powers! Such was the belief he had always been taught.

But this one had declared in a very open manner her womanly weakness, and had humbly asked for his help. What more could he ask of her than that? Still, perhaps a little test would be in order.

"This *hóta,*" he said quickly, "this back of mine, is strong, for as you say, I am very nearly a man. It is in my heart to carry your burden."

Tala thought long on his offer, for truly she could hardly walk, the baby was heavy, and the webbing that contained the sacred things was heavy as well. But at last she signaled negatively.

"No, Hawk, it cannot be done, and this is a thing that you especially should know. No one but an adult may carry the sacred things of the People."

"An adult *man*!"

"Yes," Tala agreed quickly, "an adult man, or, if one is not available, an adult woman."

"But you are Outcast!"

Tala dropped her eyes. "It is as you say. Nevertheless, I am adult, all my days I have been of the People, I love them and I love the goodness of their ways. My son, as long as I am here, I will carry the sacred burden. You cannot bear these things until you are of a surety a man. But my heart goes out in thanks that you have offered."

Hawk smiled thinly, somehow disappointed that the woman had passed his little test, and yet relieved as well. Truly he did not want the responsibility of that burden.

"Then perhaps," he suggested with a trace of anger held purposely within his voice, "I might carry the little Badger here for a time."

"Yes," Butterfly responded, smiling shyly and then grimacing at the pain the smile had brought to her parched and cracked mouth. "Do so, my brother, for—"

"I am not your brother," the boy called Hawk snapped.

Surprised at Hawk's bad face, Butterfly looked quickly up to the one who was now as her mother, and then back to the boy. "I only meant that you had become as my brother, O Hawk. I admire your courage and compassion, for truly the Badger's feet trail blood and pain. Little ones such as he should not be made to suffer, for that is not our way. And as I can, I too will help to carry him and the baby Magpie."

Ashamed of his anger and yet for some reason still upset, Hawk dropped his eyes and signaled abruptly that the conversation was ended.

Tala, however, chose to ignore the signal, and she smiled bravely through her own cracked lips. "Perhaps," she said, speaking to the younger girl, "you are right. We should think of ourselves as a family, for truly there is no one left of any of our families but us. Thus each of you will become brothers and a sister, and I will be as your mother."

"I see no reason for this," Hawk declared.

"Nor have you ever been lonely," Tala said quietly. "I have, and there is no joy in it. Additionally, my son, we will all have need of each other if we are to escape the Angry Ones. In this thing our thoughts must truly live together, just as my thoughts and those of the little Butterfly here have mingled."

Hawk and Butterfly dropped their eyes, the one in humility, the other to hide a momentary sense of shame. Badger smiled happily as he climbed onto the older boy's back, Hawk roughly took the hand of Butterfly, Tala placed little Magpie on her other hip, and the five of them pushed forward once more into the ovenlike afternoon, each resolutely placing one bloody foot ahead of the other as they fled the nightmare that followed behind them.

Often Tala tugged fitfully at the coarse fibers of the pack-net, trying to ease their abrasion of her bare shoulders, back, and forehead. She had been unable to find a tumpline and so had simply draped the coarse fibers themselves about her head. But the load was large and heavy, and the pain of the raw sores worn by the fiber would not go away.

Still she did not complain, nor dared she even look pained. Such a thing would displease the Creator, and then surely he would withdraw his spirit. No, they all needed the help of the Great One, and in the pack were the sacred things that she hoped would bring it to pass. But the heart must be right, she knew. In all things must the heart be right.

Tala considered then the things on her back—the knife, the meal, the seed, and especially the sacred water jar—and wondered how she, who was not yet truly adult herself, and Outcast besides, could bring to pass the great spiritual miracle they all needed. Tala had much respect and fear for these sacred things. They had great power, and were far more than a mere woman of so few years and so few powers should touch. Especially was that true of an evil one, a woman who had been declared two-heart and Outcast, who had brought about the death of all her People!

And Tala's heart broke open once again as she lived in her mind that recent time of horror.

15

Hitching the baby higher on her hip and glancing behind her, Tala saw only more shimmering heat waves. Four suns had passed since she and the children had begun their flight, four endless daylights and darknesses during which they had eaten only some shriveled berries left on a bush from the year before, drunk only a bit of water found in an almost-dry *koritivi,* a hole in the stone, and rested only in brief moments when their trembling legs would give up for a time and carry them no further.

But they had to keep moving, for somehow she sensed that the unimaginable killers of her People were behind her, coming on.

Of course she had heard of the Angry Ones. Tales of them were told the little ones, tales that brought quick obedience from them. But to Tala and all the rest of The People they were stories, nothing more. Things that it was rumored the Angry Ones did were beyond understanding, beyond even imagination.

Thus, when Tala had come alone from the mountain and had secreted herself in the rocks near the village as the old one had instructed, she had had no idea of what she was going to see.

Then, when the massacre had occurred, her mind had reeled. First had come confusion, for she could not grasp the enormity of the thing. It was instead a nightmare, an evil dream she was living in the same manner that she lived the dream in which she had seen the man who was to come and give her love. But unlike that other, this dream had not ended, not even after most of an entire sun. It went on and on and on.

And then had come the children, little ones who were not Outcast as she. Yet they too had seen the horror, which by then had been rising up as a great odor. As Tala saw them, saw their reactions, she had finally understood that it was real. All of the clan were *mokee,* all were dead. Then, and only then, had she felt real fear.

The Angry Ones had come because of her! It was truly as the leaders of her clan had declared. Nor did it matter what the ancient grandmother had taught her as they stood upon the mountain. She *was* a two-heart, a person filled with evil, and somehow she had brought death upon all these whom she had loved. She was Outcast even from Tiaowa, the Creator. She was a lost soul, and would be always.

Staggering under the weight of that understanding, she had begun weeping and chanting a death-chant, for truly the world for her had ceased to exist. No longer could she bear the burden of life.

And so her chanting would have continued until her death, but Hawk had stopped it with a simple statement. They were all that was left of the clan, he pointed out, and if it was to be preserved, the younger children would need her womanly help.

Tala, her mind still reeling with the horror of what her guilt had brought to pass, somehow managed to see through her own suffering to the children, and she knew that the boy called Hawk was right. To preserve the clan, to preserve at least these innocent ones, she must lead them into the wilderness, to a far and lonely place where man had not yet been. Only in that way could they avoid the hatred of the Angry Ones; only in that way might she perhaps redeem herself.

16

And so the five young ones of the People flee westward across the slick-rock mesas and the deeply cut canyons of the high plateau country. They travel with horror within their minds, they travel with fear within their hearts, they travel too with suffering and pain as their companions. Yet around them the winds of afternoon continue to blow, and if they could but free themselves of the burdens within their minds, then perhaps they might hear the gentle laughter of the Kachina people as they attempt to guide their feet.

Yet the five hear only the wind, for their hearts are very heavy indeed, they are truly young, and so they hear nothing.

And not far behind a man stands apart from other men. He is comely in appearance, but his eyes burn with an evil fire, and he is filled with anger. The woman is still ahead, and still she carries the power-things of the clan. He should have taken them when first he left the village to search for her, but the urge to find the green-eyed woman was too strong within him, and besides, he fully expected to come back to things as he had left them. But the camp where the woman had been was empty, the village was empty, and now those things are gone as well.

Angrily the man stamps his foot against the earth, grimaces at the pain from the wound that still festers on the inside of his thigh, and spins to face the others.

"There is much food back at the village," he says quickly. "We will return for it soon. Meanwhile, the sign of those who have escaped is upon the earth, and we must go after them and slay them before they warn others. I would also have the things they carry. All but the green-eyed woman are children, and she is hardly more than a girl herself. Still, as I said, her form is lovely, and after they have been taken, who knows . . ."

The well-armed men, whose heads are shaped differently and who are not at all men of the People, grin with understanding. The man Saviki, seeing this, knows they will follow, and exults once more in his great power. Truly is his mind a wondrous thing. Not only will it bring him, very soon, power over all the People of Peace, but it will bring him as well into the presence of the green-eyed witch who has so wounded and so humiliated his being.

17

The day dragged slowly by, a time of unrelenting heat, endless white glare, and uncounted stumbling footsteps. A buzzard swung in slow, lazy circles high overhead, apparently not in any hurry, and the fleeing ones ignored it and plodded onward.

They were climbing along the left slope of a steep, rocky, V-shaped draw, with the rimrock looming steep and high above them. Just ahead, a huge natural bridge arched up and down again, well hidden against a gigantic sandstone fin that thrust up from the mesa. The going was bad on the slope, but not so bad as it would have been in the boulder-choked wash below.

Almost blindly the little group staggered forward, never truly seeing, but always looking backward over the shoulder, for fear rode upon the backs of them all.

Suddenly they turned a corner in the wash and all stopped short, staring ahead. Just a few dozen yards beyond them the gully ended in a large, water-worn amphitheater of solid rock that lifted perhaps a hundred feet above them. The same mass of slick-rock extended down the opposite side of the gully, and there were no breaks in it. It was a neat, sheer-walled, box-ended draw, with the solid wall at the end only slightly less than vertical. Seeing it, the five halted and sank with sodden weariness to the rocky slope.

O Great Tiaowa, Tala cried within her mind as she saw the formidable barrier ahead of them, *can you not hear us? Can we not be seen? Listen, even the little ones cry out, and that is not a good thing. Hear this woman's plea, however unworthy. Go before us, lead us out of this place, and guide at least these little ones to the water of life.*

"Woman," Hawk suddenly declared, his voice low with disgust, "do you see where you have led us? This place is a trap, a corner where the Angry Ones might come upon us and slay us."

Tala dropped her eyes, for there was nothing she could say to the boy. He was right, and she must admit it.

"It is in my mind," Hawk continued, his voice filled with frustration and fatigue, "that we must go back to the mouth of this wash. Perhaps there we will find a way onto the top of the mesa, a way that you missed when you led us here."

Butterfly sighed regretfully, Hawk stared her down, and then slowly he got to his feet.

"Come," he ordered. "We must begin our going backward."

Badger staggered to his feet, Butterfly lifted him onto her thin back, Hawk looked at the woman Tala and at the tiny Magpie who was still in her arms, and without a word he turned away.

Tala sat for a moment, utterly exhausted, utterly discouraged, her eyes mostly closed against the pain and the understanding that so tormented her soul. But then, as she started to climb to her feet, a flicker of movement appeared in the corner of her eye, off ahead and to her right.

Automatically her eyes shifted in that direction, but there was nothing there, nothing but the abrupt rising of the slick-rock sandstone from the far bank of the brush- and boulder-choked wash.

Harder she looked, harder, straining her aching eyes, and suddenly there came into her mind a thing the ancient grandmother had once told her. She thought of that, considered it, and quickly she pulled her eyes back and away from the place of movement, focusing on the nothingness she had been seeing when the flicker of movement first appeared.

"Ha . . . Hawk, my son," she called, her voice hardly audible. "I would speak."

The youth, already several yards away, paused and looked back to where Tala sat. "Woman, there is no time for your foolish words.

Bring little Magpie, or stay and both of you perish. I can see that it will make little difference to the rest of us."

Tala still did not move, did not look up. "My son," she said, making her voice strong as she spoke, "this is a very big thing, and it is in my heart that you and the others should come back and hear this voice I wish to send out."

"Woman!" the boy thundered, "I—"

Slowly Tala raised her hand in the man-signal that demanded respectful silence from all those who were of the People. Hawk saw it, blinked with surprise that she, a lowly woman and Outcast, had so signed, and yet instantly was still.

"Come, my sons and my daughter," Tala cried weakly, "there is a thing you must hear, and then we will continue our fleeing."

Without question Butterfly and Badger turned back. Hawk watched them, kicked at a small rock with his foot, looked up at the huge wall of sandstone and then down at the woman, who still had not moved her face from staring at the ground, and at last he too returned.

"I will give ear, O woman," he murmured, "but truly will I then lead us away from this place of entrapment."

"Let it be so," Tala declared, her face down, "but first, the voice.

"My children, that ancient grandmother who lived with our people taught that we must look at the world twice. First we must bring our eyes together in front of us so that we can see each tiny pebble on the earth, each droplet of dew on a blade of grass. We must look until we can see the smoke rising from the ant hill in the morning sunshine. *Nothing* should escape our notice. That is first.

"Then we must learn to look again, with our eyes at the very edge of what is visible. We must learn to see dimly if we would see things that are dim—visions and dreams, mists, the Kachina people, animals that hurry past us and perhaps have things to tell us. We must learn to look at the world twice if we wish to see all there is. In my pain and sorrow I almost forgot these things."

"This is all very good." Hawk's voice was sarcastic, and Tala heard and worried that his face was so bad. "Still, the Angry Ones are coming," he continued, "and if we are to escape this trap—"

"My son," Tala interrupted, "would you rise to your feet and go as I show you?"

Now Hawk truly stared. "Woman, what is this foolishness?—"

"O Hawk," Tala interrupted, still not moving her face or her eyes, "the Great Tiaowa has seen our distress and has sent a *poko*, an animal to help us. But this four-legged brother of ours, this coyote, is very secretive, and in my blindness I very nearly missed the message he delivered.

"Now, my son, you must cross the wash in the direction I show and climb to the wall of stone. Do so quickly, for, as you say, there is very little time."

His face reflecting his frustration, Hawk rose hesitantly to his feet, almost refused, thought better of it, and then turned and made his way down through the tumbled boulders. Slowly he worked his way beyond them and up the far side of the wash, until he came at last to the great wall of stone.

"There is nothing," he called back quickly, triumphantly.

Tala, her head down and her eyes still mostly closed, responded quickly. "Move forward, my son. I see your form, but you are not yet at the place."

Hawk stared hard at the woman, saw the eyes of Badger and Butterfly upon him, and at last he moved forward once more, casting his eyes about as he went.

"Stop!" Tala suddenly called. "Do you see anything?"

"Yes," Hawk replied, still sarcastic. "I see much rock and earth, a little grass and a little brush, and a great wall of stone."

"Are there no tracks upon the earth?"

"None, O woman."

Tala drew a deep breath, but still did not move. "Are you close to the rock? Can you touch the wall?"

"No, I am not that close. But I can see—"

"My son, move to the wall until you can touch it. Good. Now take another step forward. Is there no sign upon the earth?"

Hawk stared down. "Nothing," he called. "It is as I said. No woman has the power . . ."

Frantically Tala thrust his murmurings out of her mind. She had seen it. It had been there, where he now stood, and she knew it. It must be there!

"My son," she suddenly called, and her voice cracked a little with her excitement, "it is higher, near where your face is. Do you not see a shelf?"

Hawk lifted his eyes and was surprised to see a tiny, almost level spot of earth, not more than two or three feet across, at about his eye level. And in the sandy soil on that shelf were the tracks of a coyote, plain and clear and fresh.

"It is here," he called quickly, "as is the sign of our four-legged brother."

"Good, my son. That will be the way of our going. The good spirit who was the coyote showed us a *hovatoqa,* a cut in the rock there, hidden well behind this other rock. That is the way we must go."

Quickly Tala climbed to her feet, leaned her body against the weight of the netted burden, and with the baby in her arms she led Butterfly and Badger down through the wash and up to the level place in the cliff. Hawk, meanwhile, had climbed onto the place, and now he looked back down, his face filled with excitement.

"O woman, there is truly a trail here. It is steep and narrow, but the sign of the coyote goes up, and so will we."

Tala looked up at him, did her best to smile, and quickly she helped the little ones up onto the shelf. Then she handed the netting to Hawk, who took it carefully and laid it to the side. Relieved of that burden she thrust her toes into the cracks in the rock and pulled herself upward, and truly was she surprised to feel the helping hands of the boy Hawk as he took her arms and lifted with her.

Perhaps, her mind declared, *the ancient grandmother was right. Perhaps, O green-eyed woman, it can be as she said.*

18

Through pain-dimmed eyes Tala watched for signs of water as she stumbled forward into the morning, doing her best to have a good countenance. But there was nothing, nothing but the soft crying of the baby she held against her breast and the crying as well of the wind as it whispered through the brush and junipers of the mesa.

For a long time she did not look back, for she feared, she truly did. Still, it could not be avoided, and so, turning at last, she looked behind.

Shocked, she could do no more than stare. The damage the passing of the day had done to the little ones was almost beyond belief. Hawk was covered with blood, and she could see that he had fallen many times. His face was scraped, and his arms as well, but his knees had sustained the most damage. They were simply a mass of torn and bleeding flesh. Yet still the boy's face was composed, and still he carried little Badger, the digger.

Badger had his head down on Hawk's shoulder, and so Tala assumed the child was asleep. Well he should be, too, for then he would not feel the great and terrible hand of thirst that was choking them upon the swollen substances of their own tongues. Little Magpie also slept against her own breast, and for that also she felt gratitude.

Tala finally looked at pretty Butterfly, and felt her heart sink within her. The young girl's eyes had sunken so deeply that now they burned like coals from the darkness of a kiva. Her pretty face was cracked and raw, and her steps, as she shuffled forward, were halting and uncertain. Her knees and hands were also torn from falling upon the rock, but Hawk still held her hand, and that alone, Tala knew, had brought the young girl this far.

Tala's heart swelled with honor-pride as she looked at young Hawk, and even though the boy held her in great disdain, still she sent a voice forward toward the sun where Tiaowa dwelt, not pleading now but thanking, giving great praise for the strength and man-courage of this boy. Now, if only she herself could muster such strength!

Pausing, she reached with her free hand into the carrying net and pulled out a small pinch of ground cornmeal. Weakly she tossed it into the air, and in her heart was a great chanting. *O Great Tiaowa, hear this voice, and see this offering of our sacred corn. There is within these little ones a great need for water. Lead us, therefore, to it . . .*

It was in the heat of midday that the new family stumbled onto the water, a very small *koritivi* in the rock of the mesa. Hawk, who was carrying the little Badger, let him drink first, giving him just a little and telling him to hold it in his mouth. They gave water to the silent baby Magpie then, pushing it into his tiny mouth through a hollow stem of grass. Butterfly followed, wetting her blood-crusted lips and then forcing just a trickle of it into her mouth. Hawk then motioned for Tala to drink, but she refused.

"But woman . . . I mean . . . Mother," he pleaded, his voice a raspy thing, "your thirst is as great as ours. Truly you need it."

Tala, surprised that the young man had used the term of mother, shrugged and did her best to smile past her thirst, though the effort cracked her lips and brought quick tears to her eyes. "Thank you, my son," she croaked, her voice little more than a whisper. "But . . . but no, you drink. Your needs are more important than my own."

Hawk looked up, his eyes wide with wonder. "No, my mother . . ."

"My son, you see how it is? For our People it is the children who must not suffer, who must be spared. I am a woman, and though wise and strong beyond understanding, you are not yet a full man. You and these others are the People of tomorrow's dawning, while tomorrow I will be gone. Now drink, and perhaps, when the four of you are finished . . ."

Hawk looked long into Tala's eyes, and then at last he dropped onto the rock, where he looked up once more. "My mother, truly the old woman called the ancient grandmother may have been right. You do not act after the manner of a two-heart."

Then he drank, and as he did so Tala pondered his strange words. Not a two-heart? The old woman? How could he know of such things as those? Besides, she was truly Outcast, and now the clan was dead. Still, the grandmother had indeed thus spoken.

At last, when the children all had a small amount of life-giving water in them, Tala dropped onto the rock and touched the tiny bit of moisture that was left. Pressing her body tightly against the rock, she inhaled the sweet odor of the wet stone, savoring it. Then, though it was painful, she thrust her swollen tongue into the bit of mud and water at the bottom of the hole.

There was no taste, for that sense was gone from her, but Tala could feel the coolness of the moisture as her tongue soaked it up. In a moment she shifted and repeated the process, and though her terrible thirst was not quenched, a little moisture entered her system, and a little strength was gained therefrom.

Finally, when there was nothing in the way of moisture left in the hole, Tala rose shakily to her feet. "Come," she signaled bravely while the children stared at her. "We must continue our flight."

Adjusting the band of the packing net upon her forehead and taking up the baby, Tala fought down her dizziness, pushed one raw and bleeding foot forward, followed it with the other, repeated the painful process, looked to make certain that the children were following, and then closed her mind to all but thoughts of walking, of getting away, of finding a *wáki,* a hiding place for the children so that at least a flickering of the life of the clan might be preserved.

19

In all the world there is only darkness. Stars, though they be many, give little light for seeing. Thus travelers, even if they are in a great hurry, must stop and wait for the darkness to be driven back. In such darkness a woman sits alone, waiting, fearing. With her are four children, but they sleep the sleep of the pure, the innocent. The woman, who has seen ugliness and all but the face of the one who will be her husband, cannot. She is too filled with dreams and with fear, and she wonders at that. How can one in such a desperate position as herself, who has seen the horror of the Angry Ones, possibly be thinking man-thoughts? Truly she does not understand, but as the stars make their slow revolution above her the woman's eyes stay open and her thoughts scatter out like dust in a twisting wind.

Suddenly she notices a soft laughter on the breezes of the night, and as she strains to hear, the gentle voices of the Kachina spirits drift above and around her head.

"Little sister," they call with a sigh as the winds whisper through the junipers. "Little sister, do you hear us?"

I hear you, Tala calls out in her mind, *I hear, but—*

There is more laughter, interrupting her thoughts. "Ho," they chuckle deeply, "but you are making a wondrous fleeing. Do you not worry, though, that you are leaving far behind you the man of your vision?"

I had not thought of that, Tala ponders thoughtfully.

"Yet we have so thought," they laugh gently. "Perhaps he comes, and yet you flee before him. Truly that would be a good joke."

But . . . but what should I do? she calls in her mind. *What is it that I must do so that this man who was in shadow will come. . . .*

But the Kachina spirits are leaving, their laughter drifting away in the night. "Do?" they laugh as they make a departing. "Who are you, little sister, that we should say? Not even you know who you are. The old woman tried to say, but you did not have ears."

But the clan! Tala screams in her mind. *They are all mokee, and it was because of the two-heartedness of this woman who now speaks. I saw!*

But her mind is echoing into the empty air. The Kachina people are gone, and in the darkness a woman sits with great tears falling freely. She is exhausted, she is filled with fear, and she is alone.

20

It was Hawk who first saw the fires of the Angry Ones. "Woman," he asked quietly, "do you see them? Do you see the red stars?"

Tala, surprised that the boy was awake, somehow could not understand his question. She had been sitting quietly, huddled against him for warmth, doing her best to trail her thoughts away from what they seemed so eager to dwell upon.

At that instant she had been thinking intentionally of her mother and father, sending her thoughts back to more happy times. In her mind she could hear the laughter of her father and the soft voice of her mother, and feel the warmth of their dwelling, which was more than the warmth of a fire. She could remember her father, a good hunter, tumbling her head over heels in the long grasses and telling her that she must never waste the good light Tiaowa had placed in her lovely eyes.

She could remember her mother singing soft songs to her even when she was no longer of an age for singing to sleep, and making her many small sandals and many fringed aprons and leggings because she was her one child and she felt she would have no other. She could remember her mother telling her that she was like no other girl because of the green starlight that was in her eyes. And always her mother had told this in the same way and with the same words, and so it had become a very big thing within Tala's mind.

Then, too, there were the words of the old woman, spoken after she was Outcast. She could truly be who she thought she was, and it did not matter what others thought or said. These things lived in the mind of Tala, and so always she had tried to be of one heart. But then had come the great killing, none but the four children of the clan were left alive, and suddenly she was no longer as she had been.

"Woman, there!"

Tala, brought back once again to painful reality by Hawk's urgent tug on her arm, looked.

"Stars, my son?" she questioned, even while her heart ached with the understanding of her evil and its awful consequences. "Surely they are all about us. . . ."

"O woman, I mean the two red stars, far across the canyon. Do you not see? They are near where we found the going-down place in the rock."

Tala stared, and suddenly the cold hand of fear took hold of her insides and squeezed. *"Urúhuú,"* she whispered. They were there, two fires winking evilly in the darkness.

She gasped with the realization of it, tried to rise but couldn't, and found that she couldn't even talk. Her tongue was useless with fear, her legs were without strength, her mind was numb with the memory of the destruction of her clan.

"Is it within your heart that I awaken the others?"

Tala slowly signaled yes. Hawk stood, placed his hand over Butterfly's mouth, and prodded her gently. The girl's large eyes fluttered open in fear, and she would have screamed except for the hand over her mouth. Hawk reassured her, she acknowledged and was silent, and then the oldest boy awakened Badger in the same manner. The baby, still asleep, he simply handed to the woman. When all were ready, he helped Tala to her feet, then the others, and then he spoke.

"The apron of Badger covers my feet as well as those of Butterfly," he said simply. "However, it is in my heart, woman, that the coverings on my feet should cover yours instead."

Tala, completely surprised at this great change in Hawk's countenance, still signaled that it could not be done. "No, my son," she declared, her voice breaking a little as she spoke. "I rejoice in your goodness, but it is as it should be. And truly, I feel no pain from my feet. It is my heart that is grievously wounded, and that cannot be bound."

And then, for perhaps the first time in her life, Tala forgot the need for showing a good face at all times. "Oh," she wailed fearfully, "the Angry Ones have found the way of our passing! We are lost! We are lost! Oh, what is there to do?"

"We must flee," the boy answered quickly, hiding his surprise at this sign of weakness he was suddenly seeing within the woman. "It must be done now, in the darkness."

"But for the space of four suns we have done nothing else," Tala cried, forgetting still the need for a good countenance. "To where do we go that they will not follow?"

Hawk dropped his eyes, for within him was no answer. Butterfly, still watching, reached down and lifted the naked Badger onto her thin and bony back.

"My mother," she whispered, "I . . . I would speak."

Tala, still watching the fires, finally responded, and so the girl began.

"It . . . it is in my heart that we should continue to go away from the star of your birth. This is my thought. Perhaps if we would also send out a prayer-voice—"

Tala silenced her with a motion of her hand. "I . . . I have done this," she responded brokenly. "But it . . . it does no good. I am of two hearts, I am Outcast, and the great Tiaowa turns away from such."

"Woman," Hawk interrupted, "perhaps a *páho,* a prayer-feather—"

"I have no feather!" Tala answered angrily and with great frustration. "I have nothing, and now they are here and I have failed even you!"

The two eldest children dropped their eyes in shame and pity, but Hawk, even though his eyes were downcast, persisted. "O woman, here is your carrying net. Our sister Butterfly is right. We must flee away from your star. Only in that direction will we find *wáki,* a true hiding place. And as for a *páho,* who knows? Perhaps Giver-of-life will provide."

"My mother," Badger said suddenly as he pointed eastward, "it grays on the mesa."

Tala, still fearful and undecided, turned and stared. The child was right! There was indeed a lighting, faint still, but very much there. Turning then, she stumbled hastily forward while once again the icy grip of fear crushed down upon her soul. They would be found! In the daylight the Angry Ones who were already as close as across the canyon would find their sign and would follow.

21

And so five of the Peaceful Ones, one woman who is not yet truly so, and four children who are not hers at all, flee in terror away from the dawn. They go in haste, for two have sandals, two are carried, and one feels no pain but the pain of guilt, and they go in fear. And yes, a spoor is left behind, a spoor of bright red blood that flows from the feet of the woman and onto the face of the rock.

The Kachina people who yet ride the early morning breezes see this and laugh. But it is a good laugh, kind and gentle. For though the woman does not yet know herself, they do, and they laugh with pride. Eagerly they move in the way of helping, and the woman staggers with great weariness, almost falling.

And so who is to say that the leaving of such a spoor is a bad thing? Truly will the Angry Ones follow, but that hurries the five along, and such haste is not a bad thing, not a bad thing at all.

22

Through the rocks and the brush and the cactus they fled, and their pain and exhaustion were etched deeply upon their faces. Across the slick-rock of a huge upthrust they made their way, then down through a rocky draw, up the far side, and onto a wide juniper-covered bench. The morning sun, as though worn from its efforts of the previous day, pushed itself wearily over the eastern horizon and stabbed with white hot lances at the lonely group, increasing their pain and their weakness. Yet still they staggered on.

Hawk and Butterfly were falling more frequently, and Tala could hear their sobs and their groanings as they dragged themselves to their feet and, still carrying Badger, followed after.

She had not fallen yet, and she knew that she dared not do so. The baby called Magpie would be injured—she could not bear to see that happen—and such a fall would surely break the sacred things that she carried in the net on her back. That must not happen! Somehow she must make the wooden sticks that had once been her legs continue to carry her. Somehow she must find the support and strength to go on.

O Great Tiaowa, she cried through her tortured mind as she sprinkled a little more cornmeal into the air as a thank offering, *hear now this voice, this voice of distress. Wa! Look not upon the two-heartedness of this woman. Wa! Look not upon the fact that there is no páho, no prayer-feather. Wa! Consider instead, O Great One, these little ones who have great need and who suffer. Wa! These are one-hearts, of good countenances, filled with courage. Give ear to the prayer-thoughts of this woman regarding them.*

And then Tala, her legs grown numb with weariness and her body nearly dead from thirst and hunger, was down upon the rock. She felt no pain, but in her heart was a fear, a fear that she had hurt the baby and broken the sacred water jar of the People.

She tried to rise but couldn't, she could hear the crying of the little Magpie but she could not get to him, she tried to see behind her, to feel if the sacred jar was all right.

And then in the darkness of her mind she heard Hawk giving quick directions. She felt him lifting the packing net from her forehead, and as she raised her eyes to thank him she was startled to see, caught in a clump of *wíkavi,* of sagebrush, a small downy feather that had come from the breast of *kwáhu,* the eagle.

O Tiaowa, she thought as her eyes widened in awe, *can it be? Can it be that you left this for us? O Great Creator, this woman of so much unworthiness gives thanksgiving.*

And once again, as they had done so often since the day of becoming Outcast, tears flowed down the young woman's haggard face. But now, strangely enough, they were tears of joy, of gratitude, and not of sorrow. It was truly a rare and wonderful thing for the children to behold.

FOUR

The Twisting Wind

23

She was there, the feather was there, and the rock was there. The rock was always there. Other than that, in all the world there seemed to be nothing. Tala felt the coarseness of the rock beneath her body and found comfort in it. She felt too the relief of pain from where the packing net had somehow been removed from her forehead and shoulders, and was grateful these things had finally been lifted from her. Then, too, there was the feather from the eagle, with which she and the children could make the *páho* they needed.

Tala struggled to sit up, suddenly fearful for the children, whom she had momentarily forgotten. *O Great One,* her mind cried, *forgive this woman . . .*

"Woman," Hawk exclaimed as Tala struggled to sit up, "what is it? What do you see?"

Clutching the tiny feather, Tala climbed shakily to her feet, facing the little ones. "Hawk," she urged in her hoarse whisper, "make, on that high place yonder, a *tútuskya,* a circle of stones opening east. Butterfly, take of this grass and twirl quickly against your thigh a string for binding. And Badger, sit here beside me and choose, from our bag of corn, the finest kernel. I myself, using the *mongwi's* ancient knife, will prepare the stick. Tiaowa has sent us this feather for the making of a prayer-stick."

The little ones, wide-eyed, hastened to obey. Soon, with the feather, the twine, the kernel of corn, and a small stick, Tala had fastened a *páho,* a prayer-feather.

"Come," she urged the children as she thrust the knife into her waist-belt and led the way to the circle of stones that had now become a shrine. "Send out a voice, my children, that in some manner we might be led to safety. I myself will turn my back, so that my own evil ways will not influence the great Tiaowa."

"O woman," Hawk declared, "do not do this. We need the strength of your adulthood. Nor will Tiaowa hear us if we are not united in our hearts. It is my desire that our voices should rise together."

Tala stared, hardly able to comprehend that the youth was asking for her help. Then Butterfly reached out and touched her arm in her own silent plea, and Tala, with tears in her eyes, made the sign of agreement.

Silently the children stood as she placed the *páho* in the center of the shrine, using three small stones to hold it in place. Then, after the manner of her people, she opened her mouth and sent her voice skyward.

O Great Giver-of-life, she chanted. *Hear the voice we send out. Wa! Hear the voice we send as an eagle flies, strong, high, full of power. Wa!*

O Great One, we seek not the destruction of these with the ways of núkpana, of evil. Wa! We seek only our safety, that the clan might go on. Wa!

Hear these our words, lifted with the strength of kwáhu, the eagle, for we know of your power, O Wise One. Wa! We know too of your goodness. . . .

24

And so the young woman called Tala, only fourteen summers old but already carrying the great burdens of motherhood and of guilt, bends her knees and with outstretched arms sits womanlike on the strong and silent rock within the circle of stones, a circle that is symbolic of the circle of the world. There the woman's faith becomes a living thing.

The children sit beside her, Hawk holding Badger and Butterfly holding the silent Magpie, and their faith joins easily with hers.

They face outward with their backs to each other, and that too is symbolic, for they are saying to the Great One that their hearts are now within the circle of love that he created, and their eyes now look only outward toward others, and not selfishly inward.

The circle of the sky watches from above, and the rim of their world rises to meet it. The level of all their eyes has dropped only a few feet, yet they are infinitely closer to the heart of the earth. They are suddenly a part of the great quietness that is yet filled with the sound of all life, and they sense the pulse of it around them.

The winds whispering through the grass and brush and junipers carry again the voices of their ancestors, and it is always so to minds who know such spirits exist. These young ones call the spirits Kachina people, and the woman especially prays that perhaps they will be her friends. They whisper, and she finds great comfort, for the whispering is soft and gentle as it begins, and such a thing is a sign to one who has prepared herself for signs and merged herself into the natural forces that surround her.

Thus the winds gather, and as a lifting thermal from the superheated rock meets a coolness that has settled within the shade of a large juniper, the air twirls around itself, moving faster and faster.

The Kachina people laugh with great delight as they ride these lively winds, urging them on, twisting, spinning with them across the mesa, lifting dust and tumbleweeds as they go, moving easily and without effort toward the small shrine of rocks with the opening to the east.

With wide-open eyes filled with awe and reverence, Tala and the children watch as the twisting wind enters the opening from the east, hesitates, plucks at the resistant *páho*, plucks harder, lifts it, and sends it soaring upward into the turquoise blue of the noontime sky. And then they are gone, twisting winds, Kachina people, *páho*, and all, and who is to say, to those whose minds have been prepared to believe such things, that the great Tiaowa did not hear, did not send the feather, did not lift it upward on the *hóta,* the back of the twisting wind?

25

Late in the afternoon of that, the fifth day of their fleeing, Tala saw the *lomáhongva,* the beautiful clouds arising. With the last bit of strength that was in her she had clawed her way over the rimrock and out of a deep and narrow canyon they had been forced to cross. Now she was lying on the stone, gasping for breath and trying to ignore the pain in her torn hands and legs and feet, content simply to let the dizziness whirl her away.

In the distance she heard the cry of *angwusi,* the crow, and closer she could hear the whimpering of little Magpie and the quiet struggles of Hawk and Butterfly as they helped little Badger over the rock. Guiltily she opened her swollen eyes and struggled to sit up, to help. But they were already there beside her, exhausted but safe, and so Tala sank back onto the rock. And then as she looked out through her aching eyes she suddenly realized that the clouds were there, lying low against the horizon to the northwest.

"H . . . Hawk," she whispered as the boy fell to the rock beside her, "my son, do you see them?"

Hawk opened his own eyes and stared about. "See what, my mother?"

"The Cloud Kachina people. Over there. Perhaps our *páho* was an *omawnakw,* a cloud-feather."

Hawk strained his swollen eyes, a doubtful look on his dirt-encrusted face. Badger looked as well, as did Butterfly, but there were no clouds. The three children looked then at each other, in fear, for truly the senses of the woman who was now as their mother had made a running away. This was the great time of dryness; there were no clouds, nor would there be any.

"Woman," Hawk responded gently, "I see no clouds. The *pongovi,* the circle of the sky, is clear and empty."

Stunned by his words, Tala struggled once more against the spinning in her head, trying to sit up. Thirst gnawed like a ground squirrel in her belly and throat. Her mouth, a great dry cavern in her face, burned with raw pain. And her body, her tired and aching body, was shriveling up and slowly dying from exposure and dehydration.

She knew this and tried to force her mind away from it, and so her thoughts roamed momentarily out and away across the mesas and arroyos and came back and were still, and again she saw the clouds.

"Hawk," she whispered weakly, lifting her arm in the manner of pointing. "They . . . they are there, low against the rock. Do . . . do you not see?"

Then, not waiting for an answer, nor even aware that she had not received one, Tala staggered bravely to her feet.

"Come," she muttered to the alarmed children, "we must hurry. Darkness will be falling about us, and we must make haste to where the clouds are making a water falling."

And Tala, with her hunger and thirst suddenly dying away within her, started eagerly forward. She felt strangely light and giddy, as if she had climbed onto some great height, and her thoughts kept fleeing away from her. And each time she would call them back, forcefully, reminding them of the need within her to reach the place of the clouds so that she might give the children the much-needed water.

She did not consider that the children might not follow, she did not think of the baby she should have carried, she forgot entirely the pack-net with its sacred burden that was now left for the boy Hawk, she did not think of the ancient metal knife that was yet within in her waist-belt, she did not even recollect her pain. She thought only of the Cloud Kachina people, showing there before her, whispering her name as they called her.

Thus obediently she followed, and with fear the children, heavily burdened, labored behind.

26

The sun dropped toward the hard-edged rock of the plateau country and the air grew still and heavy with unseen warnings. Hawk, suddenly nervous because of what seemed to be happening, carried both the baby Magpie and the pack-net carefully, and did his best to keep Tala in sight.

"Hurry," he urged Butterfly. "The woman is almost running, and we must not lose her. Her mind is wandering in the twilight, and she will need our help."

"The B . . . Badger grows heavy," Butterfly responded through labored breathing. "I . . . I can go no faster. And you, do you not fear, carrying the s . . . sacred things?"

Hawk nodded. "Indeed I fear, but I fear more the thought of leaving these things behind. They are sacred for our people, and must be preserved from the Angry Ones." He paused then, and at last continued. "I fear too for the woman."

Butterfly muttered her agreement, and in that instant little Badger lifted his head from her shoulder in the attitude of listening. "I hear them," he said in his thin and childish voice.

Hawk felt his heart grow cold with fear. He instantly stopped, as did Butterfly, and in the stillness they held their breathing and so they also heard the distant shouts of men, angry men who for some unexplained reason were seeking their lives.

Without another word the boy turned and trotted on across the slick-rock mesa. Butterfly followed, carrying the wide-eyed Badger, and the way for them was easy to see. The woman whose eyes carried the blue-green color of the star of the east had gone before, marking the trail well with her life's blood, moving in a direct manner toward the empty horizon while her feet stained the rock beneath her.

Suddenly Hawk stopped, and with his mouth open he stared down at the bloodstains. Perhaps they should not be following. Perhaps, if the woman continued to leave a well-marked trail, he and the little ones might go another way, toward a high place that lifted off to his right, and thus the Angry Ones would be misled. Without a word Hawk veered to the side and ran on, his mind a made-up thing.

Butterfly, her mouth too sore to speak, made the sign for questioning, and Hawk paused. Then he looked at her in such a way that she understood clearly her lowly status as a girl. Finally, however, he answered.

"No trail," he gasped, pointing at the rock upon which they ran. "Our feet leave no blood-sign, for we wear Badger's apron upon them. The woman is leading the Angry Ones now, and it is in my mind that we must go another way so that we might hide. We must made a *waítioma*, a running-away-rapidly, so that this, her last gift to us, is not given in vain."

Butterfly faltered, suddenly of two minds, for truly she already loved the woman of the eastern morning star. "Her . . . her last gift?"

"Sister," Hawk said urgently as he took her arm, "think on the *páho*, think long on it and on the twisting wind that took it upward. It is in my mind that the great Tiaowa has heard the prayer-thoughts we sent out, and has opened this way that the sacred things of the clan might be preserved. The woman, by giving her life to the Angry Ones, will allow the rest of us to escape and to live."

"No!" Butterfly whispered, her eyes wide with horror. "We must not leave her to th . . . them. We . . ."

"The love for this woman who has become as our mother is bright in your eye," Hawk declared, "and it is making you weak. Have you forgotten so soon that she is Outcast?"

"I . . . I have not forgotten," Butterfly answered. "But my brother, do you not recall what those evil ones did to the clan? We can not leave this one who has given so much to us."

Angry and frustrated, Hawk turned to go. "Perhaps the Creator will preserve her," he said. "These things I do not know. I feel only that we must make a hiding. Now be still and follow me."

Butterfly dropped her eyes in acquiescence. Hawk looked at Badger and asked if he would follow; the small child said nothing, only stared with great wide eyes, and so they set out once more, fleeing toward a great high place of hiding.

27

The woman called Tala staggered forward into the gathering dusk, the bright red blood of her passing showing plainly on the rock behind. Her head was no weight upon her shoulders, but her feet were heavy, and she could hardly lift them. Yet she did, over and over, again and again, and so she came at last to a huge lifting bulge of slick-rock. She did not slow, but continued up and across it, her pain a hollow emptiness within, her thoughts far away with the six-point cloud people, her eyes unseeing.

And then her right foot, reaching forward, met only air. The woman tried to pull back, but her body was beyond the will of her mind and it continued on. She plunged forward, twisted to grab the rock, missed, gave a great cry of terror, fell several feet, struck with the top of her right leg against an outcropping of stone, and with the shock unconsciousness finally took her. She bounded like a corn-husk doll out into the gloom and spun downward in a silent fall that changed only when she struck the topmost branches of a thick-limbed *salavi,* a spruce that her people called sacred.

She did not stop falling even then, but the limbs, reaching out and taking hold, slowed her so that when at last the crumpled form of her body struck the earth, the impact was no more than if she had tripped over a stone and fallen forward.

28

And so in the gathering darkness, a woman who has left an easy-to-follow trail lies still as death, while in another place four children who have left no trail at all crouch in hiding. They have heard the great scream, the cry with the sudden ending, and they truly wonder concerning the woman who has been as their mother.

And as Hawk holds the mouth of the tired and hungry Magpie so that he will make no sound, the sounds of many heavy feet and much heavy breathing whisper past. Though the children do not hear clearly the few growled words, they sense easily the evil, and know the Angry Ones are there, searching.

The winds of evening rise up and twist the branches of the juniper and pinyon, and it is easy to suppose that a very bad thing has happened to the woman who has become as their mother. She is dead—whether to the Angry Ones or to something else there is no way of knowing. But the scream was the scream of one dying.

29

The Angry Ones have trailed the blood-spoor to the edge of the cliff, which yawns deeply before them, opening only into the darkness of the unknown.

The leader of the men, comely and well-formed, but with a strange fire in his eyes, stops and pulls back, confused and afraid. Hastily he searches, but shortly he knows that he is not wrong. The spoor of blood goes over the edge and ends, abruptly. Anxiously the others look at each other, for they sense that they are seeing a great magic, perhaps even a witch-thing. The leader does not believe this, and quickly he grows angry. One man is ordered over the edge to seek a trail, but there is none, and when he narrowly escapes falling, the entire group, including the leader, draws back to consider.

This has seemed so easy, this catching of the woman who has been running on dead feet. But now she is gone, and a shiver of fear passes through each of them. The children too are considered, and it is remembered that for two suns there has been only occasional sign of their passing. There was also the circle-shrine that contained no *páho* and therefore made no sense.

"She has fallen," he of the burning eyes declares. "It is no more than that. Find a way down, and I will find her body."

The others look from him to each other and back again. The man Saviki's words made sense; this is what must have happened.

Suddenly, from the darkness of the chasm before them, a strong wind lift up, moaning eerily through a small window, an old *koritivi,* a hole in the stone where water once collected. Now, though, the hole has worn through, and the air whistles through it easily.

At the strange sound there is a great intake of breath. Each has heard such sounds before, but never in such a place, never in such a manner as this. Another gust follows the first, the moaning from the rock grows more forlorn, and to all of the Angry Ones but the leader, things become suddenly clear.

The woman, the children, all are evil spirits. They have led these men to this place, and now, in revenge for the killings at the village, those same spirits are going to slay them. These spirits are very strong, they have strange powers, they walk on the air.

In the distance lightning flashes, thunder rumbles, another gust of wind moans through the old *koritivi,* and suddenly the Angry Ones have become the Fearful Ones. Except for their leader they turn and flee backward upon their own trail, crying out their terror as they run. He runs as well, but he does not cry out. Instead he watches backward over his shoulder, and in his mind, fueled by his hatred and his lust, is a great question concerning the green-eyed woman. It seems that surely she must be dead, but somehow he cannot bring himself to believe that. He heard the scream, he followed the spoor of blood, but somehow he senses that she yet lives.

There is also the matter of the children. They must not be left alive, and Saviki is certain that they are alive. Their living could undo all he has managed to accomplish. Then, too, there are the power-things of the slain clan. Those things have great value, and must also be considered.

Slowly Saviki stops, and in the darkness he sits down to wait for the light of the sun. Those others, called the Angry Ones but in reality just as much the Foolish Ones as his own people, will run yet awhile, fleeing from their foolish beliefs. But they too will stop, and he will come up with them then.

And a little way off four children, huddled together, listen in wonder as the pounding feet tear past. They also hear the feet of the one who stops. Hawk signals in the darkness with his hands, and from that one who has stopped they begin creeping further away.

They know that with daylight he will have no trouble finding them, and such knowledge gives them great fear and also great strength.

And in another direction and far below, the woman with the green eyes of the Star of the Eastern Day Breaking lies in the manner of death. Her body is white and still, and in her form is no movement.

FIVE

The Water-Planted-Place

30

The world is a vast and empty darkness, a void awash in a sea of pain. Nothing moves, yet nothing is still. The waves of agony lift slowly as the tide of the sea, yet just as surely—rising, receding, and rising again.

In all that, the woman is there. She is a broken heap of flesh and bone floating on a thick covering of old pine needles beneath a spruce tree in a tiny hidden valley nestled in the high plateau country of the great American Southwest. She was as the *Taláwsohu* the living star of the morning, but now she is only a slight glimmering of life, floating in a place that is empty, that is hers alone.

31

In the darkness the thunder rumbled more loudly, the lightning flashed more brightly, and finally, in that one place alone upon the mesa, the rain came. With a wild rush it came, but soon it slowed until it was only a gentle falling, and so it remained. And the wetness of it was a cold dropping on Tala's face. She stirred, agony rose up and slammed into her with a fist of darkness, and in that instant she was unconscious once more.

Slowly the rain went away into the darkness. It left behind it much water, but in trade it had taken away from the rock the blood-spoor of the woman. She did not know this, for she knew nothing. She was still walking in the twilight of the world.

And then in the gray light of dawn the splashing of water over the rock awakened her at last. She lay still as the pain coursed through her body, and her eyes were wide with a growing understanding. Somehow she had lost the children.

And strangely, though she understood too that her leg was broken, that she was all alone, and that she was likely dying, her thoughts were only for the little ones, the four whom she had determined to protect. She had let them down. In their time of greatest need she had abandoned them.

O Gr . . . Great Tiaowa, she pleaded, sending her silent and faltering voice upward. *I . . . I have lost them, and I fear for their . . .*

Her words faltered, and then darkness washed once more over the understanding of the green-eyed one who was Outcast from the People, and she thought no more of the children.

32

The sun, not yet overhead, was already hot, and strangely, in this place there was no moisture in the air from the rain of the darkness before. Instead it was very dry. High on a rocky butte, flat on his stomach among the rocks, Hawk lay still and wondered where he would go now. He and the three little ones had run and climbed all night, going roughly eastward from where the woman must surely have fallen, barely keeping ahead of the single man who had apparently heard their movement and had followed.

For an instant Hawk thought of the green-eyed woman, thought of her death, and then he dismissed it from his mind. As the elders had always said, she was only a woman. Still, she *had* shown great courage.

Behind him Butterfly, Badger, and little Magpie crouched, and Hawk looked at them and then let his gaze drift past. He mopped sweat from his brow and studied again the broken cliff below him. There seemed to be a vaguely possible route, but at the thought of it his mouth turned dry and his stomach empty. For him alone it would be hard; for him and the little ones as well it might be impossible.

But coming up the opposite side of the butte, the sloping side, was the man, the Angry One, and Hawk knew they had no choice. Again he looked over the cliff. A bulge in the rock looked as though it might afford handholds. Some of the rock was loose, however, and he couldn't see beyond the bulge to see if the handholds continued. To that point, perhaps they could do it. Beyond that, he could not know.

Again Hawk looked down at the Angry One, who was moving slowly but steadily upward. He was much closer, and if they waited any longer, it would be too late.

Suddenly Hawk stiffened. There was something else, something familiar about the movement of the Angry One.

Saviki! He was the man the green-eyed woman had spurned, had stabbed in the leg! He was limping now, badly, and that was why his progress had been so slow. But he should have been *mokee,* dead with the others, back at the village. Why was he here?

Quickly Hawk took the cord that Butterfly had removed from the edges of the heavy pack-net, and though he knew it would never hold them, he also knew it would give Badger and the girl courage. That in itself made it worth the doing. First he tied it to himself, then to Badger's waist, and finally to Butterfly, and then he signed *atkyaqw,* downward, over the cliff.

Badger merely nodded and was ready. Butterfly, her eyes very large, signed agreement as well, but Hawk could see the fear that lived within her heart. Still, there was no other way, and so Hawk took the constantly whimpering Magpie and put him within the net with the sacred things. Then he draped the net over his forehead, turned his face to the rock, and slid feet first over the bulge. Feeling with his bare toes for a hold, he inched downward. If he fell from there he would drag the others with him; he knew that, and knew too that they would drop not less than two hundred feet. Close in, however, there was a narrow ledge only sixty feet down, and he hoped to reach that. It was his only hope, for beyond that he dared not think.

Using simple pull holds and working down with his feet, Hawk worked his way out over the bulge. Badger was following, doing well, and Butterfly was coming last, moving slowly and carefully.

Hawk smiled grimly at her fearful attempt at bravery and at Badger's fearless descent. That was always the way it was with women and with men. Even in small ones it was the same—courage, and the lack of it.

He took another good grip, turned his head, and searched the cliff below him. On his left the rock was cracked deeply, with the portion of the face to which he and the others clung protruding several inches farther out than the other side of the crack. Shifting carefully he stepped into the crack, pressed, and felt his foot jam. Shifting then with his hand he took a pull grip, pulling away from himself with the left fingers until he could swing his body to the left and grasp the edge of the rock with his right hand.

Bracing himself and readjusting the pack-net which was hanging behind him, he reached back and helped Badger across, and then Butterfly, though she had to wait until he had dropped a little. Then, pulling the net to the front, he tried to comfort the baby, who was now crying loudly. Magpie, however, would not be comforted, and for a moment Hawk wished for the presence of the woman. Truly he knew little of the ways of babies, and she had seemed to have a way about her.

With a sense of frustration he pushed those thoughts from his mind. Then, doing his best to ignore the cries of the baby, he began moving downward. Lying back and showing the younger ones what to do, Hawk braced his back against the projecting edge of the crack and, pulling toward himself with his hands, he worked his way down. He went step by step, grip by grip, and with each movement he quietly taught Badger and Butterfly to do the same.

Then the crack widened into a chimney whose sides had been scoured with ancient water action, and the lie-back method he had used would no longer work. Working his way into the chimney, Hawk braced his feet against one wall and his back against the other, and by pushing against the two walls and shifting his bare feet carefully, he started to descend once more.

"My brother . . ."

Hawk looked up, realizing as he did so that Badger was too small to wedge his way down. Breathing deeply, Hawk considered. He very probably couldn't do it, especially with the net, made doubly heavy now with the crying baby. But other than the thought that had come into his mind, he could come up with no other way.

Inching back upward, he signaled the young boy to climb upon his shoulders. Butterfly, seeing this, balanced herself, reached out, and wordlessly started to take the net from Hawk's head. Hawk looked carefully at her, wondering, and then signaled that she must not take it. The girl withdrew her hand, and Hawk signaled again to the boy. Badger climbed onto his shoulders, and then, carrying the net and both little ones, Hawk started down once again.

Twice he slipped, and the extra weight he carried almost pulled him forward out of the chimney. But at last Hawk and the others were well past the sixty-foot ledge, and he began to feel better about what they were attempting to do. There the chimney ended in a small overhang, and there he and Butterfly paused to let their breathing return to normal.

Hawk ran his fingers through his long black hair and wiped his brow, grinning. He had suddenly recalled the man Saviki's fear of high places, which had been a laughed-about thing among the young men of the village. Perhaps this terrible cliff would truly aid him and the little ones in their escape from the wrath of the Angry Ones.

Carefully he studied the slick drop-off below him. It was blackened and striped with desert varnish, and from where he crouched it appeared totally smooth. For them to escape they must cross that rock face, working gradually downward. For over fifty feet they would be in great danger, for the cliff was almost concave. Yet now that he looked more closely he could see that there were a few tiny handholds and other narrow ledges for their feet. If only Badger and Butterfly could reach them with their shorter limbs.

Taking a last deep breath, Hawk finally moved out, clinging to the face of the cliff and working slowly across it and down, directing as he went each of the movements of the two who followed. Sliding down a steep slab, he caught on a ledge and inched along it, with the younger ones following, to where there were further handholds. Once more he lowered himself down the face, hand over hand, until he came to another ledge, wider this time. There, chest heaving, he handed the others down beside him and then glanced up at the ridge above.

Nothing. Saviki was not yet there. Truly they might yet make a successful *waítioma*, a running away.

With his mouth dry and his throat burning terribly with thirst, Hawk started again, and in a short time was at the bottom, with an exuberant Badger and a smiling Butterfly beside him. Hawk was surprised especially with the girl's performance, but he said nothing. More than likely it was luck, that and nothing more. Girls and women simply could not do such things. All the elders had said so, always. They were only good for minding the children and other woman-tasks.

Suddenly Hawk took the still-crying Magpie from the net and thrust him toward Butterfly. Startled, she took the child, comforted him, and within moments the crying had diminished to the whimperings they had grown so accustomed to. Satisfied, Hawk turned and looked back at the great cliff.

So they had made the descending. Still, their troubles were far from over. Heat lifted up against them in a stifling wave, and Hawk involuntarily lifted his arm against it. At the same time he glanced upward once again, and now a man was there on the edge, high above, looking down.

For a moment Hawk stared, fascinated. The man was inching over the edge, going carefully, clinging close to the rock. Now he had reached the place where the rock turned back into the butte, and his legs hung suspended.

With satisfied smiles Hawk and the others watched as the one called Saviki, with a wild scrambling, dragged himself back onto the top of the butte. There he stood shaking his fist. Then with an angry shouting he notched an arrow and let it fly.

The young ones grinned more widely as it clattered into the rocks a full twenty feet away, and grinned as well as the man shouted more words of great anger.

With disdain then the young Hawk lifted his hand in the farewell signal of the People, noted grimly the man's further show of anger, turned, and he and the three children started off across the dry and brush-covered land.

33

Hours passed, and dark shadows once again claimed the valley. Winds of the evening drifted over the mesa and moaned softly through the hole in the rock. Tala lay still with her green eyes open, and the pain in her leg throbbed in rhythm with the rapid pounding of her heart, made faster because now a fever burned within her as well. Somewhere she thought she heard a call, a voice. But she listened, carefully, and there was nothing, nothing but the soft sighing of the wind in the empty sky.

Darkness filled the valley. Tala lay still and the pain found its way to her head where it pounded first against one side of her skull and then the other, constantly, relentlessly. She tightened her eyes against it, she pressed her skull against the earth for relief, yet none came. The agony was like a club, pounding down, forcing her back toward the deeper darkness of unconsciousness.

She fought fiercely, for it was large in her mind that she did not want to die. Somewhere were the children, and as the one who was acting as their mother she must find them.

The rains had long ago departed, and the winds of night wandered across the mesa. They did not drop into the valley but instead sent exploring streamers down over the bulging rimrock, seeking, feeling—and on them suddenly rode *Kotori,* the Owl Kachina, who was as a friendly spirit to the woman when she saw him.

"Who," the owl whispered as its wings drifted back and forth above her, "who are you, my daughter?" he called kindly. "Who? Whooo?"

Kotori was suddenly gone, but now the woman could see *Chuchip,* the Deer Kachina. He stood still in the white of the moonlight, his long ears lifting upward as columns of smoke, his antlers seeming to hold up the stars that showed through the spruce boughs tipping their points. He might also have spoken, but in the stirring mists of night he began a change in the mind of the woman and suddenly he was an old stoop-shouldered man with a pack on his back and a flute in his hand.

Tala was startled, for she had heard of *Kokopeli,* the hump-backed dispenser of all growing life. She had also heard that no one saw him ever, for he crept through darkness, and with sweet music that one could almost, but never quite, hear he brought sleep and therefore fertility. But now he stood before her, indistinct in the shadow of the valley, his flute in the air in the manner of a deer's horn, and with a whispering like the breeze he began a telling, a singing that filled the young woman with wonder.

"Verily, daughter, for so I name you," he chanted, "you have entered the house of my friends, without fear you have entered, longing for love. And love indeed will I cause you to feel. Wa!

"Behold the vision. In my back I put my hand and bring forth seed. White seed, blue seed, red seed, smooth seed. Then do I hold it tight and rush forth. Wa!

"I see the land does sloping lie, I see the wind follow, with breath upon me, and clouds moving down at the foot of the east, with lightning roaring from their breasts. Wa!

"Though the earth seems very wide, straight across it falls the rain, stabbing with its claws, filling the water-ways to bubbling, rushing on and on until it reaches the foot of the west. Wa!

"Turning then it sees the earth, spongy with moisture, adorned with love, pregnant with new growth. Wa!

"Thus beautifully does my vision end, for so the land once was. Thus beautifully adorned will you also be, my daughter, though the time for your blooming is not yet at hand. Wa!"

Tala, her mind swirling with the pain and the fever and the words of the strange flute player, lost sight of the humpbacked one. Pressing to see into the darkness, she was instead surprised to see, in a place of sudden great light, a young man making a walking away. The sun splashed across his shoulders, his muscles rippled with power, and she caught her breath at his beauty, his manliness. He turned then, smiling, but somehow his face was lost in shadow and she could not see, could not make out his features.

The vision! It was hers once more!

"My daughter," the voice of an old man Kachina whispered, drifting away on the wind as he called, "for this you must be of good countenance; for this you must do what you must do in order that you might live. Wa! . . ."

34

The moonlight, filtering down into the small valley, splashes brightly on the bulging slick-rock beyond the spruce. In the light a deer browses, pausing now and then to look beneath the tree. On the ledge high above, an owl is perched, its great round eyes missing nothing of what happens in the shadow of the tree.

Suddenly the figure on the earth beneath the tree struggles up to a sitting position, feels with her hands the terrible swelling near the top of the right leg, gropes about in the darkness until her hand and the ancient metal knife come together, and with a scream of fear and courage she drives the gleaming blade into the swollen flesh of her right leg.

The deer spins and flees, the owl lifts up and drifts off on silent wings, and an agony that is like terrible fire races upward through the woman. She wrenches with the knife to widen the cut, pulls the blade free, and as she falls back the evil fluids, thick and foul-smelling, gush from the opened wound.

Dizzy now beyond understanding, almost crazy with pain, yet determined to live for the man who is hers and who will yet come to this place that is now so empty, the woman of the lovely green eyes drags herself along the ground to where a trickle of water from the rain still runs. She lies close along the water, thrusts her right leg into the chill current, gasps with shock, and waits as the darkness from within her mind drops quickly down, covering the pain.

35

Hawk was totally lost. He knew where he was; he just had no idea where he was in relation to anything else. Nor did he know where he was going. At the moment he and the younger ones were crossing the mouth of a boulder-strewn canyon slashed deep into the slick-rock flank of the mesa. From the canyon extended a wide alluvial fan composed of coarse gravel, sand, and silt, washed down by seasonal rains. Ahead of them the fan was broken by the deep scar of another wash, of much more recent origin. It was toward this that Hawk moved.

Sliding down the bank, he turned back, caught Badger and Butterfly as they slid after him, and then turned down the wash. He didn't know what he expected to find, but he knew that water occasionally collected in shaded areas of washes, and he hoped he would stumble onto one of these pools.

Ahead the desert danced with heat waves and seemed to be a vast inland sea. Hawk knew the way of mirages, but he hoped this one would prove to be at least the bed of a true seasonal *pasíqolu,* a water covering the ground. Yet as he drew closer he saw that it wasn't. Instead it was only a wide alkali flat.

It was also such that it demanded a wide detour, and the heat was even more intense than it had been earlier. Hawk placed a pebble in his mouth and told the others to do the same, but the stones helped very little, and soon were discarded.

Often he looked back, expecting at any moment to see the lone Saviki following. Yet of the man there was no sign, and with each step he felt a little more safe.

"My brother?"

Hawk plodded on, ignoring the girl lest she come to place too much importance upon herself. Now that he was the leader, she needed to understand her true position as well.

However, Butterfly was not to be ignored. "My brother, is our haste because you fear that the Angry One will follow?"

Without looking at her, Hawk gave the signal for agreement.

"I fear as well," she continued, "and so I have been sending up many prayer-thoughts to the great Giver-of-all-life that he will prevent the evil one from coming after. I think he will help."

Hawk grinned tolerantly, but because of the heat and the dryness of his mouth the grin was only a grimace. Prayer-thoughts indeed! Nothing would stop that man! The girl should understand that, understand that their only hope was in making haste and in getting as far away from the man as possible.

Walking steadily, with dust rising high at each footfall, the three children turned left and skirted the alkali-covered playa. Beyond the flat Hawk could see the edge of a rocky escarpment, an outcropping that stretched for miles toward a far blue mountain. That solitary peak was the youth's ultimate goal, but first they must reach the rocky upthrust, for only in that place was there a possibility of stumbling upon a *koritivi,* a sandstone hole with water in it. Yet Hawk knew how difficult such tanks were to find, and his heart shrank at the thought. Hollowed by both wind and water, such holes were often filled with gravel and sand, and only rarely was there moisture even at the bottom. If only the recent storm had produced rain instead of just thunder and lightning!

"My brother?"

Hawk thought again of ignoring the girl, remembered her insistence, and finally turned and gave the signal that she might speak.

"It . . . it is in my heart that we should look for the woman who has become as our mother."

Hawk snorted with disgust. "Why?" he asked. "She is *mokee,* and already the fat-eating birds of the afterlife feed upon her flesh."

"You do not know that."

"You do not know otherwise." Hawk turned away, angry that a mere girl would dare to argue with his wisdom.

"My brother," Butterfly persisted, "those with good countenances would surely make a searching for one such as her."

Hawk twisted with discomfort. How was it, he wondered, that some people, even girls, could come so quickly to arguments that ended discussion? "Of course we would do that," he agreed maliciously, "but you know what a fall from a cliff can do. How could anyone, especially a *woman,* live after such a fall? And truly we all heard her fall. Besides, I do not know where that cliff is to be found."

"I know," Badger said, signaling toward the north and the east. "It is there."

Hawk made the sign of disgust. "You are only a boy," he spat. "A little boy. How do you know that?"

Badger's chest swelled with pride. "This day, from the top of the great cliff, I saw a tall standing rock that is near where the one who is now as our mother fell. I saw that rock again before we came to this evil place of dust. From that place ahead of us I will show it to you once more."

Badger paused and dropped his eyes, and at last he spoke again. "My brother," he pleaded quietly, "I too long to find our mother."

Long did Hawk look at the small boy and at the girl. It was strong in each of them, he could see, to look for the woman. Nor truly did he mind. In a strange way he longed for her nearness himself. Perhaps, if the little digger could truly point the way, and if they could find water, the attempt might be made.

Hawk paused, shading his eyes toward the end of the alkali flat. It was not much further, but his mouth was powder-dry now, and he could swallow only with an effort. The others, he knew, were at least as thirsty, and he felt badly for them.

He walked on, time passed, and he was no longer perspiring. His movements were erratic, and he stepped as if he was in a daze. Suddenly he stumbled over a stone and fell headlong. Then clumsily, with Butterfly helping, he staggered to his feet. Blinking away the dust, he pushed on through the rocks, either walking or crawling, leading the others he knew not where.

At last, at the top of the sandstone escarpment, he paused and looked around, hoping to see a *kúnya,* a plant meaning that water was near. But there was nothing but rock and brush and cactus, and so he kept on. Yet still he did his best to be alert, seeking tracks of animals that might lead the three of them to water.

The horizon seemed no nearer, nor had the distant peaks begun to show their lines of age or the rugged shapes into which the mesa winds had carved them. Yet the sun was lower now, its rays level and blasting as a furnace. Hawk plodded on, the others followed, and they walked toward the time of darkness, hoping for it, sending our fervent prayer-thoughts for it.

And then a thin whining of sound crossed the heat-seared mesa.

Hawk stopped, listening, searching the air about him with eyes suddenly clear and alert. The baby Magpie began crying, Hawk looked darkly at him, Butterfly turned away and did her best to comfort the small boy, and still no one moved.

For several moments there was nothing, and then it came again, a faint whining, and there was no mistaking it now. Finally Hawk's eyes caught the small dark spot, moving directly away, and he knew.

The whining was a bee!

Abruptly the youth started forward, following the bee. Moments later he saw another of the insects going in the same direction, he altered his course slightly, the younger ones followed, and they were still searching when darkness overtook them.

In little more than an instant, it seemed, the mountain on the horizon had grown black against the sky, its crest tinted with gold and its west side slashed with the deep fire of crimson. Scant seconds later it was full night, the stars hung low overhead, and a long way off a coyote started yapping.

In the coolness of the night Hawk stopped and considered. He knew he might go on for a time—even the others might. But the bees indicated water. If they stayed close they could find it, and it might be the last of it for days. Yes, he had to find it now. But how was he to do it?

Hesitating, he took a few steps in one direction, then one or two in another. Yet it was so dark that he could see nothing, and he knew that he could pass within a few feet of the water and not even see it.

In frustration he slumped against a boulder, wondering which way to go. His thirst and his weariness had fogged his judgment, and for some reason he could not decide. In mental anguish he cried out, the coyote voiced a shrill answer from out in the darkness, and suddenly Butterfly was beside him, her hand on his arm.

"My brother, yonder there is a chirping."

Disgusted and exhausted, Hawk turned away. "Insects of the dark sing in all places," he mumbled. "They do not need water."

"This . . . this was *not* an insect, my brother."

Hawk turned slowly toward the dark form of the girl who had become as his sister, a puzzlement on his face. "If it was not an insect, then what . . ."

Again Butterfly pressed her hand against him. "There, beyond the stones in that mound . . ."

"It is only a singing insect!"

"No, my brother. It is *pakwa,* the red spotted frog. It sings much in the manner of an insect, but its notes are lighter, and more slowly formed. It lives only near a *kisiwu,* a spring in the shadows. Thus I have been taught."

Hawk could hardly believe what he was hearing, and from a *girl,* no less. He'd certainly never heard of it himself. "Are . . . are you certain?" he finally asked.

Butterfly, smiling through cracked lips, signaled that she was. "Badger is already crawling in that direction," she said then. "Let us take to our knees and follow the sound as well. When we find the *pakwa,* the little red spotted toad, we will find water. Then we can follow Badger, for he has seen the standing tall stone again, and has marked it in his mind. In that manner we can go to the green-eyed one who is as our mother. . . ."

36

Voices awakened her. Distant voices, but real. Tala opened her eyes to another vision, this one more light, a vision of Butterfly's lovely face, floating above her in the air. For a moment it hung still, suspended, and then a look of incredulous awe was replaced by a radiant smile of joy.

"Hawk," the girl cried excitedly, forgetting the proper formalities. "She lives! The one who is as our mother is yet with us!"

Badger's face appeared before Tala next, and finally Hawk's countenance. All were smiling, all were happy, and Tala could not understand. Then there was water on her lips, sweet, cool water, and she closed her eyes to the ecstasy of the feeling.

Long she lay with eyes closed, and Butterfly dripped more water into her mouth from a hollow stem of grass. At first she could not swallow, so she held water in her mouth and lifted her head and thus some trickled down her throat. The dry muscles in her mouth soaked in the moisture and then at last she could swallow a little at a time.

Finally, her thirst partially slackened, Tala struggled to sit up. But the illness came then, from the water and the shock of the broken bone in her leg. She retched violently, and again the merciful darkness came to claim her from her pain.

That was forever, but once more time began. She opened her eyes to the true darkness of night, saw firelight flickering on the trees above her, felt the warmth of soft aprons and warm children's bodies over her and beside her, wondered at all of those things, and then at last she slept the true sleep of healing.

37

And so the chemistry of healing works within the woman while the time of darkness passes by. The gentle wind whispers through the grass and the trees of the tiny valley, the Kachina people laugh upon it, the moon-woman rises and sends her gentle light against the hard surface of the sandstone rock, insects talk to the darkness, and four of the Peaceful Ones sleep untroubled sleep, for they are secure in their valley, and it is already become a home.

The fifth of the People, a young man whose name Hawk indicates strength and speed of both body and mind, lies awake, considering.

During the past few suns he has seen much in the way of knowing and of doing bravely. What troubles him is that he has seen these things in a woman and a girl, and according to the elders of his secret society, such things should not, no *cannot* be. A woman cannot think with wisdom, cannot be brave. But he has seen—his sight cannot be argued with—these things live in his mind, and he is troubled deeply.

38

The times of sun and of darkness passed quickly, and Tala's leg grew strong with healing. Hawk had splinted it, Butterfly had found *katoki*, a medicinal plant that was working on the infection in the great stab wound, and she and Badger daily washed the evil fluids away. Thus the leg healed quickly. In the valley there was food as well, and that too helped the healing. Berries flourished on the slopes beneath the great cliff, and with snares and deadfalls Hawk caught many rabbits and squirrels.

These things brought much strength to all of them but the baby Magpie, and he did not grow strong at all. Instead he grew more thin and weak, his eyes became very large, and his cries, almost constant, were no longer loud. All of the others did what they could for the child. They found all manner of things for him to eat, they chewed up the food for him so that he would have less chewing of his own to do, they made certain that he always had water at hand, and still it did no good. The baby continued to grow more weak.

Tala worried about Magpie; she worried that the season was passing and that they had planted no sacred corn; and she worried too about water. The water in the huge rock tank, filled from the rain, remained sweet and cool, but its level was dropping rapidly, and the young woman who was as the mother of them all knew what she had to do. For all of them, but especially for the baby, fresh water had to be found, had to be started.

The children knew that too, but they held their peace and waited, sensing the dilemma Tala felt. And truly did she suffer in her mind. After all, who was she, a woman and an Outcast who was also a two-heart, to plant the sacred *móngwikoro*, the water jar?

Tala knew the tradition, knew that at the conclusion of a migration the most holy man among the People was to go without food and drink for the space of four suns and four darknesses. Then, while the People watched and sent prayer-thoughts upward, he was to plant the jar, which held sacred water-things carried always since their earliest migration. Then, if the man's heart was truly pure, Tiaowa would bless the buried pot and a spring of fresh water would issue forth. In that manner would the People of Peace always have the moisture of life.

Thus did the woman worry. In no way was she qualified to plant the sacred jar. But truly, there was no one else, and she knew it. She was the only adult. She hoped that Tiaowa would see that, and would therefore bless them.

If he did, all would be well. If he did not, if he chose otherwise and no water came forth from the jar—well, she would rather not think of that.

"Butterfly," she called on the morning she finally made her decision. "My daughter, bring to me your brothers."

The young girl, busy stripping fibers from the long, stiff leaves of the *sowungwa*, the yucca, looked upward to the place where Tala lay. Instantly she smiled and rose to obey, for she too understood the need for having a good heart and a good countenance in a time such as this.

Shortly the five sat together in the stillness of the afternoon. Tala took up the blue flute and commenced to play a prayer song, sending her heart out in her music so that the children would understand. The thin sound of the music filled the canyon, and soon a feeling of peace and togetherness settled upon them all.

"My children," Tala began when her song had ended, "it is the time for the planting of the sacred *móngwikoro*, and I would discuss it."

Butterfly watched Tala carefully, wondering. Hawk, who knew the traditions as well, also watched, and did his best to fight down the old feeling of scorn that rose within him. Acting in the manner of a man, he waited quietly, eyes unwavering. Badger also listened, but Magpie was upon his lap, distracting him, and his fingers would not leave the baby alone.

"Little Badger," Tala said quietly, speaking directly to the young boy, "planting the sacred jar is a great and fearful thing, and ought to be done by a man who is pure and holy. There is no such person here. There is no man at all except for Hawk, who acts in all things like a man should but who has not yet reached all the ways of a man. And I, the only adult, who should be a pure-hearted woman of the People, am Outcast.

"Still, this thing must be done, and it is in my heart to seek your help, yours and these others. Will you help?"

Badger, his eyes large with the pride of being asked, nodded eagerly. "I will help, my mother. Just this day I killed a squirrel with a rock, so you see I am almost a man myself. I will do what I can."

Tala smiled. "Your words are good to hear, my son. You are as you say. Now this is the way, and I send my voice to each of you. There must be a four-day fasting. I would do it myself, but within me there is not enough power. Perhaps, since no one of us can do it, we might all do it together. Will each of you join me in this fast, so that the jar might be planted?"

Instantly Badger nodded. A moment later Butterfly also agreed.

"Does the Magpie also go without food and water?" Badger suddenly asked.

Tala smiled and signaled no. "He is a baby, my son, and does not understand. Because he does not, he is not expected to make such a sacrifice."

Then the woman turned to the youth who was as her eldest son. "O Hawk, will you aid me in this, as you pleaded for my aid when we planted the prayer-feather?"

Hawk looked long at her, then arose, and with the dignity of coming manhood he spoke. "O woman, you have asked, and I would respond. Since the day of our making a running away have I watched you. I have seen your strength, I have seen your courage, I have seen your humility. These should not be qualities found in a woman, for thus the elders in my society have taught. But still they are found within you, and seeing them I have had many long thoughts. I do not yet know where my heart lives, but in this thing I will surely help."

Stunned by the boy's forthright statement, Tala dropped her eyes in the manner of a woman honoring a man. Truly there was nothing she could say, and so wisely she did not try to speak. Thus would Hawk know that her heart had heard his own, and was glad.

And so in that manner the fasting began.

39

Four suns was a long time, especially to the young Badger, who spent his days wandering near the little water that remained in the large rock tank. Tala warned him away, for she understood that it only increased his suffering. Hawk also explained that the fasting would be made more easy if he kept busy in other places, and Butterfly sternly warned him, in the way of a true little *wúti,* a woman, to stop throwing stones into the water. Yet it did no good, and for the space of four suns Badger suffered and groaned and watched the water in the tank evaporate away.

It was a long fast for the others as well, yet they kept busy and did their best to maintain pleasant countenances, knowing that such was a sign to Tiaowa that their hearts were good.

Meanwhile Tala practiced walking with the aid of a forked limb brought her by Hawk, Butterfly twined yucca fibers and strips of rabbit fur together so that they might become aprons and mantles, and Hawk prepared a good patch of earth so that, if they should stay, the sacred kernels of corn would have a home of their own in which to sprout and flourish. Thus the four suns of their fasting passed away.

In the afternoon of the fourth day, Tala solemnly lifted the sacred pot from where she had placed it beneath the spruce. Then, chanting a new song of praise to the Giver-of-all-life, she led the others in a procession dance to a cool place back against the rock above the almost-empty tank.

For some time each of them danced to the rhythm of the earth around them. Then they watched in silence while Badger, at Tala's direction, scooped out with his quickly moving hands a shallow hole. The woman then held the small vessel above her in the air, and reverently she sent out her voice in a prayer-chant.

O Great One, she declared in a very formal manner, *hear these our voices, through Bahana hear these our lonely voices. See the páho, the feather of our prayer. See the water jar, made holy by the goodness of our People. Wa!*

Look not upon our youth, look not upon our unworthiness, look not upon the fact that there is no man, no holy man, among us. Wa!

See instead our hearts, filled with what goodness we can find, and so with water fill this jar. With water sweet and pure, fill this sacred jar, that so long as it is planted here, in our pauipi, our water-planted-place, the fluid of life might come forth. Wa!

These are our words, we the Peaceful Ones, we the People. Wa!

Slowly then Tala lowered the pot into the hole dug by Badger. Gently she turned the pot onto its side so that its power might flow out and become sweet water, and then carefully, with small scoops of soil, she covered it up.

Upward she raised her arms once more, another chant she sang, and then the five, still in procession, danced back to their place of sleeping. They could not drink again before the dawning, and so they sat upon the earth and faced outward into the darkness together, their faith and hope a strong power within their hearts.

The sun sank behind the great pointed mass of mountain to the west. Dusk flowed over the hills. Tala rose and with her fire-sticks made a small fire. She revolved the one stick between the palms of her hands with its point in the hole of the other flattened stick until sparks glowed in the powdered dry *lapu,* cedar bark, around the edges of the hole. She blew on this and fed it with small twigs until the fire was burning, and then she sat back and waited, silently, surrounded by the four who were as her children and whom she already loved more than she loved life itself.

40

And so darkness falls, the light from the fire illuminates the underbranches of the sacred spruce and bounces from the smooth sandstone cliff above them, and the young ones wait. Up on the mesa a coyote calls wonderingly at the stars, another picks up the song, and for a time there is a chorus. Then it ends, the four look only downward, and much later, when the fire is only the red eye of a single hot coal and when there is no sound in the valley but the sound of their breathing and a gentle laughing that is on the wind, a new music suddenly rises into the air.

The music is a dripping—steady, quiet, continuous. That goes on, but suddenly the volume swells and the dripping is no longer a dripping but a trickling. That too grows, and soon the merry chanting of a small stream is heard, laughing its way into the deep rock tank, filling it to more than full, pushing on, ready to give life to the valley and all therein.

And the young ones, their eyes wide, wonder and do not wonder at all, for who can understand the power and goodness of the great Tiaowa, the wondrous Giver-of-all-life?

And though not understood, neither is the power of the Great One questioned or denied. The water is there, pure, cold, sweet, flowing from beneath the cliff where the jar has been planted. And now truly the valley is become a home, and in all things but one, life is as it should be.

SIX

The Dwelling Within the Rock

41

It is the morning after the coming forth of the water from the water-planted-place. The first rays from the sun are slicing across the eastern rim of the canyon, just starting to work their bright way through the leaves of the cottonwood and aspen. Tala, standing in the small field that Hawk and Badger have so painstakingly dug with their pointed and fire-hardened sticks, holds the bag of sacred *sowiwa,* corn kernels, in her hand, chanting praise and a plea for good growth.

The children watch closely, for all feel the importance, the urgency of the occasion. Already the season is well along, the kernels in the bag are not many, and to live beyond the coming time of cold they must have more of the short blue ears of corn.

Nor, for that same reason, is there time for the regular and ritualistic ceremonies of preparation, the *Wúwuchim,* the *Soyál,* and the *Powamu.* These of course have been performed the winter before by the clan, but now that seems so long ago, so far away. Yet with many prayer-thoughts Tala pleads with the great Tiaowa that he will recall the ceremonies of the People and let them apply in this tiny valley as well.

Thus in a sacred manner she sprinkles sacred meal into the air. Then she lifts the crutch that helps her to move on her slowly healing leg, casts her eyes upward, looks back down at the children who watch her silently, and then she steps to the edge of the black and upturned earth.

"Badger," she directs, "you will be the digger. You and your sister will cover the seed and mound the hills. Hawk, my son, you will drop the seed. Place no more than three kernels to the hole, for there is none to spare. And I, with this crutch which has become my *tepchomo,* my planting stick, will forge the holes in the womb of our mother the earth where the growing will begin."

So they sow the corn, and the day of the planting is for them a day of the singing of glad songs, for truly have they been blessed. In the distance dances the water, in the trees the *chosovi,* the bluebirds, sing of gladness as well, along the cliff above them the Kachina people laugh on the wind, and on that day all creation seems glad. The tiny valley and its people, at last, seem to be one.

42

"Our mother!"

The whisper was urgent, and Tala, instantly awake, rolled off the sleeping robes and onto her feet. "Yes?" she questioned staring into the dim light in the dwelling. "Butterfly, is that you?"

"It . . . it is . . . oh, Mother, the little one is . . . is dead!"

Tala's breath caught, and quickly she lifted the still form of Magpie from Butterfly's trembling arms. He could not be dead, he could not! But she could feel no movement, no heartbeat, no sign of breath.

"I heard him gasping," Butterfly explained while Tala stood with the baby in her arms, her mind numb with disbelief. "I heard, and I lifted him. But then the gasping stopped, and . . . and . . . oh, my mother!"

Hawk and Badger were then awakened, and as Tala stood swaying with the body of the child and weeping, Hawk led the little ones in the customary chant of farewell and good wishes to the little Magpie, who was leaving them to begin his long journey into the land of the Sky People.

Through the morning Tala held the tiny body close to her and wept, and the others sat nearby and sorrowed as well. When the sun was bright and straight overhead, Tala led the others down the cliff and to the sacred water-planted-place. There, while Butterfly sent out the soft voice of the flute, Tala washed the tiny body and dark hair in yucca suds. While she combed the baby's hair, Butterfly wove yucca fibers and rabbit fur into ceremonial clothing, and this Tala placed upon the small body.

Prayer-feathers were then secured to the baby's head, hands, feet, and breast, and over his face a woven mask was placed, with holes for the eyes and mouth.

"Mother," Badger asked as this was being placed, "why is my brother's face masked?"

"This mask is a cloud mask," Tala answered. "Thus, when this one, whose name we must not say for one year, returns as a Cloud Kachina to bring us rain, his identity will be concealed. Still, if our hearts are pure, we will know him for who he is."

Tala then rubbed sacred cornmeal on Magpie's face beneath the mask and placed a tiny bit of it within his closed fist, and when that was done, all was ready.

In solemn procession the four moved to the small hole that had been dug by Badger, and into that hole the baby called Magpie was placed. His legs were drawn up in a sitting position and he was placed facing east so that he might easily rise to greet the lost white brother who would one day return. Hawk then put into the grave with him a few tiny weapons he had made as toys, and a bowl containing food for his journey into the afterlife. Then, with a great prayer, the body was covered.

For the remainder of that day the mourning continued, but with the dying of the sun the sorrowing ended and the four did their best to put the name of the child from their minds. They did this that the spirit of the one called Magpie might be free to find his way to the good land, and not feel that he was being called back.

Yet for the woman Tala this forgetting was especially difficult, and she worried, as the days passed, that the child had been taken from her because of her unworthiness as a woman, as a mother.

43

On another day, and with more sunlight filling the tiny valley, Hawk began the task of cutting notches in the face of the rock that rose high above the water-planted-place. He had found a shallow cave there, had explored it, and Tala had determined that the shelter of the cave would protect them and thus should be their home.

Hawk had good thoughts about this decision, for it had been made primarily at his suggestion. Yet still the words of the woman who was as his mother troubled him. She was only a woman, after all, and should not go about in such a haughty manner, ordering him to do this and instructing him regarding that. Such was a man's task, and should remain so. And since there was no man among them, and since he was now doing all the work of a man, the instructing of them all should be done by himself. *That* was the true way of the People.

But no one listened when he spoke, except as one always listens out of courtesy to another, and deep down Hawk knew why. He had not proven himself. He would, though, and soon.

44

And while Hawk with great impatience chipped at the slick-rock with a stone hammer he had crafted, longing as he did so that he were off doing the great things of manhood, Tala searched the tiny valley, familiarizing herself with it. With her crutch she hobbled this way and that, seeing everything, examining everything, learning every detail of this place that had now become home.

She learned of the grasses that gave seed, she found the bushes and vines upon which grew berries and grapes, she discovered patches of nourishing roots and healing herbs, and she learned too the topography of the valley. In no place more than a few hundred yards wide, it was deep and still, with the high cliff running from one side to the other in a horseshoe shape.

Their cave was the largest of several. It was at the very top of the bend in the shoe, and other than up from the wash and into the valley, there were only two other entrances, two other *hovatoqa,* cuts in the cliff. One was near the cave and the water-planted-place, and the other was on the west side of the valley near the lip where it dropped off into the wash. It was near that second *hovatoqa* that Tala discovered the great bank of clay.

Elated, she filled her apron with a little of it and carried it back to the deep rock tank. There she mixed it with water and a little sand, just as she had been taught so long before, rolled the clay into coils, and in an amazingly short time she had fashioned a small pot.

To fire it she placed the pot on a small stone and then piled dry wood all about and over it. This she burned, and when the wood was consumed she was pleased to discover that the pot was not only still intact, but indeed seemed to be hardened.

One day later, however, the pot crumbled, and so the young woman tried again, many times as it turned out, each time remembering and using a different combination of clay and sand. Shortly the perfect mixture of ingredients was found, and ere long both she and the young Butterfly were fashioning many pots, jars, and *ollas.*

There was also the matter of decorations, which were not so much ornaments as they were things of importance that Tala and Butterfly wanted to record. These were carefully painted onto the dried and unfired clay with paint composed of pressed weeds and grasses and fruits mixed with a little water. In the firing this vegetable dye carbonized and turned black, the pots turned almost white, and the young women were more than pleased with the black-on-white results.

On the pottery, then, appeared the record of their lives. The migration spiral, painted with many variations, told of the fleeing and of the finding of this new home. On other pots the snake was represented, as was *pakwa* the frog, illustrated to tell of the water-planted-place, of the fertility of the soil, and of their gratitude for all of it. *Kokopeli,* the humpbacked flute player, adorned other jars, telling of their clan, of Tala's vision, and again of the fertility of the tiny valley. And finally, on a very few other jars, Tala and Butterfly painted the signs of the Star of the Eastern Day Breaking and of the Butterfly Showing Beautiful Wings, signifying their own persons and their efforts to make *kuwanlelenta,* to make beautiful surroundings of their own lives. Truly were the efforts of these two thus made lovely.

Still, within the valley there was a feeling of restlessness, a sense of some great trial waiting to happen. . . .

45

After a certain space of time Hawk finished the notches in the sheer cliff, and so with a *páho* planted to Tiaowa, the youth led the others up the cliff and into the cave.

It was small, as Hawk had described, but it suited perfectly the needs of the small family. From above, the cave was hidden by the overhang, from below it was hidden nearly as well, and the only access to it, the notches hammered out by Hawk, could be easily protected should that need ever arise. Within the cave there was ample room for building, and so within it the four would be protected from summer sun and perhaps winter winds as well.

While Hawk watched without expression, Tala laid out the plan for the building of the dwellings. It was truly her right as a woman to do so, but the very fact that she went about it so quickly bothered the youth. In her was too much strength, too much determination. The elders of his society had taught him that such should be the way of men only, and truly he believed it. Yet despite her many strengths, this woman of the green eyes, this ones who had chosen to be as his mother, had too much of the manly heart.

46

The feeling of something about to happen continued; all felt it, and all were in one way or another concerned. But then suddenly the corn was there, bright green against the dark of the earth as it greeted the warmth of the sun. And just as suddenly, Hawk and little Badger had no more time for play, for doing the things of their hearts. All day they worked, for it had become their lot as young men of the People to guard the tender green shoots, weeding as there was a need and frightening away all enemies of the new growth that would be their corn.

"Mother," Badger wailed one evening as he collapsed on the soft grass padding of his bed, "there is no creature on this mesa, whether it walks, crawls, or flies, that does not desire our corn. All are *núkpana,* all are evil! From the time of the sun's birthing to the time of its dropping out of the sky I pick off insect people, chase the wings of the air, and throw stones at four-leggeds—rabbits, squirrels, and deer. And it does no good. They come back anyway, in the time of darkness especially, and I'm *tired* of it!"

"My brother is right," Hawk grumbled. "The task is thankless, and ought to be done by the women. It is in my heart to build fires to frighten these creatures by day as well as by night. Then I will spend my time hunting, and I will be living the way of the man."

Tala was shocked to hear the two boys speak in such a bad-faced manner. Butterfly was surprised also, and turned away to hide the shame she felt for them. Hawk, seeing this, grew even more angry, and began lashing out at all of them. But most especially he lashed out at the green-eyed woman who had become as his mother.

"You are a woman," he stormed, "and nothing more! Yet constantly you forget your place. You give instructions, and it is not your right to do so. You perform the ceremonies, and men only have that power. You chant the teachings, and that too is a man-thing. Woman, I do not wonder that the elders of our society made you Outcast! From this moment I do the same."

Hawk turned his head away, and Tala's eyes dropped with shame and pity. Of course, in some things the boy was right. There were woman-things and there were man-things. Yet in this place where there was no man, what choice did she have?

It was not good that he should complain of that, but the thing that troubled Tala most of all, the most serious fault in this one who was as her son, was his bad face. This poor character was also in Badger, but he was younger and it was therefore more excusable. In Hawk, however, there was no excuse. He was indeed almost as a man, and long ago he should have learned to keep his face in a manly way. Now, though, he must be taught, as must the others, and such a teaching would be very hard.

O Great Tiaowa, she silently pleaded as she gazed up at the star-shrouded sky, *this woman is alone here, alone with three children who must be given the teachings of the People. Yet much of this is a man-thing, and should be done by a man.*

Where is this man, O Great One? Where is the man of my vision? Where is the man of my heart?

Send him, please, that the teaching, and the loving, may come full circle, may be tuwksi, that each of us may feel the complete cycle of life.

47

It was just past daylight, and Hawk was beginning his turn to guard the new green corn. He did well at the task of keeping away the wings and four-leggeds and insect people, but truly he did not enjoy it. Somehow it did not seem manly or important.

Idly he sat in the coolness of morning, throwing dirt chunks here and there and wishing that he were somewhere else, on a great hunt perhaps, bringing back a fine animal for the family. With a large wishing within his eyes, Hawk looked up at the cliffs that surrounded him, dreaming that upon them a fine big ram stood grazing.

Suddenly the boy's breath came to a stop. There, up on the ridge, was movement. Hawk watched, and before long a small deer stepped from behind a clump of brush, browsing slowly forward.

Hawk, still intently watching, let his breath out slowly, and in those few seconds the deer became, to him, a great ram that he was destined to slay. Instantly the new corn was forgotten, his new bow and short arrows were in his hand, and his self-confidence was waxing high. This deer was his. He would slay it, and then the woman would see that he was truly a man, truly one to be honored.

Quickly he took up his weapons, and with no further thought concerning anything other than the great hunt, he crossed the valley away from the browsing deer. Under cover of trees he climbed the cliff, and on top he circled carefully, keeping always out of sight as he worked nearer to where the animal had been. To his dismay, however, the deer was gone when finally he reached the place where he had seen it.

With little effort he picked up the spoor in the soft earth among the rocks, and carefully he followed, moving quietly and stealthily as the greatly feared puma. Twice he saw the deer bounding ahead of him across the mesa, but he somehow could not get close enough for a shot. Still he followed, and to his surprise the track of the deer ultimately led to the great butte upon which he and the children had so recently hidden from the man Saviki.

For a long moment Hawk considered, for his last sight of the evil one had been on top of the very butte he now faced. Still, the deer had gone ahead, and there was no chance that the one called Saviki would still be there.

He started up, and almost instantly was threading his way through huge tumbled boulders, following a narrow trail that he had not found before. So he followed, and near the top of the butte he came suddenly upon the small deer, again quietly browsing.

For a moment each stared at the other. But then, with more good fortune than anything else, Hawk let fly an arrow that struck the spinning deer directly in the heart. The animal crumbled instantly, and with his chest pounding Hawk walked up and touched it. He had done it!

With great exertion he dragged the animal off the butte, and then slowly he set off across the mesa, his mind already growing big with the deed he had done.

It was dusk when Hawk returned to the valley. Leaving the deer on the rim he slid down through the cut in the cliff, and was moving up toward the dwelling place when he noticed that the small field of corn was almost barren. He looked more closely, and to his horror he realized that during the day it had been eaten down to the roots by the creatures who shared his valley.

Thinking deeply, Hawk continued on to the place of dwelling. He said nothing of the deer or of anything else, but within his mind he planned carefully, and so he made all things ready.

Very early the next morning, while the stars yet showed, he arose and made a great noise about setting off on a hunt. There was no hunt, however, but instead there was a carefully laid trap for the young Badger, whose turn it was to watch the new corn.

With great skill Hawk marked a trail in such a way that it would capture the younger boy's attention and lead him away from the corn before he ever got to it. That finished, he smiled, climbed to where he had left the dead deer, and there he waited.

Later, long after the light of the sun had climbed down into the valley, he saw what he wanted to see. Badger was far from the corn, following the strange tracks, and Hawk knew his plan had worked.

Rolling the body of the deer down over the cliff, Hawk followed it down, and immediately set up a great shout.

"Ho," he shouted, "come and see the deed I have done! O woman, O sister, come and see this . . ." Hawk hesitated for a split second, and then he gave another shout, this one very urgent. "Badger," he called, "the corn! Are you not to be guarding the new corn?

"See," he continued, speaking now to the approaching Tala and Butterfly, "our brother has abandoned his task, and already much of the new corn is gone. I slew this deer, and in my returning I discovered, to my sorrow, that the little one has been neglectful."

Badger stared guiltily at the small field and dropped his face with shame. Tala saw the child's face and said nothing. Instead she looked with interest at the slain deer, examined the remains of the field of corn, looked long toward the ground and then long again into Hawk's eyes, and finally, without a word of reprimand to anyone, she turned and signaled for Hawk to follow.

48

Tala sat beneath the sacred spruce and signaled that Hawk was to sit opposite her. With defiance on his face he did so, and then he waited in silence, his countenance turned away.

"My son," she said finally, "my heart is heavy, for I have seen within you two hearts."

Hawk was truly surprised, and it showed clearly upon his countenance. How had she discovered his secret?

"Two hearts? Woman, I will not listen to such foolishness! I hunted a deer this morning, slew it, and—"

Tala stopped him with a signal from her hand. "O Hawk," she declared with firmness, "the deer was slain one sun past, for it is stiffened with death. The corn was eaten one sun past as well, for since it was consumed it has already pushed a little out of the earth. I am saddened by this deception, my son, for it is not the way of the People."

Hawk heard her words, but he could not believe them. How did this woman know such things? How could she guess them? His idea had been too well planned, too well carried out.

"Woman," he said, placing a great deal of anger into his voice, "I choose to ignore your words. You know how early I left this day, you know as well that I went to hunt. The deer has lain dead since before the rising of the sun, and even you should know how quickly all things stiffen in this heat. As for Badger—"

Her green eyes flashing with anger, Tala used the sign that both stopped speech and showed derision as well. Surprised that she would so signal, Hawk stopped his mouth and stared in wonder.

"My son, do you take me for a fool? I will tell you yet another thing. With these eyes I saw you this morning, preparing the trail that would lead the curious Badger away from his task. With these same eyes I saw you climb the rock and wait. With these eyes that are filled with sorrow I see your two-heartedness now."

"You have no right to speak to me in this manner," Hawk seethed. "You are only a woman, and very soon I will be a man—"

"My son," the green-eyed woman declared as she stopped his speech once again, "one part of being a man is realizing that no one escapes doing an evil deed without suffering for it. Any advantage gained by selfish means, any convenience taken, any private putting off of a thing, any insincerity, no matter how small or quick in passing, is paid for.

"Rarely is this a dramatic thing, my son. Often it is hardly noticeable. Yet always is payment made, and it is made through pain from within, it is made with unhappiness. O Hawk, a true man learns very early in his life that such two-hearted ways are not worth the price he pays for them. A true man can never be happy when doing evil. These things you have not yet learned."

Hawk glowered at the green-eyed Tala. "Woman," he snorted, "your words are of no consequence to me. Who are you, declared two-hearted and Outcast by the People, to speak to me of such things? I turn my back upon you!"

Tala stared, her eyes grew tearful, and without another word she arose and walked away. Hawk watched her go, shrugged, forced thoughts of guilt from his mind as best he could, and returned to where Butterfly and Badger were trying to dress the deer. Quickly and easily he gave orders to the other little ones, but for some reason the words and the countenance of the woman would not leave his mind, and that troubled him greatly.

49

For all of that day, Tala sat upon the top of the mesa, her heart within her hands, sending out a pleading voice to the great Tiaowa who ruled above. She needed help, oh, how she needed help if she was to reach the hearts of the boy Hawk and the others!

With the coming of dark, Tala arose and silently descended from the cliff. In the moonlight she walked to the sacred water-planted-place and knelt. Scooping out great handfuls of mud from where the water spilled out, she smeared it on her face and arms. And then, standing, she lifted her arms and her eyes to the darkened sky.

Let this be the way, her heart cried out. *Oh, please let this be the way!*

And so thus adorned with mud, Tala climbed Badger's newly constructed ladder, made to accommodate the weakness in her bad leg, and then she stood before the astonished children, who had now gathered for the night. Both Badger and Butterfly giggled at the sight of the woman, and even Hawk could not resist a look at the strange sight, nor could he resist a small grin when he saw her.

Tala, seeing that, felt her heart rejoice, for she knew that the way was opening. With those thoughts she began to act out her very foolish antics.

"My mother," Badger finally asked, "what is that that you have done to yourself?"

Tala laughed and poked fun at him. "What a foolish question, little one. You should stick to digging holes and building ladders. As you should know, this is the way of all clowns."

Butterfly was next, and Tala threw a little cornmeal into her startled face.

"M . . . Mother," the girl coughed, "why is this . . ."

Tala laughed outright. "Now you are white and yellow, O Butterfly. Your color looks much more healthy. Perhaps each morning you should dress in cornmeal."

Turning next to Hawk, she took some of the mud from her arms and wiped it across his surprised face. Instantly he was on his feet, angry. But before he could react, Tala had whirled away, laughing.

"Little Badger," she asked then, "do you not think your brother looks better now that he has been adorned with this lovely mud?"

Badger giggled. "I do, but no better than you, my mother."

Tala mimicked the look of anger that was on Hawk's face, and quickly she smeared mud across Badger's nose. The boy yelped and jumped away, Hawk finally laughed, and instantly Tala grew serious.

"O my children, with this mud I am become *Kókoyemsin* the clown, the Mud-Head Kachina. I do this to show each of you my true foolishness. I do this as well to show the great Tiaowa my true foolishness before him, for he alone knows all things, and I of myself know nothing. Hawk, with the mud upon him, is also in a position to pick up the humility he has cast aside, for truly no one of us knows all things, myself included.

"Nevertheless, Tiaowa has given us certain understandings, and this night we must speak of them. I will send out a voice to you concerning that which sustains our lives.

"Corn, because she comes from our mother the earth, is also our mother, the main support of our lives. Only Tiaowa can send the cloud people with rain to make it grow. Put your trust in him. He will come from the six directions to see our faces, to examine our hearts. If these are good, if there are no hard feelings between us, then the cloud people will gather above us in cotton masks and white robes and drop rain to quench our thirst and nourish our corn. Rain is what our corn needs most, and it will come only if we have good countenances. We must keep bad thoughts behind us and face the rising sun each day with a cheerful spirit and with united hearts, as did our ancestors in the old days of plenty.

"Recently our hearts have been hard and in many ways our faces have not been good. There is much in this valley we have been led to that is sacred, and our bad countenances mock those things. I weep because of that, I am adorned with mud to acknowledge my own sad foolishness, and I intend to change the course of my living. My heart pleads that each of you do the same.

"It is finished. I have spoken."

Hawk slowly dropped his eyes, and Tala could see the shame that was finally there. Silently she arose, took up her crutch, and slipped out of the dwelling. She was thankful that the boy felt sorrow, but she did not want him to think of her as an enemy. It was more important that he know of her love than that he remember her anger. So, near the ladder she paused, and with a smile of teasing in her voice she called his name.

"O Hawk, my heart sorrows in another thing as well."

The boy did not answer, nor had Tala thought he would. "I sorrow," she went on without hesitation and with even more of a smile in her voice, "that a youth who is almost a man of the People cannot get to the deep pool before the crippled old woman who is as his mother."

Incredulously Hawk looked up, saw her smile, heard her giggle, saw her scramble onto the ladder, and instantly he was on his feet and racing for the notches he had carved. "O woman," he shouted as he backed down the slick-rock cliff, "we shall see who will arrive most quickly at the pool!"

The other children, caught up in the game, scrambled down the ladder, and soon all four were frolicking and laughing together in the pool of cold, clear water.

And Tala, at a certain moment when her eyes came into contact with the eyes of the boy, seemed to hear him saying that he was truly sorry, and that he would make a great effort to have a pleasant countenance before her.

50

Leaving the youth Hawk and the others to swim alone, Tala slowly climbed from the pool. In silence she hobbled to the *hovatoqa,* the cut in the cliff, and up this she climbed. On top of the mesa at last, she moved to the high rock which had become their place of watching, both for the possible return of the Angry Ones and for the eagerly awaited arrival of the man of her dream.

For a time she sat silently, simply feeling the softness of the night. Hawk's fires burned like red eyes down near the corn, and they had done much to keep the night-eaters, the deer and the rabbits, away. Those fires had been one of Hawk's ideas, and he was filled with many such ideas that would truly help the People. Yet in his heart was that other thing, that anger.

Lying back, Tala gazed upward, tracing her way across the star-filled vastness of the sky. There were the *Hotokam,* the three stars in line; there too were the *Nátupkom,* the stars that were two brothers; and there also were the *Choochokam,* the stars that cling together.

Tala loved to watch the stars and usually felt a great closeness to them. But this night they gave no comfort. Instead the seeing of them filled her with a strong loneliness, a great sense of burdened sorrow. She felt so inadequate, so unable to declare the old ways that it had always been the task of the men of the People to declare. Oh, if only the man of her vision would come!

O Great One, she pleaded into the darkness, *where is he? Where is the man of my vision? This woman tries to be patient, but patience flees, and she is filled with a longing.*

Into the woman's memory then came again her vision, fresh and clear as it was when first it was given. She saw once more, in her memory, the man who was to be hers. He was tall and strong, and was making a walking away. He was in the trees, and the sunlight, filtering down, dappled his shoulders and back. And somehow, though she could not see his face, she could sense his goodness and gentleness. Her heart went out to him completely, and she called for him to return. In the vision she knew she had used his name, but that was gone from her now, and she could not remember. But in the dream he had stopped at the sound of her voice, turned, and though she could not see his face because of shadow she could sense his smile, radiant, glowing.

Suddenly Tala was weeping, for never had she loved so strongly nor ached so powerfully with loneliness. Never had there been within her such a great need.

And then, through her tears and once again into the darkness, her mind sent out a voice of love to this man who would one day come into the valley and be hers.

This day I have thought much of you, O man. I have missed you, cherished you, and needed you. O man, I have dreamed countless dreams of you and me together. O man, in my dreams we have reached for clouds and searched the stars, you and I, that we may see and climb together. O man, I have encountered many things, joy and even sorrow, that I would share, but you are not here, and I am so alone.

Yet will I save all these things, in my mind and in my heart, for one day soon they will be ours, together. O man, thus for today it is enough to say I have lived, and love you yet the more. . . .

SEVEN

The Hunter and the Hunted

51

And so many days flee past, and their going is both easy and difficult. A woman is alone, as women have been alone since time began, and over the course of that time she gives her heart to a man she has never met, never truly seen. In a sacred manner she gives herself to this man, but in the giving she also weeps, for she is very lonely. Daily she thinks of this man, daily she pledges her love to him, daily she watches for his appearing, and yet never does his face make itself known. She has even left signs for him lest he should be unable to find the way. Up on the mesa, in a high and prominent place, she has strewn pottery shards in a circular manner, thus showing him, after the manner of her people, the direction of her waiting.

Below the valley, far down on the bank of the dry wash where no sign of their dwelling or of their valley is visible, she has found a large sandstone boulder covered with ancient black desert varnish. There she has spent much time, and on it she has etched, using the hard metal knife of her clan, the sign of the four migrations of her people. This sign is a crossing of lines, turning clockwise at the ends to indicate that her own migration is in its final phase.

She has also etched a snake and a frog, in the same manner as she has painted those things on her pottery, telling of the water-planted-place that is above, and showing too that the valley has been blessed by the Creator and so is a fertile place to live.

And finally she has etched the humpbacked, flute-playing Kachina called *Kokopeli,* the other symbol of fertility and the symbol of her own clan.

These things are done, and still she waits, patiently and with a good countenance, yet with little shivers of hope as well. Soon, she is certain, the day of his coming will be upon her, and then her womanhood can be shared, the man-woman love feeling can be made manifest, and both she and he can blossom into the givers-of-life she so yearns for them to be.

And so she waits, for in that there is no choice. And as the days pass, much goodness is accomplished in the tiny valley. The woman sees this, and her heart grows big with gratitude for it.

The dwellings within the cave are completed, a room for men and a room for women, and two storage bins are completed as well. The structures are made of stone laid without mortar, plastered both inside and out with mud, are tight against water and mice, and the buildings are good to look upon.

Everything in the valley has grown lush with much water from the water-planted-place. The corn has been harvested and the stalks planted deeply. The storage bins are filled with dried corn, nuts, berries, wild onions and other roots, and certain leaves that can be boiled and eaten. There are also many baskets and jars, each filled with one or another of many varieties of seeds and wild rice. Stored also is yucca and hemp, used for fiber in weaving, and rabbit and deer hides and the feathers from many birds, all of which are used for clothing and sleeping robes. Truly has it been a bounteous season.

Below the cave, but well above the place of water, has been built the kiva: a circular, covered pit that is the winter home for sending out teachings to the children of the People. The woman gazes at the small opening in the top of the kiva, and as the chill winds of the late autumn evening tug at her hair, she wonders for perhaps the thousandth time how she will ever teach the boy called Hawk, the boy who has almost completly turned his back to her words.

The winds gust with more strength, the woman pulls her robe more tightly about her, and suddenly she is aware of the laughter, kind and gentle.

"Ho, little sister," her mind tells her that she hears, "the home that you have made is a good home indeed."

It is, the woman agrees, *but it is a lonely home as well.*

"Lonely?" they laugh. "How can that be, when there are four of the People who can laugh together?"

Sometimes we do laugh, the woman's mind agrees. *And sometimes it does not seem so lonely. Still, within one of us there is much anger, yes, and much pride. That one does not understand the ways of a true man, and his bad face makes it very hard for the other children.*

"Is it not hard for you?" the spirits question.

Perhaps, she thinks in response, *but not enough to be considered. Besides, I try to love him, though the anger in his face makes even that a difficult thing. If only the man of my vision were here! Surely such a man could teach the boy. Then, too, the man's presence might enable me to feel love for the boy a little more easily.*

Once more the Kachina people laugh, and then with great kindness they whisper a little wisdom past the eyes of the woman's thinking.

"Consider these thoughts," they say softly as the wind drifts over the rock and sighs through the brush and the trees. "Think long on them, little sister, and they will be the voice the Great One sends to you concerning your troubles.

"When your love for another is unplanned, O green-eyed woman, when it is given without calculation or without pretext, then you are neither a container of some foreign substance nor a carrier of something outside of yourself that someone else has given you. You truly feel, and that which you feel is you. It is what you do; it is what you are. You are love, and for all time, so long as you avoid selfishness, love will be you.

"That, little sister, is your power.

"No one can long resist such a power, such a giving of self, little one. Not even the boy called Hawk who is become as your son."

52

"O woman, we have need of more hides for winter sandals, and we have need as well for the horns of the sheep. It is in my heart to go on a hunt."

The words of Hawk hung solemnly in the air above the fire. Tala looked at the youth who was as her son, saw the defiance in his eyes, realized that he expected her to try to stop him, and suddenly she knew what she must do.

"It is well," she said, holding her eyes down in the manner he thought a woman should do. "When is it that you wish to leave, my son?"

Hawk was surprised, for he had expected opposition, a teaching, anything but this, this quiet acceptance. "I . . . ah . . . I had thought to leave with the birthing of the next sun," he finally replied.

"That will be good," Tala responded, "for truly we have need of the things you mentioned. Each of us will give honor to the man who brings us the power-things of the great sheep."

Hawk stared. Power-things? Man? Tala's words, and the thoughts behind them, pleased the youth very much. Truly, he thought, the woman seemed to be learning her place.

53

Hawk climbed steadily and easily, his going and his aloneness a great thing in his mind. Now he would show his manhood, and never again would he be doubted by the woman, by any of them. In two days, at the most three, he would take back to the valley the *pangwú*, the sheep with the big horns. Perhaps, if he was lucky, and if Giver-of-life would help, he would take back two of them. Then would the green-eyed woman and the two little ones know him for who he truly was.

The youth had long since left the juniper and pinyon of the mesa behind, and now he climbed steadily toward the northwest, toward the *pangwúvi,* the high, barren peaks where the bighorn sheep climbed.

He had followed a deep canyon as he had climbed, a canyon of rocky cliffs rimmed with ponderosa. Hawk had been amazed at the size of the trees, and had thought long concerning some way he and the others might put them to use. But the trees were too far off from the valley, there was no real need, and so he turned his thoughts to other things.

Hawk stopped and looked upward, doing his best to get things arranged in his mind. From low down, he knew, all on the mountain would seem clear. But once he was in the valleys and on the ridges of the peaks, landmarks would be lost and all places would appear as all others. Once up high, a man could never be truly certain of where he was—not unless he had given much thoughtful study to it beforehand. So now the boy gave deep thought to the high place he was approaching.

The deep canyon he followed ended in the foothills below the mountain, but above it and emptying into it were many smaller canyons and draws. These branched outward and upward in tortuous curves toward the barren peaks, and he knew he would need to follow one of them if he were to reach the top.

The lower slopes of the mountain were thick with brush—oak, mostly, and maple. Higher were thick stands of aspen, already gray with the losing of their leaves. And very high, as well as down the north-facing slopes, grew heavy stands of dark green timber—pine, spruce, and fir. The tops of the peaks were blue-gray with exposed rock, and that, Hawk knew, was *pangwúvi,* where the sheep with the big horns climbed.

Those peaks also hid the dwelling places of the Kachina people, and Hawk gave many long thoughts to that. He did not truly fear the Kachinas, but he respected them, and wanted with all his heart to avoid giving them offense. So he would go carefully, and would not violate anything that appeared to belong to them.

Selecting a draw that led directly toward the bare peaks, and marking well in his mind the character of the mountain around it, Hawk took up his short bow and arrows, his *atlatl* or throwing stick, and the strong spear it threw. He sprinkled a tiny amount of sacred cornmeal into the breeze as an offering in case he saw anything, and then solemnly he began again to climb.

Morning was on the land as he went, with the bright November sun blanketing the hills. Shadows of blue lay in the folds and creases of the mountain, sunlight danced on the remaining aspen leaves and on the tiny rivulets of water that sprang forth here and there, and it was a good day to be alive. Nearby a meadow lark called once, then again, and from far off in the timber a bull elk bugled his shrill challenge to the morning.

Hawk thrilled to the sacred beauty that surrounded him, and suddenly he felt a longing for the presence of someone to share it all with—Badger or Butterfly perhaps, or even the green-eyed woman who had become as his mother. How they would love this fine land! How they would delight in this high-up country that was like no land he had ever seen.

Passing near a spring, Hawk took a long drink, then sat back with eyes squinted tightly against the sudden pain in his head. Cold? The youth had never tasted water so cold, not even in the water-planted-place beneath the cliff. Yet this water, despite its chill, was somehow not so sweet as that in the valley, and Hawk thought once again of the goodness of the great Tiaowa, the Mighty One Above.

For a moment then he considered the teachings of Tala, and as always, he wondered about them. She felt differently about the gods than the men of his kiva had felt, and that troubled him not a little. To her there were actually only the two Gods, and they were very personal. Of course there were many helpers such as the Kachinas, but the woman was very careful to instruct the children that those others were helpers only, and were not true Gods.

On the other hand, the men of his kiva talked always of numerous gods, both good-natured and bad. None of them were very personal, none could be known in an individual manner, and most of the men seemed to place very little confidence in any of them.

Sign now was everywhere, tracks and droppings of deer and elk, occasionally a bear, and once even sheep. The youth knew he was getting close, yet still he did not hurry, did not rush. As the woman once had said, the trail was the thing and not the end of it. According to her, when one traveled too rapidly, he missed the very thing he was traveling for. So Hawk went slowly, with his eyes, ears, and even his nose open wide to the sensations of the land around him, and thus in a sacred manner he climbed.

54

The young man pauses once more, this time in a stand of aspen that borders a small stream. The water flashes and laughs as it dances past, he laughs with it, and the day is good. Looking up, he takes a deep breath and savors the scent of the place, a scent that speaks of moist earth and grass that is still green.

There is no place, he determines, that is more lovely than an aspen copse. The trunks of the trees, creamy white and scarred with black, stand as sentinels against the darker background of earth and pines. Elk and beaver like the bitter inner bark of the aspen, and they can usually be found nearby. Nothing, he has been told, provides more food for the animal brothers than does an aspen grove.

Always too there is dry wood for fires, for the aspen is self-pruning. As the trees reach higher into the sky, grasping for the sun, they shed their lower branches, and these dry out quickly. An aspen grove makes an excellent place to camp, and as the young man considers this he decides that, if he is able, he will spend his times of darkness on the mountain in this place.

Under most conditions that decision would be a good one, but the boy does not see the tracks upon the far side of the stream, large four-toed tracks of softly padded feet. He does not see, in the meadow on the far side of the aspen, the mounded forest debris covering the white bones and putrifying flesh of a dead deer. Nor, for that matter, does he see, in the rocks high above him, the very still form with the gleaming yellow eyes, watching, waiting . . .

55

Twice in the next few moments, Hawk saw deer. But they were not close, and he did not go after them. Still, he carried no food but a little cornmeal, and venison would taste very good while he sought the sheep with the big horns. Perhaps, he thought, if he kept his feet quiet and his eyes open he might succeed in obtaining some.

Moments later he saw more deer in the distance, a dozen of them in one bunch, and on a far-off slope, several elk. Slowly he climbed, and in the rocks of the meadows small rodents whistled shrilly. High overhead a large eagle circled, its primary feathers twisting constantly to catch each updraft from the warming slope of the mountain.

Suddenly he saw a silver-tip grizzly in the brush at the edge of the timber across the wide draw. The large bear stood to get a better view, and Hawk was amazed at its massive size. The boy felt a moment of fear, but there was much space between him and the bear, the breeze was blowing away from them both, and so at last the bear dropped down and continued to shred the old log it had been working on.

Sighing with relief, Hawk climbed a little higher, and moments later he saw his deer, his food for the time of the hunt.

Crouching down he began the stalking, and large in his mind were the words of the woman, unwanted instructions she was always sending out with her voice. He did not want to think of her words, but they lived in his mind, and for some reason he could not cast them out.

"Feeding deer are not difficult to stalk," she had said, "if the hunter moves on silent feet and with the wind in his face. When such an animal puts his head down to browse, move forward, and keep moving in a very silent way. When the tail of the animal starts to twitch and dance, it is about to look up. Be still then, do not move, and no matter how long the long-eared *sowíngwa* looks at you, it will not matter. To him you will be nothing but an *owa,* a rock, or perhaps a tree. Seeing no danger, he will return to his feeding, and then you may move closer."

And so Hawk, with those unwanted words in his mind, moved in on the browsing animal. His bow was ready as he moved, and his *atlatl* and short spear were passed beneath his waist string and ready at hand. He had killed deer in the tiny valley and on the great butte, but this one was larger, with great spreading antlers, and for some reason it seemed to be much more important than those others.

Quietly then, on soundless feet, he moved in until only a few yards separated him from the unsuspecting animal. Then, slowly, he pulled back the stone-tipped arrow.

The sun was warm on the hillside, somewhere far off a jay screeched and was still, and nearby a bee hummed around a bush. Suddenly the deer's head came up in alarm, its large eyes staring directly at the boy.

The boy froze, his eyes unblinking, the deer stared for long seconds, and at last it dropped its head once more to feed. Hawk lifted his bow a little more and took a deep breath. There was a soft twang as he released the sinew string on the bow, and less than a second later the feathered shaft was buried deeply behind the left foreleg of the *sowíngwa.*

The animal leaped wildly into the air, took three springing jumps forward, and was down. Somehow surprised, Hawk stared for a moment, then notched another arrow and moved slowly forward, expecting that the deer would rise up and flee.

But it didn't. It was dead, and as he stood above his kill, a proud but reverent youth gave thanks to the deer's spirit for its life and for its useful body. Then, with the ancient metal knife that the woman had given him for his hunt, he began the task of cleaning. And still he did not look up into the rocks that were above, did not see the piercing gaze or hear the hissing snarl of anger.

56

Later, with the meat safely hidden, the young man set out once more, seeking the elusive sheep with the precious big horns. Higher he climbed, through the tall timber and into the stunted growth of the high-up spruce and occasional fir. Here and there were the blackened remains of lightning-blasted trees, the peaks around him were ragged and gray, bare rock that had been scoured clean of earth was everywhere, and snow, black and dirty, lay here and there in the shade places beneath the rock.

There was no sound but the wind, and Hawk opened his ears as he walked, liking the sound of the silence around him. The air was clean and fresh, with a touch of chill to it, and breathing it was almost like drinking cold water. It was so very clear, too, and Hawk could see for more than a hundred miles in whatever direction he turned.

Yet still there were no sheep.

Crossing through a small pass between two low peaks, Hawk found himself in a small cirque, a little valley without growth of any kind. There was only rock there, rock and snow. Off to the side lay a small sheet of water, spirit water, he suddenly thought, a snow-fed lake that was scarcely stirred by the wind that blew higher up.

The youth shivered suddenly, and it was not only from the cold. This was a very high-up place, perhaps even the dwelling place of the Kachina people, the helpful spirits who had been the ancestors of his People. Such a thought made him nervous, for though they were helpful they might not like their secret dwellings invaded by one such as he.

Hawk paused, the wind moaned overhead and sent icy streamers down to pluck at the boy's long hair, a pebble broke loose from somewhere above him and rattled down the steep slope, and suddenly the young man wanted nothing so badly as to be gone from that place. He felt as though the eyes of death were boring into his spine, but when he spun about there was nothing there, nothing at all that he could see. His heart was pounding now, his breathing was shallow, and a cold sweat bathed his shivering body.

Another stone rattled down among the rocks, broken loose

from ages of weathering, and suddenly Hawk ran for his life. Heedlessly he sprinted toward the narrow opening that drained the tiny lake, and he neither saw nor heard the tawny form that glared balefully at his retreating back.

57

The opening through which Hawk sprang was neither a canyon nor a ravine but just a gash in the rock, a cut through which the water spilled. With a plea for protection to the great Tiaowa, Hawk also spilled through the cut, and in doing so he slid instantly down a thirty-foot stone water slide, losing his *atlatl* as he slid. He didn't notice that, however, for he was in a great hurry to escape from whatever it was that lurked behind.

Gaining his feet he kept moving downward, as rapidly as possible, and with each step his confidence filled his mind a little more. He had escaped! He had gone into the very dwelling place of the great and fearful Kachinas, and he had escaped!

Rock walls towered high overhead, closing the cut in places until there was scarcely a crack of light above him, and in those places it was like fleeing through a cave. Here and there ferns overhung the water, and often water covered the entire bottom of the cut that had now become a ravine, forcing Hawk to wade through it.

In other areas the water fell far below, and the youth found himself on a hairline trail along the cliff. Waterfalls were frequent, and the mist and spray were so thick that the youth was soaked thoroughly, and often he could not see more than a few feet ahead.

In that manner Hawk dropped almost a thousand feet. There the ravine forked, he took the upper branch, and found himself immediately on a game trail. For a hundred yards or so that snaked gradually upward, and then it opened into a small valley, narrow at first but then widening. The creek tumbled off and vanished into a canopy of trees and ferns, but the trail wound on into the valley, and Hawk did as well.

At that point the valley was no more than twenty yards wide, with steep rock walls rising on either side. The afternoon sunlight was tinting the high rock to the east, but in the bottom where the youth moved there was deep shadow.

A little farther along the valley broadened considerably, and Hawk could see that at its distant end it dropped off suddenly into a jumbled land of rocks and canyons that seemed to stretch away forever.

The canyon bottom where he strode was rich and filled with the grass of a good season. A stream watered it, springing from somewhere and tumbling, finally, off into the arid lands below. Besides the grass there were aspen, clumps of dwarf willows, and, on the benches, pine and fir. A few elk were visible, feeding peacefully across the valley. As Hawk appeared they moved off, silently and without real hurry, and they did not appear frightened at all.

Hawk once again found his heart beating loudly, for in the valley there was such a quiet, such a stillness. He no longer had the feeling that he was being watched, but there was something else, some sensation.

He moved slowly forward, skirting the trees, his short spear still within his waist-thong and his bow strung and ready. The shadows, deep and blue, were climbing higher, the far-up rim was gold with a shading of pink, swallows darted through the still air after late season insects, somewhere a marmot whistled.

And then he saw the sheep.

There were six of them, low on the opposite slope, and they were watching him. Instantly Hawk dropped to the earth and remained unmoving, and big in his mind were more words of the woman who had become as his mother.

"Sheep," she had said, "should not be hunted as the deer. The eyes of the sheep see much better and much farther, and they see always, even when the head is down for feeding.

"Now, this is the manner in which sheep should be hunted. First, spot them and determine in your mind several landmarks that are close to them and that will also be visible to you during your stalk, for you will not see the sheep again.

"With the wind in your face creep upon them, but do so in a circle route, staying all the while in the bottom of canyons and ravines so that they cannot see you. Nor must they hear you or smell you, or they will be gone like the wind after the sun rises.

"When all the landmarks tell you that you are as close as you can expect to get, then draw your bow, rise quickly to your feet, and slay the one that is nearest to you. If you have stalked well, you will then have a fine sheep.

"But remember, my sons, once you have begun your stalk, you must not look at the sheep again. Be assured that if you can see them, they will have seen you long before, and will have determined that you are an enemy. Thus will they be gone, and we will have no horns for our digging sticks, no robes for the cold."

In stillness Hawk lay, hearing in his mind these further unwanted words of the woman. Certainly she had been right about the deer, but the deer was an easy animal to kill, and she was only a woman.

And suddenly the boy decided that the green-eyed woman did not know all she claimed. She *could* not. Sheep were wild, deer were wild—there could truly be little difference between them. He had already slain one deer that day, and with a little care he would slay a fine sheep as well.

Hawk raised his eyes and took another long look at the six animals and at the terrain that surrounded them. There was indeed a circuitous route such as the woman had suggested he take, but the shadows were long and the sun was falling from the sky. Besides, according to the *mongwi* of his kiva, there was truly no need to give ear to the words of a woman, not ever. He was a man of the People, and would hunt as he chose.

58

And so a boy who thinks of himself as a man moves quietly forward from the trees, using his skills to stalk one prey in the same manner that he has stalked another. A camp-robber jay follows him silently, but the slowly creeping youth leaves no food and so the jay soon disappears, leaving him alone.

Carefully the boy moves forward across the valley and onto the slope of the steep hill, going inches at a time and taking advantage of any cover available. He slides along on his belly, for he has discovered that while three or four or five sheep feed, there is always one whose head is up, staring directly at him.

This frustrates the youth, but only a little, for the wind has come up, and it is into his face. That is a good sign, for even should they glimpse him now and then they will not flee. He will seem as a rock, or perhaps even a dead log, and his scent, blowing the other way, cannot tell them otherwise. Nor does it appear that he is wrong, for though the sheep look at him they continue to feed, and there is no sign of alarm among them.

Higher the boy creeps, now in a shallow wash, now across a talus slope of large boulders, now through a field of sedge and late-blooming wild flowers. The wind, still in his face, is only a whisper, his careful passage makes no sound at all, the raw edges of the cliffs above him gnaw at the sky with teeth flecked with a foam of snow gathered in their hollows, and still the sheep do not move.

The boy's heart races now, for he is close, very close. The woman who has become as his mother, but who is hardly older than himself, is wrong. He will bring her the great horns and the skin and the heart, and then he will send out a voice of power, declaring that she is no longer to give direction or teaching. He is the man, and will take his rightful place in the kiva.

Ahead looms a small ridge, a few feet high at best, and the youth grins. The six animals are just beyond that, and a last look shows him that a ram with great curling horns is closest, standing motionlessly and staring intently at him.

But the youth does not worry, for the wind is still into his face, and he has made no sound. That ram will be the one he will slay. That will be the one he will carry back to the woman. But first he must prepare.

With great skill the youth slithers to the back of the tiny ridge. No stone is moved, no grass whispers with the passing of his silent body. Never has he stalked better. Never has he approached so near to game such as this. Soon at least the large ram will be dead, and he will carry the horns back to the dwelling. Then will the woman Tala know of his power.

Silently he sprinkles a tiny amount of sacred cornmeal onto the ground as he offers in his mind a chant of thanksgiving. Then with great care he notches an arrow to his bow.

59

Hawk knew that no more than fifteen feet separated him from the sheep. His heart pounded, his entire body shook with the excitement of the moment, and he wondered if he would even be able to release the arrow. Drawing the bow all the way back, he paused and held his breath so that his limbs would stop shaking. Then, bunching his muscles, he leaped to his feet, his arrow already aimed at the large ram that stood just beneath the huge gray boulder.

The arrow was released instantly, the soft twang of the bow filled the evening air with its sweet music, and Hawk watched in amazement as the feathered missile flew forward and struck . . . empty stone!

The ram was on the earth, already dead, and the other sheep were not there. They were gone.

Dazed, Hawk looked around, saw nothing, heard the rattle of a stone high above, glanced up, and finally saw the sheep, the five remaining ones, leaping up the face of the wall at least a hundred feet above him.

For a moment he stood, his heart a hollow thing within him. Then slowly he moved to the dead ram.

The arrow that had killed it was similar to his own, but longer and much better made. It had entered the sheep directly behind the foreleg, slaying it instantly, and the blood still dripped from the wound.

The quiet laughter came from behind him, and Hawk spun toward the sound, his heart big with fear within his throat. There had been no one but himself within the valley! He knew that, and could not imagine why he was not alone.

The man who stood beyond the rocks was young, not much older than Hawk, but the youth could see that he was, nevertheless, very much a man. He was also well ready to slay again, for his bow was bent and an arrow was aimed directly at the boy.

"Brother," the man said quietly, and a smile was upon his face, "you seem surprised."

Hawk stared. "I . . . I . . . who are . . . you? And . . . and why do you think to slay me?"

The man's smile grew wider. "I slay anything that needs slaying," he responded, "for I am called Flies-Far. How are you called?"

"I am called Hawk. I . . . I was going to slay this great ram."

Flies-Far laughed. "Perhaps you were going to, but *I did.* The great Tiaowa was watching over me, too, and guided my arrow. You forced me to hurry my shot, for you were making such a great noise . . ."

"Noise? Never have I stalked so well, so quietly."

Flies-Far laughed again. "Well, brother, I heard you from clear across the valley. That does not seem very quiet to me."

Hawk dropped his face. "I am shamed," he said heavily.

"Good," Flies-Far declared. "Now you will go back to your father and to your uncles for more teaching and instruction."

"I would," Hawk said, lifting his eyes, "but they are all dead."

"Well, then go to the leaders of your clan."

"Brother, I have no clan. All are *mokee!*"

Flies-Far was incredulous. "All dead? You live alone?"

Hawk signaled yes. "I live alone with two children who are younger, and with a woman who mothers them."

"A woman?" Flies-Far questioned, raising his eyebrows. "She *must* be your mother. You are very young to have a woman."

"She is neither my mother *nor* my woman," Hawk responded scornfully. "She is only a young girl, hardly older than myself, she is even more foolish than other women, and I have turned my back upon her!"

"Well, brother," Flies-Far said as he lowered his bow, "I see that you are no danger to me, and truly I would hear more of this young woman and of the dead clan. Come, and let us get this ram to my camp. It will make a fine meal, and my belly cries out that it needs one badly. Perhaps you would share it with me?"

Hawk stared, then hastily made the sign showing that he was honored to be considered. Then he retrieved his arrow, found that the point had shattered, thought of the work that had gone into that one, and as he wondered what he had done that had made so much noise, the green-eyed woman's voice came once more into his mind.

"Sheep," she had said, "should not be hunted as the deer. . . ."

"Come," he said, thrusting the unwanted words from his mind, "let us go." And so together the two carried the ram down and across the narrow valley.

60

"So, tell me a little more of this woman."

Hawk spat and made the sign of disgust. "She is nothing. I do not wish to discuss her."

Flies-Far grinned. "That is your age speaking, brother. Not many seasons from now, you will find these woman creatures to be a great deal more interesting. Now describe this one to me, and tell me about her."

Hawk stared at the fire and sought for words. Down the valley a coyote called out and another joined in, and the moon was bright upon the land. He thought of the woman Tala again, thought of her up on the mesa above their valley in the same moonlight, sending out her voice to the great Giver-of-all-life that he would be protected, and suddenly, for no reason that he could understand, Hawk realized that he missed her. That angered him, and he kicked at a burning coal with disgust.

"She is huge," he answered. "She is clumsy, she is brave only occasionally, and she does not know her place."

"Her place?"

"A woman's place," Hawk responded. "That one is always trying to teach me, to make my decisions. She acts as if I am a child she must nurse along, and it angers me!"

Flies-Far grinned but did not say anything, and Hawk continued.

"She is filled with these foolish ideas about the old ways, and it caused such problems among the People that the elders of our village made her Outcast—"

"Outcast? Then, brother, why are you with her?"

Hawk rolled back and looked up at the sky. "I had no choice, my brother. Our clan was set upon by the Angry Ones, and I and three children survived. That woman also lived, and it was necessary to take her in our fleeing so that the children might have mothering. Still, I would be rid of her in a minute if I could. She is very ugly."

Flies-Far laughed aloud. "Brother, if she is ugly besides all you have told me, then truly you *are* overly burdened. What do you mean, ugly?"

"Well . . . I . . . ah . . . brother, how do I say it? She is not pleasing to look upon! Her face is gaunt, her hair is not altogether dark and is wild with curls as well. And worst of all, she has eyes that seem empty, and that are a strange blue-green in color. I can hardly bear to look upon her."

"Blue-green eyes," Flies-Far repeated as he picked up another hunk of roast mutton, "I have never heard of such a thing."

"Nevertheless, brother, what I have said is true. You are fortunate that you do not have to be near her."

Flies-Far chewed thoughtfully. "Brother," he said at last as he picked a bit of meat from between his teeth, "my heart grieves, for I have been mocking you a little. I am sorry. If she is as you say, then your position is truly one that I do not envy. And all of the rest of your people were slain by the Angry Ones?"

"It is as I have said," Hawk declared solemnly.

Shaking his head, Flies-Far leaned back. "Did you see them?" he asked.

Hawk signaled yes.

"I have heard much of these Angry Ones," Flies-Far went on. "Yet other than one man in our village, you are the only man I know who has seen them and lived. Tell me, what are they like?"

"Their hair is wild," Hawk stated as he remembered. "Their heads are long and not comely at all, and their countenances are truly filled with anger and hatred. They were even joined by one of our own people, a true two-heart. I think that he is more evil even than those others."

"Yes," Flies-Far agreed. "He would be."

There was silence, and both young men of the People gazed upward into the night. a night-hawk cried from high above them, a bat dived through the late fall air in search of some hardy insect, the fire popped, and at last Hawk broke the stillness.

"Flies-Far is a good name, my brother, a strong name. How did you come by it?"

The older young man laughed. "It seems that I was never where my mother wanted me to be," he declared. "Nor am I yet. I am happiest when I am out in this way, finding new lands, going far off to see what there is to see."

Now Hawk laughed. "I was called Hawk for the same reason. My mother declared that I was faster than the hawk in escaping from her wishes."

Both boys laughed, and suddenly Flies-Far grew serious. "Brother Hawk, you are welcome to return with me to my own village. It is strong, we have a goodly supply of water and of grain, and we are well protected from the Angry Ones. Perhaps I could be as your uncle, and could instruct you more fully in the proper ways of manhood."

"You . . . you would do that?"

"It would be an honor. Besides, we have a man who lives among us, a great man indeed. He is instructing the elders of our village in many powerful things, many things that are kept secret from the rest of the People. You would do well to learn of these things. It would be a good thing to have you as a neophyte in our kiva society."

Hawk was stunned. Never had he expected such an offer, never had he expected to be able to sit in the secret kiva societies again. It was almost too much to ask for.

"I am honored that you would ask," he stated simply. "But . . . but what of the woman and the children?"

"What of them? Are the children your true siblings?"

Hawk signaled no.

"Well, then, there you have it. The woman is Outcast and should be as one dead already. And, according to the ways we have been taught, if children have no family and are unable to care for themselves, then the rest of the People have no responsibility for them. Is that not true?"

"Yes, it is true."

"Good. Then you will come."

Hawk looked around him miserably. He wanted to go, oh, how he ached to go! Where else would he receive such fine instruction? Where else could he learn the true ways of manhood?

On the other hand, the woman and the children were waiting for him and were depending upon him. How could a true man turn his face against those who had been left so helpless? Hawk was torn badly, and it showed on his face.

"Brother," Flies-Far asked, "is the decision so difficult?"

Hawk stared at the earth, feeling awful, and signaled yes.

"Ah, it is the woman."

"Partly," Hawk responded, "though truly I despise her. It is more the children. I have strong feelings for them, and have become somewhat responsible for their lives. Small as I am, I am the only man that they have."

Flies-Far nodded. "Well spoken, brother. Perhaps you are more of a man than I had supposed. Very well, here is what we will do. For the time left to us here in this place, I will instruct you in what I can. Later, when you are able, come to our village. You will be made welcome, and there is always time to learn more of the teachings of the People."

Hawk nodded, smiling. "That is good, brother. You may be assured that one day soon I will come."

61

For two suns and two darknesses Hawk stayed in the valley with Flies-Far, learning all he could, and always hunting the wild sheep. But in spite of his efforts, he obtained nothing but scraped limbs and an aching body—those, and a great respect for Flies-Far and any other who had ever slain one of the big-horned animals. He felt that respect primarily because, no matter how he tried, he could not accomplish that great feat. Since the first kill the animals had become too filled with fear and caution, and he never got within range of even a distant shot.

At last, tired and discouraged and yet very pleased with the things he had learned, the youth gathered together the few things he had brought to the camp.

"Brother," he declared, "it is in my heart to give thanks. Go in peace, and may your hunting be good."

Flies-Far grasped his shoulder. "I wish you the same. Do not forget, O Hawk. You are welcome within my dwelling."

Hawk signaled that he understood. "And you, brother, are welcome in my dwelling."

Long the two stood looking into each other's eyes, and then with a last respected-brother touch, Hawk turned and made his way out of the canyon, over the bare spine of the mountain, and down the outer slope. Dark clouds were rising, there was a strange chill in the air that had not been there before, and Hawk sensed that snow was finally coming to the land. It was indeed time to return to the dwelling of the woman.

In the late afternoon he finally approached the alpine meadow and aspen grove where he had left the deer, satisfied that he had slain at least *one* animal to take back to the others. Now, if he could find a way to carry it that would not slow him down too much, he should be back by late the following day.

With the sun low beneath the building clouds and behind his right shoulder, Hawk moved quietly down the slope, through the heavy aspen, and to the place where he had hidden the large buck. But there was no *sowíngwa,* no deer, hidden in that place!

Stunned, Hawk stared about. Yes, it was indeed the correct place. The old stump was there, the single pine stood off to the left, the high cluster of boulders were as he had seen them.

Suddenly angry, Hawk slammed his bow and only remaining arrow into the earth. Some person had taken his kill! One who knew not the ways of a true man had taken the deer he had brought down.

Tracks! Whoever had taken the deer would have left sign, and to find that person the boy would only need to follow his spoor. On his hands and knees Hawk cast about, looking intently, but there was no trail. Instead the earth was well matted as with many feet, and here and there were tufts of deer hair.

Still looking, the youth circled outward, and came almost at once to a great mound of forest debris in the thickest part of the grove of aspen. With his short spear he pushed away the limbs, leaves, bark, and earth, and to his surprise, beneath it all was his deer, or rather what was left of it.

Grabbing the antlers Hawk pulled, and the deer came free, sliding a foot or so toward him. Great chunks had been torn from the flank, and the belly, where he had gutted it two days before, had been chewed viciously.

Chewed?

Suddenly, in the last of the sunlight, the young man called Hawk released the antlers and looked up. The hair on his neck was rising, chills were running up and down his spine, and again, as in the high cirque where it had seemed the Kachina people dwelt, he felt eyes boring into him, felt himself being watched.

Deeply he breathed, and slowly. He *knew* he should not have gone into that high place. The Kachina people must be very angry to have sent this evil upon him.

Instinctively he moved his feet together, and crouching, he reached for his bow. But it was not at his side, and with a sinking heart the boy remembered having thrown it to the earth only moments before.

Quickly he glanced in that direction, saw that he had come perhaps thirty feet, and wondered if he could get back to it.

Cautiously he took one step, then another. His spear was in his hands, his dark eyes were probing every shadow, looking behind every trunk of every tree. His heart was racing, his body was cold and clammy, and in his mind was a great fear.

Something on the ground caught his attention, his eyes

dropped, and there in a small space of earth was a track: clear, very large, well defined. It was rounded where the pad had pressed down, soft of outline, there were four toes with only the barest tips of claws showing, and the boy knew.

It was the large cat, the puma, the blood-drinking one that moved as a shadow, moved so swiftly it could never be overtaken.

Shivering with fear, Hawk looked around once more, saw nothing, took another step, and from a clump of brush behind him there was a sudden hiss, a hiss of death.

Hawk spun around, inadvertently raising his spear as he did so, and that act alone did much to save his life. The lion was there, crouched behind him, tensed for its spring. Its round eyes gleamed yellow, its ears were laid back flat against its huge head, the claws of its feet were unsheathed for the killing, and its pendant, black-tipped tail twitched menacingly back and forth.

Involuntarily the youth took a half-step backward, the great cat bared its yellowed fangs in another hiss, and in that same instant it sprang.

With a strangled cry of fear the boy tried to fall back, his foot rolled on a small stone, and he twisted downward. But nevertheless, through fifteen feet of air the lion sprang true. Its huge paws stretched out, reaching for the boy's life. But in his falling Hawk had gone a little to the side, and only one paw caught him. It smacked low into his ribs, raked downward, and as the youth was knocked away the claws ripped out across his bare-skinned hip.

Hawk screamed with pain, his twisting became a falling that threw him even farther from the cat, the lion's powerful jaws snapped on empty air instead of the boy's thin neck, and suddenly there was a sharp sting in the pad of the cat's right front paw.

The great beast landed, snarling, Hawk felt the spear wrenched from his grasp, he grabbed the haft back and instantly twisted, miraculously the two parts of the shaft did not separate, and the puma screamed in pain and anger as the sting in its paw flared at it once again.

With a horrible snarl it twisted around and sprang once more, and, wonder of all wonders, once more the stone-tipped spear was in the right place.

Suddenly, in the midst of its spring, the huge puma felt a sharp pain in its baleful left eye. Snarling angrily, it turned in mid-leap and came down to one side of the terrified youth. There, spitting and snarling and hissing viciously, the cat rubbed the side of its face into the soft earth, seeking to rub out the sting that now lived where its eye had once been.

Hawk, somehow sensing that he had little more than a moment, grasped his still-whole spear, leaped to his feet, sprinted down the hill through the aspen, and took a running dive into the heavy brush that choked the ravine.

Branches tore at his face and body, he hit rolling, lost his spear and grabbed it again, and fled downward in great leaping strides, his painful wound an unnoticed thing in his fleeing.

Behind him the puma still thrashed at the earth with loud, angry snarlings, and the terrifying sound spurred the boy onward with even greater urgency. His breathing tore at his lungs, he fell, got up and fell again, rolled under a bush, wormed out the other side, hit his feet, and took four more plunging steps before he was down once more.

Gasping for breath he lay still for an instant, and the pain hit him then, great throbbing ribbons of fire that flamed across his ribs and over his hip. The great wound was bleeding heavily, and he could feel the stickiness down his side and leg, the blood turning the earth to mud under his body.

His lungs felt as if they were tearing themselves apart, but he knew he had to move, to get off the mountain. Grasping his spear tightly, he squirmed between two boulders, dragged himself to his feet, stood gasping for more air, and was suddenly aware of the silence around him.

His breath suddenly stilled, Hawk stared behind him. There was no noise from up on the hill, no sound of the great cat's pain. Fearfully he stared about, into the bushes, into the rocks near the ravine. But there was nothing. The evening held no sounds but the small ones of his own making.

Could the puma be dead? Could there be that much good fortune in the world? Or was it out there now, stalking him?

The bank of the ravine where he stood was clogged with brush, and there were many rocks, polished smooth by running water and by the abrasion of other tumbling stones. There were many dead leaves beneath the brush, but many more still had not fallen, and Hawk could see little.

He lifted his spear, staring upward in the hope that he might see movement on the mountain. Suddenly he grew dizzy, fought it off, and was just starting to turn away and continue his descent when through the brush the great cat suddenly appeared.

Instantly it leaped, but the soft earth beneath its rear paws gave way and the puma was suddenly off-balance. Twisting to gain control, it missed Hawk completely with its long and curving claws, but the youth struck out with his spear, felt it sink into flesh, felt also the haft snap in two, and as both screaming puma and spear vanished into the brush below, the boy sprinted again, away from the ravine and down across the rock-strewn slope of the mountain.

Behind him came the awful sounds of the wounded cat, and these served only to give the boy Hawk greater speed. With feet flying he leaped brush and rocks and fled downward, never even looking back. Finally he left the steep slope of the mountain behind, but still he ran on, his course parallel to the large canyon he had followed up.

Darkness fell, and with lungs on fire the young man ran on, staggering often, falling often, yet unwilling, unable to stop and to rest. But in the darkness a large dead tree, a ponderosa, stood invisible in his path, leaning crazily against another. Hawk, his eyes unseeing because of the pain and the exhaustion and the darkness, ran directly toward the huge leaning trunk. And in that manner ended the thirteenth anniversary of the day of his birth.

62

And on the slope of the mountain, not so far behind, a huge cat crouches in the darkness, licking its wounds and hissing and spitting with pain. The beast weighs just a shade under two hundred pounds, which is large even for a lion, and is an old male trying desperately to protect its territory from encroachment.

The winds drift by above it, and on their backs ride the Kachina people. But there is no laughter now, only respect, for these know also of the strength of the great cat.

The winds drift down the mountain and the Kachina people hurry away as well, and their respect is great in their voices.

"That one," they declare, "is very large and fearsome indeed. It hunts alone, and it swings a big circle around the lands it claims as its own. It usually eats only deer and elk, though when it hungers we have seen it eat rabbits, beaver, mice, squirrels, coyotes, and grasshoppers. And yes, we have seen it eat young boys as well."

"And this one," declares other voices, "is in good health. It is a splendid, lithe creature, capable of great speed in short bursts. It is an excellent climber in trees or on cliffs, a good swimmer, and a natural taker of life. Truly should we worry about the youth."

"Yes," others agree. "That one will stalk quietly by scent until within twenty or thirty yards of the boy. Then with black-tipped tail swishing back and forth and with ears laid back it will burst forth, in sixteen-foot leaps, and will catch its prey within four or five jumps. With long claws clinging to the victim's body the puma's great jaws will then snap closed upon the neck, long sharp teeth will penetrate vertebrae and spine, and seconds later that one will have its kill."

"But should we worry?" another voice asks as the winds drop down the slope. "That young one who flees has a very bad face."

"That is true," others agree. "Still, those others depend upon him. And you know of the young woman. . . ."

"Have you seen the puma eat?" more voices whisper. "It is a clean eater, will hide for another day what it does not eat, and a large deer will last it a week. The boy will only feed it for a day or so. Such a feeding does not seem very worthwhile."

"Also," others admit, "that one will defend its territory with a vengeance, and will stalk unendingly an enemy that has trespassed, fighting viciously to destroy it or to drive it away. Should it slay the boy, it will then find the woman and the other little ones, and there will be no ending."

And as the Kachina people discuss these things among themselves, the great male puma crouches in the darkness, snarling its anger. Its right front paw is torn badly, its left eye is only an open and bleeding hole, and there is a great sting in its right flank. The small end of the spear is gone now, for the cat has torn it out with its teeth. Yet the wounds remain, none truly deadly, and in the cat's memory lives the one who was taking its kill, the strange-looking other creature who has given such hurt. Such an intruder cannot be allowed to remain. This territory is taken, and now the spoor of another lies in the air and upon the earth.

Hissing softly the cat rises to its feet, snarlingly lifts its paw as the pain strikes again, and then on three legs that have lost little of their strength it sets forth, seeking the easiest way.

EIGHT

A Life for a Life

Firelight flickered dimly against the roof poles of the kiva. Tala lay on her back watching it, sleep an unthought-of thing. Across from her two children slept soundly and warmly, but there was a third place there, an empty place, and that worried her.

Hawk was long overdue, and in the manner of a mother she worried about that. In her mind were many things that might have happened to him, things that terrified her. After the manner of a mother she considered them, and so first one thing filled her thoughts and then another. But always, no matter what she was thinking of, it was always terrible, the worst possible thing she could imagine.

In frustration Tala arose and piled more wood on the fire, wondering what she should do. Butterfly stirred, she looked at her, and thought again of how much she had come to love the little ones. Even the missing Hawk was loved, Hawk with his face that was so often bad toward her. She had so wanted him to be successful with this hunt; she had so wanted him to bring home the horns of the bighorn sheep. But now it was two suns past the agreed-upon time of his returning, and she was truly worried.

Climbing the ladder and pulling back the thatch covering, Tala climbed out of the kiva and into the darkness of the night. It was snowing, but not heavily, and she sent out a voice of gratitude for that.

For long moments she stood in silence, staring off down the tiny valley, hoping for some sign of the coming of her son. Below her the water trickled musically as it fell from the water-planted-place and into the large rock tank. Snow fell upon the bushes and trees that were near, and suddenly one spruce bough pulled loose from the white weight that had borne it down, causing a sound behind her that made her spin with alarm.

Smiling sheepishly at her own alarm, she turned her face upward and let the snowflakes come down upon her. It was so quiet, so clean, so pure. She loved the snow, loved it especially when it fell upon her face, melted instantly, and rolled downward in small beads of moisture. But what was it doing to her son? Where was he, and why had he not returned?

O Great Tiaowa, she breathed, *hear the voice I send out, hear this voice of a woman pleading. You have given me a son, I have loved him well, but now he is gone, and I fear. I fear for his life, I fear for his death. I fear that he needs me and cannot call my name. Help him, please, help him.*

64

And so a mother stands in the darkness of a frigid night and aches mightily for a missing son. All her thoughts are prayer-thoughts, all her desires are for the one who is hers. She pleads, and in the pleading she tells the powers above that, if it is possible, she will even trade places with him so that he will be well and whole.

And while she pleads and worries, the winds of winter lift up and drift down the mesa and push the snow here and there. Some is even pushed into the holes in the rocks, and for one who believes in them and accepts them it is not hard to hear the Kachina people grumble with the cold and stumble forth to get warm.

But then they see the woman, hear her pleadings, and in the manner of all Kachinas they laugh softly as they sigh past her.

"O woman," they seem to say, "why is it that you worry? If he is well he is well, and if he is not, well then, there is nothing that can be done about it."

But there must be, she says sternly in her mind. *He is my son, and there must be some way that I might help.*

Again the Kachina people laugh, and it is neither a good laugh nor a bad laugh. It is just a laugh. "Your son?" they question. "No, little sister, you have forgotten. You found him, remember? Or perhaps he found you. Either way, it is the same. He is but a youth with a bad countenance toward you. Perhaps you should forget him."

No! Tala screams at them in her mind. *How could a true woman of the People do such a thing? I love this boy as my own son, and will not forget!*

The wind suddenly picks up in intensity, a great flurry of snow blows over her, and Tala can hear the mighty discussion going on between the Kachina spirits. "No," some say firmly. "Yes," others declare just as firmly, and so back and forth it goes until suddenly the wind dies down and there is only a sighing again, a sighing that is a sound of good laughter.

"Perhaps, little sister," the laughing voices whisper, "it would not hurt to look for this bad-faced boy. That would be the way of a true mother."

65

In the gray light of dawn Hawk awoke with a start, shaking with the intense cold. Above him an icy breeze rattled through the huge ponderosa pines, and from between frosty eyelashes he gazed wonderingly at them. He was stiff and chilled to the bone, and somehow he could not understand where he was or why he was there.

Sitting up he saw the snow, everywhere, and then the pain came again like a wave of fire, tearing at his lower back and head.

Wonderingly Hawk touched his forehead, felt the large bump that was there, and realized that he must have smashed into something. Above him leaned the huge ponderosa, and that certainly explained the bump. But what was he doing there, among those big trees and in the snow? And what could have caused the wound in his back, the wound that brought such great pain?

And then in a rush it all came back, and Hawk was on his feet in an instant, staring about. The puma! It had attacked him twice, and if it was not dead it would surely do so again. He had to get moving, and he knew it. But his head was spinning, and already his legs felt like wooden sticks that would hold him no longer.

Slowly he set out, moving along the canyon and toward the tiny valley. He still clasped the hind-shaft of the spear, and this he now used as a walking stick, aiding his balance. He also pulled himself forward with it, plunging it into the new snow and then dragging his reluctant body toward it. In that manner he traveled, always moving, always in pain, and always making a watch over his shoulder lest the huge puma come upon him unawares.

Hawk thought of that constantly, and wondered what he would do if indeed the cat did come. He had only the haft from the spear, that and the ancient metal knife the woman had given him. Yet the knife was sharp, for it was the same that had opened the injury in the woman's leg during the past season of warmth.

Thoughts of the woman who had tried to become as his mother then filled his mind, and so as he made his way slowly forward, Hawk considered her. She was very strange, just as the men of his kiva had said when they had declared her Outcast. Yet within her was much wisdom, yes, and much in the way of courage. And that alone would make her seem strange, especially to those like Flies-Far, who would not expect such things from a woman.

Yet now, as Hawk thought about it, he realized that all of the things he so looked forward to seeing again within the small valley were there because of her. Truly he had helped a great deal, as had Butterfly and Badger and even the tiny baby who had departed to the sky nations. But still, the one called Tala was behind it all. It was she he felt separated from.

And so the day fled past, and the boy called Hawk staggered on as if in a dream. The great pain that was in his back was also a red haze behind his eyes, and there were times during the passing of that sun when the boy did not even know who he was or why he was walking. Yet always he went on, one step after another, and always in his mind lived the vision of the valley, of his family, of the woman Tala who was waiting.

66

Hawk did not know what made him turn. Surely it was no sound, for the great puma had made no sound at all during its stalking. Yet turn the young man did, and there, less than fifty yards behind and sneaking forward along his own trail, was the wounded cat.

For an instant each froze, and then Hawk, with a mighty shout, waved his stick in a threatening manner toward the puma. Startled, the cat took a step backward, snarling and eyeing the boy with its one good eye as it did so.

Quickly the youth looked around, saw that he was far from the edge of the deep canyon, and saw too a cluster of boulders stacked against another low cliff just ahead of him. In some past age those boulders had fallen from the face of the cliff and had spilled off in two directions, leaving a deep and fairly narrow crevasse between them.

Hawk saw that crevasse, and instantly he knew that it was his only chance. If he could just get into it before the puma got to him, then he was certain he might have a chance.

Again he raised his voice in a shout of courage, again the cat backed up, snarling and hissing, and in that instant the boy gave a mighty lunge and sprinted toward the rocks and toward safety.

He ran well, but the puma, seeing him make the fleeing, sprang forward in pursuit. Hearing the cat, the boy turned to see how close it was, and in the turning he slipped and fell heavily into the snow.

Terror-stricken, Hawk scrambled to regain his feet. But the icy snow was treacherous and he could not do it. Twisting onto his back in the snow he saw the puma coming, only two easy leaps away, and he knew that he was *mokee,* knew that he was dead. Still, there is always within man the willingness to fight for life against even the most impossible odds. And though the boy was very young, that will was strong within him.

Again Hawk shouted his courage shout, again he waved the stick that had once been his spear, and again the cat veered to the side. Scrambling backward then, the boy made a little more progress toward the crevasse in the rocks. But the big puma was close, hissing and snarling as it moved, low against the snow, back and forth, back and forth, its long, black-tipped tail swishing menacingly, reaching with its injured paw to kill this strange interloper.

Hawk saw that wounded paw, saw what the power of his stone point had done, and in the instant of seeing it he reached out and whacked the wound with the hind-shaft of his spear. With a terrible snarl the cat sprang away, and the boy made another scrambling toward the rocks.

But in the scrambling he dropped the shaft of his spear, took his eyes from the cat for an instant to look for it, and suddenly the huge puma was upon him.

He felt the heavy weight slam into him as the angry beast knocked him back into the snow, he felt the claws of one large paw sink like new fire into his leg, he looked into the deadly yellow eye and black-rimmed open mouth of the puma and realized that *túchvala,* saliva, was dripping from it, he felt the amazing softness of the tawny fur as he tried to hold the head back from his neck, he realized almost instantly that he did not have the strength to do so, and in that slow way of seeing things that is given to man when death comes close, he saw the bared fangs as they sought with blood-lust for his jugular.

Hawk screamed and kicked with his one free leg, he reached desperately for the ancient knife the woman had given him and could not find it, he pushed with his hands at the huge head that was above him, and none of those things did any good. The dripping fangs were nearly upon him.

Suddenly the cat snarled and twisted its head away, and in that fraction of an instant that was so much less than the time it takes to tell about it, Hawk saw a feathered shaft quivering from its flank. He saw it, wondered at it, wondered that he was still alive; and then he heard the screaming.

He wondered at that too, for it sounded much like the screaming of a woman, and in the instant of his wondering he felt the jolt of another weight hit and press down upon him. Through his eyes that were blurred with tears of pain and anger, and through his mind that was crazed with terror, he saw the puma above him. Against its massive body was another form, much smaller, a form that for some strange reason looked a great deal like the green-eyed Outcast called Tala.

His mind strove to accept that, he saw a bare arm circling the neck of the big puma, and suddenly the cat had spun free and he was lying alone in the bloody and trampled snow.

"Hawk! My son, hear me!"

The voice was close and yet far away, and as the boy did his best to focus on it he was aware that he could see the woman again, urging him toward the rocks with her waving arm. He would go, too, but there was a little matter of his dying beneath the fangs of the big puma. Besides, she could be nothing but a *tuawta*, a vision that had come in the moment of his dying.

But still, there was no heavy weight of death pressing down upon him, there were no claws buried in his leg, there was no stench of stinking meat on the breath of the beast.

67

Tala stood with shaking limbs, her fear a big thing within her body. The puma was gone, but only a short way and for a short time, and she knew in her heart that this was so. An old man had once told her a little of the puma's ways, and she knew it would protect its own land to the death. She also knew it was an animal to be feared, for it was a ghost animal, seldom seen, and it seldom missed its kill.

Yet if it were not slain it would be with them always, killing, killing, and always would she live in great fear for the lives of her children. She had once seen a child who had been slain by such a beast—the memory lived strong within her, and she dared not let this blood-drinking one remain alive.

But to slay the puma she would have to get past her own fear, and the woman did not know if such a thing could be done. She had thrown herself upon it before only because it had been in the very act of slaying her son. But now, now she stood still in the silence of the day, terrified, unable to move. She felt again the hot breath of the beast's huge mouth as it had turned upon her, in her mind she saw the wicked claws and the horrid fangs, and the fear still held her, its grip tighter and more tight. Fear pressed against her and her breath would not come.

O Great Tiaowa, she cried within herself, *I fear, and there is not time for that. Give this daughter who stands before you courage to slay and . . . and even to be slain herself, if such a dying will preserve the children.*

And then the wind picked up and moved the snow a little, and in the moving of the snow the woman's eyes were opened and she saw. She saw the boy who was her son as he began again his scramble toward the safety of the rocks, she saw the huge puma slide like a shadow across the snow and, snarling, leap upward into a thick-limbed tree, and she saw too the blood on the snow from her son's wounds and also from the wounds her son had given the puma.

Suddenly she stood taller. Her son called Hawk had great courage and had not feared! He had fought when he was too small to fight, when he had no weapons.

Tala's fear snapped from around her like an old rotted piece of cordage, the cold air rushed into her lungs, and with a great cry of courage she swung about and picked up the ancient metal knife her son had dropped, the knife that had come from her ancestors and that had so bravely opened the wound in her leg, and with it and her bow and one arrow she moved swiftly over the snow. A mighty strength was within her, and when she saw the blood spoor on the snow she was glad. The puma was weakened. The one who was as her son had fought bravely and well.

Carefully she moved close to the pine where the cat had taken refuge, but she was almost under it before she could see the puma. It was not more than ten feet up, lying flat along a branch, and it was spitting and glaring at her. She saw the arrow still in its flank, she saw another wound in the flank that was lower and farther back than her own, she saw that one eye in the cat's head was only a draining hole, and her heart sang with pride in the great courage of her son. Truly he had fought with the strength of a man.

Notching her last arrow, she pulled the sinew and heard the hum as it sang forth, and in that same instant the puma leaped. It wanted to leap past her, over her head, and somehow she understood that. But the bough upon which it lay was small and easily bent, its powerful muscles were weakened from the many wounds it had taken, and the great cat fell short.

Tala saw it crashing through the branches above her, she saw its huge claws unsheathed, she saw its jaws gaping open, and in the instant that it fell upon her she had her ancient hardened copper knife out in one hand and with the other she dropped the useless bow and grasped at the throat of the angry beast above her. She fell backward with the weight of the puma upon her, and as she sank into the snow she felt the tearing of the great claws at her mantle, the mantle Butterfly had so painstakingly woven from the yucca and from the rabbit.

She felt this, and in that moment she plunged the strong old knife deep into the puma's body where the soft flesh lay beneath its left foreleg. She held the foaming jaws away from her with her one hand that was filled with mighty strength, and while the claws from the puma's hind paws and its front paws too raked at the heavy mantle that was over her, she twisted the blade and plunged it in again, deeper, deeper.

She struggled then to get free of the raking claws and could not. She let go of the haft of the knife and with both hands tried to push the writhing beast away and still she could not. She tried again and again, with her hands and with her feet, and suddenly with a mighty wrench the cat was thrown free and she struggled to her feet. Hawk was standing and gulping in mighty breaths of air, for he had come to her rescue, and the puma lay writhing upon the snow.

Its claws ripped at the earth and the grasses and the snow that was over it all, its jaws snapped over and over on empty air, gradually its movements slowed, its yellow eye filmed over, it twitched a little more, and then it was still.

Tala stood swaying, gasping for breath, looking at the brave young man who was as her son, looking at the blood that was upon his body, aching within her heart that he should feel such pain.

And Hawk looked too, in an unbelieving manner, at this woman who had wanted to become as his mother. He saw the blood that was upon her, he saw the great shreddings that had once been her mantle of warmth, he saw the gore and the dead puma in the trammeled snow, and suddenly he knew how wrong the old men of his kiva had been. Never again would he doubt or question the wisdom, the courage, of this woman.

68

And so with arms supporting each other, a woman of the People and the boy who has become as her son make their way back toward the tiny valley of their dwelling. They carry the ancient metal knife, they carry the bow and two arrows, they carry the hind-shaft of the spear, and they carry also the great tawny skin of the puma. Truly has it been a good hunt.

And as they walk into the darkness of early evening the winds lift up and the Kachina people move out from their holes in the rocks and from their hiding places everywhere, and once more they are laughing. Their laughter is soft and easy, for they are laughing at a good joke that they can see and that is hidden from everyone else. The woman hears the laughter and is glad, but she does not understand.

What are you laughing at? she asks in her mind as she walks with her son held tightly within the circle of her arm. *Is it that you are making a mocking, O Kachina spirits of my ancestors?*

The winds lift higher in their laughter. "No, little sister," they whisper gleefully, "that is not it at all. We laugh because we see the other burden you carry, the one that weighs all and yet weighs nothing, and that indeed is a good joke."

Other burden? Joke? But what burden can there be, beyond my son, the weapons, and the great hide of the puma. . . .

"Little sister," they laugh softly as they drift off over the mesa and away, "the other burden is greater, and it is now carried between you, because you have each died and yet lived for the other. The joke is that you cannot see it, nor can you ever lay it down again. Do you not see, little sister?" and they laugh again as their voices grow fainter and more faint in the darkness of the night. "Well, perhaps one day you will. . . ."

NINE

Winter Is for a Teaching

It is winter in the high plateau country of the American Southwest. The red and white and multicolored rock of the mesa is crowned with snow, pure and icy. The winds of the months of cold howl and shriek like so many devils, driving the snow before them, settling it white against the ridges and filling the low places with its frigid softness. It is a time of famine and hunger, when all life shrivels up and retreats in upon itself, just holding on and barely living while it waits with impatient heart for the warm breath of spring.

Even the Kachina people are in hiding, for the winds of winter are not conducive to laughter, to happiness and joy. Many have gone to the tops of the highest mountains where they sit in council together, learning from the great Tiaowa how they might be of service to their own struggling descendants. The others crouch within the rocks, waiting for companionship, waiting for the warm winds to call them forth.

But in *Pámuya,* the water moon of January, such warm breathings do not occur, and what life there is huddles together in holes, seeking warmth, seeking companionship, seeking blessings, seeking learning.

70

The small fire burned brightly in the center of the kiva. Outside, the winds blew and the snow struck against the rock of the mesa, but within the circular chamber all was warmth and comfort.

Tala, her few scratches from the big puma completely healed, sat in the place of honor before the reflector and the ventilation chamber. Normally such a place was occupied by the priests or the elders, but now she took the position, for truly was she become the honored teacher.

On her right sat Hawk, whom Tala now thought of as a young man. Hawk felt differently, however, and so he sat as a *kékelt,* a fledgling hawk, a neophyte, for truly he knew how much he had to learn.

His wounds, very grievous, were nevertheless healing nicely, and that was due in great measure to the knowledge of Tala and the constant ministrations of Butterfly, who Tala said had the great gift of healing.

The young girl took pride in those words, and her knowledge of the ways of medicine and healing was growing rapidly indeed. Still, she humbly took her seat across the fire from the woman who was as her mother, for traditionally that was the place for the young ones of the People who were just starting their learning.

The little Badger sat on the left of Tala. He too was a *kékelt,* but his skills in the way of the earth were also growing, and already he had planned a new system of irrigation that he could implement in the following season of renewing grasses. It would allow better use of the water that flowed from the sacred water-planted-place, and would enable the family to grow on the same amount of ground even more crops than they had grown in the season just past.

And so on that day, in the warmth of the kiva which was sacred because its circular shape symbolized all round creations of the great Tiaowa, Tala ground corn on a stone before her, and as she ground she spoke, her relationship to the children being both mother and teaching kinsman.

"My children," she declared, "let me tell you something that will be useful to you—and if you listen to what I say, your life will be easier for you to live. You will not make many mistakes, and you will come to be liked and respected by all of the People you might come to meet.

"Before many seasons you will all be adult, and as you grow you must try more and more to do the things that men and women do. There are a few things that you must always remember.

"If perhaps you ever come in contact with others of the People, as Hawk did not many days ago, always remember to stop what you are doing when those who are older than you speak. Then you must do as they tell you. Such a thing applies in this dwelling as well, for that is the way of a good heart. If one who is adult says to you, 'My son, go out and gather wood,' or 'My daughter, bring me something from the pot,' you must go and do it at once. Do not wait; do not make anyone speak to you a second time; start at once.

"Again, you must get up early in the morning. Do not let the sun, when it first shines, find you asleep. Get up before the first indication of dawn, go out into the valley or onto the mesa, and make a *Talátawi,* a chant to the rising sun.

"And another thing. If by chance you should do something that is great, you must not talk of it. You must never go about telling of the great things you have done, or what you intend to do. To do that is not living in the way of beauty. Let others speak of the great things that you do, and then you will be in the path of the true way.

"If you listen to my words you will become good people, and will indeed do great things. If you let the wind that howls around the kiva blow these words away, you will become lazy and will never amount to anything."

So Tala talked through the season of cold, and as she did she kept busy at all times, doing the things that were required to keep them all alive. Nor did any of the others simply sit by. All of the children worked as well, and thus each of them learned, in many ways, the manner of the true People of Peace.

Each day brought different tasks, but always there was food to prepare and wood to gather for the fire. Besides these, yucca fibers needed to be stripped and twined into cordage; cordage needed to be braided into nets for hunting and sandals for wearing, or intertwined with feathers or strips of rabbit fur for clothing. Stones needed to be flaked into points for arrows and spears, knives and scrapers; sinews needed to be chewed into softness so that they could be used to bind points and feathers to arrow and spear shafts, and hides needed to be tanned with brains and spinal matter so that they could be made into soft leather for winter clothing and moccasins. All of them did these things.

Besides these tasks, there was always the hunting, and all worked at it as well. Nevertheless, there were man-things and woman-things to be done.

"It is the part of men," Tala declared as she pushed an antler awl through a piece of leather that would become a winter foot covering, "to obtain food for the People, and the materials for clothing them as well. This is done both by planting and by hunting.

"On the other hand, it is the part of women to prepare the food and the clothing for the People to eat and to wear. This is their honor-right, for they are mothers, and can best prepare the fruits of the true Earth Mother for the blessing of the People."

So Tala and Butterfly specialized in the tasks that belonged to women and gave them reason for being, and Hawk and Badger specialized in the tasks that belonged to men for the same reason. As Tala explained, the great Tiaowa had created men and women to complement each other, not to compete.

And so in such a manner, while a rabbit stew boiled in a corrugated pot of Butterfly's making next to the kiva fire, Tala taught the children more of the correct patterns of behavior among the People.

"Always be careful to do nothing bad in or near the dwelling," she told them. "Do not quarrel and fight one with another. The People do not do such things, for to do so is neither manly nor womanly.

"In your life with the People, remember this as well: You must always be truthful and honest with everyone. Never say anything that is not true. Do not lie—even for a joke to make people laugh.

"Do not say very much yourself. It is just as well to let other people talk while you listen, especially if they are older. Thus you will learn the ways of adulthood.

"And this is important as well: If you have a good friend, cling closely to that friend. If need be, give your life for him. Think always of your friend before you think of yourself. This is a good way to develop love, and only with love can we walk in the manner of beauty.

71

Thus the long nights of winter continued, with the four living upon the food they had stored and spending much of their time in the warmth of the kiva. Their dwelling in the cave was cold and draughty, and so the kiva had become, for the season of dead things, the center of their lives.

On another day, while all were flaking points from a stone called chert and making straight sticks for arrows and spears, Tala spoke in a manner such as this.

"Our People," she said, "believe that although man is at the center of both the spirit world and the natural world, he cannot prosper in this life unless he is in harmony with the fixed order of the universe. A person's life must follow a path that coincides with the cycle of this world, the cycle of fertilization, birth, youth, maturity, death, and rebirth into a higher order. On earth we must follow a divinely ordered path of life. At death we must follow the sacred path into the spirit world where the protection and sustenance of our People on earth is our principal responsibility.

"This is our migration through life, and it coincides with the four migrations of our people, from the point of coming forth from the third world through the great *sipapu,* the hole of emergence, and thence all the way into the four directions to the places where the land meets the sea and then back again. Having made these pilgrimages to claim the land for the great Tiaowa, we are finally to settle in the land he has reserved for us. That is yet in the future, but for each of us this is our duty, even now. We must dedicate our land and our lives to the Creator. We must live always in beauty before him. This is the true way of our People."

"I would hear," Hawk suddenly said, "of the great Tiaowa, who is the true Grandfather, the Giver-of-all-life. I would hear as well of Bahana, our lost brother, who it is said is Tiaowa's true son."

Tala dropped her gaze and worked silently at the corn with her *mano* and *matate.* "My son," she finally answered, "your request is many requests, and for it there are many answers. I do not have the wisdom to know all those answers, but I will tell you what the old woman who gave me my name told me, and truly she was a person who was filled with much understanding. Hear now the words of that old woman.

"Tiaowa is over all, for that is his place. Bahana is the great helper, for so he declared when he came among our ancestors."

"Is that all?"

"No. There is another great helper, and he is like *Huiksi,* the breath of life. He does not have a face, an identity such as we would know. But the old woman declared in words of soberness that he is a great *álo,* a true spiritual guide. His words we feel within, and he will guide us in the way of beauty.

"Beneath these three who are one in purpose are all those Kachinas of whom I have spoken, ancestors who have passed over, who have developed *nanapwala,* the personal cleanliness and purity that can come only from within. With that inner beauty comes true understanding, for these are given by Tiaowa to know the beginning and the ending of all things. In that way they have the wisdom to help us in all we do.

"They can bring the rain or hide the faces of the clouds so that we thirst. They can bring the deer or drive him away so that we go hungry and naked. They can make our lands and our seed fertile or otherwise, and they can do the same for us.

"These ancestors we desire to have as our friends, and so we honor them with the beauty of our lives, with our daily happiness, and with our winter and summer ceremonies.

"In all that the spirits do to help us, however, they do it with the knowledge and blessing of Tiaowa, for as I said, he is always first. And that is why, in all our reverencing and in all our ceremonies, we are truly honoring the great Tiaowa. He is the Grandfather. He is the Giver-of-all-life. He is the Great One.

"Thus it was understood by the ancients, thus it was taught to me by the old woman, and thus I declare it now."

"Have we always been the People of Peace?" Badger questioned.

"Yes, my little digger. Always since the coming of Bahana and the emergence of the People into this the fourth world, have we been called Peaceful. Others do not live in that manner, but we have promised to do so, and so we must."

"I . . . I do not understand what being peaceful means."

Tala smiled at the young boy. "When our village was being destroyed, my son, I saw no one attempt to return the evil and slay the Angry Ones. That is the way of peace. It is better for us to die than to take life. It is better for us to flee than to enter into conflict with another. Do you understand?"

Badger nodded, but Hawk signaled that he did not. "O Mother, such things trouble me."

"But why, my son?"

"I do not know. They just do not make sense to me. I have never promised that I would not fight. I do not like to think of that, nor do I think that taking a life is a good thing. Still, if the Angry Ones were to come to this valley, I could not bear to stand still and watch them destroy you or Butterfly or Badger."

"My son, do not speak—"

"O Mother, hear these words. A young man goes on a hunt and is nearly slain by a huge puma. A woman comes to his aid and with great strength and courage fights and destroys the puma. A woman goes to gather berries and is attacked by an Angry One. Her son goes to her aid and with great strength and courage fights and destroys the Angry One. Where, my mother, is the difference?"

Tala stared at the earth. "My son," she replied slowly, "I do not know the answer. Perhaps there is no difference at all. Perhaps for some who are not the People of Peace, such a thing is right and good. However, our ancestors promised the lost white brother that we would remain peaceful, and he promised in turn that we would prosper. O Hawk, we have prospered exceedingly, and must honor Bahana's promise by never taking life. *Halíksaí*. This is how it is."

Hawk stared downward, his thoughts in a turmoil. "Truly, my mother, I desire to understand. Yet I do not."

"Perhaps we are not given to understand," Tala said softly. "Perhaps that is part of being peaceful."

"But—"

Tala signaled for silence. "O Hawk, I can tell you no more than this. You are of the People. If your countenance is good, then Tiaowa will prosper you, and there will be no need for such worries as you have. If your countenance grows bad, then you will *not* be prospered, and I think that you will have no need for worries then, either."

Tala smiled then, Hawk returned the smiled and signaled that he understood what she was saying, and then the warm kiva grew still. Outside the wind howled past, snow beat at the kiva covering, and the world was white and frozen. Within, however, the warmth was more than the warmth of a fire, and all knew it was so.

"Mother," Butterfly suddenly questioned, and her eyes were alive with her hope, "can you tell us again the old woman's words concerning the ancient visit of Bahana?"

Tala smiled, for truly had this become one of the favorites of the voice she sent out to the children. It was one of her favorites as well, and always, as she spoke the words of the ancient grandmother, she longed for the privilege of being with those who had gone before.

72

"It was late in the day," Tala began, "and the old one and I stood alone upon the side of the mountain. Before us stretched the great mesa country, and she had just shown me how much of it had become the land of the People.

"Now she sat upon a rock that was warm with the sun, and these were the words of her voice:

" 'My daughter, the time has come to speak of things long past. These things are sacred, and must be heard in meaningful silence. So make your mind wide and clean as the eastern sky at sunrise. Wash your heart earnestly in the tears of those who have gone before, that you may be worthy of what I say.

" 'And though you shall hear these words but one time, your mind is at last uncluttered, and my story will be with you always. You may forget it in brief moments when the world is yours and things go far too well, but someone or something will shake you and you will remember. Out of the forgotten days of your young womanhood it will crawl like a beautiful baby that cannot be ignored. It will live in your mind always, and so it will shape your heart. Hear now the words of my voice.

" 'In the peaceful light of yesterday, the people lived strong and proud, wise and beautiful. Life was long and well-lived. It ended with dignity and honor, and so was worth living. This was so because the great and lovely one we call Bahana had walked among them.

" 'This great being gave the people his true name, but now it has been forgotten, and that is a sad thing indeed. Yet this much is remembered. He was pale of skin, had much hair upon his face, and his eyes were as blue-green as still water and just as changeable in their color.

" 'My daughter, his eyes were the same as yours.

" 'No one knew the land from whence he came, but it is said that he came out of the eastern sky at the time of the birthing of the sun. The light from the rising sun touched his lovely features, turning his hair red-gold, lighting it until it burned like fire.

" 'My daughter, though it is more dark, your hair burns in the same manner as did his.

" 'His face too was filled with light, and it shone brightly both day and night. He was truly a god, of high soul-stature and wondrous character, and he declared himself to be the true son of the great Creator.

" 'Strangely, though he was indeed a powerful being, no one feared him. He touched many who were wounded or otherwise afflicted, healing them. He lifted many who had died, and they lived. His strange eyes saw through all of the people, and they were not troubled. He saw easily their faults, and yet still he loved them, and there was not one who did not know this. He also forgave the people of the evil that was within each of them, for he had the power to do this. Truly did he love, and so truly was he loved.

" 'The people were humbled and filled with great gratitude that he should walk among them, and they asked this wondrous being of light how they might repay his love. He smiled, his smile lighted the earth and all of the sky, and the people wept with joy as they looked upon his beauty.

" 'And these are the words of the voice he sent out across the face of the land. "Be good. Do good. *Love* good. Love also each other in a pure manner, even as I have loved you. Husbands, love your wives in a pure manner. Wives, love your husbands the same. Husbands and wives, love your children more than you love yourselves, for truly they are already pure. Cast far from you all selfishness and greed. Lust not for power over others. Give great heed to the whisperings of the helping spirit and to all other good spirits. Let your hearts be one toward all others. Do all these things, and I will be well paid."

" 'And so the people listened, they wept, they lived this way of peace, and they were happy. My daughter, no one now remembers this great story, and so they have lost their happiness and their power. This you know, for you have seen. Remember these words, and you will have both.

" 'It is enough. I have spoken.' "

73

And so winter drifts by over the tiny valley that is high in the plateau country of the great southwest. The woman Tala, who is hardly more than a child herself, reaches far back into her memory for the things that she needs to instill within the children who have so suddenly become hers. She declared to them the ways of the People, but they are the older ways, not the newer ways which have become so ritualized and so restrictive of freedom.

As a teacher she is not always successful, she is not always patient, and she is not always correct. But always she does her best to follow her heart-thoughts as she teaches, sending out a true voice concerning the things that seem to her most right. She casts back in her mind for the words and the memories of the old woman who seemed to understand so well the ancient customs of freedom, the ancient ways of beauty.

She does this for she understands, in a far-off way, that the life she and the children are living is given meaning only by the true customs and rituals of daily living. In this the four who are living in the rock are no different from people everywhere. Only the rituals and customs are different, and who is to say whose rituals and customs are best?

With time all customs change, but unless something unusual happens, they change slowly. One could more appropriately say that they grow, and that traditions encrust them always more deeply, so that the growing becomes an adaptation of the old to the new.

For Tala and her family, this is so and it is not so. The customs change, but they change backward, and become more like the old ways that are filled with freedom than the new ways that are not. Because these four are alone, some things remain as they have always been, some things change, and some things are discarded altogether. And this too is the way of all people who are cast adrift upon the sea of life. If they are alone in the drifting that they are making, if they are alone upon the land of their drifting with only memories of former things, then finally they become what in their hearts they most want to become, of a good countenance or of a bad countenance.

74

"Mother, we must hurry before those two brothers of mine use it up."

"Use it up?" Tala questioned. "But Butterfly, what is there to use up?"

"The snow!" Butterfly shouted as she raced through the deep snow of the valley floor. "Now make haste, my mother, for we are almost . . . Ah, do you not hear them?"

Tala, running to keep up with the younger girl, could indeed hear the great shouts of the boys, coming from far ahead and over the lip of the valley.

"Hurry," Butterfly called as she slowed and turned her face back toward Tala. "Never have you gone so slowly!"

Tala had indeed slowed down, for suddenly the sun had come forth from behind the winter clouds, throwing golden light across the snow of the tiny valley. The sight was truly beautiful, and as she gazed at the barren trees, standing sentinellike and shivering in their nakedness, and now basking in the warm glow of the sun, she was almost overwhelmed.

"Mother!"

Smiling, Tala pulled her robe more tightly about her body and hurried forward, and soon she was standing with the beaming Butterfly at the lip above the great wash.

"Do you not see?" Butterfly questioned breathlessly. "The yucca mats I wove slide easily, and when I discovered that, I thought of this place. There, do you see how Badger flies down that slope?

"Hyeee! O Badger, hang on. There is a bump in that place!"

But Badger, heedless of his sister's words, flew over the bump, was momentarily airborne, and then slammed into the snow several feet below. There was a great roar from Badger and a great laughter from the watching Hawk as his younger brother rolled toward him in a cloud of snow.

Laughing, Hawk pulled Badger to his feet, dusted him off, and then the two began the laborious climb back to the top of the wash.

"Here, O Mother," Hawk panted as he handed Tala the mat. "You try it."

"Oh, no," Tala declared. "The way is too steep."

"Mother, please!" Butterfly wailed. "It is great fun, and you will enjoy it. Please?"

Tala stared at the hillside that stretched out below her, wondered that anyone would ever think of doing anything so silly, and suddenly she found herself being seated on the mat and pushed off down the slope.

"Noooooo!" she squealed as she gripped the mat, and then she was gone, down the slope and completely out of control. The cold air hit her face, she twisted and was going backward, she heard herself screaming as she tried to spin again, she was somehow past the jump that she so feared, and suddenly she was in the bottom of the wash and slowing to a gentle stop.

With great surprise she climbed shakily to her feet, smiled as Butterfly slid giggling to a stop beside her, and together the two climbed the steep hill to give the mats to the impatient boys.

For some time the family continued the fun, and as the children slid, Tala watched about her, amazed and even awed by the beauty of the afternoon. Truly the great Tiaowa had given them a lovely home, and the changing seasons made it even more so. Now if only the man of her vision were there to share the beauty with her, her joy would be complete.

"Here, O Mother," Badger said, tugging at her arm. "It is your time to go."

"No," Tala laughed, "I am an old woman, and am too tired to make the climb. You go for me."

"Woman," Hawk declared solemnly, though his eyes sparkled with his teasing, "a woman of the People does not grow tired so easily. No, nor does she force a young son to do for her what she should do for herself."

"But Hawk," Tala laughed, "I . . ."

"Go, Mother," Butterfly pleaded. "It is very slick now, and you can go much faster than before."

"I fear that you are right," Tala smiled.

"Mother," Badger pleaded.

"Very well," Tala declared. "But you, O Hawk, you with the ways of the People upon your mind, will have much explaining to do when you tell others that an old woman got to the bottom of this wash before you."

With that Tala giggled and threw herself onto the mat, and instantly she was speeding down the slope.

Hawk, with a great cry, was upon the other mat and plummeting after her, and to the shouts from Badger and Butterfly the two raced madly down the icy hill.

Faster they went, faster, and then Tala twisted slightly to the side to miss the rock that made the great jump. That slowed her a little, and Hawk, quick to take advantage, sped over the jump, lifted into the air, and dropped down onto the snow directly beside the wildly screaming Tala.

Still he could not pass her, and because the bottom of the wash was rushing toward them, he suddenly decided upon drastic measures.

"O Mother," he shouted, "make ready, for I am coming. . . ."

And with great dexterity Hawk rose crouching to his feet, balanced for an instant, and leaped for Tala. For a second or so he rode beside the surprised woman on her mat, and then, laughing and giggling, the two rolled head over heels together into the deep snow.

Finally they stopped, still laughing, both covered with snow, and suddenly Tala realized that the boy Hawk was on top of her and that his arms were about her and hers were about him.

Instantly her laughter stopped, and her heart was suddenly racing in a manner that had nothing to do with the wild ride down the slope. With serious eyes she looked up, saw Hawk's still-laughing face, felt again the strange comfort of his arms, and suddenly her heart went cold.

This must not be! This was not the way for a woman of the People to behave.

"O Hawk, my son," she whispered, and her voice was shaking with her strange and conflicting emotions, "I . . . I cannot breathe. I . . ."

"I am sorry, my mother," Hawk laughed as he scrambled to his feet, "but you see, the markings in the snow show that I was below you. Truly did the strong young man get to the bottom before the poor tired old woman."

Hawk laughed again as he helped Tala to her feet. She too laughed, but in her mind and in her heart was a great feeling of wonderment and guilt. She had had a vision of the true man, and even worse, the boy was as her son! How could it be that she would have such feelings?

75

"O woman?"

Tala, in the warm kiva chewing a prepared hide into softness, spun about and stared fearfully upward at the opening. The light was bright against her eyes, making sight difficult, yet still she saw the figure silhouetted there, and her heart turned cold.

"Daughter, I am cold and I thirst. May I enter?"

Slowly Tala rose to her feet, forcing her courtesy to overcome her great fear. "Th . . . there is warmth here," she said, "and water as well. You may enter."

The man turned his back and climbed easily down the ladder, turned again, faced the woman, and smiled.

Tala was struck by the beauty of the smile, and gradually she started to relax. Quickly she handed him a dipper of water, and as the man drank, she looked more closely at him.

He was an old man, so old that his hair was the color of the snow. Yet his bearing was straight and his face did not seem so old. He was a little taller than her, was thin almost to the point of gauntness, and his robes, though well made and clean, were very worn. He also wore much facial hair, and that was very unusual among the men of the People.

The People? Was he perhaps not of the People? Truly he seemed a little more pale, and his head was not shaped in quite the same manner.

"I give thanks," the man said as he handed the ladle back to Tala. "The water is delicious, and the pottery that holds it shows much skill in its workmanship."

Slowly then the man lowered himself to the sleeping robes, and sighing, he began to remove his well-worn leather footwear. Tala, surprised, embarrassed, and still very frightened, turned her back and made herself busy stirring the venison stew.

"Are you alone in this place?" the man suddenly asked.

Instantly fear grew larger in Tala's mind, for she *was* alone. The others were exploring out on the mesa.

"No, there are three others who dwell here as well," she quickly answered.

"Oh, yes," the man responded quietly. "The boy called Hawk, the girl called Butterfly, and the child known as Badger. They are fine children."

Tala spun about, her mouth open wide with surprise. Then, shamed by her rude expression, she turned once more to the stew. But how had he known the names of the little ones?

"They *are* fine children," she agreed with shaking voice.

"Look at these feet," the man suddenly ordered. "Do you see age there?"

Now Tala was truly surprised, her face showed it, and she no longer thought of etiquette. The words, they were the same as those used by the ancient grandmother up on the mountain.

"Are they not beautiful?"

Spinning, she stared at the man and at his bare feet, stretched out before her. Again the same words! And truly the feet were beautiful. They were light in color, much lighter even than the man's light-colored face. Even more than the ancient grandmother's were the feet beautiful—clear, clean, almost transparent in their appearance. Tala wondered at that, wondered where this strange old man had come from and how he knew the things he seemed to know, and suddenly the fear was big within her throat once more. Hurriedly she turned back to the pot, and she stirred the mixture vigorously to hide the great shaking that had hold of her body.

The man was *not* of the People! His head was a different shape, and though he looked much as she and the others did, there were still differences, many of them. But what did that mean? He might be of the Angry Ones, though he certainly did not act like he was.

"Well?"

"They . . . they are indeed lovely," Tala declared, and her voice shook as she spoke. "I . . . I will have food . . ."

"Thank you," the man said softly. "May I have another sip of water?"

Quickly Tala filled the dipper at the *olla* and handed it to the man. He drank, his soft eyes never wavering from his watching of the woman, and Tala was relieved when he handed the handle of the dipper back to her and turned his gaze away.

"Thank you," he said, rising, and Tala was surprised to see that his feet were again covered. Quickly, easily, he took hold of the ladder and climbed out of the kiva. In shock, Tala stared after him, watched as he turned to gaze back down at her, and wondered that he was leaving so quickly.

"You will never want in this valley," the man declared softly, and then he turned into the white glare of day and was gone.

Tala stared, her mouth still open in surprise. He was gone, but what had he wanted? Who was he, and how had he known what he did? Suddenly Tala remembered that the man had not eaten, and instantly she felt badly. It was customary to feed all strangers, and she had not fed this one at all. Just two small sips of water, and that was all.

Quickly she climbed the ladder into the cold of the afternoon, intending to call the man back. But as she gazed around the snow-filled valley, she could see no sign of the man. He was gone.

Now Tala clapped her hand over her mouth in true fear and wonderment. And though the strange man never left her thoughts for the remainder of the day, when the children returned she was no closer to a solution than she had been earlier.

So she buried those things in her heart, said nothing to the children, and as the days passed she wondered.

76

The snow and ice of winter in the rocky mesa country had fled, at last the earth was bright and clear with the renewed growth of spring, and almost a full year had passed in the tiny valley. The new growth of the fresh young leaves on the long bare trees was bright and glorious against the dark desert varnish of the stone walls. The sun lifted higher up and shone more hours into the hidden valley each day. It sparkled on the water that danced and gurgled out of the sacred water-planted-place. It shone warm and friendly on Badger, who had been sent to take his turn at the watching place for the day.

But Badger was not of a good countenance. He was not happy. After all, he too was a man—or at least he was a young man. It was only right that he be allowed to hunt. Somehow it did not seem just and fair that Hawk was always oldest, always largest. If they would just give him a chance, the boy thought, he could do as well as anyone. Of course he did not remember that he had spent the two days previous hunting all day. It was only big in his mind that this day he could not, and thus he was filled with bitterness.

But now the air was still save for the chants of the singing insects, the sun was very warm on his bare body, the soil where he sat was not good for digging, and so over a little time his eyelids grew heavy.

To keep awake he thought of the Angry Ones who might be coming. He imagined how he would resist bravely should they appear. He imagined that he would somehow drive them back, and, while they were trying to decide upon the best course of action against the small but formidable foe who blocked their way, he would sneak back down the cliff and warn his mother Tala and the others. Those were his imaginings, and while he was in the midst of them, somehow he drifted off to sleep.

Suddenly, close beside his head, there came a terrible crash of stone on stone. Badger, awake instantly and certain that the Angry Ones had tried to slay him, leaped to his feet and with a whine of fear sprinted across the mesa in the opposite direction from the valley.

From behind him, however, came the sound not of pursuit but of laughter, and as he slowed and turned, he was both relieved and horrified to see that it was Hawk who had frightened him, and not the Angry Ones at all.

Hawk signed for the little digger to come back, and reluctantly the young boy did so. Hawk placed his hand upon the boy's shoulder in the way of showing man-respect, and together they returned to the place for watching. There, seated together on the rock in the cross-legged manner of men, Hawk again reached out and placed his hand upon the younger boy.

"My brother, you keep a careless watch."

Badger dropped his head. "I am shamed," he said, and the way he said it reminded the older boy of a high-up valley and another man called Flies-Far who had so shamed him.

"Shame is a good thing," Hawk said quietly, "if it leads one to do better."

"I already do better," Badger grumbled.

"Do you?" Hawk gently asked. "My brother, I crept up to you and smashed the stones together to see what you would do. You did not stop to see where the noise came from, nor did you look about to see if the Angry Ones were here. You thought only of saving your own body, and started to run away. Such a thing is not better.

"A boy might do what you did, but a true man of the People does not act in that manner. Instead, he is always watching all about him so that he will know what is going to happen. Then, if he is suddenly attacked, he tries to fight. Or, if he cannot fight, he thinks more of giving warning to the People than he does of saving himself. These were the words of Flies-Far, my friend."

Badger's head was hung in shame, and his eyes were downcast in the manner of true humility. Hawk, seeing this, once again touched his brother's shoulder with a man-touch.

"Brother, do not take these words too harshly. Soon you too will be grown, as will I, and then . . ."

Badger's eyes flashed up, and suddenly his face had become bad before his brother. "Ha!" he shouted. "That is what is always said. But how can such a thing happen if I am never allowed to attempt the things of a man? I cannot hunt, I cannot work with the corn mother except to pick off bugs and direct the water in the furrows, I cannot ever make a teaching for there is no one younger than I to teach. . . . My brother, all I can do is lie here in the sun and watch for those Angry Ones who will never come!"

Hawk's eyes sparkled at the fire that was in the heart of this one who had become as his younger brother.

"Ah," he answered simply, "you desire to hunt?"

Badger eagerly signaled yes.

"Can you shoot the bow, throw the spear, or set a snare?"

The young boy again dropped his eyes. "Not well, but neither can I learn if all I do is sit here—"

"That is not a thing one such as you should be worrying about," Hawk said quickly, interrupting the young boy. "This day I will sit with you, I will tell you of my hunt to the *pangwúvi,* where the bighorn sheep climb, and I will tell you of my own foolishness during those days as I stood before Flies-Far. And while we speak we will flake points together. After all, you want to hunt, and a man cannot hunt well with the weapons of a child.

"Now," Hawk said to the boy whose face had suddenly become open and filled with hope once again, "take this piece of hide and hold it in your hand in this manner. Good. Now do as the one who is our mother showed you. Hold the stone for the point with your fingers. Hold it against the hide, press this antler tip against the edge where you wish the flake to be, and while you do so I will build a picture in your mind of that first morning upon the mountain."

And so, from the day of that warm sun onward, Hawk became as Badger's uncle, sending out a voice to him concerning all the things he was learning himself of manhood.

"This," he would say as Badger stood eagerly beside him, "is the track of the deer. You see that it has been going slowly. It is feeding, because it does not go straight ahead. Instead it goes now in one direction, now in another, even back a little, not seeming to have any purpose in its wandering about.

"Here, see this place where this brush has been bitten off? This is where he was feeding. It is called browse, and a deer's feeding is called browsing. Only rarely will the deer eat grass. Now, if we follow along, soon we will see its tracks in the mud below the sacred water-planted-place. See, they are there, and yonder is where it has stopped.

"You see, my brother, this was a big deer. Here again are his tracks. Here is where he stopped near the edge of the water to drink, and now we know that he crosses the water, for there are no more tracks on this bank.

"You will notice that he was still walking. He was not frightened. He did not see or smell any enemies. That is a good sign for us as well, for it shows that we have no enemies nearby."

On another day, Hawk stopped once more.

"My brother, these are the tracks of the sheep that in these days visit our valley. These bigger tracks are of the older ewes, and you can see that they are walking along quietly. Now notice the smaller tracks, and notice too that the ground has been thrown up around them. These tracks were made by the lambs, for they were playing and running. I do not think there was a ram in this bunch."

"How can you tell that, my brother?"

Hawk looked at the boy, smiling. "Look," he said. "Here is where this large sheep made water. Look closely at how it was done. Here and also over there each of the other large sheep did the same thing and in the same manner. Thus all were ewes, for this is the way of the ewe. If one had been a ram, you would have seen the difference in the way it made water very easily.

"Now, notice these things carefully, my brother, so that you will not forget them. When you see them again, you must know them. The tracks made by the different animals are not all alike. The sheep's hoof is sharp-pointed in front. Notice too that when its foot sinks down into the mud there is no mark behind its footprint. Remember that behind the footprint of the deer there were two marks when it walked in the mud, made by the little hoofs that the deer carries behind its foot. Always will there be such differences, and these you must learn before you can be a man of the People."

Thus Badger grew, and Hawk grew as well, for it is the way of things that all teachers grow more rapidly than the ones they teach. He became more than good both with the use of the bow and arrow and with the use of the *atlatl* and spear. Many of the deer and sheep gave their lives to his weapons, and thus he and his family lived well.

77

"Butterfly, why are you not keeping busy?"

The girl Butterfly heard Badger's voice, but she did not turn her head as she responded. "I am keeping busy," she whispered loudly as she focused her gaze directly before her. "Now be still, O brother, and—"

"Busy?" Badger questioned. "How can that be? You sit for most of a day without moving, and that is not busy."

"I have not been here for most of the day," Butterfly responded. "And I *am* busy, watching my sister the spider."

Badger laughed. "O sister, that is foolish. Why would a person choose to watch a spider?"

"Do you not recall the words of our mother, O Badger? We should be aware of all things, even the rising of the smoke from an ant village in the early morning sun."

"I am aware of spiders," Badger responded quickly, "but that does not mean I must sit and gaze upon them for day upon day. I think you should be more busy, perhaps helping in the corn."

"Brother, do you know what spiders do?"

Badger looked at his sister, surprised. "Certainly I know. They eat others of the insect people."

"Do they do more than that?"

"Of course they don't."

"O Badger, your eyes are dim. Spiders are female beings. See, this one is twining much cordage, just as I make cordage. This day she spoke to me and said, 'Ho, little sister, watch me closely, and I will teach you what a woman such as you needs to know.' Thus I am watching, for—"

Badger interrupted her with his mocking laughter, and Butterfly, upset, leaped to her feet and ran toward the dwelling up in the cliff. Back in the cave she sat and with great determination began twining strands of grass and yucca fibers into cordage, and she went at this in such a determined manner that Tala, seeing her, went to investigate.

"My daughter, why is that look on your countenance there?"

"Badger made a mocking of me!"

Tala was surprised. "I cannot imagine that he would do that."

"Well, he did. I told him that the little old woman spider spoke to me and bade me watch her spinning, and he laughed."

"That is not a good thing," Tala agreed as she sat down. "Still, boys have a difficult time understanding girl-talk, talk such as existed between you and the old woman spider. Do not let yourself be angry with him. Be patient instead, for one day he will understand. Now, what did the old woman spider tell you?"

Butterfly glanced up, saw the belief in Tala's eyes, and suddenly the excitement was back in her own. "O Mother, she showed me her cordage, and in the breeze she showed me a game that looks like such fun. I have but to do as she did. . . ."

78

"Mother, what is our sister doing back there?"

Tala, weaving fibers and feathers together into a warm winter robe, looked up and smiled. "She is being very busy, O Badger."

"I see that," the boy responded as he gazed at her through the doorway. "But what is she doing?"

"Just woman-things," Tala smiled. "She is making cordage. Would you like to help?"

Badger quickly and emphatically signaled no.

"Does she need help?" Hawk asked.

"She does, my son. The idea she has is good, but it is also very big."

"Well then, I will help. My cordage is not quite as pretty as hers, but it is strong, and I suppose that is most important."

Quickly he rose and went out into the cave, seated himself next to the young girl, and took up a handful of grass and fiber. Tala watched him, watched the attractive way he moved, and instantly she turned away, knowing that she would need to take control of her heart.

Long into the time of darkness Hawk and Butterfly sat together, chatting quietly and twining cordage against the thighs of their legs. Badger listened intently, but their words and the causes of their laughter were indistinct, and he finally fell asleep with the soft sounds of their voices murmuring in his ears.

Tala too went to sleep, thinking of Hawk and wishing that the man of her vision would hurry.

79

"Mother! Badger! Hawk! Come and see! The old woman spider truly showed me, and it works!"

Days had passed since Butterfly had begun her secret project, and now she stood excitedly at the bottom of the cliff in the early morning light. Tala quickly descended the ladder and was followed by Badger, while Hawk scaled down the notches he had cut. When they were together on the valley floor, Butterfly motioned for them to follow and then ran ahead, her face alive with excitement.

"She was right, Mother," she exclaimed as she ran toward the large trees below the sacred water-planted-place. "The old woman spider was right, and now I have become like her. Look, here it is."

Butterfly stopped and took hold of the end of a thick length of cordage which was many strands of cordage tightly woven together to become one. The cordage rose upward to a large limb of the tree that extended many feet above them, and as Butterfly stretched her cordage tight, they all looked upward.

"My sister," Badger declared indignantly, "this seems very silly, tying that tree to the earth."

"No, Badger," Hawk declared teasingly. "Can you not tell that the roots are loose? If it is not tied, then perhaps it will get away."

Tala laughed easily, but Butterfly saw nothing humorous in her brothers' words. "You are both foolish," she declared angrily, "and have clouds where your minds should be!"

Hawk, surprised at her anger, immediately apologized, though Badger would not.

"Butterfly," Tala then questioned, "tell us what you have done."

"Well, this is how it is," she said carefully. "The old woman spider called me, and when I got to her she was busy making cordage. Much of it she used in her home, as I intend to do. But then she wove a great length, hung from it, and the breeze pushed her back and forth as though she were flying like the wings of the air. I saw, and heard as she told me I could fly in the same manner. Now watch and I will show you."

Quickly then Butterfly took the end of her cordage, climbed onto a rock that was above the sacred water-planted-place, pulled the thick strand tight, leaped out, and to the amazement of her family she flew easily out over the water of the deep tank, swung around, and returned to them.

"Urúhuú," Tala whispered in fear. "My daughter, you are truly like the wings—"

"I want to do it," Badger suddenly cried. "I want—"

Butterfly silenced him with the silence signal. "Hawk, would you like to fly?" she asked quickly.

Hawk stared first at the rope and then at his younger sister. "I . . . I . . ."

"I do!" Badger declared.

"Hawk, do you hear?"

"As a man of the People," Hawk finally said, "I will do it."

Hesitantly he took the thick rope and climbed to the rock. There he gripped it tightly, leaped out, and swung even farther out over the pool. When he alighted, he was grinning widely.

"Truly," he breathed, "I am as a wing of the air."

"Mother," Butterfly asked excitedly, "would you care to fly?"

"I do! I do!" Badger repeated.

"My brother," Butterfly declared, "your face has been bad toward me and the old woman spider as well, and I see no reason why you should be allowed to do this great thing. Now, Mother, would you like—"

"Butterfly!" Badger wailed, "I did not mean to have a bad countenance. I have never had the old woman spider speak to me. I am sorry, and will help you in all things from now on and throughout my life."

"Well . . ."

"Butterfly, let him do it. Then perhaps I will have the courage to try."

The young girl Butterfly looked up at Tala, suddenly smiled, and quickly she handed Badger the rope. He took it, leaped onto the rock, and instantly was off on a grand swing across the pool.

At last it was Tala's turn, and so with her heart in her throat she took the rope, climbed the rock, gripped it tightly, closed her eyes, and swung outward. Suddenly there was nothing below her but the air, and in terror she opened her eyes and looked downward.

Water! Below her was the tank filled with water!

And then the woman's hands slipped, the watching children caught their breaths, and Tala dropped with a great splash into the water of the deep rock tank.

Gasping and sputtering, she clawed her way to the surface, shook the water from her hair and face, and saw the children staring anxiously down at her.

"Th . . . that was truly ex . . . exciting," she gasped as she trod water. "I th . . . think it is even more fun than . . . than . . .

And Tala could not finish, for the children as one forgot her, grabbed the rope, and climbed to the rock. Butterfly went first, swung out over the deep pool, and dropped down, to come up splashing and laughing. Then Badger got the rope and did the same, Hawk came last, and so while Tala lay on the rock and watched, all the children laughingly made a great game of Butterfly's new cordage.

Truly, she thought as she watched, the valley was a wondrous place to be.

80

And so the tiny valley that was hidden high in the rock country of the Southwest grew more and more to be a home to the woman and the young ones who were growing with her.

The Kachina people also made their dwelling there, and their laughter and their whispered instructions drifted always on the gentle winds of the valley.

Yet far across the plateau country, in a village where none but one or two knew his heart, a man sat pondering, and the anger in his belly grew to be a black and evil thing. He spoke of this to no one, but he thought long and secret thoughts, he favored the old wound in his leg, and within his mind he made careful plans for the time he felt certain would one day come.

TEN

The Coming of Flies-Far

"Hawk! Hawk, come quickly!"

Hawk, on his hands and knees weeding the corn, scrambled to his feet in response to Badger's cries. Wiping the sweat beads from his forehead, he stepped out of the field of corn and watched as the young boy ran frantically toward him.

"My . . . brother," the boy panted as he slid to a stop. "See, there is a smoke from down in the great wash. I saw it, and it does not go away."

Spinning, Hawk squinted against the brightness of the day, and quickly he too saw the thin wisp of smoke.

"I see it, my brother."

"Do you . . . think it is the . . . Angry Ones?" the boy panted, his face showing his anxiety.

For a moment Hawk stood, watching intently. "No," he finally answered. "They would simply attack. This is more like a signal."

"A signal?" Badger was surprised. "But who would be signaling? Our mother and Butterfly are busy with their pottery, and there is no one else who knows of us."

"In the days of our village there were many traders, O Badger. It was the custom for these traders to signal with such a fire before they entered into the place of our dwellings. Perhaps this is such a trader."

"But Hawk, how would they know of this place? We have told no one, and it is very well hidden."

Hawk was silent. What the boy said was true, and so he was worried, truly worried. Still, would an attacker make his approach so obvious?

"Badger, we must go carefully, and see if this fire is made by a friend or an enemy. Let us climb out of the valley and approach from another direction, so that we will not give ourselves away without reason."

Badger nodded, and so together the two took up their weapons, climbed the cut in the cliff, raced across the mesa, and quietly descended the great wash. Silently they moved forward, and at last, through a screen of willows, they saw the solitary man seated near a small fire of green and smoky wood.

For an instant Hawk stared, and then he broke into a grin and lowered his bow. "Come," he whispered to young Badger, "this man is no enemy. This is Flies-Far, my friend of the mountain valley. Let us go very quietly, and see what he has to say."

82

"Ho, brother."

Flies-Far, his back partially to where Hawk stood, spun to his feet in surprise. Then, seeing Hawk, his face broke into its familiar smile.

"Brother," he called, "you are getting better. Your feet are light as the wind, for that is the only sound I heard."

"This one called Badger is the stalker," Hawk answered. "He can tickle the hind feet of a sheep with his finger, and the sheep will think it is only the touch of the grass. It is he who led me to you."

Badger stood proudly, and solemnly Flies-Far nodded. "That is a good thing to know. I honor his skill, and I honor as well his teacher. Well, brother, is your dwelling near this place?"

"It is," Hawk responded, feeling suddenly nervous.

"I thought as much. I remembered your description, and the writing upon the stone over there said much the same."

Hawk signaled his understanding. There was silence then, as the young men simply looked at each other and then away into the distances down the great wash.

"You are no doubt wondering at the purpose of my visit," Flies-Far finally said.

Hawk smiled. "I wondered, but a man does not want to be impolite."

Flies-Far signaled his understanding. "I have thought much of the ugly woman you are forced to live with," he grinned. "It is in my heart that I should see this great ugliness for myself."

Hawk started, and then guiltily he looked away from the staring Badger. Now surely would the woman know of his evil words against her, spoken before he had learned to see the true person who lived within her heart.

"Well," he said lightly, "you said I would get older and thus see things differently, and perhaps I have. She does not seem so ugly to me now."

With a great laugh Flies-Far grasped Hawk's shoulder in the man-to-man honor grasp. "It is as I thought. And you do seem to be more tall. Still, I would throw sticks with you that your first description is more accurate than this nondescription you give me now. Come, lead me to your dwelling, so that I may see for myself."

Hawk signaled that he was ready, Flies-Far shouldered his pack, and with Badger following, he led the way up the steep slope of the wash.

"Brother," Hawk said as they climbed, "I would know the true reason for your visit. I cannot tell the woman that you have come to see her great ugliness."

"No," the man agreed, and his smile was still within his voice. "That would not be wise. Perhaps you could tell her instead that I have come to gaze upon her great beauty."

"She is very perceptive, my brother. She knows that I do not think of that, and she would be very doubtful if you claimed that you did. Nor do I think that is the true reason for your visit."

"Well," Flies-Far declared, "you are indeed growing older, my brother, for your wisdom is increasing. Truly I did come to see the woman, but there is also that which is in this pack. Recently I have come into a little wealth, and I intend to increase it."

"Wealth?" Hawk questioned. "Then you are representing your village."

"No, brother, I represent only myself."

"But . . . but how does one man have wealth? Among the People, all things are shared by all who are of the village, and thus all prosper or all suffer together."

Flies-Far laughed again. "O Hawk, that is the old way that is past. In the new order of things, each man prospers according to his own management. You see, I have much fine sky-stone, and it is in my mind to trade it for other things of value. Thus I will grow in wealth. I hope to show it to you."

"I would like to see it," Hawk declared. "And perhaps the one who is as my mother will be interested also. But I still do not understand."

83

Hawk had never seen the woman Tala appear so flustered, and he could not understand it. Nor could he understand why Flies-Far would not take his eyes from her. It made no sense to him, and therefore he was bothered by it.

"My mother," he declared after introductions had been made, "this one who is as a brother has brought much sky-stone for us to see. Perhaps if . . ."

"O Star of the Morning," Flies-Far declared, "this brother does the stone injustice. It is *fine* stone, and much of it would match with exactness the wondrous color of your eyes."

"M . . . my eyes?" Quickly Tala dropped her face to hide her sudden embarrassment. What was happening to her? she wondered. Why did the words and the look of this man affect her so?

"Truly had I thought to trade them," Flies-Far continued. "But now, my Star, I would make a gift of them all if I could but know that they would always enhance your great beauty."

Hawk stared, Butterfly and Badger giggled, Tala squirmed nervously, and Flies-Far smiled with a smile as wide and innocent as the eastern sunrise. Truly was this woman unusual, and though her beauty was different from that of any woman he had ever seen, it was still, to his mind, a great beauty.

"My brother," he said, "before I show the sky-stone, I have a small gift that might be of some use to you."

So saying, Flies-Far reached into his pack and drew out the two huge horns of the ram he had slain the year before. Hawk's eyes grew wide, for these were indeed a marvelous gift.

"Brother," he declared solemnly, "my home is always your home, and all that is mine is yours. Truly does my heart give thanks."

Flies-Far humbly signaled his response. And then, to gasps of wonderment and joy, he spread upon a tanned hide the wondrous blue-green stones from his pack.

84

"Brother," Flies-Far spoke into the darkness, "no longer will I trust your judgment. Truly is the one called Tala a woman of great beauty."

Hawk lay still, thinking long thoughts about the man's words. Out on the mesa the small wolves yipped at the moon-woman, somewhere a rabbit squealed in death, the stars shone brightly upon the tiny valley, and in the dwelling up in the cave the woman sat in darkness making new music upon her flute. The sound of it was faint, but it was there, and Hawk wondered at it, he truly did.

"This is a fine valley," Flies-Far suddenly declared. "How did you find it?"

"By chance," Hawk replied honestly. "It is where we ran out of strength from our fleeing."

"You were fortunate to find such a bountiful supply of water."

"There was no water when we came here, except for a bit of run-off. This is a water-planted-place."

Flies-Far laughed. "Brother, this is me, remember. You do not need such tales with the one called Flies-Far."

Hawk turned his head, surprised. "It is no tale," he said earnestly. "The woman declared to us the teaching, we all fasted and planted the sacred jar, we all joined our hearts in the chant, and within a day the water was flowing freely."

"Well, then you were fortunate to hit in your digging a hidden spring," Flies-Far muttered. "Water cannot flow eternally from a little jar!"

"It is truly a wondrous thing," Hawk agreed. "Nevertheless, it is true. We hit no spring. The great Tiaowa blessed us with that water."

There was silence, and at last Flies-Far spoke again. "I am surprised that you believe that foolishness, my brother."

"When one is thirsty and the water comes, it does not seem very foolish," Hawk answered quietly.

"Well, I can understand that," Flies-Far declared. "Still, the one who has become our *mongwi* has told our secret societies the tricks behind many of these seemingly great things. If he were here, no doubt he could explain this very quickly. My brother, this *mongwi* is a great man, wise beyond his years. He knows the true meaning of life, and is filled with much power. I would be honored, upon my return, to take you to him."

"Return?"

"It is so. I go on a long journey, one that may last two or more full cycles of the seasons. It is my intention to visit all the villages of the People. I will learn much, and will become wealthy in the process. Those are the words of the great *mongwi* of my village."

"He sounds wise," Hawk agreed.

"It is so. He truly is. It is he who has shown us the foolishness of those old ways you speak of."

Again there was silence, and nearby the quiet chuckle of water from the water-planted-place sang into the darkness, accompanying the distant sound of the flute. For some reason that he could not understand, Hawk felt angry. He felt also like a little child who had been chastised, and he did not enjoy the feeling at all.

"The planting of the sacred jar is one of the old ways," he declared defensively, "and I do not think of that as foolish. In this place we honor the great Tiaowa by following the old ways as well as we know them."

"The old ways were good ways in their time," Flies-Far agreed quickly. "I do not speak against them, my brother. I say only that the old days are gone, and many of the old ways should go with them. Truly we have learned much, and this new knowledge should help our people greatly. Yet it cannot do so if we stick so closely to outdated thoughts and ideas and customs."

"But surely you accept the goodness of the great Tiaowa, the all-knowing Grandfather. Surely you wish to keep a good countenance before Bahana, the lost white brother who will one day return and accept our good hearts."

Flies-Far sighed deeply. "Brother, these things trouble me. I accept them, as I accept the old ways. But . . . but now I find myself wondering if they are not foolish traditions."

"How does your heart say concerning them?"

"I do not know. I think it says to remember and to accept. But my mind says otherwise, and the leaders in my secret society have trained me to follow the powers of my mind. It is very confusing. Yet I will say that I lean toward the strength of my mind, for that is the way of my village."

Hawk thought of this, and truly he did not know how to reply. Perhaps with the coming of daylight, the woman who was as his mother would know.

"Brother," Flies-Far suddenly stated, "enough of that. Let us discuss something else. It is in my mind to take the woman Tala to wife."

"To . . . to wife?"

"You sound very surprised, O Hawk. Remember, it is done all the time."

"But she has said nothing. She might not want . . ."

"Brother," Flies-Far said with great patience, "as you know, what she might say has little to do with anything. She pleases me, and that is enough. Still, it is within her eyes that I please her as well. I do not think she would mind such an arrangement at all."

What he said was probably true, and Hawk knew it, for he too had seen the strange look in the woman's eyes. Still, the thought of her leaving with Flies-Far gave him a strange sense of emptiness.

"Brother, she cannot go with you."

"Why is that?"

"The . . . the little ones! She is as their mother. She would not leave them."

"She would have little choice. Besides, they are not actually her children. I do not think that would be such a great problem either."

"Well, then you do not know her heart as well as I know it. Brother, if you took that one for a wife, then you would have two children as well."

Suddenly Hawk had a thought, and in the darkness he smiled. "With those three, your traveling would be very slow indeed. You might be away for as many as five cycles of the seasons, or even six."

In the darkness Flies-Far was quiet, thinking. "You are right," he finally declared. "I will wait, and upon my return I will take the star woman to me."

Hawk breathed more freely, though for the life of him he could not understand why. Still, for some reason he did not want this good friend to take the one who was as his mother to wife. Somehow, he knew that such a union would not be a good thing at all.

85

Tala could not remember ever having felt as she felt that morning. She had slept little, yet with the light she was fresh and filled with great energy. Furthermore, her thoughts would not stay with her body, but were always fleeing outward to where the man Flies-Far stood with young Hawk, conversing.

Nor could Tala explain this. She had seen the man's eyes, had seen the hunger in them, and truly had she found it exciting. That he might be the man of her vision was almost more than she could bear to consider.

She had watched him very carefully, and truly he might be the one. He was strong and comely in appearance, he stood tall and very straight, his voice was gentle and filled with sweet words, and surely, she felt, such a man would understand the proper meaning of love. Yet there was the other thing, the lack of a face on the man of her vision. How could she tell if this man were the one that was to come?

"Woman," the one called Flies-Far suddenly called, "I would send out my voice to you before I leave."

Tala took a deep breath to still her pounding heart, and slowly and with downcast eyes she made her way toward him.

"Little One," the man said, using a rare form of endearment. "Here are the sky-stones that are my gift to you."

"I am honored," Tala responded. "And here, friend of my son, is a jar of my own making. It is my gift to you."

Flies-Far took the jar and examined it carefully. "Never have I seen such work," he declared truthfully. "It is beautiful beyond description. I am honored in the accepting of this gift."

There was a moment's silence, and then the man spoke again. "Woman, in one seasonal cycle, perhaps two, I will return. At that time I will take you to wife."

Tala's eyes flew up in surprise. "To . . . to wife?"

"Of course. I find you very desirable, so I have made this great decision."

"But . . . but . . ."

"There is no need for words. I have spoken with this one called Hawk, and it is planned."

Now Tala looked Flies-Far directly in the eye. "And have I no say in this?" she asked quietly.

"Why should you say? That is not the way of the People."

"Whose people? Not our people, O man; not the People of Peace."

Tala turned away, seeking words that would help this one to understand the things that were within her heart. She did not know why, but it was suddenly very important to her that he do so. It was very important that he see that the old way was indeed the true way.

"Friend of my son," she finally said, "hear my voice. The children and I live in this place, and in all things we are the People. In this place we each have a say in *all* things, for that is the ancient way."

Then the green-eyed woman turned to the one who was as her son. "Hawk, are his words true? Have you agreed to this?"

The boy dropped his head. "In a manner of speaking, my mother. We did discuss it, but . . . I did not agree to it."

"You see," Tala stated, turning back to gaze into the eyes of the one called Flies-Far. "This one knows well of our ways here, which are the proper ways.

"You may return to this valley, O man, and you are welcome to do so. But remember this. Whether or not you take me to wife will depend upon a great many things, and one of them is my own feeling toward you. Thus it is. I have spoken."

"And what is that feeling?" Flies-Far asked as a smile lingered upon his face.

"I do not know at this time. Perhaps, when you return, it will be more clear to me what I am to do."

Flies-Far stared hard at the woman, and at last he threw back his head and laughed. "Truly you will make a good wife," he declared. And then without another word he lifted his pack, placed the carefully constructed jar within it, turned, and started down the valley. Yet while he walked he thought only of the bold look of her strange eyes, a look that was most certainly a challenge.

And while he walked away, the woman called Tala stared after him, and within her pounding heart were the man's words of endearment, and the strange look that was within *his* eyes while he laughed.

Book Two

ELEVEN

In the Way of a Waiting

86

The grasses and the leaves and the shoots of new corn were fresh and green and the sun was warm and the rains were soft and did not last overly long and food was plentiful and good and the days drifted through the seasons, and the waiting and the growing went on. Then again the snow was cold but not too cold and the kiva was warm and there was always so much to be done and so many days to be spent considering the changes in the valley and in the People and so many nights to be spent watching the red-eyed glow of the fire, remembering and waiting.

Then the days were warm and gentle once more and the nights were soft and always the moon-woman climbed over the rock wall of the tiny valley and shone kindly into the strange green eyes of the young woman who continued to wait, encouraging her, reminding her of the things she had seen and of the things she had felt concerning the one who was to come.

And then the snows were there again, soft and cold, and then the grasses that were bright green with new growth—the years became two and then three and then four since the great fleeing and the coming of the strange man to the kiva, and still the waiting continued. The man called Flies-Far had not returned, nor had any others of the People been heard from, and in the woman's heart an understanding was beginning to come.

87

"Mother, why is it that you sit alone, day after day, sending out the soft voice of the flute? There is a strange sadness in your eyes, and we who are your children feel a deep wonderment."

Tala had been sitting near the large tank in the rock beneath the water-planted-place, cooling her feet, playing the flute that was the symbol of her clan, and considering the fact that even while nothing seemed to change, all things were in fact becoming different. Four full cycles of the seasons had passed since she had fallen from the wall above, four journeys of the sun to the land of *Palatkwapi,* the lost red city of the south, had passed since she and the little ones had prayed over the sacred water-planted-place. In that time the valley had changed dramatically, and as she saw those changes she wondered at them.

The grasses below the tank were thick and luxurious, the trees were varied and of great height and gave much shelter in all seasons, the cleared ground for their corn was everywhere, even up on the dry mesa, and the winged ones of many nations filled the warm air with their pleasant voices. The insect people thrived and were always busy, the four-leggeds had multiplied so that, in spite of the great hunting done both by Hawk and by Badger, their numbers were still more than abundant. Indeed the valley was a place of sacred beauty.

But the man of shadow, the man of her dream, had remained away. Not in all those seasons had he revealed his face. She thought often of the man Flies-Far, wondering if it were he.

"Mother?"

Tala glanced at the youth who now sat beside her, and with a start she realized how much he too had changed. He had grown tall with the passing of the seasons, tall and strong. Nor had his unusual powers of wisdom diminished. He was truly a unique young man, this great son of hers, and she never ceased to marvel at the thoughts that grew always within his heart and at the words that fell like gentle rain from his mouth.

Yet how could she tell him of her dreams? How could she explain the memory of a faceless one who never stopped haunting her thoughts?

Despite his wisdom, Hawk was one of the People, a People who did not discuss such things, did not even understand them. The concept of love, when discussed at all, was as a peace between men, nothing more.

Of course there was often a fine affection between a man and his woman, but it was never spoken of, not even between the man and the woman who shared it. To do so was considered, for the man especially, as a sign of weakness.

Marriages were made between two well-suited people in order that children might come forth and strengthen the clan. Usually for the man and always for the woman, the union was arranged for by others, and there was little in the way of emotion involved. Such had the custom become.

And that custom, as much as any other single thing, had been why Tala had been declared Outcast. She had defied it. She had demanded the right to send out a voice, she had spurned an order for marriage and had vocally declared a dream and a love for a man that had come from that dream. In all those things she had gone against the *mongwi* and the elders, and so she had become Outcast.

But now her son Hawk had asked concerning the dream, and though she had never spoken of it to any of the children, this one was of an age and of a temperament to possibly understand.

"My mother, I have seen much pain in your eyes, and much longing. Furthermore, there is a great loneliness in the voice of the flute. It is in my heart to offer what small help I can offer."

Tala smiled. "This woman who has been as your mother sends

out a voice of deep gratitude," she replied. "Give ear now to the voice of my flute."

As Hawk watched, she blew gently into the hollow wooden flute, her fingers dancing up and down on the holes as she played. The melody that came forth was lovely, but it was also very lonely, and it spoke of the pain that lived within her heart.

"My son," she said when she had finished, "do you see how the wind carries the music out and away? See, a low sound that is of despair floats down and lies in the wet earth before us. Another, higher in sound and of greater happiness, alights in those trees yonder. And that last sound, highest of all, is filled with joy and hope, and it floats out over the great wash and away. I can do no more than that, and I know that it will never be enough. Thus my sadness."

"But mother, I do not understand. Perhaps if you will send out a voice to me. . . ."

"Ah, my son, it would do no good to speak of such things. In spite of your wisdom, I am certain that you could not understand."

Hawk was silent, his eyes downcast. In the trees above, a *chosovi*, a bluebird, sent out a happy voice in response to the flute, and out in the valley, Badger, also beginning to grow tall, shouted with great consternation as he drove a flock of birds from the maturing corn.

"My mother," Hawk said at last, "I would speak."

"My ears are listening, my son."

Hawk took a deep breath and carefully held his eyes down in the attitude of humility, for truly he was about to speak of things that always went unsaid.

"This son of yours has observed," he finally began, "that your pain is a great loneliness. That is what we have all seen in your eyes. The others and I have discussed this often, and for many seasons we have felt that this pain has been brought on by the deaths of our People.

"But now much time has passed, those deaths are a long-ago thing, and still the loneliness remains within you. I have given this much consideration, in my mind is an old memory, and I would send out my voice concerning it."

Tala looked at her son, questioning. What memory could he be speaking of? What could be in his heart?

"Speak," she responded hesitantly. "I would hear the words of your memory."

"My mother, the words are these. Long ago a small boy sat as a *kékelt,* a neophyte, among the priests and the elders in a Bow Clan kiva. A young woman with strange green eyes had been raising many eyebrows among the People, and that night she sent forth a voice concerning a powerful dream of a man-to-come, a man who would come to her with love."

"You . . . you know of my dream?"

"It is so."

"But how? I spoke of it to no one but them, them and the old woman."

"My mother," Hawk answered softly, "I was the *kékelt* in the kiva. I heard your words, and of such is my memory. That night more eyebrows were raised, many in anger, one voice especially was raised powerfully against you, and you were made Outcast."

Tala's head dropped. "It was so," she replied quietly.

"I have also thought," Hawk went on, "that your sorrow was because of being Outcast. But now I think not. I think this man who has not come has made the loneliness in your eyes.

"O woman, I have seen the pottery strewn on the mesa, and I have seen the markings on the stone in the deep wash as well. I know your thoughts, my mother, and since this man you dreamed of has not appeared, it is in my heart to offer myself in his place."

"No," Tala whispered as she dropped her eyes in shame, "this cannot be so."

"But . . . I do not understand," Hawk declared, suddenly aware that he had committed a great blunder. I thought only to ease . . ."

"Your heart is good," Tala declared as her mind filled itself with memories of her strange feelings for this young man, feelings that were wrong but that she had never been able to completely discard. "I thank you, O Hawk, but such thoughts are not good."

"But mother, I long only for your happiness—"

Tala held up her hand signaling silence, and instantly Hawk grew still.

"O Hawk, I am deeply moved by your love, and even though the thing you suggest cannot be, I honor you for considering it. Still, your eyes tell me that you do not understand, and so I will tell you this. Between that man and me would be a love that is different from all other love. It would be a man-woman feeling, and I know of no other way to describe it. Such a feeling could not exist between you and me."

"Is it . . . is it the one called Flies-Far?"

Tala looked up, surprised that he could see her thoughts so easily. "No, my son, not wholly, though I do indeed see his countenance very often in my mind. Yet it is the great dream, the vision, that turns me away from you. It was real, as is the man who was shown to me. And though the great Tiaowa has taken the love of my life away from me because of my great evil, yet always must I honor the possibility of his coming."

"Mother," Hawk declared, rising to his feet. "You are *not* evil! Strongly I send out my voice that this is not so!"

Tala smiled. "Like yourself, your words are kind, my son. Yet still I know better. It was declared in prophecy by the *mongwi* and other village leaders, and in all things that prophecy came to pass. Because of my evil the village was destroyed, and in punishment, Giver-of-all-life has prevented the man of my vision from coming to me. Now I am certain that he will never come! My two hearts of evil have forced me to spend all the days of my life in loneliness, and never will I know the man-woman feeling of love. These words are hard, I know, but they are filled with truth."

Slowly Hawk shook his head. "I do not agree, my mother. You are no evil two-heart! You cannot be! How can evil come forth from someone who is good?"

"My son—"

"No, I cannot bear to hear you speak these words. Nor can I bear to see any further unhappiness. Somehow I will find a way to ease your loneliness! Thus it will be. I have spoken."

Swiftly Hawk turned and walked away, and Tala stared after him, a strange emptiness within her heart. Truly was the young man Hawk a fine son. Truly was he filled with love.

88

Later, as the family sat in the gathering darkness of evening, enjoying the fullness that comes from a good meal and the warmth that comes from close companionship, Hawk suddenly spoke.

"My mother, this day you spoke of a thing you called man-woman love. You declared that it would live between you and the man who was to come, the man of the shadows. This is a thing which I do not understand, for such a thing was never spoken of in the secret society of the kiva. What does this thing mean, that a man and a woman would live in love?"

Wiping her hands and taking a deep drink from a pottery ladle of Badger's making, Tala looked up into the face of this young man who was as her eldest son.

He is so large, she thought suddenly. *Perhaps he will understand this love. Perhaps he will understand too well, and will leave this place in search of one that he too can love. Oh, where have the seasons gone, that these my children have grown so quickly? Have I taught them well enough? Have I given them love enough?*

She was aware of the intense silence that had suddenly dropped around them. Butterfly was listening, and Badger was giving her his complete attention as well. A log popped on the fire, and in that moment she decided to send out her voice directly to Hawk, for only he could truly understand her words. Then too, only he truly needed them.

"My son," she finally said, "to you I send out a hard voice, for the words I will declare are not easy to understand. In all the days of my life I have heard these things from but one other, the ancient grandmother who gave me my name.

"Truly it is as you say. No longer do the People speak of this love, this man-woman feeling. Nor do they even consider it. It is indeed one of the forgotten things of our People.

"But the ancient grandmother knew many of the old ways. They were more than sacred to her, and always when she was with me did she speak of them. Still, it was not until after my *tuawta,* my vision of the man-who-was-to-come, that the old one chose to tell me of this man-woman feeling of love.

"The voice she sent out was a chanting, a very old chanting after the manner of a prayer. It was sent out in ancient times by either the man or the woman, and was by way of rejoicing over the love they shared.

"Hear now the chant":

I wake to see the morning from within our dwelling, from beside you, from within me. Wa!

I walk at dusk waiting to greet Bahana, God of the dawn. His star lies there giving light, giving life, giving love, for I am beside you in understanding. Wa!

To Bahana I send my voice. I want to live of the warmth of the earth, of the flash of the water, of the arch of the sky, of the body of my love. Wa!

And I will give forever the soles of my feet, the words of my mouth, the sweat beads of my skin, the prints of my hands, the yearnings of my heart, the tears of my eyes, the birthings of my children, to the one I love. And thus I give to him of the Dawn Star as well. Wa!

In peace I go now, in peace will I walk, in beauty will I walk, for I walk beside you, my love, forever. Wa!

There was another popping from the fire as a pocket of pitch in the burning log was exploded by the heat. A few sparks swirled upward within the smoke, a prairie wolf called out up on the mesa and was answered immediately by another, farther away, and in silence the woman sat with the three young ones. Again the small wolves howled, and at last Tala spoke once more.

"Do you hear them?" she asked. "Do you hear the four-leggeds as they make their chantings? This man-woman closeness is the way of all nature. The insect people live it, the wings live it, and the four-footed ones live it as well. It is also the true way of the People, but with them there must be a great deal more. That more is what the old ones called love. The ancient grandmother told me that this teaching was had directly from Bahana himself.

"All living things are brothers, are sisters. But of them all, man is highest. In this man-woman closeness he cannot be as the lower creatures. As in all else he must remain the highest, or he will cease to be man. At all times must his heart be pure and his countenance pleasant toward his wife and so toward all other women. At all times must a woman's heart be pure and her countenance pleasant toward her husband and so toward all other men. Thus declared the lost white brother.

"So my son, from the ancient grandmother came the understanding that this love is a heart-feeling, a deep and abiding reverence or respect for another who is also a mate. In such a union the quiet thoughts of each touch lightly, as two wings nesting together after a storm. You will know those who so love by their laughter, but to each other they speak more often through solitude and gentle silence. If they find themselves apart, they dream of being undisturbed with each other, or wrapping themselves warmly in each other's comfort.

"For reasons that are never clear to either, it is said that each accepts without hesitation the other. Each knows of the annoying traits and private habits the other strives to hide from view, and each loves beyond them. Neither guards against much when with the other, for each sees the true person behind the words. Each somehow sees the other clearly, even when their eyes are open.

"To each of them, the old woman told me, the other becomes more precious than life, and each of the two in such a union must feel as I have described or love does not exist. Each must be to the other as the Dawn Star is to the birthing of the sun, going before in a constant and faithful manner. . . ."

"My mother," Hawk responded as Tala's voice drifted off into silence, "this is something I have not yet felt."

"I know, my son. Nor have I felt it. Always I have longed to do so, but now I know it will not happen."

For a long moment Hawk gazed silently into the fire. "My mother, you have spoken of the words of the ancient grandmother. What of them? Have you not told us that her voice declared the destruction of the village as well, and prepared you for it? And have you not told us also that her words declared your oneness of heart? O Mother, what of those words?"

Tala dropped her eyes. "I . . . I do not know," she answered. "It is in my mind that she was mistaken. . . ."

"But woman, she was not mistaken. In all things have her words been fulfilled. In all—"

"No they have not!" Tala cried as she signaled Hawk to silence. "The man has not come, and I have never known of that love. Oh, my son, do you not see? If he were going to come, he would have done so long ago, when he was most needed. He did not, and the understanding now fills my mind that he will not! It is my punishment for turning against the *mongwi* and the others, and for speaking with the ancient grandmother and even for speaking with each of you after I had been declared Outcast. You see, even now does my evil continue, and I cannot cease. My love for you is such that I will always send out my voice—"

Hawk, in a manner he had not used in all the seasons since the fleeing from the Angry Ones, suddenly signaled Tala to silence. "My mother, you must not ignore the words of the ancient grandmother. That does not show a good countenance."

"But Hawk," Tala declared, and her face and voice were filled with anguish as she spoke, "can you not see? I am beyond those words. No longer do they have meaning for me!"

"Then," Butterfly suddenly declared, "there must be more words, words of power that will have great meaning. I will construct a *páho,* Hawk will plant it in a circle-shrine of Badger's making, and these others and I will send out a voice to the great Tiaowa that he will send new words to take away your pain and your loneliness. We will do so this night."

"It will be so," Badger solemnly agreed.

Tala stared in silence, unable to fathom the depth of feeling she was seeing within her children.

"Butterfly and Badger are right," Hawk declared. Then, resolutely, he rose to his feet and spoke. "And woman, there is more. If this man of yours cannot come to you, then I will seek a man out from among the scattered villages of the People. I will find a good man, one who understands the old ways, and I will bring him to you! It is so, for I have spoken."

Tala's heart beat wildly with sudden fear and she started to protest. But the tall young man was already walking away in his mind, his heart set on perhaps the most difficult hunt of his life. Yet still he would go, for within him was a great love for this woman who had become as his mother.

89

And so in the soft glow of a small cooking fire on a warm summer night in a far-off valley high in the plateau country of the great Southwest, a woman struggles with herself and with those who are as her children, trying to understand her deeply felt emotions.

The winds of evening drift down through the valley, sighing over the bulging rock of the mesa and wafting off through the trees and the grasses below. And on the winds ride the friendly Kachina people, their laughter a happy sound in the silence, their wisdom a pleasant whisper in the darkness.

"Love," they declare in delightful appendix, "is never ownership of another. It is a declaration of trust in another's good sense and good intentions. Love does not restrict, but grants greater freedom."

The woman of the strange green eyes hears these words and knows in her heart that the Kachinas are speaking to her of her eldest son. He must go, she knows. But oh, the pain of seeing him leave!

"Little sister," the spirits who ride the wind now laugh once more, "do not fret. You have given love, and in the doing have expanded this young one who is as your son. He sees much more, he enfolds much more with his wisdom and his understanding. He truly has blossomed as have the wild roses within your valley."

But there is an emptiness, she cries in her heart. *How can I bear this great pain and emptiness when he goes?*

Night birds call out from down within the valley, there is a scurrying as some creature moves away from the sweetness of the water-planted-place, and as the Kachinas drift off and away she hears their voices again, pleasantly teaching.

"It is well, our little sister, that you have given such love. Now it will be yours to learn, after the manner of all true one-hearts, that the giving of love can be very painful. It is the burden we spoke of so long ago, the burden you and the young man Hawk will always carry between you. Still, love is a good burden, and so we have seen to it that the more you give of it, the more you will also possess."

90

"My son," Tala declared soberly as Hawk and the others faced her across the small fire, "hear my voice that will not cease. You are now a man. You, Badger, are nearly so. And you, Butterfly, are nearly a woman. I now see that it is time for me to set you free, for you are behaving in the manner of men and of a woman. You have been as my sons and my daughter, but truly I do not know you. I can dream great dreams for you, but my dreams are not your dreams. Your life is not my life. Yours may end today in ways I have not dared to think, as did that of the baby so many seasons past. I know this, and I fear.

"My sons and my daughter, because the voice I send out is clear and steady, do not think I feel nothing. Because my eyes are free from tears, do not consider that my heart is the same. Just to know there is little I can do when it comes to the destinies of each of you, just to know that terrible things could come about, these thoughts make me ache inside, and cause many tears to fall within my heart.

"I wish I could be with each of you forever. But my children, all I can do is cry with you or even for you when you feel pain. And though this may sound like a cruel thing for me to say, and though it may also be difficult for you to hear, it is true that while I would give my life for you, would willingly die for each of you, yet, my children, I can never live for any of you. I can only give thanks that the Great One, in spite of my evil, gave me a little of your lives to share.

"Go forth, therefore, walking always in beauty, and I will truly rejoice for all of you. And my son Hawk, even though I know your errand of love is destined to fail, it is in my heart that perhaps you will find a woman who walks in the way of beauty. Then your own life will be fulfilled.

"It is finished. I have spoken."

TWELVE

The Visitors

It was in the heat of the late fall day that they came, when the sun was hot upon the mesa and when even the coolness of the tiny valley did not seem to be enough. Hawk and Badger were out on the mesa on a last hunt, though the season was truly too hot for good hunting. Still, it gave Hawk a last day to be with Badger, and he was anxious for that. Butterfly was also gone, far down the valley, digging within the clay bank for another supply of pottery material. Tala was therefore alone, and was feeling the weight of it upon her shoulders.

All morning she had considered the words she had finally managed to utter the day before, words that admitted that the man of her dream was not going to come. She had also considered the words she had sent forth concerning the reasons why, and within her heart she knew that they were true words. She was indeed being punished for her great evil, and the punishment would continue for the remainder of her life. All of her days would be lonely, and never would she bring forth a child of her own.

Of course, there were also the words of the young ones, words spoken with great power and conviction. They had truly offered up a *páho,* all were convinced of the rightness of their desire, and she wondered at that. Still, it could not be so. Too much time had passed.

"Daughter."

With her heart in her throat Tala spun about, and then in great surprise she took a quick step backward toward the cliff, and then another. Three men stood facing her, three strange men, and one of them was—*the man from the kiva!*

All three were pale of feature, though in most ways they appeared to be like men of the People. The one she had seen and one other were of nearly the same height, while the third was much taller. All wore long hair that seemed very fine and well-kept, and all wore facial hair. On the taller of the three and on one of the others the hair was gray, and the hair of the other, the one she had seen before, was almost pure white. And most amazing of all, each of the men wore a long robe of white that was made of some sort of fine-twined linen such as she had never seen before.

Tala stared at the men, very frightened. Who were they? she wondered. And how had they come to be within the hidden valley? Had the one brought back these others so that he might have more strength? Were they the Angry Ones? Could that be so? But no, there was a look of gentleness about him and the others, a look of kindness. The Angry Ones could never look like that.

"Might we find water in this place?" the man with the white hair, the one from the kiva, asked pleasantly as he took a step toward her.

Involuntarily Tala took another step backward, her fear of them big upon her face.

"Do not be afraid, daughter," the man of the white hair said. "We mean you no harm." He smiled then, a pleasant and unusually radiant smile, and suddenly Tala felt all her fears tumbling away.

"Do you not remember me.?"

"I . . . I do."

"Good. We all thirst. Is there still sweet water in this valley?"

"Here," she said quickly as she motioned toward the great stone tank. "This water is . . . is always fresh and cold and very good, for it is a gift to us from the great Tiaowa."

The man smiled again, and suddenly Tala remembered the good ways of her People. "My . . . my brothers, drink as you wish. I will get you a little food."

Each of the men nodded and smiled with gratitude, and so quickly, with her heart racing, the woman Tala climbed the cliff to the dwelling, gathered a few corn cakes and a pot of still-warm stew, and with these upon her back and head she returned to the rock tank below.

The strange men were seated upon the ground when she arrived, and in silence they accepted her meager offering of food. The bread they broke and ate, the stew they hardly touched, and every few moments one or the other would take another sip of water.

"The water is very good," he who had been with her before finally declared. "The Father has blessed you indeed in the giving of it."

"The Father?"

"Yes, he whom you call Tiaowa, the Grandfather."

Tala signaled her understanding, and in the silence that followed, she looked very closely at this man who again sat before her, speaking. Other than his clothing, nothing about him had changed in the time that he had been gone. His skin was still more clear than pale, and though at first she had thought he and the others were all old, now she wondered. This man's hair was white, yet the look upon his face was a look of youth, of endless strength. It was the same with each of the others.

It was the eyes of the man, however, that amazed her. They were not dark like the eyes of the People, but lighter—not at all like hers, but very clear, very bright. And more, they seemed to see through her.

"Daughter, you carry the sign of the Creator within your eyes."

Startled, Tala looked at the man, and then quickly dropped her gaze. He *knew!* He truly knew! How could such a thing be?

"Within your heart you also carry a great burden," the man went on, "a burden an old woman told you not to shoulder."

"It is so," Tala whispered fearfully. "But . . . but, *who* are you that you should know such things? Who—"

"Daughter," the man interrupted, and his voice was like sweet music as he spoke, "the old woman once mentioned us. Do you not recall?"

Tala, her mind whirling and her eyes open very wide, silently nodded. "Wh . . . why," she then asked, "did you . . . did you remove your footwear?"

The man smiled. "To show you that the old woman was known to me, and I to her."

"But you said nothing."

"You were too filled with fear, my daughter, and I could not."

Tala dropped her eyes, ashamed.

"We three are merely wanderers upon this land," the man continued gently. "That, and only a little more. Nevertheless, we have seen within your heart, and feel to send out to you a voice of understanding. Yes, and perhaps a voice of explanation and of instruction as well. Can you find it within your heart to give ear to our words?"

Tala breathed deeply, looked long into the man's piercing eyes, and at last, with a little shiver, she signaled yes.

"Good," the man said, smiling again. "Then when we have finished, perhaps we might speak with you a little concerning a few things of the future."

"The . . . the future?"

"Yes, daughter. The days of tomorrow. That is another thing that we do. Now, let us make a beginning.

92

"Do you not know," the tall man then asked, and his voice was more deep than the other man's and just as musical, "that the one you call Tiaowa cannot reward evil with good?"

Tala nodded, but her eyes were down and her thoughts were heavy with the understanding of what the man was going to say. It was as she had determined. The man of her vision, of her life, had been withheld in punishment, and these men had come to make it finally clear.

"Daughter," he then asked, "how has your life been in this place?"

"It . . . it has been very happy," she said, looking up in surprise.

"Why is that?"

Once again Tala dropped her eyes. "It is the children," she answered.

"The children?"

"It is so. Their hearts are good, and all they have done has made me happy. In spite of the great evil that has lived within my heart, truly has Giver-of-all-life blessed me with their love."

The man nodded, smiling, and then looked around. "Is not this valley comfortable?"

"Oh, yes, it is indeed," Tala responded. "You have tasted the water, which is sweet and more than plentiful. The soil is fertile, the hunting is easy, there is more than enough here in the way of food, the cliffs are high and give good protection, and we are well hidden and so have not been molested by the Angry Ones. The Creator has more than blessed us here, and daily we give thanks."

"If all this is so," the tall man said quietly, "and truly it seems to be, then these others and I do not understand."

Tala made the sign for puzzlement, and so the man continued.

"Daughter, you have said that the Creator can only reward good with good, and what you have said is a true thing. Then these others and I look around this place that the Creator has given you and see only good. You say the children who are not yours but who have been given to you by the one called Tiaowa have given you much love, and that is also good. Daughter, if Father can reward only good with good, and if all within your life here is so good, how can you feel that your heart is filled with evil?"

Tala's face was down, and she did not know how to answer.

"Daughter?"

Slowly the woman looked up.

"Would you like to send out a voice concerning the man who has not come?"

With sudden tears filling her eyes, Tala looked away.

"Perhaps his coming is only delayed—"

"No!" Tala interrupted, turning back. "There has been more than enough time. I know that now. I will not have his love because I must be punished for being a two-heart, for not living as Outcast, and for bringing death upon my people."

"Who told you this thing?"

"It . . . it was spoken by . . . by the leaders of my village. They sent out the voice, I heard and ignored, and it happened. . . ." And finally Tala broke down and the tears came, tears that had been building for season after season within her heart. The tall man, seeing this, rose from the earth and placed his hand gently upon her head and blessed her, and with the blessing Tala wept even more.

93

"My daughter," the man continued gently, "those words you remember are the words of the one called Saviki, and they were not true words. Those who were destroyed suffered such because of an evil that also made you suffer.

"Hear now my words, for this is the evil. In those secret societies of your village were a few men who sought selfishly for power. Saviki encouraged such selfishness, it grew large within each of them, and of such was the evil that brought to pass their destruction."

Tala was aghast. "O man," she whispered, "do not say such things. You *must* not. You cannot know them—"

"My daughter," the third man interrupted, speaking for the first time, "we have seen this evil growing through all the seasons since you were declared Outcast, and for uncountable seasons before. And because of what is truly within your heart, we have come to you with words that must now be spoken."

Tala started, for big in her mind were the voices of Butterfly and of Hawk, who had planted a *páho* that new words would be given her.

"The grandmother," the man went on, "declared to you in words of soberness that in ancient times the one you call Bahana, the true white brother, came to our people and gave them all needful knowledge and understanding."

Tala stared, and the questions were growing larger in her mind. "How do you know of her sayings?"

"Her voice," the man went on, gently ignoring Tala's question, "declared to you that in those ancient days the people were happy. Daughter, the old woman's voice was true. We know of it, for we saw and felt it all.

"She declared as well that the happiness became sorrow when the two-hearted ones appeared—men and women who chose a path other than the path laid out by the one called Bahana. The one heart of goodness was not in those people, for they sought secretly, through works of darkness, their own selfish ends. Through secret oaths with each other they sought power and gain, and their evil brought about famine and wars and great destruction. It was from that time that the clans of your people, in sorrow because they were no longer one, went their separate ways. My daughter, are not these the things the old woman declared?"

Fearfully Tala signaled her agreement. How could he *know* these things?

"My daughter," the gray-haired man continued, and the smile was gone from his face, "You can see that the village of your own people was also polluted with two-hearts. Some who were in your secret kiva societies were such."

"But . . . but how can this be? Why do you say such things? How do you know them?"

The man arose and stepped to the edge of the great stone tank, where he stared long into the deep and clear water. Tala sensed that there was within him a great sorrow for the evil of the two-hearts.

"This, our daughter, is in our hearts, and it is heavy within us. As wanderers we have seen this selfishness grow many times, and always it ends the same. As your friends we send out a strong voice and declare it unto you. Hear these words carefully.

"The *mongwi* and a few others of your village sought power and gain. They hoped to achieve this by denying knowledge and understanding to the remainder of the people. In their secret kiva society they agreed among themselves to do this, and they agreed with a solemn oath that their plan would never be revealed.

"They understood, my daughter, that if all the others lived in ignorance, they themselves, because of their superior knowledge, would be much in demand. With this demand would come power, they could command as they wished, they would no longer be forced to labor for their own support, and their lives would be much more easy and much more filled with pleasure. Such was the darkness of their thinking.

"Can the eyes of your understanding be open, my daughter? Can your heart see? You were not made Outcast because you were two-heart. You were declared Outcast because you would not accept ignorance, because you would not give those evil ones your obedience. You sought knowledge and understanding, you defied their commands, and thus you threatened their power."

"And the one called Saviki?" Tala whispered. "Was he as the others?"

"Yes, my daughter, and more so. Among the people of your village, Saviki was as the first seed. His words were very strong, and even the *mongwi* paid heed when he sent out his voice.

"He truly spoke of obtaining kingdoms and great glory, and his words held much power of persuasion over the others, even to the undoing of their own thinking. He administered the secret oaths to many, though many others never knew of them. Always the words of those oaths are the same, for they are designed by the powers of evil to keep people in darkness, to help such as seek power to gain power, and to murder, and to plunder, and to lie, and to commit all manner of wickedness. In all things such secret oaths seek the overthrow of freedom and goodness, and such a desire is what lives in Saviki's heart."

"Lives?" Tala quickly asked. "But he . . . the people, were slain. . . ."

"Such is not so, my daughter. Saviki lives, and is one now with those you call the Angry Ones. The son you call Hawk once saw him, and with the others of your children fled from him. Hawk has not told you because he does not want you to live with fear."

Tala sat silently, her mind reeling. These were new thoughts to her, revolutionary thoughts. Almost they were more than she could accept. Yet she could not doubt these men. There was a spirit about them, a feeling of truth.

"What of the others?" she suddenly asked. "Did no one else see this great darkness that the one called Saviki held within his heart? Could no one else see that he was leading our people to dwindle in unbelief?"

"A few saw these things, my daughter. Some of the men in the society saw, and refused the oaths. In that, they were fine men. The ancient grandmother who gave you your name also saw, and sent out a loud voice against it. However, the *mongwi* declared that her mind had gone to walk in the twilight, and from that day forth most of the people heard her words no more.

"Nor was your village alone in this evil. Selfishness spreads everywhere, as it has so often in ancient times. Even those with no understanding of the ancient oaths set about secretly to climb above their fellow beings with power and great knowledge. Each creature seems to be grasping to be more than his or her neighbors, and in this, the Creator feels much displeasure. Thus he has taken away the greenness from the land."

"The . . . the sign," Tala whispered.

"The sign that is within your eyes," the man agreed. "Already the Creator has dried up the mesas, and the People suffer much with hunger and thirst. So also does the Father scourge them by the ones you call the Angry Ones, for truly he allows the wicked to destroy the wicked.

"Soon, my daughter, because of this great evil that the people have allowed to fester and grow among them, they will be driven from these mesas. Many will die, and the few who do not will be taken to a land where the living is harsh and where humility and unity will be required for survival. We three will lead a few of the Bear Clan to that place, and there the migrations will end."

For a moment there was silence, and the water fell with a chuckling sound into the great rock tank. Tala stared ahead, and still her heart was troubled.

"This that you have declared," Tala finally said, "is a heavy weight upon me. Surely if what you say is correct, this great evil would have been seen by many, and many would have resisted it."

"Did you see it, daughter?"

Tala dropped her eyes. "I did not."

"Do not feel badly. A thing like that is hard to see. Still, many did see, and even now are choosing to do nothing."

"But why? Why do they not resist it?"

The man of the white hair smiled. "The question is a wise one, and the answer will give you even more wisdom. Hear now the words of my mouth, and as you hear these words, think of your great dream and of the mocking so many sent out toward you.

"It was given us to understand, by the great Bahana, that we who are of the People. . . ."

94

And so an old man who is beautiful and youthful in all his ways sends out a voice of teaching, declaring to the woman one of the strange ways of mankind. And the way is strange indeed, for it is as if men and women do not want their own minds. Most seem eager to receive their attitudes from someone else. If a man does not like something, and declares that dislike to another, the other will often assume the dislike. This is especially so if the expressed opinion is negative, and if more than one declares it. Always such a popular and negative opinion is assumed to be the height of intelligence.

For instance, a man thinks his own thoughts and so discovers an uplifting truth. With great courage, he sends out a voice concerning it. Another, a critic who longs for the praise of man, says the truth is too simple to be a truth. It is too emotional. It is too brief. It is too lengthy. It is too inspiring.

Others, hearing this critic, take his mind as their own, for it is fashionable to be negative, it is fashionable to be intelligent, it is fashionable to be critical.

And so the truth does good for very few, not because it is not truth, but because so many fear to hold and to defend their own thoughts and hearts concerning it. They fear the scorn of their fellows, and so because of that fear which is the pride of the world they abandon this truth, which could have made such a difference.

The woman hears these things from the old man who is one of three, they are very reasonable things, and so they live and grow in her mind. And as she considers them, the winds of morning drift down the valley, carrying upon their backs the Kachina people. But there is no laughter among the Kachinas, only awe, for this that they are seeing and hearing is a great thing indeed.

"Listen," they whisper to the green-eyed woman. "Give heed to the words of power that come from these three. Remember your vision. Let it flourish again, for these who are prophets have nourished it. Let it grow with hope, little sister, for the days of a person's life are never so long as they seem."

THIRTEEN

The Man Who Asks, "Who Are You?"

As Hawk walked into the afternoon, the juniper-studded sandstone ridge across the creek to his right began growing higher. On his left, however, the land flowed away like an ocean after a storm, in heavy rolling waves of red and white rock and splotchy brown grass. The sky was losing its blueness under a wafting yellow scud, but the sun burned through surprisingly hot after the chilly morning.

It was the hawk moon of November, *Kelmuya,* and he had finally pulled free of the tiny hidden valley and the three who remained behind. The leaving had been a hard thing, for the ties that bound him to Tala and the others were strong and buried deeply. Hawk understood his own reluctance to leave, however, for he knew that if he did not find the shadow-man, he would not go back. The cycle of his life, at least as it involved them, would be finished.

Dropping to the earth near the bank of the small stream, he took a drink, a deep one. Many times that morning he had done this, for he would be leaving the water soon and wanted to have as much of it in his system as possible.

His thoughts then went to Flies-Far, as they had so often in the recent past, and he felt his stomach tighten with jealousy. The man did not understand goodness, and he was far too certain of himself around the woman Tala. No, among the men of the People, Flies-Far would be the last one he sought after. He would go to the village of Flies-Far only if he had failed to find the right man in any of the other villages in the vast mesa country.

There was also that other thing. Flies-Far had promised to return, Tala had waited, and the returning had not come. Not in four cycles of the seasons had the man returned. Of course, there might be many reasons for this: death, another woman, a longer-than-usual journey. But no matter. Tala was deeply saddened that the man had not made another appearance in the tiny valley—the sadness was upon her face, and Hawk could not bear to see such sadness.

Strangely, in some perverse manner he was also glad that the man had not come. He liked Flies-Far and respected him deeply, yet when it came to thoughts of him taking the woman who was as his mother to wife, his mind refused to consider them. So, for as long as it took, he would look elsewhere for this shadow-man who would come and make the woman Tala happy.

Standing again, Hawk moved up and out of the wash, faced the land where each morning the sun had its birthing and which was away from the village of Flies-Far, and resolutely he set out across the dry and rolling plateau. He went quickly, yet always he chose his way with care, keeping off the ridges and skylining himself only when he had to and then only for the briefest possible time. He was not hiding, but as he had long before explained to Badger, a man never knew when caution would be needed.

For one sun and part of another he had followed the deep-cutting stream, and he was certain he had gone far enough. Now, by going toward the morning sun place, he would come ultimately to other dwellings of the People, *his* people, who were those of the Bear Clan. For even though Tala's village, where Hawk had lived, had been of the Bow and Blue Flute clans, his own lineage—from his mother—was through the Bear Clan.

Hawk thought of this, wondered why he had never spoken of his true heritage and clan to Tala, and then he shrugged off the question. The answer to it was obvious. The woman had not been told because it had never been important. To her, it would have made no difference at all.

"Each person has his strengths," she had said, "as each season has its tasks. But always should that person be loved, for always it is the season for love."

Hawk smiled as her words echoed in his mind. She was a strange person indeed, and he knew that the time would never come when she would cease to have influence in his life.

The November sun bore down, and the young man continued away from the direction of its ultimate setting. In his hands he carried his strong bow and his carefully crafted stone ax, in the belt of his apron was a stone knife, and on his back were the *hótachómi,* his arrows held together. He moved carefully, for he was by nature and training wary. Yet still his thoughts fled backward away from the path of his going, and without conscious effort he found himself thinking still of the tiny valley, and of the wondrous thing that had occurred within its walls.

Three men, Tala had declared. Three old men who were not old, who wore strange clothing, and who were pale of feature. No, more even than pale. There were times, Tala had declared, when their skin seemed so clear that she had thought she might see right through them.

Even more unusual, they had spoken of things no man could know, and they had done this easily and with great confidence. Tala had declared these things to Hawk and the others when they had returned, and the words of the men still filled his mind. Nor could he consider them easily, for in doing so he forgot all else, and this was no time to be forgetting where he was and whom he needed to watch for.

So Hawk continued in silence into the afternoon, a lonely buzzard keeping pace with him. And as he walked, his mind made a traveling of its own.

96

It was dark and the young man Hawk was lying back upon his cloak, staring upward at the star nations. He had come far, but other than empty dwellings, most of them very old, and pottery shards that showed the way of the going of those people who had dwelt within those ruins, he had found nothing. Nowhere was there indication that his clan or any other clan yet inhabited the vast mesa country through which he had passed.

Again he focused upon the stars, upon the white pathway that crossed above him, and he wondered how the world would look from such a place as that. The great Tiaowa would know, for his dwelling was somewhere within those stars. Surely from such a vantage point he could see the various villages. Perhaps if a *páho* were planted in such a manner as the woman had shown him, his way might be made clear.

Tala again! In the darkness Hawk grinned. She was even more deep within his memory than he had supposed. Always did his mind turn to her, to her teachings, to her smile, to the strangeness of her eyes, to her gentle love.

He thought then, again, of the three men who had come, the three whom only the woman Tala had seen. Her words concerning them had been strange, more strange than any voice she had ever sent out.

There had been a time when he would have doubted her words, when his face would have been bad toward her. But that had been long ago, and was no more.

He thought then of the gentle falling of rain that came to the valley and, so far as he knew, to nowhere else in all the land. And interestingly, the rain came only after he and the others had performed the ceremonies that called it forth. He had seen that, had helped in the chants and the dances, and then had gone to stand a little way off on the mesa and watch. There he had seen the cloud people hovering only over the small area of their living. There too he had seen their prayers and their lives blessed. Truly such sights had given him reason to listen to the words of the woman.

And when rain had come, all of them would quickly climb to the top of the mesa and go to the high watching place. There, in the old circle-shrine with the opening facing east, Tala would lift her face to the falling rain and chant her gratitude.

O Great One, she had always begun her song, *hear these our words, hear these our words of joy. Wa!*

He comes, riding on the wind, kicking up the dust, bending the trees, blowing past with power, fleeing to a distant rumble of rain. Wa!

She comes, pregnant with water-child, quietly, softly, gently, following after, giving birth to tiny droplets of rain. Wa!

He will come and go, she too will make a leaving, father sun bursts forth, mother earth will awaken, and all of us rejoice with new life. Wa!

Thanks we give to the wandering stranger. Wa!

Thanks we give to you. Wa!

So no longer would Hawk even think of doubting her words. There was too much power in them—yes, and too much truth. Yet none of those words had been so unusual, so full of power, as the voice she had sent out only one sun before when the family had gathered to hear of the three strange men. And finally, after so many seasons, he had understood the meaning of the woman's thanks to the wandering stranger.

Hawk considered the chant, placed it deep inside his mind where sacred thoughts were kept, and considered as well the words the woman had sent out afterward.

"My children," she had declared, "hear my voice. These are the words of the three whom the Kachinas whisperingly called prophets.

"Many of the People will die, those three declared, and the few who are left will abandon these mesas. The men who told me of this will lead them to another place, an inhospitable place, where they will dwell in great discomfort until they can learn to remember and to live the old way of beauty, of love for all. Or, if they will not learn these things, they will dwell in that place through the seasons until all have dwindled in unbelief. Then, finally, all of them will be gone.

"They also declared another thing, my children, a thing that even yet I do not understand. The tallest of the three sent out a voice, a strong voice. He declared that if the People were not in some way, by some person who was of one heart and of a pure countenance, brought to a remembrance of those old and sacred ways, then surely would the dwindling of the People come to pass.

"My children," and now Tala had been whispering in awe and even a little fear, "the tall one declared that the teacher of those old ways of beauty would spring forth from . . . from my womb."

Butterfly had gasped. "The dream! My mother, the man of your dream is to come!"

"Yes," Tala had responded, smiling. "One day . . ."

"One day soon," Hawk himself had declared. "Now I know I will surely find this man, and I will bring him to you."

"But my son, what if that is not the way?"

"Then I will fail. But Mother, it is in my heart to go forth."

"I too will go," Badger had suddenly declared.

"I would rejoice in your presence," Hawk had responded. "But brother, if we both go, then what man is there to protect these two? What man is there to do the things of a man in this lonely place? No, my brother, you must stay here, though in my heart you will always walk beside me."

Badger had dropped his face, and in the late afternoon the silence had hung heavily upon the valley.

"My mother," Badger had suddenly asked, "where are the three men? Why did none of us see them as we returned?"

"Ah," Tala had whispered, and Hawk could yet see the look of wonder in her strange green-blue eyes, "hear my voice, for that is perhaps the strangest thing of all.

"We stood speaking, the three of them and I, and I was filled with silence. I had many questions, but my mouth was stopped and I could not find utterance. Confused, I looked away at some sound, and when I looked back, the men were gone.

"Badger, they did not make a walking away, or even a fleeing. They went into the air, where the Kachina people live, and I saw them no more."

97

Hawk, still upon his back, looked at the stars and considered those strange words. Yet within him there was no doubt concerning them.

There were many things that he did not understand, and that was but one of them. Nor did that worry him. He had seen the joy in the eyes of the woman Tala concerning her shadow-man, and if the three men had done nothing else but confirm that dream to the one who was as his mother, thus bringing her happiness and peace, then he would honor their memory forever.

So now he would find that man, or he would die in the trying, and that also was as it should be.

98

Three suns from the stream in the deep wash, Hawk found the first fresh signs of other people, and one sun more had not passed when, with his heart pounding in strange excitement, the young man approached the village of another clan of the People. Truly it was, for him, a momentous experience, for he was now about the task of finding the man who had been taught as Tala had been taught.

"Brother," the Kachina people whispered as they drifted by on the wind, "be very careful. These people are not quite as you are. Perhaps even now they lie in wait to deceive."

Hawk, hearing their silent words, nevertheless pushed them from his mind. He had much to do, and it could only begin if he entered into these dwellings of the People.

99

In the tiny valley the seventh day of Hawk's departure dawns clear, cold, and very lovely. The winds off the mesa moan through the old *koritivi* in the bulging sandstone cliff, and in the watching place a woman stands still, with arms uplifted. After the manner of her people she is chanting, sending out a voice to greet the dawn.

She is also, from old habit and long-unfulfilled desire, supplicating the Creator to send to her bosom the man of her dream, her vision, the shadow-man who will, with a love she does not even understand, complete her life and make it full. Yet even as she prays, her heart aches with loneliness, for her eldest son is gone from her life and she fears. She thinks of the three men and remembers that she could not ask them the question that tears at her heart, the question concerning when the shadow-man would come. She listens to the sighing wind, hoping for some sort of consolation and answer from the laughing Kachina people. But alas, they are also silent. There is no laughter, there is no joy, there is no softly worded instruction. There is only the wind, blustering now and cold, and the loneliness she feels for the youth who has gone.

And in the valley, near the water-planted-place and the deep rock tank, the lovely Butterfly and the tall young Badger watch silently, and with prayer-thoughts of their own they join their mother who stands so far above.

They too feel the loneliness, they too feel fear for the excellent life of their departed brother. And besides all of that, there is something else that all three feel, some nameless, haunting dread of an approaching evil.

100

In the darkness the rhythmic beating of the drum had an otherworldly sound, and Hawk shivered involuntarily. The stars hung brightly against the chill blackness of the mesa, and the young man stood with the watchers as the procession of masked dancers wound past and on into the walled village.

It was *Pámuya*, January. It had been over a year since he had left the valley, and the purification ceremony that made the People of this village ready for the blessings of the coming season of planting was in its concluding stages.

Hawk watched intently, as he had during all the suns and darknesses of the season of cold he had spent in this particularly large village, and again his heart was troubled. The ceremonies, as performed, were proper and flawless. But somehow they also seemed devoid of life. The people moved mechanically in their tasks, without joy, and everywhere there seemed to be a feeling of gloom.

The masked dancers represented the Kachina people, but on so many of their faces there was painted anger and darkness, not at all like the gentle spirits who lived on the winds of the tiny valley.

As Hawk followed the Kachinas into the large kiva, he found himself thinking of the ceremonies as Tala and he and the others had performed them. There was simplicity to them, and joy, for in all things they pointed to the great Tiaowa and to his son whose true name was lost and who was called by the People Bahana.

But in these people there was no joy, no apparent reverence. Each of the participants was told what to do by the *mongwi* or the society elders, and each simply obeyed. Of such a nature were the rules. It was not true worship; it was not true prayer. It was instead only blind obedience given out of fear and ignorance, and again Hawk realized how vast was the difference between these ceremonies and the true worshiping performed by Tala and the little ones.

As the ceremonial destruction of the sand painting in the kiva ended on that night, and as the Kachinas began their bean dance, Hawk made his way from the kiva and out into the cold night. For a time he simply stood in the darkness, trying to understand his mind. Then, as he started toward his place of sleeping, a man suddenly appeared out of the darkness.

"Who moves?" the man challenged harshly.

"Hakomi," Hawk answered, using the name the People had given him.

"Why are you not in the ceremony?

Again the voice was harsh, angry, and Hawk wondered if the man spoke to all the People in such a manner. "I grew tired," he finally answered, "and would sleep."

"Not on this night, Hakomi. All are to be at the ceremony. Those are the *mongwi's* orders. And though you are an outsider and a searcher, nevertheless, that order includes you! Now, back into the kiva!"

For a long moment Hawk gazed into the man's set face. Then,

without another word, he turned and climbed back down into the huge kiva.

As the dancers swayed and fed the others their newly sprouted bean plants, Hawk found his thoughts fleeing once more to the tiny hidden valley. He thought of the freedom he had lived with, he considered the openness that had existed between them all, he recalled the responsibilities each had shared, and he felt again the warmth of the love that had bound their lives together.

How different it was in this place, how restricted, how filled with sadness! Nor was there much difference in any of the villages he had visited. Not in any of the villages had he found such a way of life as he sought.

Hawk considered again the underlying feeling he had found within the people, the feeling that was so destructive, and he knew that it was fear. In many of the villages this fear was great and terrible, for the rumors of the Angry Ones had come. "Who can stand before the Angry Ones?" the people thus wailed. "Behold, they sweep the earth clean before them, and all of us are doomed."

And so they seemed to be. Always they waited in anguish, and their lives were a mockery of anything that was joyful.

In others of the villages the fear was a different sort of fear. It did not show itself, but lingered quietly just below the surface of the minds of the People. This fear was not of the Angry Ones, but of the few elders of the secret societies who controlled all of their lives.

Still, in all of those villages had Hawk looked for the man he so longed to find, the man he yet sought.

Strangely, he also found himself looking more and more upon the young maidens of the villages, and the laughing words of Flies-Far came back into his mind. And many were the young women he saw and found beautiful, many were the maidens who were available for the taking and the bearing of children. Yet nowhere had he found a maiden who would speak with him as a friend, as one person to another. Rarely had he even found one who would walk beside him instead of behind, or who would look directly into his eyes instead of staring always at the earth when in his presence.

Some truly seemed to want to do these things, for Hawk was

attractive and his fame had spread. But still they could not. Either they did not know how, or they feared the anger and scorn of the *mongwi* and the leaders of the secret societies. They had been taught what their proper roles should be, and not one could be persuaded otherwise.

Then too, Hawk was often offered a daughter or a sister or even a wife of one man or another to take as his own wife. The young woman would be brought before him with downcast eyes and told to go with him, and without expression she would obediently step forward.

These offers Hawk consistently refused, and in the refusing received much ridicule and much mockery from the men of the secret societies.

This too troubled him, for he saw true injustice in the hearts of these men, and a great ignorance of that injustice as well. He saw that while he and the other men were well-fed, the women and the children ate what was left of the food when the men were finished. He saw that while he slept in a warm kiva, the women and the children slept in the upper rooms of the village. No fires were allowed in those rooms because of the danger of burning all the dwellings; the rooms were cold and damp, and many of the occupants were consumed with sickness and even death.

Additionally, under no conditions were the women given more than the barest shreds of knowledge concerning the past of the People, knowledge upon which they might construct the attitudes of their lives.

Nor did many appear to be bothered by any of this. The women were not concerned because they knew no better, and the men were not concerned because it was much more easy and comfortable to keep things the way they were.

"Why worry about the women?" he was asked again and again. The lineage of the clans passed through them, such a passing from mother to children made their existence important, and what more in the way of importance and recognition could a woman possibly want? Such questions as he asked were foolish questions indeed. Women were property—they went about their tasks willingly enough, and could easily be replaced if they did not. That had always been the way of things, and it certainly wasn't going to change.

Of those men who were truly troubled by the things Hawk described, most had very good hearts, and he saw that a growing number of them lived in great fear. They did not dare to defend the women, they did not dare to declare their choice of whether to hunt or to farm on any certain day, they did not dare to send out a voice of preference concerning what part they would play in any of the great ceremonies, they did not dare to choose which of the necessary skills they would master. These men feared the power of the village and clan leaders, and because of that fear, the power of those few leaders grew ever more strong.

Hawk considered these things deeply, he watched the haughty, devious, and secretive attitudes that lived among the People, and always he tried to declare to them the things the ancient grandmother had taught the woman Tala so many seasons before.

"Do you not remember the old ways?" he would ask the men who sat within the kivas. "Do you not recall that in ancient times the People had one heart toward each other, and men and women were considered the same?"

There would follow much laughter. "What you say may be true, our brother," someone would usually respond. "But these times are not the old times. These are the now times, and the now way is much more pleasant."

"It is so," another would add. "Our brother, do not stir things up. We are comfortable and happy, and the women do not complain."

"Nor do they dare," another would grin. This would be followed again by laughter, and finally the *mongwi* would speak.

"Join us, our brother. Your fame has proceeded you, and you would be a great addition to our village. In such a way, you too can enjoy this good life that is ours."

Hawk would look long at the earth, and then at last, in a very quiet voice, he would declare his heart.

"My brothers, I cannot. Such a thing is not within me, for I have been taught by the one who has been as my mother to live the old way, the higher way. I cannot do otherwise and be happy."

Within the kiva there would be a great silence. Hawk would know the meaning of that silence, and, sorrowing that his words had fallen only upon the empty air, he would take up his journey once again.

Nor was that ever a difficult thing to do. Each village was happy to see him leave, for he was known already as Hakomi, the man who asks, "Who are you?" in an embarrassing way.

Thus he moved from village to village, and so he learned that in each of them the secret societies had gained much power over the people. Each society clutched its bit of knowledge or power selfishly to itself, each vied for initiates, each plotted against the other societies for more power, all of them considered men far superior to women, and none of them realized what they were doing.

Still Hawk searched, for somewhere, he was certain, he would find a village whose inhabitants lived still in the true manner of the People. Somewhere he would find a village where the countenances of the people were good and happy, where each had but one heart toward all others, and where the man-woman love lived in their dwellings. In that village would he find the man who would stand beside the woman Tala in beauty.

FOURTEEN

The Evil One

Hawk had found the woman, *his* woman!

He was certain of it. He had come to a small village far off and across the great river, had been made welcome, and had found within the dwellings of that place much of the peace that he had known in the tiny valley.

For many days he had stayed, making himself useful with his hunting and his other unusual skills, and in that time he had become aware of the eyes of a young maiden. Constantly she had cast her gaze upon him in a smiling manner, and quickly Hawk had realized that she was indeed pleasant to look upon. Moreover, she did not fear him much, but walked beside him when he asked. As well, she occasionally gazed for long moments into his face without looking away, and that was indeed a rare thing.

And so now they stood together in the darkness beyond the edge of the village, and her scent was strong within his nostrils. Hawk's heart beat fast, and in the light from the moon-woman he looked long at her, wondering. She was very lovely, her eyes sparkled with humor, her hands were skilled at many crafts, her smile lighted up her entire face, her form was comely, her mind was quick with intelligence.

"My Hakomi," she suddenly asked, her voice low and throaty, "where is it that your mind travels?"

Hawk gazed down at her, and within him was a longing he had never known. She was so beautiful, so desirable. Slowly he turned his face away, and at last he spoke.

"My thoughts were walking within your soul," he answered simply.

"My soul? What is that?"

"It is . . . it is that which lives within you."

"How is it that you can get within this . . . this soul?" she asked. "What is it that you were seeking?"

Hawk sighed. "I do not know, my little one. Since my coming to this place, you have lived more and more within my mind. It is in my heart to wonder if . . . if there is, between you and me, the man-woman feeling of . . . of love."

There was silence, and at last the young woman's gaze fell away.

"I do not know of this feeling," she answered honestly. "I have not learned of it."

Again there was great quiet, and the young *wúti,* the young woman, sensed, somehow, that this was a very big thing in the heart of the tall young man who stood beside her. Desperately she wanted to please him, for to wed such a famous person, such a well-known searcher, would give her great status among the other women. There was also his appearance, which was good and manly. Such a person could father many fine sons and many lovely daughters, and these too would enhance her position before the others of the People.

Of course the *mongwi* must give his approval for the marriage before anything could be done, for he had final say in all such things. But the young woman smiled at that thought, for she knew the chief of the village was favorably disposed toward the one called Hakomi. And even if he weren't so disposed, there were other ways of getting his approval. There were always ways.

Still, the man Hakomi had spoken of this feeling between a man and a woman, a feeling she truly knew nothing of. "I know of love," she said, her face suddenly brightening. "I know of love for a man, my Hakomi."

Hawk looked back to her, his own face brightening. "That is good. Will you tell me what you know of it?"

With humble pride the young woman dropped her eyes, for truly she did know. "It is the honor, the respect that a woman must have for a man," she answered quickly. "A woman is to pleasure a man in all things, and always she is to do so with a good countenance. That is love."

"And the man?" Hawk asked quietly.

The young woman glanced up. "The man? What is it that you ask, Hakomi?"

"The man," Hawk repeated. "What has he to do with this love?"

"He has nothing to do with it," the woman responded quickly and surely. "He has only to be there and to demand. The task is the woman's."

"That is not so," Hawk retorted fervently. "For it to be the man-woman love of which I speak, each of the two within the marriage must feel the same things for the other. The task is the man's as well as the woman's."

Now the young woman stepped back, a fearful expression upon her face. "These words you speak are *núkpana,* they are evil, O Hakomi. It is good that I alone can hear them, or you would be judged most harshly by the *mongwi.*"

"There is no evil in what I say," Hawk responded, his heart feeling tired. "Only truth. This love-way that I speak of was so in the old days, but now the way is becoming lost, and few recall it. Selfish men drive this two-hearted way along, this two-hearted way in which you have been trained, and I fear for the freedom of the People. Such a losing of the way is indeed a great evil."

The young woman turned her back upon him, and her voice was filled with fear. "O Hakomi, I cannot hear these things. Your countenance is bad, and mine soon will be. I fear what would happen to me then. . . ."

"We will leave this village," Hawk declared as he gripped her arm. "There is a place I can take you to, a tiny valley, and there you will learn of the true way, the old way. There we can learn to share this great man-woman love feeling."

The young maiden pulled her arm free, and with a choking sob she turned and ran toward the village. Hawk, his heart tearing at his chest, watched her go, started after her, stopped, started again, stopped, and with his head down and with great tears filling his eyes he turned and walked slowly away across the mesa.

102

The moon-woman dimmed her face behind a cloud, the darkness gathered around him, and still the man Hawk continued forward, his heart tearing, his thoughts reeling, his eyes not seeing. The village shrank to a dark outline behind him, and then across the mesa the winds of night arose. The Kachina people came out of their holes in the rocks, and with a gentle laughter they passed around him and above him, their voices a soft mocking within his mind.

"Ho, little brother," they called, "it is a good time for a walking, is it not?"

Angrily Hawk strode forward, and the laughter grew louder. But still it was a good laughter, and he could not help but notice that this was so.

"Make this a lengthy walking," they laughed. "Perhaps in the time you are away from that *wúti,* her heart will change. Perhaps, little brother, you too will learn a new thing. Remember, your quest is for the man who will fulfill the life of the woman who is as your mother, not for the woman who will fulfill your own."

I understand that, Hawk declared in his mind, *and truly I have been looking. It is just that such a man is not to be found.*

Perhaps, little brother, you are looking in the wrong places. There is another, one you have not been willing to consider."

No! Hawk's heart cried. *Not he!*

"Well, little brother, at least it is something to consider."

And then they were gone and the wind was only a cold thing against the back of the sorrowing young man who had become Hakomi, he who asks, "Who are you?" Somewhere, he knew, a village of the People would be found where the true way was yet lived. Was it, then, to be the village of Flies-Far? Was it truly to be there that he would find the man he sought?

103

Three moons later, and almost two years from the time he had left the tiny valley, Hawk was led into the kiva of a small village that had been built out on the edge of a towering mesa. It was far to the north of the village where the young woman resided, and Hawk had no idea of where he truly was.

The light in the kiva was dim, and his eyes had not adjusted fully when a man across the fire suddenly leaped to his feet.

"Hawk! Brother, is it truly you?"

Hawk stared. "Flies-Far?"

Quickly the man leaped the fire and grasped Hawk by the shoulder. "Brother, you have truly grown. But for your eyes, I might not have known you. Tell me, what brings you to this place?"

Hawk looked directly into the face of the man who had been his friend. "I seek you," he said simply.

Flies-Far stared hard. "Well," he finally declared, laughing lightly. "Now I am found. Tell me, brother, why it is that you seek me. Has the woman changed her mind?"

"Brother," Hawk answered, looking around at the silent faces as he did so, "I would speak in private."

Now Flies-Far truly laughed. "Private? Hawk, this is more than private. These men see and hear nothing that I do not tell them to see and hear. Now send out your voice, for I grow impatient."

Hawk dropped his gaze and stood in silence, Flies-Far glared at him, and finally, with a signal of impatience, he sent the other men scrambling from the kiva.

The man seated himself again, indicated that Hawk should do so as well, they each ate a bite of food and took a sip of water in the customary manner of old friends greeting each other, and finally Flies-Far spoke.

"You seem to have come a long way, my brother."

"It is true. I have traveled for the space of two full cycles of the seasons."

"To find me?"

"In a manner of speaking, my brother. Tell me, are you *mongwi* here in this place?"

Flies-Far laughed again. "No, brother, though such a thing could be, if I should choose. I merely instruct the *mongwi* and the others in the true ways of our people."

"You seem to have much power."

"A little. And I am learning more of that power all the time."

"How is it done?"

"Well, brother Hawk, this is how it is. I have something, and these people want it. That gives me power. I give it to them, and that gives me wealth. Or, I give them only a portion of what I have, tell them it is all, and I have both wealth *and* power. It is a very easy rule to understand."

Hawk nodded. "And what are you trading, brother?"

Flies-Far laughed again. "Brother, you have many questions, and is is within my mind that this started with my questions. Truly you have grown clever. Now tell me, why have you sought me out?"

"You did not return to the valley," Hawk answered simply.

"And you have come to take me back?" Flies-Far asked incredulously.

"Perhaps."

"But . . . but *why?*"

Hawk again dropped his eyes. "The woman Tala grows very lonely," he said heavily. "Still she waits for the man of her dream."

"Her dream?"

"Yes, brother. Long ago she was given a dream, and in it she saw a man who was to come to her and give her true man-woman love. She waits for this one."

"And I am that man?"

"Perhaps. You are in her thoughts."

Flies-Far sat pondering Hawk's words. "Is she still as comely as she once was?" he finally asked.

Hawk signaled yes.

"And is she still stubborn and proud?"

"Only when she chooses to be. If you were that shadow-man, you would never see that in her."

"Shadow-man?"

"It is so. In the dream, the man's face was covered with shadow, and could not be seen."

"Ah," Flies-Far breathed in understanding. "That is why she does not know."

"That is why."

For another moment Flies-Far stared into the fire. Then, with a smile upon his face, he rose to his feet. "Come, brother. My heart beats strongly with anticipation. If I am to take the woman Tala to wife, there is much to be done. I must return to the village of our people and send out a voice concerning these men here. They are very willing men, and—ho, brother, this will give me the opportunity of presenting you to our *mongwi,* who is truly a great man. This is something I have long wanted to do."

"I go willingly," Hawk said as he too rose to go. "Though truly, brother, my heart hesitates."

"Do not fear," Flies-Far smiled. "I tell you, this *mongwi* is filled with goodness and wisdom, and you will learn much from him. Now come and let us be gone."

104

The village where Flies-Far dwelt was larger than any of the villages Hawk had yet seen. It was built back within a wide and shallow cave, high above the floor of the narrow valley that led to it, and was within seeing distance of a great high mountain that rose into the blue dryness of the sky. Truly was the man Hawk impressed.

"This is my village," Flies-Far declared as they approached. "Within those walls live many people, and slowly the great *mongwi* is teaching them the new ways, the ways of freedom and life."

"What freedoms are those?" Hawk asked.

"Freedom from the burden of making all sorts of choices—or the freedom to make those choices for others. That, and freedom from fear. Here in this place we are safe. Here the Angry Ones cannot come. Here we can live as we choose."

"That is good," Hawk agreed. "Yet I wonder, brother. In all my wandering I have seen no village where fear of one sort or another does not exist."

"Now you will," Flies-Far assured him. "The Angry Ones cannot come here, for the *mongwi* has so promised, and all his words are filled with power. Thus we do not fear."

"That is likely true," Hawk agreed. "But brother, there are other fears that are just as bad. As an example, what happens in this village if one disagrees with your *mongwi*?"

"Why . . . he is worked with, taught until he understands the error of his thinking."

"And if he does not come to such an understanding?"

Now Flies-Far looked hard at his friend. "That cannot happen. The understanding of better ways comes to all."

"But brother, what if it did not? Would a secret death then occur?"

"O Hawk," Flies-Far laughed, "those are foolish words. Have you forgotten that we are the People of Peace?"

"I have not forgotten, brother, but many have. I have heard many rumors of such things happening."

"But not in this place," Flies-Far assured him, smiling. "Now come, and I will present you to the *mongwi*."

Again Hawk followed, and his eyes were everywhere as they walked and climbed, taking in the wonders of this great village. Dwellings were built upon dwellings and more dwellings were built upon them, sometimes as high as five or six dwellings tall. Ladders and people were everywhere, working, busy at the tasks that filled their days. Corn was being ground, robes woven, here and there the men gambled or worked on their weapons, and everywhere the children played. They did this laughingly, as was the way of children, but Hawk noticed that this laughter did not extend to many of the men and women. There was a seriousness in their eyes, a great fear.

105

"O *mongwi,* may I present this man who is my friend. He is called by the name Hakomi, for he is the one who asks, 'Who are you?' as he wanders."

There was a quiet ripple of laughter in the kiva, and from the darkness a voice bid Hawk welcome. At the sound of that voice Hawk started, and as his eyes finally adjusted to the gloom of the kiva, he suddenly realized that he was in serious trouble.

Across the small fire, black eyes gazing up at him from an intelligent face that was yet seared with evil, was the one who was known as Saviki, the one who had chased him so many seasons before.

In the firelight the man's eyes glittered, and Hawk felt the chills start low and work themselves up along his spine. In all the seasons since he had first seen that look, it had not changed. It still did to him exactly as it had done so long before.

Nor had the man himself altered, even with age. He looked exactly as he had looked the night he had demanded possession of the green-eyed Tala, the one he had later called *powáqa,* a witch. Nor had he changed since the darkness and the sun during which he had pursued Butterfly and the baby and Badger and himself over the cliff and into the searing desert.

Those memories troubled the young man, but he was troubled more by the man's presence in the kiva. Saviki was evil, a two-heart who had almost certainly joined forces with the Angry Ones in the great slaying of his clan. His hands and his heart were polluted with the blood of many of the People, yet the man Flies-Far was associated with him and considered him great.

"He has come," the man Flies-Far continued, "to request that I take the one who is as his sister to wife."

More laughter rippled around the circular room. The one called Saviki silenced it with a motion of his hand, and only then did he speak.

"We bid you welcome, Hakomi. I am *mongwi* of this great village, the chief, and we who greet you are of the Black Bear Clan."

Hawk started, for never except once from his own mouth had he heard such a blatant lie, never among all the People. Saviki was of the Bow Clan, had gone through the initiation rites for it, and had been admitted to the *Soyál* observances and so to adulthood from it. Now he was in this place, claiming to be of the Black Bear Clan, and he was also the *mongwi.*

"My brother," Saviki said suddenly, and his voice was as a purring, "the face you wear is troubled. It is in me to question why."

"It is nothing," Hawk replied evasively. "An old memory came to mind as you spoke. That is all."

Saviki nodded. "I too have a memory, my brother. I have heard of you, and to have you here is not a surprising thing. Yet in my mind there is something else, a feeling that your face is familiar. Is it that we have met before?"

Forcing himself to relax, Hawk made the sign for ignorance. "In the great migration of life," he answered, "all things are possible. I am one who wanders, seeking a certain man, and so I have been many places. Perhaps in one of them—"

"No," Saviki interrupted. "It is more of an old memory, almost a haunting . . ."

Again Hawk signed ignorance. "Who knows?" he responded, forcing into his voice an ease he did not feel. "I too am of the Bear Clan. Perhaps it is only that our lineage is the same."

Saviki stared hard at him. "Perhaps," he finally responded. "And this man you seek? Is it that you have found him in Flies-Far?"

"One hopes so," Hawk answered, "for truly has my search been long."

"Then the wandering has been in behalf of the one who is your sister?"

Hawk, his eyes steady upon the face of Saviki, signaled yes.

"That is a great deed," Saviki declared. "Either this sister is very ugly and has need of much help, or you have strong feelings for her."

Flies-Far laughed. "She is not ugly, O *mongwi.* She is very comely in appearance, and her form is good to look upon."

"Then you have seen this woman."

"It is true. Once, long ago."

"It is why I have come at last to him," Hawk declared. "The woman has fond memories of his visit."

"And I too," Flies-Far responded.

"Ah," Saviki said thoughtfully, still staring at the young man Hawk. "So, Hakomi, have you thought yet of where we might have crossed paths?"

"I . . . think it must be that I remind you of some other man."

"Perhaps. If such is so, I will know of it before long. If it is not, my brother, if my memory is searching for a true remembrance, and you have deceived me, I will know that too. You will also know it, for I will not be deceived.

"Flies-Far, take this man to your dwelling and see that he is comfortable. Then I would hear the voice you have to send concerning that small village."

106

"Brother," Flies-Far said seriously as he and Hawk shared a small meal, "it is in the *mongwi's* mind that he truly knows you. How can this be so?"

Hawk stared at the pile of robes upon which he sat. He wanted to answer, but for some reason he did not dare. Flies-Far was a friend, but Hawk knew well the power of the man Saviki. No, he could not reveal anything until he knew more.

"Well," he answered as he chewed, "there is much about all of this that I do not understand. This *mongwi* truly seems to be a great and wise man. What name is he called by?"

"He is called The Eagle Flies High. Truly did his mother give him a fitting name."

"That she did," Hawk agreed, wondering even more at the many lies that had fallen from Saviki's mouth. "Brother, do you accept all of this *mongwi's* great vision? Do you know all of his wisdom and knowledge?"

"I accept it," Flies-Far answered quickly. "Still, there is much about it that I do not understand. I have not yet been told all of the power-things that he knows, nor have I been admitted to all of the secret ceremonies. The time is quickly coming, though, when that will be so."

Hawk looked up into the face of this man who was his friend. "Brother," he suddenly declared, "do no more with this man. He is evil, and the truth is not in him. His name is Saviki, he is of the Bow Clan, he is the one I told you of on the mountain who joined with the Angry Ones to slay the people of my village. I am certain he is still with the—"

Flies-Far suddenly made the signal for silence, and Hawk instantly closed his mouth. "Brother," the man whispered, "You must not say these things. They are wrong, and they show you to be a two-heart."

"They are not wrong, my brother. I know, and I send out the voice of truthfulness to you. You asked how he knew my face, and I will tell you. Long ago we were of the same village, and—"

He was interrupted by the sound of feet upon the roof of the dwelling, and as the two men looked up, a man dropped through the entryway and stood before them.

"You are made welcome," Flies-Far declared.

"It is accepted," the man stated gruffly. "The *mongwi* directs that this wanderer come alone to the kiva at once."

"I choose not to go," Hawk replied.

Flies-Far stared at him in surprise, and then quickly he turned to the messenger. "He does not understand our new customs. Of course he will accompany you, as will I."

"You are to remain in this dwelling," the man interrupted. Then, turning to Hawk, he signaled that he should arise and go forth.

Hawk gazed long into the eyes of his friend Flies-Far, arose, and with the messenger following behind, he climbed the ladder out of the dwelling of his friend.

107

"So, my young Hakomi, have you decided to tell me what I wish to know?"

"My mouth is closed against you," Hawk responded quietly.

There was complete silence within the kiva as his defiant words sank in, and Hawk was aware of the sudden intake of breath from the other two men, and from the messenger who stood behind him.

"Hyeee!" the man Saviki yelled, his anger bright upon his face. "This one is more than impudent. What say you others?"

The men on each side of Saviki solemnly made the signal for agreement. "Truly," one then said, "he has need of learning manners."

"It is so," Saviki agreed, smiling. "O Hakomi, it is my order that you open your face toward me, or else . . ."

The man broke off his threat in mid-sentence, for down into the kiva came the first of three young women, bearing food. Saviki turned his gaze upon them, and even more did Hawk feel the chill of evil in the air.

As the women turned into the small circular room, the man Saviki, in an unheard-of manner, began treating them lewdly. The women laughed with it, the other two men did likewise, and Hawk was aghast. Such a thing as he was seeing was truly *núkpana,* truly evil. No one who was of the People would even countenance such behavior, let alone consider it or indulge in it. Occasionally a rare individual was found guilty of *chunta,* adultery, and was made Outcast. But this gross evil he was witnessing was blatant, beyond comprehension.

Hawk knew instantly that he must take Flies-Far and make a running away from that place. Furthermore, he must do it quickly. The man Saviki was very wise in the ways of the two-heart, and Hawk did not doubt that the man would learn his true identity before much more time had passed.

The time of darkness would most likely be best, he determined as he stood within the kiva, his eyes downcast with shame. Then these men would be asleep, and he could leave without hindrance.

"Here is *noosioqa,* nourishment," Saviki suddenly laughed as he signaled toward both the women and the food. "Come, brother Hakomi, and join us."

The young man could not move, could not lift his eyes because of the great shame that was before him, could not speak because his throat was squeezed tight with the horror of what his eyes had beheld.

"Yes," Saviki continued, "my memory still searches, my brother, and though it has found nothing, yet I *do* know you. It will come. Until then . . . your eyes seem downcast, as if with shame. Is that a true thing?"

Hawk remained silent, and Saviki laughed. "I thought as much. You have not learned the new ways of freedom and happiness. My brother, hear this my voice, for upon it hangs your life! It is said that you seek after the old ways, the foolish ways of the ancients. You have said that you seek after a man to take your sister for a wife. Well, my brother, I think you seek something else as well. It is in my heart that you also seek a woman for yourself, someone to ease the strain of loneliness under which you live.

"Well, brother, my heart is happy for your good fortune. Your lengthy search, at last, is at an end. You have found the man Flies-Far, and now here is your other finding.

"The old ways are dead, and we can all praise Tiaowa for that. Here are three women, all good to look upon, all wise in the ways of pleasing a man. Choose one, or choose all three if you prefer. It does not matter. But choose now, my brother, and take her, or we will know that your heart is not good toward us."

The silence in the kiva was profound. Hawk's heart beat fast, and a great fear was within him. He knew the man Saviki would take his life, and he was not anxious for death at all. Yet he could not, *would* not, raise his eyes and acknowledge his acceptance of the evil that was before him, that was offered him in so hideous a manner. His mind was strong against such a thing.

"Take him," Saviki growled to the man who had been the messenger. "Take this searcher and hold him, for as you can see, my brothers, he intends great evil toward us. He must be destroyed, just as he would destroy us if it were within his power."

"Do you wish his destruction immediately?" the messenger asked.

Saviki signaled yes. But then, as an afterthought, he spoke once more. "But first, my brother, I would know his true identity. Determine it for me."

The man nodded, and to Hawk's great surprise he was grasped, dragged forth from the kiva opening, and bound. Then in a heartless manner he was taken to an unused storage pit and thrown inside, where he lay seething with fear and anger and hurt pride.

Never had be been treated in such a way, not even in the villages where he had spoken out so strongly against the selfishness of their ways. Men of the People would never behave in such an ill-mannered way. Surely the men in this place, men such as Flies-Far, could see that.

Struggling to his feet, Hawk leaned against the ladder until he was rested. Then, with his hands still bound, he started slowly to climb.

He never saw the blow coming, for his head was down and against the ladder so that he would have balance. One instant he was climbing—the next the whole world had exploded within his head. There was a brilliant flash, a burst of pain, tiny pinpoints of light that pricked in the darkness, and that was all.

Much later, in the darkness of the night, Hawk's mind came slowly back. He still floated on a great sea of pain, his eyes would not open, his muscles screamed with a great agony, and yet through it all he knew where he was and what had happened. He had been beaten and left where he had fallen.

"Well, Hakomi," a voice growled, "are you ready to reveal to the *mongwi* your true identity?"

Within the young man called Hawk arose a great anger. "Tell that man," he mumbled, "that I spit upon him!"

He struggled to rise then, and from out of the darkness there was laughter, and then another vicious blow. He fell, blackness rose around him, and through it, as his mind floated away, he heard more laughter, cruel and evil.

108

The man called Saviki stared into the fire, thinking. Somewhere he had seen the man who was called Hakomi before. He knew he had seen him, for the face was a very familiar thing, and that troubled him. Yet he could not remember.

Glancing up, he stared at the man called Flies-Far, who had been brought before him. The man had just been brought in, was still bathed in sweat beads, and so had been well prepared by the others who watched for him.

"Yes?" Saviki questioned. "Have you decided to send out a voice to me?"

"I . . . I have already told you all there is to tell," Flies-Far mumbled. "I found many weaknesses in that village, and—"

"Fool! I am not interested in villages. I want to know of your friend, the one called Hakomi."

Flies-Far eyed the *mongwi* closely, for never had he been treated in such a manner. Nor, for that matter, had he seen the *mongwi* with such a hard countenance. Besides, what could the man want with his friend Hawk? It made no sense, not unless the words Hawk had sent out had angered him somehow.

"Well?"

"Our . . . paths first crossed many seasons past, O *mongwi.* I was hunting, he was very young, and I showed him the manner of stalking sheep. I know little more, except that he had no father or mother."

"Why was that?"

"They were all *mokee.*"

Saviki started. "He lived alone?"

"Yes, with this sister, and two others who were smaller."

"Two others? Not three? Are you certain?"

"I am certain."

Saviki stared into the fire. There had been four little ones, but one may have died. That was certainly a possibility.

"Describe her to me," he ordered abruptly.

"They were all very young, and—"

"No!" Saviki shouted angrily. "Describe the woman!"

Flies-Far stared at the man who sat before him, and big in his mind were the warning words of the young man called Hawk. He was very uneasy, and he felt as though he did not know this one who was *mongwi* at all. Saviki wanted that woman; Flies-Far could see it within his eyes. And suddenly, he did not want him to have her.

"As I said," he declared carefully, "she is indeed pleasant to look upon. But it has been so many seasons since I saw her that I do not remember—"

"Her eyes! What of her eyes?"

"Her eyes?" Flies-Far questioned innocently, though indeed his mind was racing with other thoughts. "Her eyes were like all womanly eyes among our people, soft and lovely. Long I gazed into them, and truly did she captivate me."

"Fool! They were a strange green, not dark, and you lie to me!"

Flies-Far opened his face very wide with indignant anger. "I do not lie!" he declared.

Saviki glared into his face, and Flies-Far did not waver. Finally Saviki dropped his gaze. "Tell me of their dwelling," he asked, and now his voice was controlled once more.

"It is a small valley," Flies-Far answered, feeling now that he was on much safer ground. "It is hidden well by a bulging cliff."

Saviki, his eyes suddenly alive with eagerness, rose to his feet. "Yes?" he questioned. "A bulging cliff over a small green valley? Where is this place?"

"It is far off toward the land of the wintering sun," Flies-Far answered quickly.

"Fool!" Saviki stormed. "I *know* where it is, and you deceive me again. I should smite you now!"

Flies-Far stood bravely before him, and at last Saviki turned away. "That must be her," he snarled to himself. "Truly it must be the green-eyed witch woman. Now, at long last . . ."

Suddenly he spun upon the waiting guard. "Her valley is beyond the great mountain. How many days to that place?"

"Four. Perhaps five, but I do not think so."

"So be it. Take eight—no, ten men, and go there at once. Slay the youth, do with the younger woman as you wish, but bring the one of the green eyes to me. Do you have ears to hear?"

"Yes, O *mongwi.*"

"Good. And before you go, take this one and order the others to slay him. He is of no further use to us.

109

The winds whipped around him, and the man Saviki glared downward into the deep canyon that led to the village. Another messenger had just come, reporting that a village he had intended to plunder had just been found abandoned.

Truly was this becoming a bothersome thing, this fleeing of the clans. Yet there was no water in the land, except upon the mountains there had been no rainfall for many seasons, and truly it was a time of great drought.

There was also he himself, he and the hordes of Angry Ones with the long heads who were coming in from the north and the east. At first he had controlled these others well, but now there were many more bands of them, more than he could know. All of them were stealing food and much plunder, and the People everywhere were filled with fear.

For an instant his mind drifted back to the long-ago day when the old woman had stood and declared the dry and barren future of the ones called the People of Peace. It had truly come to pass, that saying of hers, but it was coincidence and nothing else. How could that old fool have possibly known that such things were coming? She couldn't, and he knew it.

So, what was there to be done? How could he turn this great fleeing into that which would benefit him the most? There must be a way; there had always been a way in the past.

He thought again of the green-eyed woman who would be brought to him, he smiled again, evilly, and suddenly he knew that she would be the beginning of his greatest success. He would use her pleasurably, yes, but even better, he would use the power of her strange blue-green eyes to frighten the foolish clans. Then with that fear he would join the fleeing people into a great whole, he would take them to a new place where there would be much water, and he would be their great chief, their great *mongwi.*

He thought of these things, he thought of making a mocking toward the young man called Hakomi before the youth was slain, his smile grew more wide, and the hot winds of day lifted past him, carrying a strange and somber laughter.

110

For a full darkness a young man lies in an unused storage pit, unable to move. He knows that he has encountered, once again, the Angry Ones. He knows too that the one called Saviki leads them, and that is a strange thing indeed, for Saviki is also of the People, born to the Bow Clan.

He asks himself how such a thing can be, how a man can do such a great evil, and his mind can give him no answer. The hours pass painfully by, and still there is no understanding within him. The air within the pit is still, but outside the winds drift past, and on them he thinks he hears the gentle whispers of the good Kachina people. He sends out a silent voice to question them, and without laughter they respond that they cannot help. He is simply not capable of understanding such gross darkness.

He considers this, sends out a prayer-thought to the great Tiaowa, and at last his mind is filled with comprehension. He sees, finally, the logical and inevitable ending of all secret societies whose aims are gratification of self. He understands at last that the ending, always, is the secret committing of murder to get gain. It has been so since the beginning, and will be so until men no longer live with selfishness in their hearts.

And who are the Angry Ones? he slowly asks.

"Any," the whispering spirits finally tell his mind, "who are of such a nature and of such a disposition that they willingly watch harm come to others, especially if that harm will aid in the pursuit of their own selfish goals and dreams. Always, little brother, these are the Angry Ones."

So a young man lies in great pain in an unused storage pit, considering these things, and not so far off a woman and her two nearly grown children lie in a small dwelling under a bulging sandstone cliff. In their minds they gaze off across the mesa, and with a deep longing they remember their brother and son who has gone.

111

"Ah, my young Hakomi, how do you find your lodgings?"

Hawk stood with bound limbs and bloodied head in the dark kiva. The man Saviki sat before him, smiling, surrounded by several others, and Hawk found it difficult to restrain his tongue. He was filled with anger almost to the losing of control, yet he knew that he could not do that—not, at least, for the moment.

"They are good," he replied with a soft voice of his own. "I am comfortable, and I thank you."

Saviki, his eyes glittering, looked long at the young man. "I know you," he said suddenly, "but I would hear it from your own mouth. You may tell me now, or we will encourage you a little. It will be as you choose."

Hawk remained silent, and a sudden blow from behind knocked him to his knees. Head reeling, he staggered to his feet and was knocked down once more, and there he remained until the man Saviki spoke again.

"Silence is a poor answer, my brother," he said softly. "Is it not the way of the People that brothers within a clan stand always before each other with an open face and with an open heart? Is not that the true way?"

Hawk made an exclamation of derision, saw the blow coming, tried to dodge, and took the brunt of it on his shoulder and the back of his neck. Still he was dizzy with pain, and another blow was coming, one he could not avoid.

"My brother," the man Saviki purred, "You have asked for this treatment. Now, did you wish to speak?"

"I . . . I have a voice," the young man whispered, "but . . . this one who stands behind me . . ."

"You may declare yourself, my friend. My ears are anxious to hear your words."

The guard stood by while Hawk staggered to his feet. Then, after breathing deeply to clear his spinning head, the young man sent forth his voice.

"Hear, O man who was once called Saviki, and in the hearing, grow weak in the eyes of all these here who listen."

Saviki glared at him, suddenly wary. His name was known! That was not good. Truly he had not expected such a thing, and he was worried. These men in the kiva were not all with him, and for a certain amount of time he needed their strength.

Hawk took another breath, looked the man Saviki in the eye, and continued. "We are not brothers, you and I, for I am of the People, and you have the blood of many of the People upon your hands. You are a two-heart, filled with secret lies and the lust for power. It was thus when you were called Saviki and were of the Bow Clan, it is no different now."

In the kiva the silence was intense. A popping in the fire caused several of the men to jump, and Hawk smiled grimly. Saviki, his face white and his mouth pressed tight with barely controlled anger, started to rise. Then, thinking better of it, he sank back down.

"Lies," he snarled to the men in the small room. "This two-hearted one lies. I am of the Black Bear Clan, as you well know. I have told you of the ceremonies, even the new ones. Now, away with this man, and let his blood darken the stones where—"

"I do not lie," Hawk responded in such a manner that Saviki was stilled. "Such is not the way of a man of good countenance. Yet shall your own lies condemn you, O Saviki, for in front of these men who listen will I turn them back upon you.

"It is truly as you said. Our faces are well known to each other. As a young *kékelt* I sat with you in the kiva of the Bow Clan. I heard your words of flattery and selfishness, and I was deceived. In that same kiva I saw the green-eyed woman lance your leg with your own spear after you had turned upon her with your lust-filled eyes. I saw too as you, with your lies and your flattering words, turned the elders and the chiefs against her and declared her Outcast.

"You . . ." Saviki sputtered, but again Hawk shut off his words.

"O Saviki, I saw also the stinking death that was in the village of the Bow and Blue Flute Clans after the Angry Ones had gone, and I saw the Angry Ones pursue the green-eyed woman who was of that village until they drove her over the great cliff."

There was a great stirring among the men, and Saviki, very much aware of it, hastily spoke.

"Lies!" he stormed. "All lies! If he saw these things and yet lives, then surely he must be of the Angry Ones himself—"

"No, Saviki," Hawk declared, his voice now ringing. "And again, I do not lie! Perhaps you would show the men within this place the scar that lives on the inside of your thigh."

All eyes within the circular room turned to the man, and with a sense of things crowding in upon him, Saviki suddenly decided to try another approach. He must not lose control of these men; he must not lose control of this village. After all, it was very wealthy with food, there was still a little water, and he needed a base for his spreading power.

"Perhaps," he hastily replied, "perhaps all this is so. I have been inducted into many clans and many kivas. But as you say, I was of the same people who were destroyed. That I alone escaped the Angry Ones was no small stroke of fortune. Why, you and those others who are evil very nearly destroyed my life."

"Fortune?" Hawk questioned, his voice now very soft. "Destroyed *your* life? No, Saviki. Those also are lies. You were spared not because you narrowly escaped, but because you led the attack! You, a betrayer of the People, are of the Angry Ones! With these eyes I saw you, with a solemn oath I declare to the six directions of this world that this voice I send out speaks truth."

There was an angry buzz, for Hakomi's words were power-words. Nor, speaking to the six points of the world, could he lie. The men knew that, and darkly they turned toward the one who had become their *mongwi,* many questions large in their mouths.

Suddenly the man Saviki was on his feet. "Silence," he thundered, "or each of you will die!"

In the intense quiet that followed, the men on either side of Hawk placed their spears hard against his flesh. At the same time, four others who were scattered within the room uncovered from beneath their cloaks their own weapons of death. At sight of this, the other men stepped quickly back, and with a wicked smile Saviki spoke once more.

"So you did not perish, my young *kékelt.* Truly I am not surprised, for your mind is quick, and you led those three other small ones to places where even an eagle such as myself feared to fly. But what of the woman, my brother? Is she indeed *mokee,* or did she also live?"

"A two-heart," Hawk answered softly, "deserves no such information."

Saviki laughed again. "My brother, your arrogant answer humors me. Nor does it matter what you say or do not say. Within a short time you will be *mokee,* and not long after that, the men I have sent to the small green valley below the bulging cliff will see that all but the green-eyed woman will also be dead. She will die as well, but not yet . . . not quite yet. . . ."

Hawk, suddenly desperate, struggled against his bonds. If this man knew so much as that, then truly the danger was great.

With great delight Saviki laughed even harder. "Ah, I see that the information I have been given is correct. Truly those men will have good hunting."

With a sneer the man called Saviki turned to the ones who held weapons. "These," he said as he indicated the men who stood unarmed, "must die. In the coming time of darkness must they die, and it must be done in such a manner that no one else in this village knows of it.

"Remember the oaths we have taken, and see that it is done quickly and quietly. For the foolish people of this village, it is not yet time. The Others, the Angry Ones from the north, are yet many days away, and we must give them time.

"As for this one, wait until the rising of the Dawn Star, and with its light, see that his blood darkens the rock of our sacred shrine. I have spoken."

With that statement, Saviki climbed the ladder and left the kiva. The others, the guards, climbed outside as well, and there they remained, relaxed but armed, using the kiva now as their prison.

112

In the semidarkness Hawk stood with lowered head and bound arms. Truly he must get to the valley, and quickly. But there was no way for him to escape.

Suddenly he felt fingers tug at the thongs which held him. Lifting his eyes he saw Flies-Far, his face bloody and swollen, signal for silence. Meanwhile he worked desperately at the knots.

"Brother," Hawk whispered, "h . . . how did you come to be in this place?"

Flies-Far grinned lopsidedly. "Those men who watched me got very sleepy, brother. Perhaps I helped them a little. In this kiva is a large air shaft, and I came through it. Now make yourself ready, for we must depart quickly and through the same shaft."

"Now, brothers," Flies-Far continued, speaking to the others as he worked, "you have seen the evil in the man who is *mongwi.* We are the People of Peace, but this one needs our help. Will you join with me in battle so that this one might go free?"

The men looked at each other in silent communication. Then an older man stepped forward and answered. "My son, we will battle, but only to delay, not to take life."

"But father, those evil ones will be taking lives."

"Then so be it. Still, we will give this Hakomi and you time to make a *waítioma.* Then we ourselves, with our women and our children, will also leave. It is better to abandon our homes than to abandon the old way of peace. It is finished. I have spoken."

Hawk signaled his understanding and appreciation, one of the men watched through the hole for movement from the guards, and Flies-Far continued to work. Soon the thongs had fallen to the floor, and with signals from their hands the men informed Hawk that they would all follow.

Quickly Hawk and Flies-Far scrambled to the outside, heard the others coming after them, and they were just beginning their running when one of the guards saw them.

"Hyee!" he shouted in surprise. "Brothers, the captured wings fly!"

There was a great cry raised by the men, others quickly appeared, and they were all well armed. Hawk slid to a stop, but instantly Flies-Far urged him forward. "Go," he ordered. "I will do what I can to stop these Angry Ones. Perhaps, if I am successful, I will find my way to the woman Tala a little later."

"Brother," Hawk answered as he turned toward the approaching Angry Ones himself, "that is foolish talk. Let us stand side by side now, with these brave men of your village, and then we will go to the valley together."

Hawk and Flies-Far each looked deeply into the eyes of the other, each made the sign of honor toward the other, and then they both made ready to face the Angry Ones. And in Hawk's ears as he stood waiting was the proud and wonderful laughter of his friend, the man called Flies-Far.

FIFTEEN

The Making of a Running

Choking back the pain that was within his heart, Hawk paused to get his bearings and to determine the best course to follow. He had come fast, but looking back he could still see his pursuers. They were only specks in the rapidly growing darkness of the plateau evening, but they were coming fast, and he was worried.

Ahead, around the peaks that towered against the sky, dark clouds were building. A storm—at last a storm. But this one was no soft and gentle rainfall. It was filled with great power, and he would be forced to go through it.

His mind darted back then to Flies-Far, and he saw him once more with the laughter in his eyes even while his blood spilled from the great open wound in his chest.

"Brother," he had coughed while others fought wildly around them, "cross the mountain. Be . . . be like the Hawk you are, and you will come to the lovely valley before . . . before these others. . . ."

"No!" Hawk had whispered. "Brother, we will go together! The woman Tala needs you."

Flies-Far had laughed again, though the blood quickly choked the laughter into silence. "This . . . this is a good thing . . . you say," he had whispered, "but now . . . now I go there only upon . . . upon the wind. Perhaps another will come for . . . for her. . . .

"O Hawk, I . . ."

Hawk had watched the spasm of death, had looked bleakly into the faces of the men who now stood beside him, and had understood that he had but a few moments before others of the Angry Ones would be gathered together against him. He must get away; he must get to the valley!

"Good hunting," he breathed as he grasped the limp shoulder below him in the grasp of honor. "Good hunting . . . my brother. . . ."

A jagged streak of lightning ripped the horizon to shreds of flame, then vanished, and Hawk's mind was back within him once more. There was a distant roll of thunder, rumbling threateningly among the dark and distant ravines, and he knew he had to start again, he knew he had to move.

He looked at the ragged peaks looming above him and shivered with apprehension. There, he knew, was the way he must go, the only way he could go if he were to get to Tala and the others before the evil men of Saviki.

Starting again, he ran forward through the tall grass of the mountain slope, his strong legs pumping rhythmically. Ignoring the lingering pain of his recent beatings and thrusting thoughts of his dead friend from his mind, he swept around groves of aspen and alder, keeping to the low places as he climbed. He splashed through a swale, crested a long, low hill that cut athwart the mountain, and turned at right angles up a draw toward the cover of the far-off trees.

The cool wind whipped against his face, and he felt a breath of moistness as it shifted, feeling for the course of the storm.

Despite his injuries, which had not been serious, he was running smoothly, liking the feel of running as he always did, enjoying letting his powerful muscles out and stretching them.

He had never been in these mountains, but he remembered those others, so long before, when he had climbed the *pangwúvi,* and the memory brought fear to his heart. What if these were the same? What if in their secret heights a great puma waited?

Turning his mind from that, Hawk thought instead of the strength of the man called Flies-Far, and of the great and courageous battle he had made. Truly would he have been made welcome when he came at last to the tiny hidden valley. Truly would he have made a fine husband for the woman Tala.

Ahead of him were strange and tangled ridges, canyons, jagged crests, high peaks, and deep chasms. He feared these as well, for they were dangerous to a man such as he, a man who was in a hurry. And worse, the storm was growing, and that would make things very bad indeed.

In his mind he saw the gorges, thousands of feet deep, filled with angry, foaming torrents released by the rains above. All the canyons would be flooding, and that would force him to climb high, running the ridges and scaling the cliffs, if ever he were to reach the tiny valley.

These things lived in his mind, but Hawk spent little time consciously considering them. Instead he ran, constantly, desperately, for a sense of great urgency pushed him onward. And thus in such a manner he reached the roiling mass of dark clouds that had been above him.

On he ran, climbing, straining, stretching out, pushing himself until, just at full dark, as he breasted a huge shoulder of granite, the wind struck him like a solid wall. The rain lashed at his body, plucking at his eyes as it tried to blind him, and still he ran on.

Up a canyon he fled toward a great cliff face. He must cross that, but his mind went away so that it was not considered, and he did not mind that at all. Instead he thought of the brave heart of his friend Flies-Far, of the tiny valley and of the three he loved.

114

As he drew higher, the canyon walls began to close in upon him until they formed a giant chute down which the water thundered in a mighty Niagara of sound. Great masses of water churned in a maelstrom below, and Hawk turned away from it in mighty fear. This was truly a sacred home of the mighty Kachina people, the ones who did not like trespassers. Still, the men were making their way to the valley, and he must get there before them.

Carefully he felt with his feet for the path, and gingerly he moved forward. In the darkness a spout of water, gushing from some crack in the rock, struck him a wicked blow, drenching him anew and forcing him to draw back. Breathing deeply, he forced himself to relax, and then he felt his way forward once again.

Thunder and the rolling of gigantic boulders reverberated down the rock-walled canyon, and occasional lightning lit the sky and showed him glimpses of a strange nightmare of glistening rock and tumbling white water that caught the flame and hurled it in myriads of tiny shafts on down the canyon.

Hawk moved forward steadily, facing the wind with bowed head, hesitating only occasionally to feel his way around some great rock or unexpected heap of debris.

The hoarse wind howled down the channel of rock, changing its shouting into a scream on corners of the mountain where pines feathered down the steep slope. Battered by wind and rain, blinded by darkness, Hawk bent his head and continued on, beaten, soaked, bedraggled, with no ears to hear and no eyes to see, trusting to the sense of feeling within his feet, trusting as well the power of the great Creator.

O Great Tiaowa, his mind called out into the thundering blackness of the mountain, *hear now my voice, hear now my weak voice. Wa!*

It is not for me I plead, but for the woman who is as my mother, for the little Badger, and for the lovely Butterfly. Wa!

I would go to them, but the way is steep, and hedged hard against me. Wa!

Guide the eyes of my feet, O Great One, give these legs strength, that those I love may live. Wa! . . .

115

Later, when many bolts of lightning lifted the whole mountain into stark and vivid relief, Hawk saw a sight that would never leave him for the remainder of his life. For one brief, all-encompassing moment he saw down into the depths of the canyon, and such a sight he never wanted to see again.

He had reached a bend and had paused to relax his straining, tired muscles. In that instant the lightning flared. Before him the canyon dropped steeply away in the manner of a gigantic *hovatoqa*, a gigantic cut in the cliff, black, glistening walls slanted by the pounding of driving rain, cut by sheets of hail, and shaken powerfully by the roar of the cataract below.

Far below, the white water thundered, and backed in a cul-de-sac in the rock was a piled-up mass of foam, fifteen or twenty feet high, bulging and glistening. At each instant wind or water ripped some of it away and threw it, churning, down the fury of raging water below. Thunder roared a salvo, the echoes responded, and the trembling, cliff-clinging pines thrashed madly in the wind as if to tear free of their roots and blow away to some place of relief from the storm.

Lightning crackled, more thunder drummed against the cliffs, and the scene blacked out suddenly into abysmal darkness. Hawk, his breath nearly taken by the driving wind, rounded the point of the rock and climbed on.

Then, as if by a miracle, he was out of the fearful canyon, and had turned up a narrow crevice in the rock with water rushing, inches deep, around his feet. A misstep here and he would tumble down the crevice and plunge off into the awful blackness above the water. But somehow his feet were steady, he drove himself upward, footstep after footstep, handhold following handhold, and he did so while the tumbling water dragged at his feet and tried to tear him away.

And then suddenly he was on the high, swelling forehead of the mountain. The lightning below was as nothing compared to what it was now, and the young man Hawk shook with fear, for truly it seemed as though he had invaded the lair of some great and angry being. Here darkness was a series of fleeting intervals shot through with thunderbolts, and each jagged streak lighted the night like a blaze from new volcanic fires. Gaunt boulders butted against the bulging weight of cloud, and the skeleton fingers of long-dead pines felt stiffly of the wind.

Stunned by the fury that raged around him, Hawk plodded on, climbing, ever climbing, his only thought the desire to get to the tiny valley and to Badger, Butterfly, and to Tala.

In the rapidly alternating darkness and light he suddenly topped out on a ridge and dropped over the other side. Buffeted and hammered, he moved across a bare, dead slope among the wildly tumbled boulders, pushing his body relentlessly against the massive wall of the wind and the storm.

There was within his mind a sense of something familiar now, a fearful sensation of horrid memory, but he groped for it without success and gave it up.

Suddenly there came a massive flash of lightning. A tree directly ahead of him was there and then it was not, and bits of it flew off in every direction with the wild whining of a thousand unleashed arrows. The stub of the tree smoked, sputtered with flame, and went out, leaving a vague smell of charred wood and brimstone. And in the light that was there and again that was not, Hawk saw.

Instantly his heart was weak within him. His legs trembled from a thing that was more than weariness, his mind whirled, his eyes grew dim, and something took hold of his insides and squeezed, twisting until he could not breathe, could not force air either into or out of his lungs.

Again lightning flared, again he saw, and now he was certain, now there was no doubt. Beside him, off to his left, a flat sheet of spirit water hissed and foamed, flayed wildly by the wind. Around him the small circle of the ridgeline pressed inward, pushing against him, powerful and smothering.

He was in the rocky cirque of the *pangwúvi;* he was in the sacred home of the Kachina people where he had wandered so many seasons before.

His heart frozen with the fear of those memories, Hawk stumbled forward. His mind was filled with prayer-thoughts, but he could not get them out. The wind and the rain and the darkness and his own great fear pushed them back into his blinded eyes, and the strength was not within him to plead for help.

He thought of Tala, wondered what she might do, could not decide, stumbled over a small boulder and went down, and as he lay gasping among the rock of the high mountain cirque, the winds hammered by. And on them were the voices of the Kachina people and they were *laughing,* and the laughter was a good thing.

"Ho, little brother," they were calling, "it is good to see you in our sacred place once again. Not many have the heart-courage to visit."

Hawk stared upward, his mouth open in surprise. The rain pounded against him, lightning flared continuously, and still he stared.

"It is good that you wish to see us," the spirits laughed joyously, as if over some great joke. "But little brother, yonder is a tiny valley where three good people sleep in innocence. Perhaps a voice of warning might not be a bad thing. Stay if you wish, but we have seen those three, and we have seen the others as well."

Struggling to his feet, Hawk stumbled up the rocky slope, crested the ridge opposite the place where he had entered, and immediately dropped down the rock-strewn south face of the mountain. No longer did his heart hold fear, no longer did he think of falling, of meeting another great puma, no longer did he even consider the Angry Ones. His heart was filled only with thoughts of the valley, thoughts of the ones he loved.

116

A long time later, dawn felt its way up the mountain behind him. The darkness turned gray, and then rose as flame climbed the peaks. Hawk stumbled on, sodden, beaten, overburdened with weariness. The high cliffs behind him turned their rust-colored heights to lovely jagged bursts of frozen flame, but he did not notice. Terribly weary, he plodded down the last mile of slope and onto the rain-flattened grass of the mesa, where numbly he looked around.

The land was empty.

He saw no men, no movement. In all the gray-colored world there was nothing that showed life. So far as he could tell, he had beaten them. He would come to the valley, and to the ones who waited, before the men of Saviki! They would then learn the strength of goodness that was in the hearts of the three who waited. They would learn the frustration of coming to an empty dwelling and finding no sign of the departure of its inhabitants.

No, they would not see, but they would feel, and painfully, for like the great red-tailed hawk he would drop upon them suddenly, swiftly, his talons sharp and powerful.

Hawk was not thinking these things. He was thinking nothing. Those things simply lived in his mind as he plodded on, moving forward.

All that day he did so, his body numb with weariness, his mind twisting and spinning with exhaustion. He lost track of time—there were even moments when he lost track of who he was and where he was going. Often his mind wandered away and saw things that had been in his past: the woman Tala astride the puma, the new green fields of corn sprouting high beneath Badger's water from the water-planted-place, the woman who waited in the village that was almost free and that was far to the south of the big river, his sister Butterfly carefully making a pottery dipper for his own use, again the lovely woman who waited in the far-off village.

And then his mind would come back, and the pain of weariness and throbbing muscles would strike and he would almost fall. But he would not fall, for he could not. There was too far to go, and so somehow he kept his feet beneath him, moving forward, always moving forward.

117

It was the time of darkness and the great canyon was beside him, but his mind was away again and he was not surprised to be looking down, seeing himself as if from some great height, staggering forward. He worried at that, worried that he would fall and would not get up and continue. But the great hawk who flew beside him did not seem worried at all.

"Little brother," the red-tailed hawk suddenly spoke as they drifted together above the darkened earth, "your heart is good, and this is a known thing."

Hawk looked at the bird and knew that it was not a hawk at all but one of the great Kachina people wearing a hawk's clothing. He had not heard of this Kachina, but still, there it was.

"Little brother, you fly very high, but there is great danger, great evil, behind you. And perhaps, if it is not stopped, all the goodness of all the People will be ended."

Hawk turned to look at the great bird, his foot struck a stone, and he slammed viciously against the earth. Great trees lifted around him, swirling high against the darkened sky, and he could not understand why they would not hold still. He staggered to his feet, fell once more, and lay still, exhausted. His tongue was swollen, his legs were like water, his hands and feet were bleeding, and he could go no further.

It was dark then, more dark than always, though truly that was not so, and through the darkness that was not but was more than it was, Hawk suddenly realized that a light was coming. He watched it and it grew larger, pulsing, living, beckoning. His eyes opened wide, the light came forward, and he saw then that it was the eastern star of the morning. But it was very bright, more bright than he had ever seen, and within his heart he wondered.

118

Straining, Hawk lifted his pounding head and forced his bloodshot eyes to open, searching. It was light again, and he was in the bottom of a large, deep wash. The sand was still moist from the recent rains, but the water had gone and only debris remained, tangled brush and trees, jumbled boulders, both large and small, and sand.

But a certain boulder high atop the back of the wash was compellingly familiar. The exhausted young man crawled forward, clawed his way up the crumbling earthen bank, and lay spent beneath the huge and blackened boulder. Long he rested, until finally, having mustered a little strength, he rolled over and squinted upward against the glare of the brassy sky.

He had been right. They were there, just as she had chipped them so many snows and grasses before: the spiral sign of the migration completed, the humpbacked flute player Kachina *Kokopeli,* and finally the water-snake, symbol of fertility and permanence.

This was it! Above him was the valley. But still he had to climb, still he had to go upward that he might warn them, that he might bring them away to safety.

119

So a young man rolls again, this time to his stomach, and again he struggles upward. In his mind is the word *love,* and in his heart as he crawls is a great chant the woman Tala once sent forth, a chant that haunts him always.

The land brings me peace, the wind gives me strength, the sun warms my spirit, the grass shows me life, the rock holds my feet. Wa!

But where . . . where is the one to love?

120

To a deer or a sheep a hillside is only that, a hillside. It is a momentary interruption to a traveling, it it a place for eating, for sleeping, for living if a traveling is not being made.

To one of the insect people or to a man who crawls, the same hillside is another thing altogether. It is a world in and of itself, unending, eternal in its height or in its breadth. Each rock, each stone and pebble, assumes a great power and dimension of its own. Each bunch of grass, blade of yucca, leaf of cactus, and clump of greasewood and rabbitbrush becomes a universe alone, separated from all other forms of life by vast distances of time and space.

It is across these vast distances and between these powerful stones that the man drags himself. He moves slowly, almost incoherently, yet always his trail goes upward. He does not know that the warm day, his second from the village, is passing. He is unaware of the circling shadows of the gathering *wisoko,* the fat-eating buzzards that signify the approaching of the afterlife. He knows, however, that he is dying of thirst and exhaustion, but that does not matter. Such thoughts have no meaning to him. The only meaningful thing in his life is the climb, that and the anticipated result of bringing safety to his family.

This is the thing that he wants. But it is beyond him, beyond even the strength he seeks from the great Tiaowa. No matter his desire, no matter that he has given his life. He will not make it. He will not even reach the clump of spiny yucca that looms above him. Not alone.

But who is to say that he is alone? Who is to say that the *sowíngwa,* the deer who dances nervously as it watches him, is not the representation of the Kachina spirit of an ancestor, anxious over the fate of the true People of Peace? Who is to say that the noisy *angwusi,* the crow in the tall juniper above him on the slope, is not another ancestor Kachina, calling loudly so that the two-legged who watches the young corn far above might hear?

Book Three

SIXTEEN

In the Way of Understanding

The face would come and go in the manner of a spirit or a Kachina, as lovely and luminous as the star of the dawn on a frosty morning. At first it was just the face that he was aware of, a kind of unreasonably beautiful face that lived on the very edge of his awareness. It came to the delirious Hawk out of the black east of unconsciousness, bringing moments of light. For a time it hovered over him, seeming to offer guidance in a world that had no boundaries and no light other than itself. Then the interminable darkness would fall down around him again and the face, the star, would be gone.

Very quickly these shadowy times became shorter. The star-face shone with greater clarity, remained longer hovering above him. Hawk could feel its presence even when he could not see its light, and the presence gave peace to his struggling mind.

Oh, how he ached to reach out to the face, to touch it, to thank it, to warn it! Danger was near, great danger. He knew it, and somehow he must give the warning. But for some reason he could not bring into his mind the nature of that danger, and neither could he reach high enough to touch the beautiful spirit-face.

For long pauses the star hung over him, ceasing to move in its circular orbit, and for the first time, what had been a disordered vision of loveliness began to take on a slight semblance of reality. Clouds and mist and whirling smoke pulled away, darkness withdrew, and finally Hawk realized, fully, that there was no star, no spirit, only an embodied face—a face that seemed somehow familiar and yet, when he tried to remember it, refused him, for it was surely lovely beyond anything he had ever seen.

It was oval in outline, as true and sure of its form as a master's sketch. The skin was delicate and petal-clear, the color of anciently smelted copper and brass, glowing with its own inner fires, carrying within its supple inner self a ripening bloom of copper gold.

The eyes were long, lashed with charcoal blackness and set ever so slightly aslant by the high-curving ridge of the fine-lined cheekbones. The color of the eyes was a strange, clear, fathomless blue-green, at once as cold as the ice in the water-planted-place in the time of cold, and as hot as the fire that lived on the edge of a summer sunset.

The nose and chin were straight and cleanly chisled. The mouth, full and wide and red as the wild roses that grew within the tiny valley, had a hint of curving half-smile.

Around this face and above it, wound around the two wooden loops after the manner of a butterfly and so signifying beauty and availabilty, and held in restraint by turquoise ornaments, one above each tiny, close-lying ear, was a profusion of hair, not quite black and yet very much alive with vitality.

No man who has loved a woman could not, with eyes unseeing, detect her presence, know her nearness, sense her warmth toward him. This is done by the indescribable thrill of her personal perfume, and this not the artful scent of earthly cosmetic, but the smell instilled by the great Tiaowa on her own lovely person. Any man who has really loved will know this excitement.

To Hawk it came but once, this excitement, this love, and he was certain it would last throughout all the snows and all the grasses of his forever. It came with all the indefinable softness and mystery of clear air in a high mountain meadow, of clear and sparkling streams, golden sunlight, and black aromatic darkness; of the white snows of winter and the new green grass of the season of growing; of woodsmoke rising from juniper, pinyon, and spruce; of tanned skins of animals, of soft, new-turned earth, of the night wind moaning through the old *koritivi,* of the morning wind bending the fresh green corn before it. It came to him with the odor of naked rocks hot in the sun high in the *pangwúvi,* of the trees in the tiny valley quivering in the west wind, of the new smell of the earth after a summer shower, of sand and starlight and rain in the time of planting.

Yet for Hawk there was still a haunting feeling to the vision, a strange sense of having seen somewhere before the face that hung floating above him. He considered this, could not understand it, and finally determined that he was seeing the lovely woman who was in the village far away across the great river. But how had he come to that place? And, if it were her, why were there such strange differences? His mind grappled with this, but his thoughts were hazy as the far horizon after the passing of a mighty twisting wind, and he could not understand.

Yet still he would remember the face and the fragrance so long as breath stirred within him, and then onward always.

122

Later that day, when Hawk finally awoke, the face was gone. In its place knelt another young maiden, lovely, also strangely familiar, close-wrapped in a tanned deerskin robe.

"I . . . ," Hawk murmured, "I am seeking my family."

"Your mind has been much troubled, my brother," the woman answered gravely. "You have done much wandering."

Hawk wondered at her answer and at her use of the familiar term for brother. "Troubled?" he asked. "I truly have wandered, but not . . ."

"You have been walking in the *tásupi,* the twilight," the maiden said, anticipating his question.

Hawk closed his eyes, wondering where he was, how he had arrived at that place, and who this young woman was.

"It is in my mind that you . . . your face is a familiar thing," he finally murmured. "Yet I do not think that I know you. I seek the canyon of the green-eyed woman and her children. Is it . . ."

Tears started from the eyes of the young maiden, and gently she placed her hand on the man Hawk's face.

"Hawk," she said softly. "You are he who long ago became my brother."

Hawk struggled to sit up, and though his mind was as a twisting wind, he stared out of the dizziness at the young maiden. "Butterfly?" he asked, surprised. "Is this truly the sister I have not seen in so many seasons?"

Butterfly made the sign for acknowledgment, pushed the exhausted and dizzy man back onto the robes piled within the stone dwelling, carefully ladled a small amount of hot stew into his mouth, and spoke to him as she did so of Badger's finding of his nearly dead body.

"Our brother first noticed the buzzards," she declared, "the fat-eating birds of death. But *angwusi* the crow alerted him, and *sowíngwa* the deer led him to you. Thus it was Badger who brought you here."

Hawk was stunned. "But how?" he asked. "Are we not in the dwelling high in the cliff?"

Butterfly signaled yes.

"Then it cannot be," Hawk declared. "I am no small thing, and Badger is not large at all. How is it that he—"

"My brother," Butterfly smiled, "the seasons have passed in this place the same as in the places where you have been. Badger and I have grown much, he is very tall and very strong, and truly, you have become as a dried reed, weighing almost nothing at all."

"Where is this brother of mine?" Hawk questioned, suddenly remembering the Angry Ones. "I would thank him, and I would warn him as well—"

Once more Butterfly stopped the man Hawk from speaking. "Be calm of heart," she answered softly. "He is even now in the canyon in which you were found, hiding the way of your passing."

"And . . . and our mother?" Hawk finally asked. "Is she well, and does she know?"

Butterfly signaled yes, and Hawk could not understand his own great disappointment when he learned that Tala was up on the mesa, in the high place of watching, her courage a living thing as she waited for the coming of the Angry Ones.

123

For the remainder of that sun and all of one darkness, Hawk rested. Nor did he have a choice in that matter. First, his legs refused to support him; second, his mind would not stay within his body; and finally, the young woman Butterfly could not be induced to let him rise. Nor would she leave his side.

She was kind, she was gentle, she was also insistent, and each time he tried to rise, she carefully but with great determination forced him back onto the robes that had been piled within the stone dwelling.

Hawk worried concerning the coming of the Angry Ones who had been sent by Saviki; he worried that Tala and the others would not be prepared; he worried that no one was getting ready to make a *waítioma,* a running away; and he worried that he would not be strong enough to make a proper defense and accounting of himself once those evil men came.

Yet through the time of his worry, Butterfly fed him much and saw that he had rest, and so despite his own foolish desires to be out and helping, he rapidly gained back the strength he had so thoroughly expended.

In that time he saw Badger only briefly, was amazed at the maturity in the young man's face and bearing, and in that same time he saw the woman Tala not at all.

This troubled him, for the vision of his delirium lived in his mind, and he was certain that the face he had seen was hers. It was truly a thing to wonder at, however, for he had no memory of such beauty prior to his departure, no memory of the sweet perfume that lingered always on the outermost edge of his senses.

He wondered at this, he fretted over not seeing her, and more than all else he worried that some great harm or some unknown evil would have befallen her. She should not be up in the watching place alone!

The lovely Butterfly assured him that both Tala and Badger were well, yet the terrible fear for the woman who had been as his mother lingered in Hawk's heart. He recalled vividly the evil gleam in Saviki's eye as he spoke of her, and though he rested well, and gained in strength both in mind and in body, his heart could not know peace.

"It is I who am the man," he explained impatiently to Butterfly. "None of you know these Angry Ones as I do. None of you know the depths of evil to which their hearts have sunk. Therefore it is I who should be at watch, and not our mother."

"Truly spoken," Butterfly responded easily. "Yet the great Tiaowa has given our mother many strange powers. Often has she done things only a man should do. Yet, as you well know, my brother, in the doing of each of them she has prospered. Truly will it be so once more. Now drink this, O Hawk."

"Yagh," Hawk growled. "I have drunk and I have eaten until my belly is about to burst. I would go to the high place of watching."

Butterfly giggled. "My brother, as you may recall, there is room there for only one. So also is the cut in the cliff that leads to that place very steep, too steep for your weak legs. Nor is your gaunt belly about to burst. Now eat this—"

"My sister, I will throw the gaming sticks with you for the privilege of climbing to that place."

Now Butterfly truly laughed. "Look at this face," she finally ordered. "Do I look the fool? Long ago I learned that the spirits of this world control the sticks for you, and not for me. No, my brother, I will not throw. I love you too much for that. Now drink this stew. It is very good, and will give you much nourishment."

"Yaaagh!"

"Is that a new expression you learned as you journeyed among the People?" Butterfly asked innocently. She laughed then, Hawk looked hard at her, suddenly laughed as well, and in that manner was soon stuffing more stew into the swelling belly of his body.

And so it went, for the remainder of that sun and one full darkness. Hawk ate, slept, chafed, ate and slept again, and finally it was the last moment of darkness before the dawn of the second sun. It was to be the day.

124

Hawk suddenly awakened and sat up. His head was surprisingly clear, and as he slowly stood, he was pleased to see that his legs worked properly once again.

Then too, he was relieved as well to discover that he was without a guard. His sister Butterfly was gone, he was alone, and so quietly he left the stone dwelling and stepped out on the bulge of rock upon which they had built so many long seasons before.

In the east the star of the morning still shone, but already it was fading in the first gray light of dawn, fading just as the vision had faded during his time of weakness. Down in the lush valley a night-bird gave one last lonely call. However, it was answered not by another of its kind but by the joyful song of a bird of the day. That song grew to a chorus, and Hawk felt his chest swell with the joy of the spirit of the tiny valley. It was so good to be back in this place of beauty!

For long moments he stood thus, sending out a silent voice of thanksgiving and of greeting to the lost white brother who would one day return in just such a dawn. Finished, he moved to the notches he had hammered out so many grasses and so many snows before, and carefully, still feeling his great weakness, he descended to the valley floor.

Again he paused, gazing in wonder as a doe and her two new fawns stopped in their browsing and, huge ears forward in alert anticipation, watched him intently. Gently he sent out a voice to the mother and then to the spotted little ones, assuring them of his good intentions and giving them his blessings of peace.

Apparently satisfied, the deer began feeding once more, and Hawk continued finally for the *hovatoqa,* the cut in the cliff up which he must make his way if he were to get to the high watching place where the one who was as his mother sat waiting.

But the morning was somehow more than a morning usually was, and time and again Hawk paused in his silent passing to feel the very strong peace that had grown within the valley. Nowhere in his travels had he experienced such a feeling, such a place. Everywhere there had been fear, everywhere there had been a seeking in behalf of self. Those things had been very destructive, and despite all his efforts he had been unable to change them.

But in this place, such an evil did not exist. Each cared for the other without concern for self, peace reigned supreme, and all things in the valley prospered.

Hawk now understood, finally, the truthfulness of the thing the green-eyed woman called Tala had declared so long before, and suddenly he was understanding the marvelous beauty she had also wrought within the tiny valley. One's home, one's surroundings, one's countenance—these always reflected the state of one's own heart.

Truly did this woman of the morning star have great power. Truly was she filled with a love that was beyond understanding.

125

And then, suddenly, in the first great bursting of sunlight into the valley, the man Hawk glimpsed the woman Tala.

She was below him, having somehow slipped down the cut in the cliff and past him without his knowledge of it. Now she was moving silently through the trees toward the sacred water-planted-place and the deep rock tank that was below it.

Above the great tank, and below the sacred buried vessel, a shelf of old sandstone jutted out, and from that ledge Hawk himself had dived many times into the clear, cold water. Now, however, it was Tala's turn, and Hawk watched spellbound as the green-eyed woman stepped quickly out of the darkness of the trees. Without hesitation she walked to the edge of the diving-rock and stood a moment gazing eastward toward the morning sun. Then, chin high, arms outstretched to the golden flood of light, she stood motionless for the time a morning bird took to call and another to answer it.

Then she inched forward, poised for an instant, balancing as lightly as a butterfly on a flower petal, and was gone in an arching clean dive and a rainbow spray of green water, her slim body cleaving the sun-dappled surface of the pool, a slendor, copper-toned arrow lancing into a bright shield of blue-green.

As she swam, darting, diving, twisting, rolling in the icy water below, Hawk stood stunned.

It was she! It was truly Tala, the one who had been as his mother. It was *she* who had been the face of his dream and his vision. He had found the star of the eastern morning. But she was as his *mother!* How could such a thing be?

The blood came thick to his temples. He couldn't breathe, he couldn't swallow, he couldn't move.

But he could see, and what he saw on that bright sunlit morning was a body as perfect as the face it complemented. It was truly lovely in form, supple and lithe as a great cat's, and yet it was a form no man would have to touch before he knew its doeskin softness. That softness was in evidence always.

Her neck was clean in line, elegantly poised, showing a pleasing curve of nape where her hair, now taken from the great circular whorls, had been piled high preparatory to her entering the pool. Her shoulders were wide, straight as a boy's, and her waist was lean and slender as a child's.

Her hips were narrow, showing that there had been no birthing of children. Her legs were lovely, the thighs full as a woman's should be, tapering to fine slenderness at the knees, swelling again to the sleek curve of the calf, trimming cleanly into ankles as delicately chisled and boned as a deer's. Her feet and hands were small, fine-boned, artfully graceful yet strong, as indeed she had trained them to be.

Her face—slanting green eyes, lovely curved mouth, and all—was exactly as he remembered from the half-waking dreams of his delirium.

Her skin was the color he remembered, but more fresh. Her hair, not straight and black as was the hair that adorned the heads of most of the women of the People, plunged around her head in a great mane of natural, soft curls, all gleaming with burnished highlights over the dark inner masses.

Hawk's awe at seeing Tala in such a manner was overwhelming. Through many seasons he had sat quietly at the side of this woman, he had spoken with her, worked with her, watched her as she involved herself in many tasks, striving to teach him and the others. He had seen her in sunlight, he had seen her in moonlight, he had spoken quietly with her in the firelight of the small kiva. He had even swum with her in the great rock tank. And yet never, never had she looked as she looked to him that morning.

Below him the sounds of girlish gasps at the coldness of the water floated up, interlaced with bursts of high musical laughter and plain, simple boyish shouts of shock and pleasure.

And then she was back on the rock, her entire body diamond-dewed with myriads of sun-glancing droplets of clear, clean water. She stood for a moment then, with her arms to the sun, slender legs tensed on tiptoe, trim back arching in a curve to bring a pulse thick in a man's throat.

Then she was gone, into the thickness of the spruce, and Hawk's long-held breath expelled itself with an explosive burst.

He did not know what madness impelled him then, for suddenly he forgot the proper ways of the People. In haste he leapt down through the trees, lunging on unthinkingly toward the thick spruce that had closed around her. He must see her again, he must tell her, he must explain the feelings that had blossomed within him!

The blind spell passed and his mind suddenly cleared, but not before he burst through the inner cover of the trees and stood, dumbstruck, before her.

The woman Tala froze as she had been at the instant of his appearance, leaning slightly forward to retrieve her clothing. Her great green eyes widened perceptibly, the ripe berry lips falling apart in wonder. Yet no alarm or any other emotion marked her movements.

Slowly she stood, the long-lashed pools of her eyes holding

Hawk's eyes unwaveringly, while her arms hung quietly at her side. Then the haunting, half-curved smile of his dreams bloomed into a radiantly happy countenance, and her arms lifted.

"Hawk," she said easily. "My son lives and is upon his feet. It is *so* good to have you with us once more."

"My . . . my mo . . . Tala," Hawk responded impetuously, forgetting again all the old decorum. "I have come to you. With my heart in these hands, beating like the wings of a wild bird, have I come to end the seasons of your waiting."

Tala's wide smile remained frozen for an instant in time that seemed to the waiting Hawk to be as long as eternity. Then slowly it vanished, her eyes dropped with personal shame, and her voice, when she spoke, was filled with consternation.

"I . . . I . . . ," she stammered. "I . . . my son, I am cold. I would cover myself."

Instantly Hawk's mind snapped back to reality, and in a manner that showed clearly his great embarrassment, he turned his back and gazed at the earth beneath him.

"My mother," he finally said, his voice low with self-reproach, "for this poor behavior, for this bad countenance, this son whom you have raised sends out a voice of shame.

"Yet . . . yet woman," and now the man Hawk truly struggled for words so that Tala would clearly understand his heart, "there is this great thing within me, and . . . and when I saw you on the diving rock and again in the pool, I . . . I could not contain myself. It was no longer as if you were the one who had been as my mother. It was . . ."

"Hawk."

The voice, gentle as always, perhaps even more so, washed warmly over the young man's being, and slowly he turned to face the fathomless depths of Tala's lovely green eyes.

"Your eyes have beheld me in the pool before."

"That is so, my mother. But . . . but never in a manner such as this. It was . . . it was as though the great Tiaowa gave me new eyes with which to see and a new heart with which to feel. I saw you not as my mother but as a woman, a lovely and most desirable—"

"My son," Tala interrupted, holding her delicate hands toward him in a manner that stopped his speech. "This thing you have felt, this thing you have seen, cannot be. Surely you of all the People, you with your great wisdom, must understand that."

Slowly Hawk dropped his eyes once more. "The dream of the shadow-man," he replied without emotion.

"Yes, my son. That . . . and more."

"I understand," Hawk declared, "but I do not feel as you feel! My heart is as the water-planted-place, gushing forth new feelings, new thoughts! O woman, for two full cycles of the seasons have I searched among the villages of the People for this man you have seen. Such a man does not live!"

"There was once a man," Tala breathed, "a man who promised to return. I have considered—"

"That one was truly such a man," Hawk respectfully declared as he avoided the use of Flies-Far's name. "He is *mokee.* I myself watched him die."

Tala caught her breath and looked away.

"O woman," Hawk went on slowly, "that one was truly a man who would have loved you. Furthermore, he was ready to come and to be one with all of us. Had he done so, always would I have been content with your happiness. Yet now there is no one else, and truly have new thoughts toward you been given birth within my heart. You are no longer as the one who has been my mother. It is as I said. Truly I see you with new eyes."

"My son," Tala spoke, and now her voice broke and she could not find utterance. "I . . . I am . . . honored, and within my heart is a strange feeling that I cannot . . . describe. I do have love for you, more even than I can understand. . . .

"Yet this . . . this cannot be! You are not the man of the *túawta,* the . . . the vision. The great Giver-of-all-life has shown me on two occasions the man I am to love with the man-woman feeling, and it . . . it is not you. O Hawk, to be true to all I am, to be a one-heart, it is for him that I must wait. Of a truth there can be no other.

"Besides," and now she smiled a little, "you know the custom, my son, for I have sent out a clear voice on many occasions. I have taught you as well that the custom is good. In the event that your long absence has dimmed your memory, it is this. People who are of the same clan may not marry."

"But Moth . . . I mean, Tala," Hawk tried to interrupt. But once again Tala silenced him with the powerful signal for obedient stillness.

For a long moment she gazed into his eyes, trying to see, to understand, and even to help this one who was as her son to understand. Despite one's feelings, a person could not go against the thoughts that the great Tiaowa had planted in the heart. But Hawk could not see, Tala understood that, and she knew that her words, no matter how she sent them out, would bring pain. And strangely, she would feel the pain as well, for she longed to hold this one, to comfort him.

Still, those words that would drive him away must be said. "This is not a matter for discussion," she declared firmly. "It is the way of the People, and I will not give myself a bad countenance before Tiaowa and go against it. Thus have I spoken, and thus will it be."

126

And so in the bright, clear sunlight of early morning a young man turns away from the only woman he has ever truly felt the heart-stirrings of love for. A great quiet settles over the tiny valley that has been made lush and green and filled with plenty by the multitude of blessings from the wise Tiaowa.

A quiet settles over the woman as well, for as the man Hawk looks at her with a great pain in his eyes, she feels a huge thing being torn from her heart. This thing that is torn from her, this strange love-feeling for the man Hawk that is different from the love feelings she has had for the other children, seems pure as snow on the tallest rock-strewn mountain, white and clean as the moon-woman when she is high up and drifting between the darkness of two clouds. It has been within her for a great deal of time, comforting her, aiding her. She has wondered at it, she has told herself that it is evil to feel it, she has tried to cast it from her heart but has not been able to do so. And now, suddenly, it is gone.

Hawk turns away and his feet begin to move, and in an agony the woman with the strange green eyes steps forward. Her hands are outstretched, her mouth is open with the words that she has felt for so long. But no voice is sent out, for big in her mind is the vision, the true dream, and she knows this feeling for the one who has been as her son is wrong, and cannot be.

For long moments she watches the young man's back as he climbs away from her, going toward the cliff and, finally, out of her life. She can hardly bear that, for the love for this one is strong within her, and very real.

Almost she calls out, almost she runs to him.

But no! She must not! She must bide her time and wait, always with a good face, for one day the great Tiaowa will send her the man who will bring the understanding of man-woman love. And truly, then will she know.

Slowly the woman called Tala turns away, and in doing so she glances once again at the retreating Hawk. He is already beyond the spruce, striding upward through the dappled shadows of the new-leaved aspens, his shoulders down with discouragement.

But something somehow moves between them, and suddenly Hawk turns his head for one final look at the woman whose face is as the great star of the eastern direction of purity in his life. He is in the strong early-morning sun, and the golden light plays across his back as his powerful muscles ripple like peaceful water beneath his skin.

The woman of the strange green eyes sees this, her breath catches, and in that single instant that seems longer than all eternity she sees as well that the man Hawk's face is in deep shadow and so indistinct. Yet he is smiling in a manner that tells her that she still lives strongly within his heart, she somehow knows this even though she cannot see it, her hand claps over her mouth in absolute amazement, and her heart leaps with the unbelievable joy and rightness of the thing she is seeing and feeling.

127

"Well, little sister," the Kachina spirits call laughingly as they drift past her on the morning breeze, "did we not tell you that we would bring him here to you?"

Tala still stares, unable to comprehend, to believe.

"And did we not warn you," they continue, laughing more loudly than ever, "that the love between you and that young man would become as a great burden, one that you could never lay down?"

Yes, she thinks, *but surely this is a joyous burden.*

"More so than you know," they laugh good-naturedly as they drift away. "Now, what is it that binds your feet to that very small piece of earth? Go to him! Go to the shadow-man of your dreams, for now he is here. Now your waiting is over."

128

"Ha . . . Hawk," she suddenly called, her voice little more than a strained whisper. "O Hawk?"

The young man stopped and turned, saw the wondrous expression upon the woman Tala's countenance, and great questions formed instantly within his heart. His smile of manly defeat vanished, and was replaced with a look of wonder, of unfathomable love.

"O Hawk," Tala called again, more loudly, and suddenly she was running up the hill toward him, his name a repeated thing within her mouth.

The young man Hawk, normally swift as the winged brother after whom he was named, was too surprised to move quickly. Slowly he took one faltering step forward, then another, and suddenly the more-than-lovely woman of his heart and his dreams was pressed tightly against him, her arms holding him desperately close to her.

"O my Hawk," she wept, her voice instantly filled with tears. "At last . . . at last you have come to this place, you have come to me. . . ."

Still not understanding, Hawk stood with his arms around the woman Tala, feeling the deep pounding of her heart and the delightful pressure of her arms and listening to the strange but wonderful words of this one whom he had always, until only short moments before, considered to be as his mother.

But now, he noticed, her voice, always gentle, had become soft and cool and musical as spring water among moss and small stones. Her green eyes, always soft, had become warm and supple as the newly taken fur of a winter rabbit, and his mind wondered at these things.

"You have come to me," she continued, her words almost as a song, "and my heart is like a hummingbird's wings within my breast. Oh, my strong Hawk, the seasons of my waiting are at an end, for I have found at last the shadow-man of my vision."

The man Hawk could say nothing, think nothing, only stand there, dumbstruck by her words. He didn't know what he had expected, if he had expected anything at all. Possibly there would have been the silence of shame, possibly there might even have been a stern reprimand. But this, this wide-eyed thrilling acceptance, was more than he could dream of.

And so he continued to stand, open-mouthed, his eyes open but not seeing, his ears wide but not truly hearing.

"But this . . . this cannot be!" Tala cried, suddenly pulling away. "We are of the same clan, you and I, and—"

Hawk stopped her with the signal for silence. "Woman," he said gently, "I tried to send you these words, but you would not hear. You are of the Blue Flute Clan, and by birth I am of the Bear Clan."

Tala stared upward, her eyes wide. "Can . . . can this be true?"

Hawk smiled at her wide-eyed wonder, realized that he felt the same wonder himself, and suddenly they were together once again. How long they stood thus he could not say. Surely it was no more than a few seconds. Still, in that perverse way a man's mind has of working when it is completely nonplussed, he thought not of her words and of their meaning, not of the differences of their clans, but of the strange fire that was suddenly burning from deep within the frighteningly green depths of her eyes.

Hawk had never seen that fire, could not yet know its meaning, and so he gazed, dumbfounded, as the woman who had taught him to love all others, and who had taught him almost all else of true importance, now suddenly and more than willingly shared her own great and personal love with him.

And so, in the brilliant light of the warm spring morning, as she stood holding tightly this man who had come at last to her heart, the woman Tala sent out a great but silent voice of thanksgiving and love.

O Great One, he is here, he is here! Wa!

My heart leaps high, like a young deer it leaps high, for the one of my heart is here. Wa!

O Great One, if ever two were one, then surely we are. If ever love did live, then surely it lives here. If ever woman was filled with joy, then surely it is me, for this one who is a man is come! Wa!

Out of the white of the east he is come, out of the red of the earth he is come, on wings of mighty eagles he is come, on the soundness of his strength he is come. Wa!

Rejoice with me, O Great Tiaowa, for he is come!

129

Nor do the following moments matter. Let it be said only that two voices are sent upward with great joy, for at last both understand that the *túawta,* the vision, is finally fulfilled. The man with true love in his heart has come at last to the tiny valley of the lovely green-eyed woman, and the love-thing that lives between a man and a woman lives between them now, growing and increasing always.

And only a little way off, moving away through the sacred spruce and the cottonwoods, the morning winds carry the friendly Kachina people who are as the ancestors of these two. They are laughing, for there is much in the way of rejoicing that is going on within the tiny valley. Yet the spirits are worried, too, for not very far off are several men, and there is no joy in the hearts of those men, no goodness at all.

SEVENTEEN

The Returning Winds of Darkness

The peaceful stillness of the quiet morning ended abruptly, and a feeling of great oppression dropped like a heavy hand over the quiet land. Somewhere back on the great rock mesa a hunting coyote, out for mice in the morning grass, lifted its head and sampled the freshening freeze moving eastward across the mighty plateau. The coyote yapped once, noisily, and was answered only by its own echoes. It whined nervously, not liking the too-quiet feel of this particular morning.

Suddenly it decided that there were other mice and other mesas. It turned, slinking away eastward with the wind through the tall brush bordering the hidden valley. It was best to work far windward of that rising rimrock breeze this morning. For some reason it was stale and disturbed, hanging badly in the nostrils.

And the smell of death lay heavily within it.

131

Tala and the man Hawk, breaking suddenly apart, looked into each other's eyes for a long moment, and then as one they turned and ran for the notches in the cliff.

Badger, up from the edge of the great wash, met them there, and seconds later Butterfly stood among them, a small *olla* filled with pure water slung over her shoulder.

"All is ready for our *waítioma,*" she said simply.

Hawk, his heart small and hard like a stone, stared first at Butterfly and then at Tala. "I do not understand," he declared.

"O Hawk, we must make a running away. The Angry Ones will be here soon."

Hawk signaled the woman to silence, looked carefully around the valley, saw again the amazing beauty of the place, turned his gaze back to Tala's wondrously lovely visage, and at last he broke the silence.

"The Angry Ones are indeed near," he said simply. "Too near for us to make a running away. Nor is it in my mind that we should do so. The great Tiaowa led us to this valley, and it is strong within me that this should remain our home."

"But," Tala protested, "we cannot slay them, for we are the People of Peace. Do you not remember—"

"I remember, O woman, and I understand. I also understand the Angry Ones, for I have seen them, and I have seen their ways. We must not make a running away, for once we do, they will never stop from coming after us.

"Tala, you and Butterfly climb to the dwelling and hide yourselves there. Badger, take your hunting tools and climb partway up the *hovatoqa,* the cut in the cliff. Defend this valley from the place we prepared so many seasons past. I myself will wait where the valley drops off into the great wash. Perhaps from there I can lead them away so that they will never see this lovely place that is our home.

"However, if some should get past me from below, my brother, hasten to this place where the dwelling is, that thus the women will be defended."

"Must . . . must this truly be done?" Tala asked quietly.

"O woman," Hawk answered, "they are coming. There is no time,"

"But surely there must be another way."

"Not any more," Hawk stated. "Nevertheless, Badger, do what you can to respect the lives of these men, for indeed a life is a sacred thing. I will do the same, for truly I do not know how else to be an honorable man of the People."

There was a brief silence, Tala turned her face away, and Hawk thought of the men of the village of Flies-Far. Perhaps he was wrong, perhaps it would be better to flee.

"Be it as you say," Badger responded. "But my brother, truly I would rather stand beside you."

Hawk signaled his acknowledgment. "My brother, I would rather you be there as well. But on this day, such a thing cannot be. I know these men, and perhaps my heart understands them a little. They have been directed to this place by that two-heart who is called Saviki, and the hearts of all who follow him are dark with evil. He is most intent upon the capture of the woman who has been as our mother, who humiliated him so many long seasons past. Do then as I have directed, and perhaps, if the great Tiaowa smiles upon us, there will once again be peace within this valley."

Tala, her eyes now open wide, stared at Hawk. "Saviki?" she asked in a hoarse whisper. "The three prophets said he yet lived, but always have I hoped . . ."

"Indeed he lives. His men slew the brave man who was my friend. I have seen him, and he has sought my life as well. The wound you inflicted upon him still burns, my woman, not with pain but with hatred. His heart is filled only with great visions of himself, he wields much power, and he is truly one to be feared."

"And he is coming to . . . to this place?"

"He is, though I do not . . ."

Tala was stunned, and her ears heard no more. "But . . . but you must *not* sl . . . slay him," she whispered. "You must not, O Hawk. I would rather perish than to see you do this thing."

Hawk signaled that he agreed, but that there were other things to be considered. "I do not think he is with these men," he declared. "But should he be, and should he thrust himself upon me, then woman, I will have no choice."

Hawk then reached out and touched Tala in a manner that showed his great respect, and his man-woman feeling of love as well. Badger and Butterfly, surprised, glanced quickly at each other and then back again.

"O Tala," Hawk declared. "hear my voice. It is not within my heart to slay, not Saviki or any other man. Still, when all I love is threatened, when it is in the heart of another to take away the freedom that is mine by the gift of the great Bahana; when it is the evil desire of another to take not only the life of the ones I love, but also to take from them that purity which is most sacred according to the old ways, then I have no choice. Against such a threat, I must stand forward."

Tala dropped her eyes in sorrow, Hawk gazed tenderly upon her, and then he continued. "My family, I strongly desire that all will be well. I do not know, however, that such will be. But know this. My heart is singing, like a wing in the trees above the water-planted-place it sings, for the woman Tala and I have discovered the touching of our hearts. This day our souls are at peace, for all good things have come together in our lives. If perhaps we should die as we stand against evil, then it is a good day to do so."

Tala choked back a sob and struggled to present a happy countenance to this man of hers who had come to her at last, and who was now already preparing for a leaving. Butterfly and Badger did the same, and after touching Tala's face gently with his fingertips, Hawk turned and fled.

He ran swiftly down through the valley, his tools of hunting were in his hands, and his heart was big within his throat.

He passed the sacred water-planted-place, he passed the ordered fields of new growing corn, he ran beneath the spreading bright green of the new-leafed trees, he ran through the lush softness of the fresh spring grasses, and so he came at last to the lip of the valley that hung in such a hidden manner above the deep and empty wash below. There he paused to hide himself, and there he waited.

132

And so a man waits. He is on the bare slope of the hillside, below the lip of the valley, in plain view of the men. He has his bow, his arrows, an ancient metal knife, and a stone ax. Beside his face is a small grouping of prickly pear, near his hip is a boulder that is about the size of a man's head, and that is all the cover he has.

He considers this, worries, and the winds, drifting above him, are filled with the laughter of the friendly Kachina people.

"Ho, little brother," they laugh, "that is a very strange place for a man to hide. This is a fine joke you play on yourself, but we do not think the woman Tala will find it funny when your body is brought to her."

This is no joke, Hawk declares, his thoughts high above these good spirits who pester him.

"No joke? But surely," they laugh, "the Angry Ones will see you in such a place as this."

Hawk squints his eyes against the glare from the rock-strewn slope. A fly buzzes near his face, lands somewhere, remains briefly, and begins to buzz again. A swarm of tiny flying insects pesters him briefly. Ants and others of the insect people become evident then, busy about their daily tasks as they always are, for rarely are insect people affected by the comings and goings and the doings and the undoings of man.

"Well," the Kachina people question, their laughter a little less as they grow perturbed, "is it your thought, little brother, to give us no answer? And that after we have done so much."

My brothers, Hawk finally thinks, *where is the best place for a man to hide?*

There is a silence, and suddenly many answers come forth. In rocks, behind trees, in a hole, behind brush. These answers all come at once, and Hawk laughs quietly.

"Why is it that you laugh?" the spirits ask with great anger in their whispers.

I laugh because this is a thing that you do not know, Hawk responds easily. *Yet go to the spirit of my friend who is even now beginning the journey to join you, and he will tell you that this is true. He was a brave man, and he declared this truth to me.*

"And what truth is that, little brother?" the Kachinas ask, sounding doubtful but no longer angry.

The truth is this, Hawk responds quietly. *The best place for a man to hide is in the mind of another. I lie in this place precisely because it is the last place in which those who come will think to look.*

There is a strange silence upon the wind, and then the laughter comes again, more loud than ever. "Truly this is a good joke," the Kachina spirits laugh among themselves as they drift away. "Our little brother is indeed wise, for the joke will not be upon him this day. Truly it will be upon those who come."

133

In a very short time, Hawk saw the first of the Angry Ones coming up the slope from the deep wash below. Shortly there were many of them, stretched out single file, and they were led by a huge man of thick body and close-cropped hair who wore nothing but a string about his waist and whose face showed his vicious temperament.

Hawk's heart raced faster and he felt a great fear, not for himself but for those whom he loved who waited above. It these men could not be stopped, then surely they would destroy the women, and that not pleasantly. And Badger too would be lost.

But then, with his mind filled with a prayer-thought to the great Tiaowa, seeking courage and also forgiveness because he was about to do battle, he rose to his feet in the manner of the woman Tala's instruction, just as if he were hunting the great sheep, and with no hesitation at all he released in a powerful manner his stone-tipped arrow.

There was an instant when nothing happened, and then, as the huge and evil man who led the group turned to the side to see what had moved in his peripheral vision, and to see as well what had caused the soft-sounding *twang,* the well-shot arrow drove powerfully forward, severing the hamstrings of both his legs.

With a great cry the man fell backward, his legs completely useless. The others of the Angry Ones scattered, and with a mighty lunge Hawk was running. Up and along the lip of the valley he sped, then up the steep sandstone cliffs that bordered it.

There was a shout from below, an arrow and the feathered shaft from an *atlatl* shattered against the boulders near his face, and then he was on the mesa top and running, swiftly and easily.

He had a long way to go if he were to get to the place he had in mind, but the Angry Ones were very cautious and did not hurry after him. They had seen the closeness of his hiding place, they had seen the force of his arrow, and they could not imagine that he was alone.

And so they came slowly after him, ready to flee or to attack as their judgment might tell them, and they watched carefully as they followed.

Hawk ran swiftly and well, for he was not tired. His crossing of the mountain had taken much strength from him, but Butterfly's care and Tala's love had more than replenished it. Thus his legs moved as did the legs of *sowíngwa,* the deer, and he fairly flew over the slick-rock and the rocky soil of the easterly mesa. Through the junipers he ran, and the pinyon. Over the sage and the rabbit brush and the greasewood his strong legs lifted him. Around the cactus and the yucca and the great cities built by the ant people he sped, and there was a laughter in his mouth because of the speed that had come to his legs.

The Angry Ones too now hurried a little more, but each time they came to a place where Hawk had been, he was far ahead and they could not see him. Still, his spoor was upon the earth, and so they followed, wary, ready.

134

Hawk came at last to a narrow gulch that led to the right and forward. Holding his body low to hide his head he followed it, for the gulch was strong in his memory. Along it he had crept many seasons before when he had tracked the small deer. Nor in the passing of the seasons had it changed, and so he followed it once again.

The Angry Ones still followed, searching over the ground. It was not difficult to find his tracks, for in running he could not hide his way. Here and there between stretches of slick-rock or clumps of green grass they found where his leather-covered feet had pressed into the earth, and they followed. They scattered out and searched and found no other tracks, and a great shout arose among them. From a high place they looked all around, and there was no one else.

This man was alone!

There was the spoor left on the earth by only one man, and that was all. With another shout they dashed forward, for now he was theirs.

They lost a little time at the small gulch where Hawk had turned, for in their hurry they ran past it, taking it almost in stride. But suddenly the spoor was gone, so they stopped and searched the ground. One dropped into the gulch and saw the tracks in the bottom sand, gave his courage-shout, and quickly all of them dashed along the twisting way.

Hawk, far ahead, was out of the ravine and creeping through the thick grasses toward the high stand of tumbled rocks, the butte where he had first escaped from Saviki and where he had slain his first deer. It was a great butte of perhaps three hundred feet in height, and a good sprint long, and the mass of boulders and hidden corners that built it up made it seem almost *núkpana,* almost evil. He had thought such thoughts as a youth when he had come after the deer, and it had taken much self-persuasion to go up into it. Now, perhaps, these Angry Ones could be made to feel the same.

Hawk heard the shouts of the Angry Ones coming to him on the wind. He crept along and lay flat on the earth and was very still, for it was still his thought that these men looked where they thought to look. And once more he was right. They swept past him and dropped out of sight where the earth rolled downward, and he jumped to his feet and leaped forward toward the high rocky butte that was to be his *wáki,* his place of hiding.

He ran leaping and striving, his breath coming rapidly, and strangely he was filled with a sadness for those men who followed and for the great fear that lived within them. If it had been they who had known the gentle Tala instead of himself, if it had been they who had been taught the words of the ancient grandmother, they would not be seeking his life.

The rocks were ahead of him, rising in their strange and fearful formations. Behind him Hawk heard shouts, and though he did not look back, he knew that they had seen him and that they knew also that he was alone.

They shouted and ran toward the rocks, but Hawk reached them first and leaped, climbing and twisting upward among them. And as he moved through the gullies and the strange and fearful shadows, his breath came short and suddenly he could run no more. He stopped, gasping, with his back against a huge sandstone abutment, and there he waited. He held his *atlatl* ready and his bow was in his hand and then there was laughter in his mouth that was like the brave laughter of Flies-Far who had been his friend, and it rang out, bouncing through the strange formations of rock.

135

There was no sound of the Angry Ones climbing after him. Then there was a whisper as of something such as skin brushing against rock, he laughed again, the whisper turned into footfalls pounding away, and suddenly Hawk knew that he was alone. There was no sound but the low moaning of the wind as it drifted between the rocks and up the steepness of the small hill, gnawing as it climbed.

He crept to a jutting point of carved stone and looked back down the way he had come, and there he saw them. They were a little way off, standing on the slick-rock back in the direction of the little valley. They were gesturing and talking, and now and then one would point his weapons at the butte that was a pile of rocks and there would be more discussion and then another would point his own weapons off across the mesa toward the tiny valley and there would be another discussion.

The man Hawk saw this, saw them turn and drop out of sight

into a deep ravine, watched for signs of their emergence and saw none, and within his heart he knew that they were making a drawing out. They had baited a trap with their disappearance, and now they were waiting for his own eagerness to trigger it.

He laughed again, loud, delightedly, and then he settled back to wait. He knew they were in the ravine, for it was short and he could see where it headed and also its mouth where it became part of another and larger one. That did not worry him. What worried him was that these men of the Angry Ones might tire of waiting. They might grow hungry or thirsty or even they might grow more fearful, and in such a way they might turn back toward the tiny valley. Truly that was a thing to be considered.

For a long time he watched from his high vantage point, and the Angry Ones did not appear in any direction. Not anywhere on the entire mesa could he see them. Nor could he see any other living thing. They were gone and it was a vast and empty space before him, and behind him climbed the strange rocks of the butte, where long ago he had slain the deer when he should have been watching the corn.

Hawk considered that memory, considered the way the woman Tala had taught him with such gentleness, and the great love that lived within him for the wondrously lovely green-eyed woman expanded until it filled his being. It choked the air from his throat, it made his eyes burn with tears, and in a solemn and sacred manner he sent out his silent voice of gratitude.

O Great Tiaowa, hear now this voice, hear now this voice from one who has so often been of two hearts. Wa!

Yet now, O Great One, he is of one heart. Wa!

In this one heart is gratitude, in this one heart is love, in this one heart is pride in the lovely Tala, the one who is as the light from the star of the eastern morning. Wa!

136

The sun was slanting down the western sky, and Hawk knew that this thing must be concluded. If the time of darkness came, the Angry Ones could do as they chose, and he would not know of it.

Climbing to his feet he turned and worked his way up through the morass of rock. Perhaps he could go by another way, down the cliff he had descended so many seasons before, and could get to the valley before them.

Slowly he moved along the old trail the deer had shown him, working upward, past huge boulders black with desert varnish, beneath strangely shaped columns of stone carved by the wind and rain of eons past. In the light of the late slanting sun it was not a hard way to go, and yet each step grew more difficult. On one side of him the hill rose steeply, on the other the path fell away quickly and a great crevice opened and dropped *atkyaqw,* far down.

He hesitated in that spot, the wind whistled, and he seemed to hear the Kachina people laughing. But their laughter seemed hollow and mocking, and suddenly he was filled with bad feelings. Perhaps he should not go that way. Perhaps he should turn and meet the Angry Ones.

Still, in his heart he did not want to fight, and the high cliff was far ahead of him and offered a way down and back to the valley in time to make a fleeing.

He took another step, hesitated, took another, and suddenly the earth gave way beneath his foot. With a quick grasp he took hold of a projecting stone and stopped his falling, and here he hung, breathing deeply.

At last and without great difficulty he pulled himself back to the trail, and there he stood, breathing deeply, worrying deeply. His bow and arrows were now gone, dropped in his almost fall, and so he was without proper weapons. But at least he still had his *atlatl* and spear, he thought, reaching for them.

But it was not so. The throwing stick had been broken between the weight of his body and the hardness of the rock he had slammed against. And the stone point on the feathered spear shaft was also broken. He was left with only his ax and the ancient metal knife.

137

And so a man hesitates and wonders. The wind that blows above the mesa moans unceasingly and grows stronger. It sends streamers through the cracks in the high rocks, and with a hollow sound the Kachina people who ride them laugh and chuckle among themselves.

"O little brother," they seem to ask, "do you not think that the falling we gave you is a good joke?"

Hawk glances nervously about, and in his mind he is saying that it was no joke at all. He wants only to escape from the men and to get back to Tala and the others. He chooses not to fight if it can in some manner be avoided.

There is more of the laughter on the wind, the sun drops from sight in the far-off west, and with a soft chuckling the Kachina people drift away, their laughter an easy thing.

"Little brother, do as you wish, for it is said that you are wise. But were it us, we would go back the way we came."

138

In the first deep darkness of night, Hawk moved out from the base of the rocky butte and onto the mesa. He carried his ax in one hand and in his other there was nothing, for with that he must feel his way. He moved cautiously, for this was near the place where the Angry Ones had vanished into the deep wash, and he knew that they were clever and relentless enemies.

He moved a short distance and waited and listened. He moved again and waited and listened once more. Still there was no sound. A night bird called from a long way off, a coyote yipped from far across the mesa, a small four-legged brother scurried in the brush very near his feet, and there was nothing else. On all the mesa there was silence.

Reaching down he felt around, found a large stone, lifted it, and threw it as hard as he could. It landed far to one side of him, for he heard it thump sharply against another rock. He listened, heard a screech owl call from near where the stone had hit, heard another answer and then another, and instantly he turned and ran back toward the butte.

He ran straight for the high, jumbled mass of rocks, knowing that he must get to them or he would have no chance. Behind him and gathering to come after him he heard other feet running, many of them. He thought of the strange counsel of the Kachina people, wondered at it, and then he was in the rocks, leaping and striving up and among them.

But this time he heard the feet continuing behind him on the hard earth. They were close, very close, and Hawk knew they would not let him escape. Desperately he leaped and stumbled, the ax clattered from his grasp, and he was falling. He hit, rolled, caught himself, and crawled quickly into a deeper pocket of darkness among the rocks.

He crouched silently, doing his best to still his labored breathing and pounding heart. He could hear them searching, and they were very near. They were poking beneath the rocks with their stone-tipped weapons, whispering, and at each moment they drew more close.

The man called Hawk considered this, and as his thoughts went outward the Kachina people heard them and came whispering beneath the rock where he hid.

"O little brother," they asked, "why is it that you worry? Have we not made all things ready for you? Have we not helped you in your great joke?"

Joke? Hawk thought wonderingly. *Perhaps you have, O spirits, but I do not understand. You have led me back to the evil ones, and I am without weapons.*

The Kachinas laughed. "That is so," they whispered gleefully. "Save for the ancient knife, we took those weapons from you. And that knife should remain in your waistband. As a man of the People, you have no need for it. It is sacred, and must never be used in anger."

No need? Hawk questioned. *Sacred? But—*

"Little brother, think of the joke you played in the great wash. Deal with these men now as you did then—in their minds!"

In frustration Hawk tried to understand. *In their minds? I do not . . .*

But the Kachina people were gone, he was alone once more, and the Angry Ones were drawing closer.

Desperately Hawk sent out a prayer-thought for wisdom, and into his mind came suddenly the memory of the great puma. He saw it clearly as he had when he stumbled and went down into the snow in that long-before season of cold. He felt the huge claws dig deeply into his leg, he experienced the heaviness of the animal as it pressed down upon him, he smelled the fetid breath, he watched the saliva drip from the open mouth, he saw the huge fangs as they struggled toward his neck, seeking his life-blood.

And in his mind he saw too the slim arm of the woman Tala, the skin petal-clear and the color of anciently smelted copper and brass. He saw it snake around the roaring puma's throat, squeeze closed against its air supply, and then with greater strength than a man would guess, and greater courage than a man could ever know, throw the great puma to the side and away from the young boy who was as a son.

Hawk saw these things, he saw the green-eyed woman who was now the woman of his life as she fought without weapons against odds that were truly not even imaginable, and suddenly his heart was big within him and growing rapidly bigger.

A man who planned to take such a woman as his wife did not lie like a prairie dog crouched in terror within its hole. If he were to die, then he would die honorably with his face toward the Angry Ones, and they would know who it was they had slain because he would face them with no fear, just as his friend Flies-Far had done. And if he were not to die, then they would know his identity as well, for they would hear his laughter, and that would live always in their minds.

Minds?

Suddenly Hawk understood, and in the darkness his face grew into a smile. Their minds—their minds!

The Angry Ones were almost upon him when Hawk sprang forth from beneath the rock to meet them. In his arms was the strength that had been the woman Tala's when she had thrown away the great puma, and in his mouth was the brave and mighty laughter of his friend Flies-Far.

O Kachina people, he shouted as he sprang amongst the startled men, *do you hear my laughter? It is brave and it is good and it is the laughter of my friend who will soon be with you and it is what will work in the minds of these men. Take heed, for I would that the woman should know what happened here.*

Hawk brushed aside the first lance as if it were one of Badger's old toys. He seized the first of the Angry Ones within his bare arms and he raised the man off the ground and held him and threw him mightily among the others. They scattered, but instantly he was among them once more, striking with his hands to the right and to the left. There was more laughter in his mouth, strong laughter, joyous laughter, and though there was also a sudden wound in his side, such a little thing did not matter. With much power he laughed again, grabbed a jabbing spear and broke it easily with one hand, and caught and threw two more men away into the darkness. Then he sprang back and waited for the men to come.

But they did not.

In the dark the Angry Ones were confused, and because of the great laughter of this one man, they were also afraid. They spoke to one another of this and the fear was plain within their voices.

"This is one," they said, "who laughs when he is alone against many. This is one who hides where there is no cover. This is one who strikes down such a one as has never been struck down, not even by the *mongwi* Saviki. This is one who calls upon the spirits."

They were more afraid, and they took another step backward, and then another.

"This one is a demon," they said, and their voices were now hoarse whispers. "This one is a demon who has taken the form of a man to deceive us and lure us to this place where he can slay us."

With a great cry the Angry Ones turned then and ran in a direction that was away from the tiny valley, and their running was more of a falling and a rolling and a tumbling than it was a running, and the laughter that followed them was a ringing in their ears.

They reached, finally, the flatness of the slick-rock mesa, the heavy pounding of their feet died off into the darkness of the night, and the tale they would tell grew large within their minds as they ran.

139

And in the winds that floated above the rocks and chuckled down between them, there was also great laughter and great mirth. "This is a very good joke," the Kachina people howled with much hilarity. "Truly, little brother, it is as we declared. This is a very good joke indeed."

EIGHTEEN

And Thus a Beginning

Marriage, among those who are called the People of Peace, is a serious custom indeed, for upon it rests the future of the clans, of the People. There is much in the way of preparation, much in the way of ritual, much in the way of time spent, and many who are kinspeople both of the young woman and of the young man become involved. Cornmeal is delivered to the mother of the young man, and the young woman grinds corn for three days to prove her ability to do so in a home of her own. During this time the relatives of the young man are weaving wedding robes for the new bride, and so all is in preparation.

On the morning of the fourth day, before sunrise, the mothers and other relatives of each of the young ones who will be wed come together in one place to each wash the hair of the child of the other. The hair is washed in yucca suds and rinsed, and during this washing and rinsing, the hair of the two is woven together, and so the symbolic union of the young man and the young woman has occurred.

The couple then take a pinch of cornmeal and walk together to the edge of the mesa. As the sun rises they each breathe on the cornmeal, toss it toward the sun, and offer a prayer to the Great One that their union will be blessed.

141

Hawk grunted as the pain from the wound in his side stabbed downward, yet still he did not move. Nor could he, for the strong hand of the young man called Badger held his head down near the water of the sacred water-planted-place. Next to him, kneeling and sputtering with great mirth, was Tala, and she was undergoing the same treatment at the hands of Butterfly.

"H . . . Ho," Hawk sputtered as his face was pushed once more beneath the water, "it is sometimes considered necessary, my brother, for a man to breathe."

"A man, perhaps," Badger teased, "but what of you, O wing of the air?" And with a great laughter he pushed Hawk's head once more beneath the surface.

Hawk struggled and came up again, gasping with laughter, and Tala, kneeling next to him, laughed as well. "What you do to this man is good," she encouraged Badger. "Perhaps if you do it well enough, I will not have to worry ab—ouch! Butterfly, must you scrub so hard? Because I am about to become a wife does not mean I no longer have need for my hair."

"I understand," Butterfly responded laughingly. "Because you will soon be an old married woman, my mother, your hair will never again be beautiful. But that does not matter. Such ugly hair is still very good for the weaving of nets, and you will need many such to keep the handsome Hawk near your dwelling."

Tala sputtered in mock anger, there was much laughter at the jest, and so the washing and the rinsing continued. Then, as the strands of hair from the heads of each began at last to be woven together, the laughter vanished and much seriousness prevailed.

Tala and Hawk knelt facing each other, their eyes only inches apart, and never had either of them seen so deeply into the soul of another. No, nor had either of them seen greater devotion, greater man-woman love. Yet truly, for both of them, it was only a beginning.

142

And so two people stand together on the edge of the bulging slick-rock that looms in a protective manner out and over the tiny valley. Their hair, black and black with dancing burnished highlights, is woven together, their hands are woven together, and in a sacred manner their hearts are woven together as well.

Between their two palms is a pinch of sacred cornmeal, and they hold it out together, waiting solemnly for the moment when they can first send out their prayer-thoughts as one. Their hearts beat rhythmically with the music of life, the air around them is filled with the joyous singing of many wings, and truly is the beginning of this day lovely.

Finally the first diamond flash of the rising sun bursts upon them, and as it does so their hands lift, together, and the cornmeal scatters and drops, carried outward on the gentle morning breeze.

O Great Tiaowa, Hawk breathes, *hear the voice we send, hear the voice we send at last, as one. Wa!*

Give this love between us tenderness. Wa!

Give this love between us honesty. Wa!

Give this love between us playfulness. Wa!

Give this love between us power. Wa!

Give this love between us excitement. Wa!

Give this love between us meaning. Wa!

Give all this love to us, we plead, forever. Wa!

143

The man Hawk and the woman Tala were alone in the stone dwelling, high in the bulging cliff above the tiny green valley. They were alone, and truly they could not look at one another. They tried, and always their eyes turned away. Hawk rose to his feet and stirred the small fire, placing two new logs upon it. The fire did not need those logs, but it was something to do, and that was better than feeling foolish about being shy, about doing nothing. For Hawk was shy, he was afraid, and he did not know what to say.

He lay down on the pile of robes that had a new woven covering spread over them, and still he was afraid. When he turned his head he could see Tala across the room, and though her back was to him he could tell that she was shy and afraid also. She did not speak, but instead kept very busy putting things away and arranging things that she had rearranged three times already.

Tala was very beautiful to him in the firelight, and as he looked upon her his heart beat a strong rhythm within his breast. How could such good fortune ever come upon such a man as he?

144

With great fear and great shame for that fear, Tala stared into the corner of the small room that was the corner away from the piled robes that would be their place of sleeping. Her mind told her to turn and go to her husband, but her heart beat wildly and noisily and her legs were as water and there were tears within her eyes and she could not recall ever having felt so shy and so afraid. This shamed her, and desperately she wished to hide herself, to flee down the valley and into the deep wash and go on always, never returning.

Oh, why had she so longed for this time to come? Surely she would never have pleaded that it come if she had known it would bring such shyness and fear. Nor could she understand her feelings. She loved this man Hawk more than she loved life itself, but . . . but . . .

Quickly she reached out and moved another seed bowl so that she would seem to the waiting Hawk to be busy, but she was not busy at all. She was only afraid, and that should not be the way of a new wife.

"Tala?"

Slowly she turned, and the firelight was strong upon the face of the man she loved. His countenance was good, and there was no mockery in it for her shyness or her fear. She stepped closer, gazed deeply into Hawk's eyes, and was surprised to see within them another great shyness, a shyness of his own. That truly was surprising, but perhaps it was also good.

Tala stood now near the pile of robes that had the new woven robe spread over them. She looked down upon her new husband and her thoughts were plain on her face. She was a woman, and according to the new custom of the People it was not her right to decide what was to be done.

Yet she could see that the man Hawk wished her to be comfortable and happy. He would choose the old way, she knew, and give her the choice.

Truly her love for this good man waxed strong, and her desire to please the one who was as a new person in her eyes grew strong as well. She was shy and she was afraid, but still, she would do as her husband decided.

"O Tala, my *wúti,*" Hawk said softly, and in his voice was almost a stumbling, "I . . . I am afraid of the newness as you are afraid. It . . . it is enough that you lie here beside me. Thus we may grow accustomed together to the newness of being alone with each other in the night."

Tala, her green eyes wide in the firelight, stood motionless for a long time. Finally she lay down beside her new husband, and gently he pulled the covering over them. He put his arms around her then, and was still. Slowly the stiffness went out of her body and she was quiet and relaxed beside him, and then as the winds of night drifted laughingly past their dwelling, the two who were becoming one quietly talked in the darkness and the newness of being together.

145

It was the third night of their being together alone in the dwelling. Butterfly was constructing another dwelling a little way off, still under the bulging cliff, and that one would also have two rooms, a room for the man and a room for the woman. But for now she slept in the kiva below. Badger, on the other hand, slept where he wished, always out under the stars. It was a new order for the family, but it was a good order, and there were many smiles and sideward glances during the day concerning it.

But now Hawk and Tala were alone in the firelight once more, and there was a great quietness in the air. Hawk had finished the working of several new arrows, had eaten the sweet mutton stew prepared by Tala, and had pronounced it very good. He had also stacked much firewood should his new wife find need for it.

Tala had ground a great deal of corn and had swept out the two rooms of the dwelling, thus making much dust. That had quickly settled and so had made things about as they had been before, and thus she too had kept very busy.

Hawk lay on the robes, watching his woman, wondering once more that someone so lovely as her would feel the man-woman love feeling for such a one as him.

Her hair this night was loose and not cut or in the braids that signified a married woman, and so it cascaded loosely about her beautiful face in a manner that set his heart to pounding. In the firelight her green eyes, set within the perfect oval of her face, danced with a strange and intentional mischievousness, and not once did she appear to even know of his presence.

And then Tala glanced at him, shyly, and with her rose-red lips curving into the half-smile he so well remembered from the time of his delirium, she turned and came to the bedding and lay down beside her new and suddenly frightened husband.

"It is my wish," was all she said.

146

In the quiet of the tiny canyon the times of daylight pass quickly, and never has there been such a happiness. The hunting is more than good, for game is abundant and arrows fly more straight than ever before. The corn grows taller and carries bigger ears, the berries are larger and more plentiful, the basketry and the pottery become exceedingly fine, and the season is very good.

There is a fine magic in the times of darkness as well, for always the two are alone together in the dwelling, and always it is good for them both. The winds of night blow softly across the mesa, and often they send searching fingers through the old *koritivi,* bringing out the moaning that is a good sound to the people of the valley. They drift down then, past the open window of the dwelling, and on them ride the Kachina people, laughing their pleasure at the happiness of these their children.

"Listen," Hawk whispers, "the Kachina ancestors are talking."

Tala, with a frown of delight in her voice, answers. "I hear only the wind. There is nothing else, my husband."

"But you must surely hear them," Hawk responds earnestly, unable to see the joking that is in her eyes. "It was you who taught me of them so many seasons past."

"Perhaps that is so," Tala teases, "but now I hear only the wind. Tell me, O Hawk, what is it that they say?"

"They say, they say, 'O little brother, we pity you. It is sad that you were stuck with such an ugly old wom—ouch!' "

There is then a great deal of giggling and scuffling, and at last all grows calm and quiet once more.

"Do you see?" Hawk states. "They are still laughing around their words. No doubt they are making a laughter of us as well, for one of us is acting very foolish."

"No doubt," Tala declares quickly, "and it is within my heart to plead with you to stop such foolish behavior, my husband."

There is another tickling, another giggling scuffle, Tala allows herself finally to be subdued within the two strong arms of her husband, and at last she speaks once again.

"Ha! Perhaps I do hear the laughter, my husband, but truly I can not make out the words. Can you not help a poor, ugly woman to understand?"

Hawk releases the woman who is now his wife, rolls onto his back, stares intently up into the blackness of the cave ceiling, and at last he solemnly speaks.

"Hear now their words, my woman. They say, 'Little brother, it is good that you lie now with this most beautiful woman who is our little sister. Now the great good in this valley is fulfilled.' "

In the silence the winds race down the valley, and the Kachinas dance upon the winds, their happy voices loud with joy.

"I hear them once more," Tala whispers, "but still I do not understand. Do you tell me, my husband, what it is that they say now."

"They say, 'Little brother, the woman who is your wife is better than any woman in a dream or a vision. She is lovely as the sun on the fresh green leaves of the aspens. She is fresh and pure as the water in the sacred water-planted-place. She is warm as the summer sun against the rock of the mesa. She is playful as the breezes drifting in and out of the old *koritivi.* She is comfortable as a warm fire and many robes in the kiva on a cold winter night.' "

"That is foolish talk, my husband. It was I who saw *you* in the dream, not you who saw me. That is how I know they would not say that. But still, it is good talk. Tell me more of what you say they say. . . ."

147

"My Hawk, you must leave this valley very soon and bring for me the soft skin of a young deer."

It was already the season of harvest, and Hawk and Tala and Butterfly and Badger had been very busy with that. The wild plums and cherries had been dried and stored for the season of cold. The berries, of many varieties, had been picked and pounded on a stone and made into flat cakes and also stored. Wild grapes had been gathered, nuts of pinyon and other trees were plentiful, and the corn was more than any of the four had ever seen.

It was also, once again, the season of love, for Badger and Butterfly had determined to wed. It was not right, they declared, for Tala and Hawk to be having such a fine life, and for them to be left out altogether. Besides, it was coming upon the season of cold, there was only one warm kiva, and so there was much in the way of preparation and much in the way of being busy in the tiny valley. Nor were there many days left until the corn would be gathered in. And then would come the grinding of the meal and the weaving of the robes and the washing of the hair.

"A young deer?" Hawk asked, his mind elsewhere. "Why must I do that? We have much meat, and many hides as well."

"Listen, my husband," Tala whispered in the darkness, her green eyes dancing with mischievous joy, "do you hear the Kachina spirits whispering outside?"

"It is only the wind," Hawk replied as he smiled in the darkness at the old game. "There are no voices out there. And what has this to do with a young deer?"

"Much, my husband. Perhaps the voice is from the Deer Kachina, or perhaps it is the humpbacked one called *Kokopeli.* Do you not hear the words?"

"I hear only the wind," Hawk answered, growing impatient. "But in case it is more than that, tell me what they say."

Tala lay back with her hands upon her belly, took a deep breath, and at last she spoke. "They say, 'Little sister, it is good that you warn this man who is your husband, for he is very foolish, and may not understand.' "

Hawk leaned up, turned, and looked closely at the woman who lay beside him. "What is this? What kind of words are these. . . ?"

"They say," Tala went on unheeding, "that it must never be the case, after I am fat and ugly, that we grow weary, or impatient, or fearful, of sitting and talking about our love. They say, 'Remember, O man, that sitting and talking and learning, together, was the manner of the discovery of your love in the beginning.' "

"That is a good warning," Hawk agreed, lying back. "But I do not understand what it has to do with us, or with a young deer that you said you needed."

"This is the reason for my words, O husband," Tala declared as she rose to her feet. "I must make a small robe of the tender young skin, for I am certain at last. We will have a child before the winter snows have melted and the warmth has come back to our valley."

Tala stood straight and tall and proud, for within her she was doing what a woman alone could do and what made her as important in the home dwelling as ever a man could be.

Hawk stared, his mouth open wide with astonishment. Then, suddenly mindful of his foolish countenance, he dropped his eyes in shame. And in that moment the winds came up, strong, forceful, and there was a laughter on them, a strong laughter and a strong voice of pride in the life of this one who was coming.

Hawk suddenly stood tall before the woman who was his wife, and his words were strong. "It will be a son," he said, his voice now filled with power and with pride. "It will be a son, and we will call him Stands Alone, for truly he will stand alone among the People. We will teach him the true ways, the ancient ways, and he will go out among the clans and send out a voice to those who yet remain, declaring the way of happiness where he goes.

"Truly will he be considered a great man, for he will bring a message of peace, saying, '*Haliksai;* listen, brothers, this is how it is.' "

Now Tala smiled. "My husband, it is to be so. Now indeed must the two of us grow close."

"And in what manner can the two of us do that?"

In the darkness Tala smiled, and gently she circled her arms about the one she loved. "In a manner such as this," she whispered. "in a joyful manner such as this."

148

And so the man and the woman stand together, their thoughts wide with wonder that such a thing can happen to them. Yet truly have all things happened as it had been declared so long before, and surely they must continue to do so.

But not very far from the valley, a small fire burns in a deep wash, and over it crouches a man. He is alone, for those who followed him are either *mokee,* dead, or they have with great fear made a fleeing from his presence.

He is bitter about this, and confused. Throughout the land that was to be his he can find only abandoned villages and much broken pottery. The People, those who have not died of starvation and disease, are for the most part gone, their footprints dwindling into the distance toward the south. Truly there are none left for him to make afraid, and he does not understand why this should be so.

The winds of afternoon drift by, and though the Kachina people who ride them do not care for this man, they try to tell him the reasons so that perhaps he will see.

He and others like him have contaminated the People of Peace, the spirits declare, filling them either with fear or with gross wickedness, so much so that the great Creator has verily turned away his face from them. Tiaowa has, with very few exceptions, withdrawn the moisture from the face of the land. And too he has withdrawn his great hand of protection, and the People are now buffeted from all directions by the Angry Ones, so much so that those who yet live are making a great fleeing from their homes, a great abandoning of their dwellings.

Thus, this man has lost all he had once thought to gain, for the great evil master whom he has served has now abandoned him to his own devices. Yet still he does not see this. Still he believes in his power, his great intelligence and strength. Still he believes that if he can but find and destroy the man who escaped, the one who is called Hakomi, and as well possess the body and the mind of the green-eyed woman who lanced his thigh so long ago, then he will once again have great power and force among the People who have fled.

So now he crouches silently, preparing something to eat, and his mind spins in dark circles. The evil, lusting selfishness that has lived within his heart fills him with frustration, for it has grown over the seasons until it is as a consuming fire. Nor will it ever go away.

Still he prepares, for he is close now, and the foolish ones of the tiny valley do not know that this is so.

NINETEEN

Another Part of Living

The arrows came out of the cloudy morning on the last day of the harvesting of the corn, and each arrow found its mark. Badger, tall and strong and thinking much of the coming day of his wedding, did not notice the warning cry of *angwusi,* the crow. Nor did he notice the silence that had settled upon the tiny valley. His hands were very busy and his mind was more busy still, and he did not see, did not hear.

And so the softly whispering arrow slammed like the sting of a thousand angry hornets into his back, high up, between his ribs. He grunted with surprise, started to cry a warning, realized that the blood within his mouth would not allow him to do so, reached back for the arrow, and then he was down upon the earth, his breathing a ragged effort in his throat.

Hawk, through the corn, had noticed both the *angwusi* and the silence, and was standing still, listening. He heard Badger's grunt and his fall, and desperately he ran to his brother's side. Kneeling, he jerked the arrow free, and though the stone point remained imbedded, the angry opening at least was clear.

Quickly he gathered a handful of earth, and he had just packed it against the wound in the gasping Badger's back when the other arrow whistled out of the sunlight. Hearing something, Hawk started to turn, and that alone saved his life. Instead of plowing deeply into his abdomen and spine, as had been intended, the swiftly flying missile tore across his back, slammed into his pelvic bone where it formed the hip, and then it glanced away.

Yet the shock was great, and with a cry of surprise and pain Hawk spun and went down across the young man who was as his brother. For an instant he lay thus, struggling, felt the shock of another arrow strike his body, and as darkness closed around him he saw the form of Saviki rise from the brush on the side of the valley wall and move quickly toward the sacred water-planted-place and the dwellings above it. And truly was he smiling.

150

There was water on his face. From far off there was the rumble of thunder, and there was still the water on his face, trickling down, nourishing the thirsty ground all about him.

Opening his eyes, Hawk stared for a moment into the gray sky, wondering at the gentle rain, his mind a blank. Surely the great Tiaowa was prospering—and then it came back; Badger, the arrows, Saviki.

"Tala," he murmured as he struggled to sit up. "The evil one has come for Tala, and I must warn her. I must . . ."

Suddenly Hawk was aware of the still form that was beneath him. Quickly he turned and lifted the head of the one called Badger, holding him tightly, seeking for signs of life. But there was no movement, no breath in the body. His brother the little digger had taken his last great journey to the west.

"Hyee, my brother," Hawk breathed as tears filled his eyes. "So soon you have begun your journey to the land of the sky people. So soon . . . so soon. Go now in peace, and . . . and good hunting. . . ."

Staggering to his feet, Hawk turned toward the high, bulging cliff that sheltered the dwellings and the storage rooms. He did not look back, for he knew that Badger was no longer there. He who had been Badger was now gone, and now poor Butterfly would be left alone.

But Butterfly lay where she had been slain, and Hawk's heart turned small and cold within him at the sight of her battered head. Truly had this been the work of Saviki.

"Hyeee, my sister," he whispered, and he wept as he said it, "now you also are gone on your journey, leaving us here alone. Go quickly, that you might come upon Badger and so travel together. In that, you will find much happiness. Go in peace, my . . . my sister. May your pottery be fine . . . and your cooking be always of an excellent taste. Go, my sister. . . ."

Rising, Hawk looked around the silent valley. His side ached and his mind was spinning, yet he knew he must go on. Again he dropped his gaze to the still form of the young woman who had been as his sister, and he was surprised to see the ancient metal knife of the Blue Flute Clan lying near her body. He picked it up, looked at it, thought first of his anger toward Saviki and then of the whispered advice of the Kachina people that the knife must not be used in anger.

Slowly, with a look of fierce determination on his face, he placed the knife back upon the earth. Then he moved forward, his mind beyond the knife and filled with fear of what he would find of the woman who had become his life. He could not bear to consider those thoughts, but they would not leave him alone.

What would he do if he found her as he had found his beloved sister Butterfly? How could a man remain a man of peace under such circumstances? Even more important, how could a man go on living?

151

Hawk found the place of capture near the water-planted-place and the great rock tank. He followed the spoor to the *hovatoqa,* the cut in the cliff, somehow he climbed that, and once on top he set out after the one who had taken the woman, the one who was called Saviki.

Hawk had been wounded twice. He knew that, but strangely he could find only one injury. He thought about it as he could, though it was not an easy matter, keeping his mind within his body. Still, the other arrow, the second one, must have struck within the same wound created by the first arrow. Somehow, without remembering it, he must have removed the second arrow.

Pain gnawed at his back and side like a hungry rodent, but the man Hawk did not stop. He dared not. He could not! In his mind lived the memory of Saviki's lustful evil toward women, and within his own breast was growing a great fear, a great anger. The woman Tala was now as himself, truly part of him. He could feel within himself her pain and her fear, but even more he could feel her great shame that such a one as Saviki should lay hands upon her. Thus the anger became a great blackness within Hawk's heart, and his muscles grew strong with the carrying of it.

The rain stopped, the earth dried out, and soon it was as if there had been no rain at all. Dust from the way of his passing rose up, settled upon him, and caked with his blood and perspiration. His head ached, his mouth was dry, yet still he pushed on across the slick-rock mesa. The heat waves pushed in close around him, blotting out the distance, leaving only a vast shimmering waste, and slowly he staggered across it.

Twice, for short times, he rested his throbbing body. Yet his mind would not be still and so he pushed on, the foot-spoor and the blood-spoor already dry on the ground before him. He wondered whose blood was upon the earth, told himself that it must be Saviki's, and for some perverse reason was certain that it had to be Tala's. His heart ached with the thought of that, his mind wanted to flee away from the understanding of it, and yet with great courage he held it close, keeping himself alert with the pain of it, knowing that when he came up with the two of them he would need to think, to plan.

He carried no weapon but his anger and his pain for the suffering of the woman of his life, and those were also his strength and the power of his going. Thus armed, he moved forward through the heat of the day. His head throbbed heavily and continuously. His mouth was more than dry, his lips parched and broken. His body was unnaturally hot—he could feel it and knew that it was fever. His great wound still bled, but often he clapped great quantities of dust against it. That helped the bleeding, but the agony gnawed at him constantly and relentlessly, and soon he could not remember when it had not been so.

His hands felt large and his head heavy and awkward, and in his mind was the worry that he could not go on.

His mind worked with startling clarity, yet he distrusted it, knowing this clarity was the beginning of delirium. He felt his weakness, knowing he needed rest and water and time to treat his wound. But that could not be so, for the green-eyed woman of the morning star was somewhere ahead, held captive by the evil Saviki.

And then a wash opened before him, he stumbled into it, saw that the spoor turned and followed the twisting course of the ravine, and so he did as well. And suddenly it was in his mind that he had been in this place before.

He glanced up, his eyes red-rimmed from sun-glare, his face whitened by alkali dust and his muscles heavy with weariness, and it came then into his memory.

The butte! The rocky butte where he had escaped from Saviki, where he had first slain the deer, and where he had fought, as well, the evil men Saviki had sent during the time of new green growing. Now he was back here once again, and his mind wondered, for truly all things seemed as a great *pongovi,* a great circle in time.

But the tracks in the sandy soil did not go as he had expected. Where he had thought they would turn toward the great butte they veered away, and Hawk suddenly realized that the man Saviki was going to go around it rather than attempt a crossing. He remembered then the man's apparent fear of heights, shown before himself and the other three children so many seasons before, and for the first time a hope began to build within his heart.

He would take again the hidden trail, and if he could manage not to fall, it would save the longer journey of going around and he could draw even more near.

152

The top of the butte is a narrow, flat tableland, rubble-strewn and sloping away toward the south. It is littered with cedars and is not as large as the man remembers it. But it has been many seasons of growth since the time of the great fleeing, and things seen as a child have a way of shrinking when seen again through the eyes of adulthood.

Hawk sees this and does not think of it, but hastens as rapidly as he can through the quickly gathering twilight across the mesa to where he can see off and down.

Far below the mesa grows dark, and Hawk's heart sinks within him. It is too late. They have passed, or, if they have not, they will do so in the darkness and he will have no opportunity to reach them, to stop them. Nor can he climb down the great cliff in the darkness. Surely all the good Kachina spirits have turned against him. Have not his brother and sister been slain by this evil one? Surely even the great Tiaowa has turned away his face, leaving him completely alone, helpless and unable to go to the one he loves.

In desperation and exhaustion he sinks to the earth, the darkness of night drops down, the winds lift their playful heads above the rimrock, and on them ride the Kachina people who, despite the man's despair, are yet as his ancestors.

"Ho, little brother," they laugh as they whistle by, "is this not a lovely night? Have you perhaps glanced at the stars?"

Then they are gone, still laughing, and Hawk knows all is over. He is near delirium, his mind is whirling in a great pounding circle, the stars of the night spin above him, and even the small red star that winks below is dim and flickering.

Small red star? Below?

Suddenly the words of the Kachina people return to Hawk's mind, and he is again upon his feet, for truly there is a star below, a red star of a fire. The man Saviki has stopped. He does not know that there is a pursuit, and he has halted for the darkness. Hawk sees this, considers again the evil that lurks within the heart of the man, and knows something must be done. Perhaps Saviki's attention can be taken from the woman, even for a time.

153

Swiftly the man Hawk glanced around. Poised on the rim of the butte was a huge boulder, much larger than himself. He thought of that, discussed with himself all that might come of what he was considering, and decided it was his only hope. Perhaps such a rolling and such a noise would drive the man into further flight, but it would also stop him from such evil as his heart delighted in. The woman Tala could not bear such an evil.

Leaning down, Hawk got behind the huge blackened boulder, trying its weight with his hands, testing.

Far below winked the fire, and Hawk knew Tala was there, waiting for him, praying that he was alive, counting on his strength and wisdom.

Stooping, he took the strain, paused to gather strength, and then he heaved. The old rock tipped, grated, and then hung still. Overhead the stars shone bright, and Hawk's body throbbed with an aching weariness such as he had never known.

His toes gripped the stone beneath him, the calves of his legs bulged out, he strained even more, the rock grated, and then it leaned further out. Alone then he stood, the veins swelling in his brow, throbbing powerfully within his throat. Suddenly there was a stabbing pain in his side where the great wound lay, he sucked in his breath, heaved once more and staggered away, defeated, and then surprisingly the rock rolled free.

Hawk went to his knees, gasping, his mouth wide, the feeling of the blood coursing down his body a large thing within his mind. He could not lose much more, not if he was to have the strength to win back the woman Tala. And win her back he must, and quickly too.

The boulder tumbled off and vanished into the vast blackness below, there was a rattle of smaller stones, a long silence, a great and splintering crashing, a brief clatter of other rock following along, a distant pounding and rolling, and then at last all was still.

Hawk listened, and then looked out and away from the butte. There was no fire, no red star in the night.

Now Saviki would know that he was not alone with the woman Tala. Perhaps he would flee once more, but now he would know, and for the woman Tala, at least, there was yet a little more time.

154

The moon-woman had risen beyond the mesa, and the earth shone white beneath her, a beautiful white like a great garden—a garden of death. A bat dipped and darted through the still air; somewhere in the darkness a pebble rolled loose and rattled down among the rocks, and in that moment Hawk came finally to the scattered remains of the fire.

The odor of burned wood was still strong in the air, but the fire was gone and so too were Tala and the evil one who had taken her. For a long moment Hawk stood, his exhausted mind trying to grasp the meaning of the empty clearing. His mind no longer worked well, but was almost always walking in the twilight. Now, however, he stood tall and called it back, and in the brief span when his thoughts cleared and were his own again he looked about, then knelt and felt with his hands for the spoor of Saviki.

Not satisfied with the little sign he found, he looked farther, and finally decided the man had continued in the same direction he had been going earlier. Stumbling, Hawk started to follow, and it was only much later that he realized he was going in circles and making many other strange wanderings.

Beneath his feet there were no tracks in the sand and the dust, before him there was no evil one, nor was there the woman of his life. They were gone, in a horrible way they were gone, and always again would he be alone.

155

Yet there was a laughter on the wind, Hawk heard it and wondered, and the Kachina people cried out with great mirth that he was playing a very good joke indeed. But these made Hawk angry, for it was no good joke at all!

Fools, he yelled out within his mind. *Can you not see that the woman whom I love is gone! Truly that is no joke.*

The spirits laughed again and teased him for having such a small understanding. But Hawk ignored them, for he knew he must continue. Never must he stop, not even to listen to the spirits, for then the woman who has been his love would be lost forever.

Suddenly he fell, heavily and with almost no pain, for that at last was gone. But gone too was his strength, and when he tried to rise he could not. He tried again, somehow reached his feet, stepped out, and again his mind left his body and raced far away. His head was spinning more, the stars above were a lovely wheel of light, the star of the eastern morning was gone.

"Brothers," the Kachina spirits said to one another as they watched, "truly does this younger brother have great courage. Now, though, that will not be enough. Do you not remember the old days? Perhaps it would be a good thing if we helped again. . . ."

156

From the east a weaponless man comes staggering across the mesa. The day is bright with the light of a new morning, but he does not see that; he does not see beauty anywhere. He falls, for he is weak from the lack of sleep and the loss of blood from the great wound in his side. He drags himself to his feet by instinct alone, and once more he staggers forward away from the morning.

His heart is empty, for the evil man and the woman Tala are gone. She is now *mokee,* as are the ones who have been his unborn child, his friend, his brother, and his sister. Such evil slaying has always been the way of Saviki, and it will not change now.

Thus, though the arrows did not destroy him, he himself is

mokee as well, for with Tala and the unborn child gone, he has nothing left for which to live. His heart is truly dead, and so too, because of his great weakness, are his eyes. Thus there is much on the mesa that he does not see.

Before him, yet still some distance off, the sandstone bulges out and plunges sharply downward into the hidden valley. It is there that the man Hawk goes, though even he does not yet know that. He knows only that he must go forward, that for some reason he must place one foot before the other.

157

Before Hawk also, but much closer and very carefully concealed, lies the man called Saviki. He has waited long for this, he has lain still since before the first breath of daylight touched the distant blue mountain, and now he prepares.

The green-eyed woman, carefully bound and gagged, lies close behind, and it is in Saviki's mind that he will taunt the man one more time with her fate, kill him, and then use her and the hidden green valley with its plentiful water for as long as he chooses.

Taking over the tiny valley for a place of living has not been in Saviki's thinking for long, but this man who follows, the one whom the People call Hakomi and who should have been dead, has done some very troublesome things in the past few hours. And strangely, this run of ill luck started with the younger of the two women, the one whose head he crushed.

Saviki glances down at his aching shoulder and wonders as he lies on the rock of the mesa that such a light flick with the ancient metal knife could do such damage. He had hardly seen the woman move her hand; he had reached for her, thinking to take her along with the green-eyed one, and suddenly the wound was there. Angered, he had thrown the maiden to the earth, taken up a stone, and had slain her. Then he had chased down the green-eyed one called Tala and had dragged her from the valley, his goal the fleeing clans scattered somewhere to the south.

So his thinking has been to hasten in that direction, enjoying the woman as he traveled. But the wound has bled much, has throbbed powerfully and continually, it has slowed his travel, and he has been unable to enjoy anything!

Isn't it strange, his mind declares with great bitterness, that the only two wounds of his life have come from women. And both of these wounds slow him still, so that he has not the strength he wishes to have. Women, then, have made him less of a man!

Yes, but they have paid, the one with her worthless life and the other with whatever sport he will choose. But still the wounds caused by those two women have been the beginning of his poor luck, and he can do nothing about it!

Then of course there was the boulder, coming out of the darkness like so many devils. Besides frightening him, it had come very close to the fire, and Saviki himself was almost slain by its crushing weight. Then the man called Hakomi had come too, even when he should have been dead had he come. And despite his great wounds he has come more rapidly than anyone would have thought a man could travel.

He has also followed during the time of darkness, and no matter in which direction he, Saviki, and the struggling woman have gone in the hours since, that one has always and in a very strange manner stayed close behind. It is almost as if the man Hakomi has been led by someone.

Thus since the falling of the great boulder has the hated sound of Hakomi's footsteps pounded into his ears. Even now the man follows like one who is dead, staggering, falling, rising, staggering forward, and for a moment the man who is called Saviki worries.

Perhaps it is as those Angry Ones claimed when they paused in their fleeing to claim the food from the so recently abandoned village. Perhaps this one is a spirit, a demon.

But no, such a thing cannot be! Such things are for foolish ones to believe in. Still, there is also the strange laughter that has been drifting past on the wind, laughter that seems to become at times the voices of people enjoying a good joke. That truly is a frightening thing, and Saviki trembles as he thinks of it.

But now it is the time for truth, not for foolish fears. There is no longer time for wind, there is no longer time for the strange laughter it carries. There is only time for the wounded man who staggers forward toward him across the mesa, coming always more close to his own swift ending.

158

And so the man Saviki watches the man and does not see the woman Tala as she lies bound and gagged behind him. He does not see her struggle helplessly against her bonds. He does not see her eyes, filled with tears not of pain but of sorrow, he does not see the wild beating of her heart as she listens to the staggering approach of the man whose child she carries.

He does not see, but again, it would make no difference to him if he did. Such things would only make him laugh with delight, for truly has he wished to hurt, to humiliate.

159

Tala knows that the man Saviki's heart has died, for she has seen the fullness of evil that lingers upon his face. Since the moment of her capture has she watched him, and it is always there.

She considers this, she shifts a little as she tries once again to free herself of her bindings, she hears the staggering footsteps drawing ever closer, and the hand of fear clutches tightly around her body.

O Great One, she pleads within her mind, *hear these my words, hear these my frightened words.*

From this sacred shrine I send forth my voice, from the sacred circle shrine of the earth and the sky send I forth my sorrowing voice. And I myself am the unworthy páho. Wa!

See the man, see the man who staggers. Wa!

This is the one you sent to end the days of my waiting. This is the one you sent to bring fulfillment to the valley. This is the one you sent with the pure heart. This is the one you sent to be the father of my children. Wa!

O Great Tiaowa, remember the words of my vision, remember the words of Kokopeli, remember the words of the three prophets. Remember as well that this one called Saviki has lost the light of goodness from his eye. Truly has his eye become empty of goodness. Wa!

Help this one who staggers, O Great One.

Thus she waits, the sun climbs higher and grows more warm, the soft chanting of prayer goes on in her mind, and always the wounded and weakened Hawk staggers forward.

160

With a lunge and a great cry the man Saviki was on his feet, crouched low, his knife in his hand and a smile of anticipation upon his face.

Surprised, Hawk staggered back a step, then another, his eyes staring in an almost drunken manner at the grinning apparition that loomed before him.

"Ah, my foolish Hakomi," Saviki snarled, "we meet again so soon. Tell me, is it within your heart to make another *waítioma*, another running away?"

Desperately Hawk tried to focus his eyes, yet he could not. The man was an unclear thing that danced ahead of him, almost like a *túawta*, a vision. Yet the voice was there, more cold than ever, and the wounded Hawk knew that again he faced Saviki, leader of the Angry Ones.

"Can you not speak?" taunted the knife-wielding evil one. "Is your heart so filled with the fear of death that your voice has fled from you?"

Suddenly Saviki lunged, Hawk staggered to the side, and as his knees buckled, his mind strangely cleared. All at once he knew what had to be done. There could be no turning away, no shrinking from this thing called a killing. The man Saviki was evil incarnate, and therefore must be destroyed. It was for the good of all the People.

"That was good, my brother," Saviki taunted again as Hawk climbed to his feet with a dry stick in his hand. "That was very good. Perhaps you do not fear death as much as I had supposed. Perhaps, however, you do fear what I shall do with the green-eyed witch when you are *mokee.*"

Green-eyed woman? What he shall do . . . and then even more was Hawk's mind made to clear. Tala was not *mokee,* she had not been destroyed by the evil one! She was still alive!

Suddenly Hawk's anger blossomed into a red flower in his mind, and his strength flooded back into him. With a quick snap of his wrist he threw the dry stick, and as Saviki stepped easily to the side of the harmless missile, Hawk launched himself into the man's legs.

Together they crashed to the earth, rolled over, the stone knife flashed in the sunlight, and Hawk kicked suddenly out. His sandaled foot caught the wrist of Saviki a numbing blow, and instantly the knife was sent spinning.

The two came to their feet together, circling warily, each watching for an opening to the other. Hawk feinted, Saviki was not fooled, and then Saviki's foot sent Hawk sprawling to the earth. Painfully he scrambled to his feet, and in Saviki's mouth was an evil laughter.

Hawk's breath was coming in ragged gasps, and his new strength was going. Suddenly he felt sick and empty, his head was pounding unmercifully, and for some reason he was having difficulty recalling why his body should be hurting in such a terrible manner.

Now Saviki feinted, Hawk stumblingly dodged to the side, and his knees gave way once again. He went down hard, tried to roll over, and an instant later the evil one was behind him, his arm across his throat, shutting off his air.

Hawk gagged, fought blindly and without results, felt his mind grow dark and become filled with piercing, flashing stars, and then with what he was certain was the last of his strength, he heaved himself to his feet.

In him was suddenly a great desperation, for the man Saviki was still astride him, still choking him, and he could find no way to shake the man free.

With monstrous effort he dragged his hands up and dug his fingers into the straining wrists of the man who clung to his back. Harder he pressed, harder still, forcing the wrist into an unnatural angle, and in his mind was the picture of an arm encircling the throat of a great cat. Would he be as that puma had been? Would the straining arm of Saviki close off his life?

Suddenly there was the terrible sound of snapping bones. Saviki screamed mightily, loosed his grip, and with a powerful heave Hawk sent the evil one flying into the brush a dozen feet away.

For a moment then the darkness fell down over the mind of the man called Hawk. The pinpoints of light were back, piercing more deeply. He fell into the brush and the rock, thinking of Tala as his body slammed down. And then there was a great silence upon the mesa. In all the world he could hear only the ragged sound of his own breathing, could feel only the pounding of his own tortured heart.

In the darkness of his weakness there was no will to move, no will to rise. Instead there was only a great wishing to hear the laughing of the water in the sacred water-planted-place, only an aching desire to stand once more beside the lovely green-eyed woman and smell the fresh growing scent of early morning in the valley. Hawk felt only a throbbing urge to stand beside the woman of his life and chant the *Talátawi,* the song to the rising sun that was a symbol of Bahana.

161

The mesa smelled of sage and warm rock and blood, and there was a wafting of the scent of greenness from the tiny valley below. It was the smell of his dying, and Hawk knew it. Yet the thought lived within his mind that he could not die, not until he had cleansed the land of the evil Saviki.

No man who understood the man-woman love feeling as he did, no man who had the strength of limb that was his, had a right to lie down and die before that was accomplished. No man who had such a woman behind him as he did had the right to lay down and die without preserving for that woman her freedom and her happiness.

Such a thing was unthinkable. It would not have been the way of his brother Flies-Far nor of his brother who had been called Badger. It was not the way of honor, it was not the way of the People who carried always a happy countenance.

A feeling of great pride in those who had been slain suddenly rose up within the man Hawk, and with a shout of laughter in his mouth that sounded very much like the laughter of Flies-Far, he rose slowly to his feet.

162

So the wounded and weakened Hawk steps forward toward the edge of the valley, forward toward the crouching and snarling Saviki. He endures the swift stab of pain that strikes his side, and the sickness too. Before him, some fifteen feet away, Saviki slowly rises to his feet, and Hawk sees once again the flash of the stone knife in his hand.

He has found it. Saviki has somehow found the knife. But such understanding has no bearing upon the mind of the man Hawk. It has no more bearing than does the seeing of the dangling and useless hand, the bloody shoulder, or the small trickle of blood from the corner of the evil one's mouth. He sees those things only with his eyes, and not with his mind. That has fled to some place far away, and what remains is only a shell, seeing before him only the man who must be slain.

163

Saviki too sees only the blood-covered man before him, staggering slowly but inexorably forward. He stares, unbelieving, for no one who is mortal can have such great strength and endurance. Still, now that he has the knife, the battle will soon be over.

164

And so neither of them sees the woman Tala as she lays silently on the rock. They do not see her eyes, open wide, tearfully sending out prayer-thoughts with great hope and faith. They do not see her, they do not see that she is a *páho* that has been accepted, they do not hear the stillness that suddenly lives on the heat-shrouded mesa.

Hawk draws a step closer to Saviki, Saviki moves as well, and still the two of them are oblivious to what is happening nearby. They do not hear the whispering of old tumbleweeds as these begin to dance across the mesa, they do not feel the pluckings as the advance breezes brought on by the morning heat tug at their hair, they do not see the rapidly growing twisting wind.

"Ho, little brother," the Kachina people laugh as they twirl around the man Hawk, "this has been a sad but good joke, this thought of yours to make a killing. It is good that it is not within your heart to do so, for that is not the way."

Hawk stops, staring around him, for truly he does not understand. Saviki stops as well, for the laughter is loud, ringing, and even he who does not believe can hear something strange.

But this man is evil, Hawk declares in his mind. *He is núkpana, and he must be destroyed.*

"Quite so," the Kachina people laugh as they dance and twirl faster and faster in a circle that grows smaller and more small. "Quite so, little brother. But there is a little sister of ours who lies bound. Lie down for now, then see to her, and that will be enough. This one with the stone knife and the stone heart does not believe in our existence, and as you may know, that is a very foolish thing. We will see to his disbelief, and we will see as well that the name of Saviki is remembered for evil throughout all the coming generations of the People. Now, brother, if you will allow us . . ."

And as Hawk is forced to the stone, staring upward, and as Saviki glares about him, the winds twist even harder and slam down with great force upon the mesa, burrowing, digging, lifting, throwing.

165

These winds are not seen, nor are the Kachina people, for who can see winds and spirits? The dust is perhaps seen, the tumbleweeds are seen, even the bending of the brush and grass is seen. But the twisting wind or the Kachinas? Such a thing is very unlikely.

But perhaps one man does see. Perhaps the evil one called Saviki, just as his body is plucked up from the rock by the mighty twisting wind and cast off the bulging cliff to hurl down amidst the dust and the tumbleweeds and the laughing Kachina spirits—perhaps he does see. It is certain that he sees something terrible, for as he plummets to his death there is a great scream of fear in his throat, a scream that goes on and on.

166

With aching limbs and wide-open eyes the man Hawk stared at the empty cliff. Saviki was gone! Saviki, the evil, two-hearted slayer of the People, was stopped at last.

Finally convinced that his mind was not playing jokes upon him, Hawk turned and stumbled to the bound form of the green-eyed woman who had become his life. As he removed the cords which bound her, and as he helped her to her feet, it was in his mind that he had never seen anything more beautiful in all the days of his life.

Hawk put out his hands and then took hold of the hands of the woman Tala. For a long moment they stood looking at each other, and silently they sent out voices of thanksgiving.

"My . . . brother and my sister have taken the long road into the twilight," Hawk said at last.

"I . . . I know this," Tala answered as her tears welled slowly into her eyes. "The evil one made a great boast. . . ."

Tala could not continue, for her voice had gone away. Hawk drew her into his arms in a comforting embrace, and in that manner he held her tightly against his body.

"O woman," he said softly, "it is a good way that those two have been given, walking into the land of the Sky People together."

"That . . . is so. It is never good to be . . . to be alone." Tala paused and took a long breath, then buried her face against her husband as her body shook with great wracking sobs. "O my Hawk," she wept with relief. "O . . . my Hawk. . . ."

Long moments later Tala was still sobbing quietly, but Hawk sensed the difference and he knew that the tears were no longer only from sorrow but from joy and relief as well. These he also understood, for he too felt much the same way.

So he felt those emotions, and he felt as well soft lips, soft cheeks, and soft silken hair against his mouth. Suddenly he was alive once more, and his heart laughed with the pure joy of it.

Tala looked up in wonder, and so he released her and held her back from him so that he could gaze upon her once again.

"You are lovely," he declared softly. "Truly, my woman, these eyes have never beheld such loveliness. For all the days of my life will I send out a voice of gratitude that you have graced my living."

"And I will do the same," Tala whispered through her tears as she reached up and wiped a spot of blood from the man's face. "Indeed, there have never been two people who loved more."

And perhaps there have not been. Who knows, other than the great Tiaowa, he who knows all things?

TWENTY

A Very Fine Joke Indeed

Wind brushed his face, a cold wind, and icy. Hawk opened his eyes and looked up at logs and woven brush, and at firelight flickering against them. Everything was peaceful and still.

He lifted his head, and then he became aware of someone nearby, watching. He turned slowly, saw the most lovely oval face in all the earth, saw the petal-clear skin that was the color of anciently smelted brass and copper, saw the deep blue-green eyes brushed with long black lashes, saw the fine lifting of the nose, saw the rose-red lips lifted in a half-curving smile.

"My husand," the woman said softly.

"T . . . Tala?"

"It is time, my husband. The pains are steady, and grow stronger."

Hawk threw himself off the robes, hardly daring to believe what he had heard. "The child? It is truly the time?"

Tala smiled and nodded, and then she grimaced as the pain doubled her over.

"O woman," Hawk cried anxiously, "what is it that you wish me to do? There is no one else, no woman . . . and I do not know how . . ."

Again Tala smiled weakly. "I . . . I do not need another woman," she declared. "In a moment I will stand, and . . . and then you must hold me so that I do not fall. Shortly after that, your new son who is already called Stands Alone will be here."

Hawk stood fretfully, for truly he did not know how such a thing as this would come about.

"My husband," Tala said as she smilingly took his hand and placed it upon her swelling belly, "this one within me is ready. There, did you feel the great kicking? This one is truly to be a son who is filled with the strength of the rock which surrounds us."

Wonderingly Hawk felt again the kicking beneath his hand, hard, constant, and as his eyes lighted with a smile of anticipation for this son of his who was almost ready for birth, Tala sprinkled sacred meal into the air and made herself ready.

And as she did so, the winds drifted above the kiva opening, picking at the ladder and the opening cover and dumping a little of the season's last snow inside. And on the winds the Kachina people laughed with delight, for this was truly another good joke, this believing by the two from the rock that a son was coming, when instead there was a daughter, one with petal-clear skin of the color of anciently smelted copper, fine and waving hair, and eyes of a deep and frosty blue-green.

Epilogue

So you are there when you wish to be, in the tiny valley that lies high in the rock-filled Colorado plateau country of the American Southwest. Time has passed, but not much, for the People of Peace do not live for great lengths of time. Perhaps, far to the east and across the great sea, it is the Christian year 1306. If it is, then England's Edward I has one year left of his life, and in that last year will whip and expel some 100,000 Jews who have remained since his expulsion order of 1290. He will also order a Londoner tried and executed for burning coal within the city. He is a very civilized Christian.

In France, all Jews will be arrested, stripped of their possessions, and expelled, and in Italy the painting *The Lamentation* by Giotto di Bondone will be completed for Padua's Arena Chapel. Again, civilization.

Perhaps, however, it is 1307. If that is so, then the Italian poet Dante Alighieri will have begun the work that will become famous as *The Divine Comedy.*

If, on the other hand, it is 1314, then London will see the completion of its famous St. Paul's Cathedral. And if it is 1315, the world's first public dissection of a human body will take place under Italian surgeon Mondino de Luzzi. In that year also will begin a famine that will last three years and will decimate the population of Europe. This, as you can understand, is the time.

In the tiny valley also, much has happened. But the recordings of these great events have been kept in minds and hearts, and so have received less attention. Still, so that you will know, there have been many births and a few deaths, there has been a great deal of joy and laughter and pleasure found in each day, for as the woman Tala often declared, if one saw only the destination and did not take time to enjoy the little things of the journey, then the end would have little meaning. Within the valley, therefore, there has been much understanding of the meaning of life. There has also been much in the way of pain and of tears, and that too gives meaning. These are the ways of living, and these have been what have occurred in the valley.

That is also the time.

But now, save for the humming of insects and the soft splashing of water, the valley is silent. Deer browse without fear in the thick brush on the hillside, rabbits romp freely in the tall grass of the valley floor, corn grows without help in the unworked fields, beans and squash grow wild below the water-planted-place, and not anywhere is there the sound of human laughter.

In a manner that shows his age, an old man shuffles across the mesa to the hidden cut in the cliff. He pauses, turns and backs into the cut, and slowly descends to the valley floor. His hair is the white of winter snow, his face is wrinkled and tired, his clothing shows much wear, yet his eyes are clear, and in them is a great anticipation.

In the valley at last, he stops and looks around. He sees once more all the things that have made this such a fine home, and his heart is made glad. For long moments he watches the early sun splash across the deep rock tank. It is still filled with sweet water from the sacred water-planted-place, and in his mind is the memory of the woman Tala, splashing, laughing, diving away.

He steps forward, ready to call her name, but there is nothing there but the sunlight, and he turns away, feeling foolish.

Slowly and with bowed head he makes his way to the notches he cut in the rock so long before, and these, very carefully, he climbs. At last, on the ledge before the low cave, he pauses.

It has been one year since he has been to this place, one full cycle of the seasons, and for him it has been a lonely time indeed.

With his heart pounding hard within him he enters, pauses, and slowly he relaxes and smiles. Nothing has changed. All he sees is as he left it, all he sees reminds him of the woman who for so long has been his life. The bowls and jars are neatly stacked, an *olla* dangles from the hanging shelf, and everything is as it should be, as the woman Tala always kept it.

Carefully he steps into the next room, his room, the room Tala once made, unknowingly, for him. It is not neat and tidy, for he has never been so. Nor, out of respect for his way, has Tala ever demanded such. Instead she has lived here too, and has told him often that she cherishes the room because it brings thoughts of him to her mind.

The man remembers that, smiles again, and suddenly two tears fall.

Slowly he drops his gaze to the empty shell that has been his life, the too-still form that he has loved since almost before he can remember, the soft and tiny shape that has always been his Tala, his green-eyed woman of the morning star.

She is seated exactly as he left her, comfortable on her robes, facing the window to the east, her eyes watching and waiting.

But for the past year those eyes have been closed and her spirit has been gone, walking in the twilight as she takes her journey to the land of the Sky People, leaving him alone, alone with his grief.

A strand of wavy gray hair is loose, and in a manner that shows his love, the old man reaches out, lifts it from the still face, gently feels of its texture, and places it behind the small right ear. More tears fall and the old man is not ashamed. Truly has he loved, and just as truly, he knows, will he always love. Still, his life now seems so empty.

Long he stands, his eyes unseeing, his heart looking backward over the days of his life. He sees the woman as she laughingly holds her green-eyed daughter and then her sons, he sees the girl child smiling, he sees her growth and her loveliness, and he sees the day of her leaving, with three younger brothers, for the land to the south. He sees blue-green eyes that sparkle with humor and joy and love, and he sees young men who are tall and strong and think more of the life of their sister than they do of their own.

These, his mind tells him, are the important part of him and the woman Tala, walking forward into a new life.

Of course he does not know of the doings of these young ones. He does not know of the high thoughts of his sons and of the honor-way they feel toward all women. He does not know that they are thus setting forth the old way that the men of the People are slowly adopting as the new way. Nor does he know that the green-eyed woman who is his daughter is sending out her voice in such a wise and loving manner that the scattered but gathering clans, because of her great goodness, already revere her memory. Nor does he know that after his daughter has passed, the People will, through untold future generations, fondly remember her by the honorable name of Spider Woman.

The old man called Hawk does not know these things, and yet he does, for he and the woman Tala taught their little ones well.

Tala.

O woman, his mind cries out, *from this world you walk to the east, where the sun rises and there is new life. No one has spoken your name for one year, and now that time has passed. I have told myself never to forget you. I never will.*

I hear you when the night wind blows through the old koritivi, I see you in the dreams of my sleeping, I know you are always with me, and I am not afraid.

It is said that the journey to the land of the Sky People is a hard one, and there is work to be done. In one year's time your tracks on this world must be covered.

Memories cling and images fade, and except for in this valley and wherever the little ones are, no sign of you is left. One year has gone by quickly, and I still feel your presence. Yet now you must leave, and tears swell my vision. My throat is coarse and dry. I can hardly speak. I cannot make . . . the signal of . . . of farewell.

Our people are told not to cry. Our tears put out your fire, and thus made tired, you cannot climb. But my tears are no longer sad ones, for I realize that you are always with me.

O woman, I am not afraid. . . .

Slowly the old man sits down beside the still form of the more than lovely woman who was called Tala. He is suddenly tired, and as he rests he considers once again the loneliness that is now his. His old heart aches, and as two doves begin their cooing of love down by the water-planted-place, his tears start forth anew.

Suddenly the man jumps, for he senses, he feels a presence beside him.

And then a hand, warm and soft, enters his own and clasps his fingers tightly. The old man turns in surprise, and finds himself gazing into the sparkling depths of the most lovely blue-green eyes he has ever seen. Red lips, full and fresh, smile with joy in a face that is smooth and young and the color of anciently smelted copper. The hair that frames that face is wavy and silken-dark with burnished highlights, and as he sees these things he hears her laughter, bright and fresh as ever it was.

Together then, and without a word, for words are no longer needed, these two stand, easily, quickly. And with hands clasped tightly together and with joy on their faces they step forth from the rock of their home.

The seasons fade swiftly into other seasons, these pile constantly upon each other, and the valley lies still and quiet. The winds of morning and of evening whisper through the old *koritivi,* carrying upon their backs the lonely Kachina people and much fine dust as well. This drifts into the stone dwellings and covers everything with a thick layer of dryness, and so in the process all that is buried is preserved.

Centuries pass, four and then five and then six, other winds stir up the dust and carry much of it away, the Kachina people sleep deeply now, for no one has need of them, and suddenly it is 1910 and there is another who stands at the old window facing east.

Arah Shumway stands still, looking but not truly seeing, his thoughts far away and in another time. Hours have passed since he has first entered the old dwelling, hours that he has not even been aware of. Instead his mind has been with the man and the woman who sit before him, and in a manner that he does not even begin to understand, he has seen them in their living and in their laughing and in their loving.

Truly he has found what he has been seeking. Those two who are in the dwelling have given him a hope, a quiet assurance that it can be done. Distance and silence between a man and a woman are not necessary at all. His beloved and eternal land of rock and trees and sky can draw a man and a woman together just as surely as it can thrust them apart. And one day, he and his yet-unfound wife, together, will find the way he knows these two old ones have found.

In the wash that was far below, his horse stomped impatiently, Arah started at the movement, and then guiltily he remembered the cattle. Hurriedly he nodded his solemn good-bye to the two, stepped quietly from their dwelling, climbed down the cliff, took a quick drink of the clear sweet water, moved through the tiny green valley, and dropped into the wash below. And even after all sounds of his departure had died away, the valley remained tranquil and serene, a place of beauty and of peace.

And so we leave as the Old Ones left, going eastward up Bullpup Canyon, lifting upward and upward on the laughing wind, crossing Alkali Ridge and Devil Mesa, lifting above Montezuma Canyon, going on until the land grows wide and flat beneath us. And around us always there is a joyful laughter, soft and good, and if we listen with more than our ears we may be fortunate enough to hear the exuberant words of the Kachina people.

"Come ride the winds with us," they declare with great mirth. "You will need to, for those you seek have also ridden. O give ear, you who follow. They are ahead, not behind in that old stone dwelling. Is that not a great joke? These two from the rock who are almost not even remembered as People, are so very far ahead in their living and their loving. But perhaps if you hurry, and if you will be willing to learn as they have learned. . . ."

And who is to say that the spirits who ride the laughing wind are not correct?